Finding Hope FOR TOMORROW

KATHRYN MᶜNEILL CRANE

Finding Hope for Tomorrow
Copyright 2016 Kathryn McNeill Crane

Cover Design by Ashley Baumann
For more information visit Ashleybaumann.com

Formatting by R.A. Mizer of ShoutLines.
For more information visit Shoutlinesdesign.com.

ISBN: 0692676074
ISBN-13: 978-0692676073

Dedication

This book is dedicated to Dottee Mackie. Thank you for showing an angry, surly teen with no friends, in a new town, the perfect example of God's love. By taking me under your wings, you gave me the chance to grow and encouraged me to fly. You fought the good fight, my friend, and I know you rest easy in the arms of God. Your memory lives on in all those blessed to know you.

To Keyna and Shelley for years of happy memories and crazy teenage antics. Wanna cruise?

To Gail and Tootsie for loving me like I was yours and for raising two incredible daughters.

To Missy and Michelle for not letting me go no matter how hard I pull.

Love you!

I thank my God upon every remembrance of you.
Philippians 1:3

Acknowledgments

This is truly the hardest part of the job. Over the course of the last two and a half years, so many people have had a hand in bringing Liam's story to life.

Praise to the Lord, the Almighty, the King of Creation. You were, You are, and You will be. Thank you for my many blessings.

To Chan for feeding me, replenishing my wine supply, and not nagging about all the things I avoided when I sat down to write. For all those who say insta-love is a crock, guess our twenty-three years together show 'em. Love you, babe.

To Brittany, Zachary, and Elizabeth for interrupting me, not doing the dishes, and loving me even when I was grumpy. I'll never love you less than I do right at this moment.

To Grayson and Carson for bringing sunshine into my life. Remember, Nonnie is the smartest woman there is. Ask your mom.

To my mom and dad, Bill and Faith, for letting me grow wings and encouraging me to fly. Thank you isn't enough for all the sacrifices you've made for me.

To William (Liam), Rebekah (Bekah), and Sarah (Maggie) for helping mold me as I grew up. You taught me what sibling love really means, along with how to chew tobacco, eat too many blueberries, and how to use hairspray as a weapon. Love you!

To Cat Graham for responding to my texts and meeting me at the bus stop early to make sure my medical facts and terms were correct. I owe you some Rocky's Hot Chicken.

To Melisa 'Missy' Case Garren for walking me through some serious brainstorming. Those conversations with you are the reason I was able to finish telling Liam's story. Talking with you is always a highlight in my day.

To Michelle for porch time. You always seem to know when I need it.

Julie, we did it. Can you believe it? Without your help and support, your gentle guidance and tough love, Liam would have died in a car crash in chapter two. My day's not right without talking to you.

Debbie, our early morning phone calls have allowed me to travel the streets of Boston. I look forward to hearing you order cod for many years to come. Thanks for letting me borrow your brain so much.

Mel, I'm pretty sure it's time for another marathon call while I'm driving the Interstate. You keep me on my toes, encourage me, brainstorm with me, and love me despite my weirdness.

To the betas who helped me and encouraged me along the way, I'm not naming you because the great 'Zon will swear we're manipulating stuff. Just know that your feedback, both negative and positive, made such a HUGE difference in this book. I hope you realize how much I appreciate the time you sacrificed for Liam and Elizabeth. AND I hope you're around for the next one.

To my girls in Indie Chicks Rock and FTN, this has been a long, slow ride for me. Thanks for answering questions, encouraging me, and making me laugh.

And you, the reader. Bleeding words is never an easy task, but knowing someone loves and appreciates your doing so by READING your work. Wow. Thank you for taking the journey with me. Please take a few minutes and leave an honest review at the retailer where you purchased Finding Hope for Tomorrow. Thank you in advance.

Every person's life tells a story.

Some are uncomplicated, straightforward, and easy. Things fall into place with a simplicity that boggles the mind.

Others twist and turn, and every day is centered on fighting and scraping, yet never *finding* victory.

And then there are those who gain an inch only to be knocked back a foot. They love. They fight. They stumble. They fall. But through it all, they stagger to their feet, step back on life's path, and push through until they win. For these people, happiness is not an illusion. It's a truth, a promise, worth any effort, any scars, but just out of arm's reach. It stands at the end of the path, taunting and teasing, tempting them to take one more blow.

And in the end, the battles make victory sweeter. More valued. More precious than ever imagined. More than any one person could *hope*.

This is Liam's story.

Loyal, protective, shoulders stronger than Atlas'.

Broken, worn, battered.

Win or lose, he's ready to fight for what *tomorrow* brings.

Life. Love. Healing. Hope.

He tasted of
strong man,
bright sunshine,
everlasting love,
and
hope eternal.

Radio Broadcast

"Gooooood morning, Highlanders! You're listening to the local news on WHLD, AM radio 1250. Today is Friday, January eighteenth, and these are your community updates.

"First Presbyterian Church wants me to remind you that the annual Souper Bowl Drive begins tomorrow. Don't forget to grab a couple of extra cans for the local Food Pantry when you're doing your grocery shopping. Remember, every three cans donated can be redeemed for one ticket to the Souper Bowl party, and trust me, you don't want to miss out on the chili and chicken noodle soup cook-offs. Folks, last year's event raised over five thousand cans to help feed those in our area who need a little help. Let's see how quick we can beat that this year.

"And speaking of soup, His Hands Soup Kitchen is in need of some volunteers throughout the week. If you've got time, Mrs. Hattie will surely put you to work, so give her a call at 828-555-5656.

"Folks, last week, Odele Freeman slipped on his icy driveway and broke his hip. Debra says he's feeling better physically, but his spirits are down and her nerves are frazzled. She may have mentioned something about him being a big, old, grumpy baby, but don't tell her I told you. Anyhow, she's hoping some of his VFW buddies will come around for a few games of checkers and give her a little time to get out of the house.

"And parents, don't forget that school is closed next Monday to honor Doctor Martin Luther King, Jr.

"I will close out the local updates with this quote from Doctor King. 'The ultimate measure of a man is not where he stands in moments of comfort and convenience, but where he stands at times of challenge and controversy.'

"Now on to the national news …"

Chapter 1

The rear end of the old truck skidded on black ice when Liam turned into the driveway. If Tripp—his late brother-in-law—knew how bald the tires were, he'd haunt Liam. The two years since Tripp's untimely death had been hard on everyone, and Liam wasn't immune to the grief. Every time the dog tags hanging from the rearview mirror clanked together, his mind drifted to happier times. Unfortunately, reality had the knack of slipping back in and slapping him in the face.

Through the windows of his twin sister Wrynn's house, light spilled out and sparkled on the white blanket of snow, giving the illusion of diamonds sprinkled across the yard. Come bright and early the next morning, Liam would be shoveling slush and throwing salt on the porch and steps. The last thing he wanted was for one of his nieces or Wrynn to take a wrong step and end up with a busted head or a broken bone.

The forecast for Highlands predicted winter to last for a few more months. Everywhere he looked, snow piled up, and the temperatures held steady below freezing. Before one layer melted, another fell. Beneath the pristine, fluffy surface, hid a solid, slippery sheet of ice. Much like his life. Folks saw the happy-go-lucky guy who loved and took care of his family and worked hard at his jobs.

But underneath the shiny exterior was what he hid from the world—a lonely heart gripped with fear.

Lately, every day seemed the same. He woke up, worked late, visited his parents or Wrynn and the girls, then went to sleep to start the cycle again. If there was one thing he could count on, it was his boring life. The monotony had never bothered him much before, but his best friend Zack and his wife Ashton were expecting their first child, and their excitement reminded Liam his own future was bleak and dreary. He was the only person who could do anything about changing the outcome. It wasn't like his dream girl was going to slam into him and knock him off his feet. Although, as thickheaded as he was, it might be exactly what he needed.

Maybe the time had come to put his hermit life to rest and make an effort to be around people more? Yeah, he wasn't looking forward to doing anything of the sort, but hey, didn't he deserve a brighter tomorrow? What surprised him was his lack of desire and energy to do anything about changing what had become his version of normal. Rejection and dancing around sensitive subjects were on his top ten list of things to avoid. Few women his age appreciated or honored the old-fashioned teachings he clung to. Was he perfect? No, not by any means. But when life threw a lesson his way, he learned from it and refused to make the same mistakes again. The way he figured, he'd saved himself a little heartache and a whole lot of trouble.

Good grief, he needed to crawl out of the funk he was in before heading inside. Wrynn had enough to deal with, without him adding more to her plate. Lord knew his nieces expected a happy, loving Uncle Liam, not the morose, gloomy creature he was finding himself to be more and more often. His only excuse, though flimsy, was the summertime blues had sunk its claws in him, and dreams of sunshine and temperatures in the eighties taunted him. As a landscaper, his working out in the cold didn't make matters better, either. At twenty-eight, he was much too young to be so exhausted or to feel so old.

As he slammed the truck door, laughter filtered out through

the still of the night. The knots of tension in his neck and shoulders loosened at the joyful sound. The front door flew open and Maggie's little head appeared. His youngest niece was growing like a weed. Because of her two older sisters' influence, she was smarter and more mature than most two-year-olds. Nothing coming out of her mouth surprised him anymore. He dreaded the day she discovered the circumstances surrounding her birth. Knowing the news of her father's death put her mother in labor might dim the spark of life in her eyes.

"Da pwince is here! Da pwince is here!" She jumped up and down, and her little body shivered from the cold. "Hurry, Unka Wiam befoe I fweeze. It's told." Her blonde corkscrew curls danced around her little pixie face as she shivered from head to toe.

Liam climbed onto the porch and lifted her quivering, pint-sized body in his arms. "Does your mother know you're outside?" He glanced down at her wiggling, shoeless feet. "And barefoot, to beat it all. You trying to catch a cold?" As he kicked the door shut behind them, he kissed the top of her head, barely missing getting smacked in the nose.

"Siwwy pwince. I paint de toes. See?" She folded her body, grabbed her ankle, and pulled her foot up to his face. "Spartle pink." She beamed a radiant smile at him, and her little teeth gleamed like pearls. "I wike spartle pink. It's my favowite."

Her smile was contagious, and Liam's face split into a wide grin, his earlier woe-is-me moment disappearing. Yeah, he was in the best place to make him feel better.

"Looks good on you, sweetie. Sparkle pink is perfect for a princess. Now, where's your mom?"

She wriggled in his arms, and he lowered her until her feet met the floor. "In da kitchen. She gwumpy." Her cute frown and squinty eyes made him chuckle. "Tonight, eat tacos. I wike tacos." Her frown changed to a smile, and Liam's heart sighed.

Maggie hugged his legs before darting to her sisters, Annie and Bekah, who were on their knees at the coffee table. Color-splotched cotton balls and vibrant-hued polishes scattered along the surface, and the light scent of acetone and lacquer filled the air. A man could get high from the fumes in the room.

He pulled his toboggan off his head and stuffed it into his coat pocket before hanging them up and running his fingers through his messy, auburn hair to get rid of the static electricity.

"Uncle Liam, can you help me?" Annie's panicked voice broke through the girls' chatter. "I keep messing up." She held her right hand up, tilted it back and forth as she inspected it, and frowned. Sure enough, red nail polish smeared the tips of her little fingers.

"Umm, well, does your mom know you're using *that* color?" He grabbed her small hand to inspect the bright crimson. "Isn't that just a little too grown up for you?"

Annie narrowed her eyes and tilted her chin up at him. "I am. Nine. Years. Old. Uncle Liam." Defiance etched every word.

Uh oh, looks like we have a diva in the making.

A grin threatened to take over, because the older she grew, the more Annie's moods changed, reminding him of his sister when they were young. Before he could open his mouth to retort, Wrynn yelled from the kitchen.

"Anne Marie Tidwell, I heard that! You know better than to talk like that to anyone, much less your Uncle Liam."

Annie's eyes widened and filled with shame. Her lower lip trembled as she whispered her apology. "Sorry, Uncle Liam. That wasn't very nice of me." Her body curled into itself, and she grew smaller right before his eyes. Tears slipped down her cheeks as her tiny voice cracked. "Daddy wouldn't be very proud of me, would he?"

"Aww, honey." His heart melted. That her first thought was of what her father's reaction might be didn't surprise him. He longed for the day when she would accept that Tripp wasn't coming back to them.

Though she tried to be strong for her younger sisters, the burden was too heavy for Annie to carry. Like her mother, she still struggled fiercely with her dad's death. As the oldest of the three girls, her father's memory whirled through her mind on constant repeat. Even though more than two years had passed, she sometimes waited beside the door, hoping Tripp would walk through and sweep her up in his arms. More than once, Liam had caught her carrying on a conversation with her dad, reminiscing about the time they'd spent together. The past Christmas had hit her hard, and her uncle had spent most of the day with her tiny body snuggled on his lap, attempting to soothe her and encouraging her to enjoy the day.

No child should need coaxing to open her gifts.

He leaned down and tipped her chin up, forcing her to look him in the eyes. "Baby girl, if your daddy were here, there wouldn't be enough room to hold the pride he'd have for you." The sight of her glistening eyes and wet face slammed against his heart. Pain shot through him, and a single tear traced a path down his cheek. His voice cracked under the weight of his grief. "He would see you growing up, being such a good big sister, and helping your momma all the time." He thumbed the tear from his ruddy cheek, lifted her off the floor, and carried her to the couch.

"And he would snatch you right up and tell you just how proud he is of you, how much he loves you." His arms tightened around her, trying to calm her shuddering sobs. "I know I'm not him, and I never will be, but I love you, and I'm so proud of you. You're such an amazing little girl." He chuckled quietly and tickled her side. "Or maybe *not* such a little girl, as I've been recently reminded."

His joking words produced the result he wanted. Blinking her eyes at a rapid pace, she looked up at him and cracked a small smile.

"Thanks, Uncle Liam." She settled back against his chest, her words coming out in choppy huffs. "I really am sorry I was mean to you. I just miss him so much." Her breath hitched, and her petite body melted against him.

"Oh, sweetheart, I know you didn't mean it." He brushed a kiss on the top of her head. "And just remember, there's nothing wrong with being sad or missing your daddy. We all miss him, every single day."

He may not be their dad, but he loved those girls more than life, and his primary goal was to ensure their happiness and wellbeing.

Liam squeezed her close as his eyes drifted to the kitchen doorway. Wrynn leaned against the doorframe and mouthed *thank you*. Her mahogany hair was tangled and unkempt. Stains dotted her sweatshirt. Liam wouldn't be surprised if those were the same clothes she'd slept in the night before. What he wouldn't give to see her happy and carefree again. Because grief had a way of aging a person, she looked much older than their twenty-eight years. Her pale face flushed as she wept.

Glad I have Wrynn's girls to fill the empty. Don't know what I'd do without them.

His thought made him grimace. He tried not to dwell on his lack of family, but at times, when he was with Wrynn and his nieces, it became harder to fight back the desire to have his own. He often wondered if he was meant to live his life alone because he'd yet to meet the right woman he wanted to share in his life, his love, his family.

"Okay, guys and dolls, let's eat." His sister's hoarse voice broke through his musings.

He wrapped Annie in one arm, grabbed six-year-old Bekah in the other, and turned sideways on the couch to help Maggie climb on his back. Satisfied all three were safe and secure, he stood to his feet and lurched toward the kitchen with giant, fumbling steps. Giggles rang out around him. He placed Annie and Bekah in their chairs, then leaned forward and flipped Maggie over his shoulder. Lifting her above his head, he nibbled on her toes. As her laughter increased, he blew raspberries on her belly before sitting her down and strapping her in her booster seat.

Liam set the table while Wrynn put the food out, and after he said grace, he dished out tacos for the older girls while Wrynn helped feed Maggie. Though the girls' chatter never lessened, his sister didn't say much at all. Liam glanced at her, and when he saw her rosy cheeks and glassy turquoise eyes, he pressed a palm to her forehead.

"Sis, you're burning up. What the heck? Why didn't you tell me you were sick? I'd have brought supper with me."

Fever-glazed eyes peered at him. "I've been a little run down the last few days." She rolled her watery eyes and barked a sharp laugh, which turned into a deep, rattling cough. "Who am I kidding? I've been run down for two years. But I've felt like I was coming down with something the last few days. I'm sure it's just a cold, but I feel like crap."

"This is the second time you've been sick since Christmas, and that was only a couple of weeks ago. Why do you have to run yourself ragged all the time?" Irritation sparked in his voice, and he wanted to yell at her to at least try to get a grip on her grief, but three little girls focused their attention solely on him. Since he was always happy and fun, they didn't understand his angry tone or know what to expect from this strange Uncle Liam. His frustration was unusual, and he blamed it on the nasty winter weather. He sucked back any harsh words flitting through his mind, calmed the ire, and finished in a soft voice. "You need to slow down, sis. The girls need you. Sometime soon, you're going to have to make an effort to deal with this better than you have been."

Wrynn's face crumpled, and she dropped her chin to her chest. "I'm trying I promise, but if I slow down, I have too much time to think," she whispered. The anguish in her voice was thick enough to choke him. "I know you're right, but it's so hard to wake up every morning, knowing he's not going to be here to share my day. Every single day starts and ends with missing him, and I just don't know how to get past it."

Liam crouched down and wrapped his arms around her. "I know you miss him. We all miss him." His lips brushed the top of her head. "But, honey, we miss you, too. For the rest of us, most of the time it's like we've lost two people, even though you're technically still here with us. It's time you saw the therapist again." A sniff brought his head up, and when he saw Annie wiping her eyes, he realized he had said too much. "We'll finish this later, but for now, let me get you something for that fever."

He gave her some ibuprofen, and she swallowed them. The pained look that crossed her face made him wince in sympathy.

"You going to eat anything?" He pointed at her full plate, but his eyes roamed over her hollow cheeks and the dark circles smudging the tops of them. She looked like death warmed over.

She scrunched her nose and shook her head. "Hurts to swallow." Her hand drifted to her throat.

"Well, you go take a shower and go on to bed." When she opened her mouth to argue, he held up a hand to stop her. "Nope, I'm qualified to wrestle these three little monkeys, and you need your rest. If I need you, I'll come get you." He helped her stand, hugged her to him, and kissed her forehead. "Holler if you need anything, sis."

Wrynn shuffled out of the kitchen, and minutes later, the sound of her shower drifted down the hall. He and the girls finished eating, then he helped them bathe and get ready for bed. Maggie raised her hands to him, and when he picked her up, she settled her head on his shoulder and, in seconds, fell fast asleep.

After tucking the girls in bed, reading them a couple of stories, and washing the dishes, he locked up as he left and headed to his place. The short trip around Wrynn's house to his humble abode in her basement, never failed to show him just how lonely his life was. When Tripp died, he'd moved in to help Wrynn with his nieces. What began as a temporary solution, seemed more and more permanent every day.

As he entered the back door, Liam stopped to let memories wash over him. Happy days when this was Papa and Nana's house. He and Tripp drawing racetracks on the dirt floor of the basement. Homemade ice cream and lemonade under the trees in the back yard. Tire swings hanging from the limbs of the tall oaks. All those things added up to the things he valued most. Love, family, and happiness. If the walls could talk, they would tell the story of triumph over fear and laughter after heartbreak.

Every time he heard the pitter-patter of little feet scurrying on the floor above his head, it brought a smile to his face. The warm oak floors and wainscoting created a homey impression, and masculine touches definitely proclaimed bachelor. The whole picture screamed for the need of a woman's touch. Sure, Maggie's muddy handprints right inside the door added a definite flair. Colorful drawings covered every inch of his fridge.

At times, the walls closed in to remind him that, while he was a part of someone else's puzzle, he had yet to find the pieces of his own. Whatever it took, he refused to lose hope, because hope was one of the few things he had left.

He tasted of
strong man,
bright sunshine,
everlasting love,
and
hope eternal.

Chapter 2

The incessant clang of the bell over the door shattered the silence of the lobby. The irritating sound seemed to take forever to stop. Elizabeth Pittman stepped out of her office to see a regal-looking woman stomp across the weathered oak floors, leaving a trail of melting snow in her wake.

"Welcome to the Endless View Farm and Inn!" Elizabeth smiled at the haughty, intimidating woman. "I'll be with—"

"Hmph, I don't need your help, young lady." Her narrowed eyes and upturned nose created a harsh look of disdain, surprising Elizabeth with the strength of the vehemence pouring off her. She walked through the front lobby but turned back as she reached the hall. "I know why I'm here and whom I need to see. Why you feel the need to speak is beyond me." She sniffed and rolled her eyes as she disappeared from sight.

Shock tinged with a small measure of anxiety traveled up Elizabeth's spine. In her short time in Highlands, every single person she'd met had welcomed her and made her feel as if she'd been there forever.

Glad I don't have to deal with her today!

Elizabeth went back to the tangle of numbers displayed on the monitor, but the slamming office door followed by raised voices fought hard for her attention. Not a nosey person by nature, she tried to ignore the conversation, but the loud shouts made it impossible.

"We've had this discussion before, Mrs. Tidwell, and I'm still not interested in joining your little vendetta." The rumbling anger made Elizabeth sit up straight. Seldom had she heard her grandfather Roger raise his voice, but she was certain, if she stepped outside on the porch and closed the door, the volume of his words would carry through to her. "I own this place free and clear, so you have nothing to hold over my head."

The door of the owners' quarters flew open so hard, the knob banged the wall and caused the framed pictures to rattle. "You have got to be kidding me." Tootsie, Roger's wife and Elizabeth's grandmother, rushed into Elizabeth's office, anger written all over her face. "How long has she been here?" Her eyes sparked fire, and Elizabeth was glad she wasn't on the receiving end.

"Honestly, she walked through the door less than two minutes ago, Grams." A look of confusion passed over Elizabeth's face. "She acts like she owns the place," she whispered.

"Sounds like that hateful, old biddy. Figures." Tootsie frowned when Roger roared in anger. She straightened her petite, five-foot-nothing frame, propped her fists on her hips, and stalked out to the counter. Anger twisted her mouth, and her eyes shot daggers at the closed office door. "And trust me when I say, you do *not* want to know that woman. She is trouble with a capital T."

"You will do as I say or your business will suffer. This is my last warning." The voice got louder as the woman stepped out of Roger's office, and the click-clack of her heels preceded the human tornado. The infuriating, pushy woman halted, glanced back at Roger, and threw her parting words over her shoulder. "Mark my word, we're not finished here. I *will* be back."

"Thanks for the warning, you bitter, old shrew. I'll know to hide next time." Roger's sarcastic words blasted through the room. His body shook, and his breath hissed in and out through clenched teeth.

Ice-cold winds blew in and scattered papers to the floor as she marched out the door.

"Who *was* that?" Elizabeth rushed around to gather the strewn invoices and placed the pile of clutter on the edge of the desk.

"*That* was Mrs. Tidwell, known around these parts as Tidwella Deville." Roger snorted. "She's someone you'd be much better off not knowin'. My advice? Stay far, far away." He wrapped an arm around Tootsie's shoulders, pulling her close to his side. "Toots, I see fire in your eyes. You know you can't let her bother you."

"Not let her bother me?" she grumbled and pressed a hand to Roger's cheek. "Sugar, your shoutin' woke me from my nap, and I was dead to the world. I've never heard you yell like that, not even when Mike asked for Keyna's hand in marriage."

"Surely it wasn't as bad as all that." Roger choked out a laugh as a faint blush washed over his face. "And yes, I know I yelled at Mike, but that's my baby we're talking about. I like the boy, but ain't nobody good enough for my girl."

Elizabeth bit back a laugh at her grandfather. The legend of Gramps' reaction when her father asked for her mother's hand was something she'd heard often since she was little. She was pretty sure anyone in a twenty-mile vicinity had heard it, too. According to her mother, Gramps had headed for his shotgun, and Mom and Dad had run out the front door.

Tootsie grinned at Elizabeth. "Keyna and Mike have been married nigh on thirty years, and it still gets his goat to talk about giving his little girl away." She shoved Roger away from the counter. "Now, I think we need to check your blood pressure, and if it's high, I'm going after that old bat myself."

"Aww, I'm all right, but I should just let you take care of her for me." He winked at Elizabeth and tugged his wife to him. "You may be a tiny little thing and not even weigh a buck, but I'm pretty sure you could take her, Toots." When she pulled on his hand, he followed her. "My blood pressure's fine, hon, but we need to talk about this whole boycott thing she's trying to organize around town.

I don't know what that nice young man did for her to set her sights on him."

"You just put it out of your mind and…"

Their voices drifted off as they walked into their living quarters. Her grandparents never failed to amuse her. Elizabeth stared at the door for a moment before shaking her head and getting back to her computer. After all, upgrading the computer systems and reconciling the accounts were part of the reason she moved there after Christmas.

She occupied herself with the inn's current cash flow until everything surrounding her faded to the background. The shrill ring of the switchboard drew Elizabeth from the numbers dancing on the computer screen. When she straightened in her chair, her lower back protested her movement. While rubbing the grit from her tired eyes, she reached out to answer the phone.

"It's a beautiful morning at the Endless View Farm and Inn. This is Elizabeth speaking. How may I help you?" The practiced spiel flowed from her tongue without hesitation.

A light chuckle traveled through to Elizabeth. "Sweetheart, it's not quite morning. You might want to change your greeting to good afternoon."

A smile bloomed as Elizabeth glanced at the clock, but her mouth dropped open when she saw how late it was. "Oh, my goodness, you're right. Good afternoon, Momma." Elizabeth yawned, stood from her desk, and dug her fist into her aching back. "Gosh, I can't believe it's so late. I've been hunched over my desk for hours."

"How's my baby girl doing today? I saw on the news where you're supposed to get more snow tonight. You staying warm? You know I don't want you getting sick. You didn't grow up with all this cold and snow, and I worry about you. Are you able to drive around in this mess? Did you get the snow tires put on your Jeep? I swear, if this weather doesn't break, your dad and I–"

Elizabeth's laughter cut off her mother's words. "Take a breath, Mom, or you'll suffocate. Your sentences are running together." She smiled when she heard her mom snort. "I'm doing fine, Momma. Otherwise, Grams or Gramps would have told you by now."

"True. Knowing you're there with them is the only thing giving your dad and me some peace of mind. They'll look out for you."

"Oh, Momma, before I forget, this woman came in here this morning, just a raising Cain, acting like she was the boss of me. All yelling and getting up in Gramps' fa—"

Her rush of words stopped when the door to the owners' quarters opened. Tootsie stepped out into the foyer and walked over to the office.

"Momma, can you hold on for just a second? Grams just walked up." Without waiting for a reply, Elizabeth laid the phone on the desk. "Everything okay? I kind of got lost in this week's reconciliation. I had no idea it was so late."

"I was wondering why you were still here. You shoulda left a couple of hours ago." Tootsie pointed to the clock on the wall and wiggled her eyebrows. "Now, let me talk to Keyna. You get on out of here before it gets too dark and have a little fun."

"Okay. Let me just tell Momma bye." She grabbed the phone and spoke as she gathered her purse and coat. "Momma, Grams told me to get outta here. She wants to chat with you for a sec. I'm going to go grab something to eat, and if I don't fall asleep, I'll call you later. Love you."

Tootsie stretched her arm across the counter, and Elizabeth gave her the handset, shut down the computer, and kissed her grandmother on the cheek.

On the way to her cabin, she saw the landscaper's truck and heard the scrape of his shovel in the parking lot. His broad shoulders and deep auburn hair had caught her eye a couple of weeks ago. Yes, she didn't mind looking at him at all, and wondered if she could convince Grams to let her work the front desk so she could meet him. What impressed her most, though, was his working in below-freezing temperatures so close to nightfall. She shivered at the icy wind biting through her coat and hoped he was warm enough. Then thoughts of hot cocoa to ward off the chill spurred her to her little cabin.

Chapter 3

Blue skies and a bright, yellow orb greeted Liam when he walked out of the fire station. The sight was so rare those days, he stopped in the middle of the sidewalk and tipped his head back to bask in the sunshine. Though the blinding rays were plentiful, the below-freezing temperatures prevented him from absorbing any of its heat.

The harsh winter weather kept most people inside where it was warm. That meant fewer accidents on icy roads, but the flipside was more chimney fires during the evenings and nights. Three such calls had come in during his shift the night before, and even though Liam was exhausted, icy walkways and parking lots waited for him to salt and scrape.

Liam figured they could wait a little bit longer. Buck's Coffee and a jolt of hot caffeine were calling his name. The two-block walk passed quickly beneath his long-legged stride, and the smell greeting him at the door put a smile on his face. When he reached for the knob, he heard a small shriek, and a body slammed into his back, smooshing him face first into the glass.

"Oh my gosh, I'm so sorry." A soft, sweet feminine voice from the face pressed into his back drifted to his ears. "I slipped on a patch of ice and couldn't stop sliding."

Liam reached behind him, got a good grip on the elbow digging into his waist, and steadied the woman as he turned. The top of her head barely reached his shoulder. Intrigued and more than a little puzzled by the burning sensation traveling through his hand, he bent his knees to get a better look.

Draped around a beautiful, heart-shaped face, long, blonde curls framed flushed cheeks and sparkling cornflower blue eyes. Her teeth gnawed the corner of full, pouty lips. Recognition was instant. It was the pretty, soft-spoken young lady who'd caught his eye when he delivered invoices to the Endless View Farm and Inn. Dwarfing her body was a long, puffy, white down coat. The bright red of the scarf looped around her neck matched the color of her cheeks.

At least she isn't cold.

"This is so embarrassing," she whispered. Her blush deepened, and her gaze drifted to the sidewalk.

"Hey, there's nothing to be embarrassed about. I can just about guarantee you, with the winter we're having, this happens to lots of people several times a day." Liam wrapped his hand around her cheek, and his first thought was her skin was like silk. "You okay? You slammed into me pretty hard."

She mumbled something about strong arms and pretty, turquoise eyes, but her voice was too soft for Liam to hear everything she said.

"Pardon? I didn't quite catch that."

She gasped. "Oh my gosh, did I say that out loud?" Her eyes avoided his, and the tips of her ears burned bright red. "I'm so, so sorry."

"Don't give it another thought." Her cute murmuring made him want to laugh, but he didn't want her to be even more uncomfortable. "I'm Liam Broun, by the way. I've seen you in the office at the Spiveys' inn several times." His thumb traced her jaw, and he pressed her chin higher. A faint buzz hummed in his ears, leaving him slightly dizzy and off balance. "You just visiting the area or you here to stay?" A deep buried part of him hoped Highlands was a permanent part of her future.

Good grief, Liam. What is wrong with you?

Excitement flashed in her eyes. The smile she beamed made his breath catch, and his heart thud in a strange rhythm. He shook off the strange vibrations whirling in his veins, opened the door, and ushered her into the warm coffeehouse.

The pop of static sizzled through the air as he slipped off his wool cap. Imagining his hair resembled a porcupine, he tried to tame the unruly mess, but froze when she ruffled her fingers through it. Her touch sent a whole different kind of electrical zap through him, and he squinted his eyes, fighting the strange sensation.

"Well, yes and no." She giggled and bounced up and down on the balls of her feet as they waited in line.

"Hmm?" Confused by the whirlwind of whatever the heck she was doing to him, Liam struggled to wrap his mind around what she was saying. "Yes or no, what?"

"You asked if I was here to stay. My answer is maybe. My grandparents own the Endless View Farm and Inn. I just finished my degree in December, and you'd think a twenty-three-year old woman would know what she wants to do with her life, but I have no idea. They needed some help, so here I am. Besides, I've been visiting the area since I was a little girl, and I L-O-V-E, love Highlands. I guess you could say I'm a little excited to be here."

"So, you're Roger and Tootsie's granddaughter?" Liam grinned at her enthusiasm.

"Yeah. You know them?" Her head tilted to the side, and her eyes squinted in question.

"Everyone knows the Spiveys. They've owned the inn, what," he searched through the names, dates, and useless information in his head, "twenty, twenty-five years now. Almost long enough to be considered locals." He shot her a playful wink. "Course, being as they're from down East, I'm not sure if they'll ever truly hold that title."

She stepped up to the counter, scrutinized the menu, and ordered a maple & smoked sea salt cocoa before turning back to him. "Yeah, yeah, I've heard something along that line just about any time someone asks where I'm from. You mountain folk sure don't like us Flatlanders." Her button nose crinkled, but her eyes sparkled with humor as she moved aside to let him choose his coffee. "You'd think being born and raised here in North Carolina would mean something, but nooooo. It's not like I've got an accent or anything. We talk the same." Amused sarcasm laced her words.

Liam chuckled loud and deep. While her accent was Southern, it most definitely wasn't the same as the mountain locals, and it was obvious she was well aware of that fact. Now that her initial nerves were gone, she was quite the spitfire, and he discovered he liked her bubbly personality. Of course, he noticed how pretty she was, even if her coat made her look like The Michelin Man braving the harsh, cold tundra. As sweet as she was, Marshmallow Girl was probably a more appropriate nickname. Yeah, that sounded much better.

His chance to reply disappeared when Elle, the barista, called out her order number. As she grabbed her cup, she glanced at her watch and her eyes widened. "Oh my gosh, I gotta run. Grams needs a few things from the store, and I've been gone way too long." She hitched her purse strap over her shoulder and beamed another beautiful, bright smile. "It was so nice to finally meet you and talk to you, Liam. I hope we get to do it again real soon." And with that, she scurried out the door.

Liam's eyes stayed glued to the spot where she disappeared as the flicker of interest in his brain sparked to a smoldering ember. He leaned his head back and grinned at the ceiling. "Is that *Your* idea of knocking me off my feet?"

She was pretty and somewhat shy. Her sense of humor was sharp and witty. The pink on her cheeks when she was embarrassed was adorable. She obviously loved his mountains, so that was a big plus. As a matter of fact, only one thing bothered him about their whole encounter.

With all the crazy shenanigans going on in his brain, he forgot to ask her name.

Over the next several weeks, Liam's mind refused to shut down the thoughts. Images of her radiant smile and her bubbly personality intruded when he least expected. Life would keep him from finding out more about the mysterious girl, but glimpses of her around town would taunt him.

Liam walked out of the corporate office of Serene Escape Spa and Rejuvenation Center, too bewildered to notice the snowflakes dusting his cheeks. His gaze locked on a distant mountain range while his mind struggled to work through the puzzle of what happened moments ago.

The actual spa covered over thirty acres. Luxury, tent-like yurts and cabins situated around babbling brooks, and small waterfalls created a calm, healing atmosphere in a natural setting. For the past twenty-one years, his family's business had cleaned up winter's debris and planted the numerous lush meditation gardens. The job took several weeks of preparation and a full month to complete. Not to mention, it provided a solid third of his annual income. Because of this, Liam always made it the first stop for his spring scheduling.

The Huáng family leased several businesses in the area, including the spa, and Liam's company handled the landscaping at each of their locations.

Until that morning.

When Liam walked in for their annual planning session, Mr. Huáng surprised him by saying a group out of Asheville would handle the needs for all the family properties for the upcoming season. Liam's questions—and he had more than one since he'd never received a single complaint from them—went unanswered. Mr. Huáng ended the short meeting by saying things weren't what they seemed. As he walked out of the office, he warned Liam to keep his friends close and his enemies closer.

Liam prided himself on providing quality service in his hometown, just as his father did before him. Because businesses opened and closed all the time, the Huángs weren't his first loss, but they were the first to go elsewhere with no explanation or reason. Wrapping his head around losing his largest client was impossible.

With no family of his own and minimal expenses, he would be more than okay financially, but dang if it didn't sting his pride. The more he reflected on it, the more frustrated and confused he became. Questions bounced around in his head, tennis match style, but the answers were beyond his reach.

Icy wind cut through the layers of his coat and clothes, and a violent shiver drew him out of his miserable thoughts. The tips of his ears burned from the cold, and snowflakes gathered on his eyelashes, reminding him he needed to get to work instead of standing around feeling sorry for himself. He tugged his toboggan down over his ears, pulled the collar of his coat higher on his neck, and headed to his truck.

Out of the corner of his eye, he caught a glimpse of bright color moving down the dreary street. He turned to see what it was, and for the first time that morning, he felt like smiling. The *what* was *her* leaving the convenience store, eyes to the ground, her long, blonde hair hiding her face, and her red scarf trailing the ground behind her. Each of her careful, precise steps down the street took her further away from him

Her sweet voice and happy laughter were exactly what he needed to smash his sour attitude to pieces, and it certainly wouldn't hurt him to see her beautiful blue eyes again. With that in mind, he rushed after her, focused on the direction she was going, and watched to see if her path was clear.

But not his path.

Or Mr. Shelling's path, who chose that moment to walk out of the doctor's office, straight in front of Liam. Hard, young body slammed into soft, elderly body. With a fraction of a second to spare, Liam rotated to take the brunt of the fall, smashing his hip and elbow against the unforgiving concrete, but saving the retired high school principal from a nasty injury.

In the minutes it took Liam to get Mr. Shelling back on his feet, she was gone. And with her went the rest of Liam's day.

Elizabeth waited in the checkout line at Bryson's Grocery, furious over the events she'd witnessed earlier in the day. That crazy Tidwell woman was relentless in her visits to the inn, and Grams and Gramps refused to involve their granddaughter in the dealings. After her morning appearance, the menace stormed out, yet again. Grams and Gramps attempted to pacify Elizabeth when she asked questions, but *that* woman was close to pushing her temper past its boiling point. Instead of unleashing her anger, she hopped in her Jeep and headed into town, thinking boiled peanuts, hot cocoa, and a brisk walk would calm her. And if she were honest with herself, she hoped to run into Liam again, but not literally. Okay, since she was being honest with herself, that wouldn't be so bad, either.

As she stepped up to the register, a strange prickling sensation traveled down her spine. Someone was staring at her. Her gaze whipped to the end of the checkout, and there he stood, right beside the exit.

Liam.

His turquoise eyes lit up, and his lips curved in a warm smile.

She was captivated by his stare, and everything else faded to the background.

Until he took a step toward her.

Nestled against his chest was a small head full of caramel blonde, Shirley Temple curls. Thumb clutched firmly between her lips and eyes closed in sleep, she looked like a little angel.

"Hey, you're hard to track down." He inched closer, but stopped when the child in his arms wiggled.

"Your little girl is precious." Her heart hurt a little, but her words were sincere.

"Oh, she's—"

Liam's reply ended rather abruptly when the little angel lifted her head, cried out, and then proceeded to throw up all over his chest.

His eyes shot wide open and filled with alarm, and Elizabeth giggled. When his nose scrunched against the strong odor, Elizabeth choked back a sympathetic gag at the smell. She sighed as he rubbed soothing circles on the little girl's back while he spoke words of comfort.

Like a good father, he showed no panic at the situation. While she was happy about that, she was also disappointed, because when she was with him at the coffee shop, he certainly hadn't acted as if he was married. She thought she sensed interest on his part, and she knew, without doubt, she was more than a little curious about him. Judging by the way he held the precious bundle in his arms, his heart belonged to someone else.

The toddler's whimpers made it obvious where his attention needed to be. His eyes traveled from the little girl to Elizabeth, and his face fell.

"One day, I'll get this right." His shoulders slumped as he gave Elizabeth a half-hearted wave and walked out the door.

Too bad he's taken.

"Not yet, but Liam Broun's sure gonna make some girl awful lucky one day."

Elizabeth whirled around to the register and realized she'd spoken her thoughts out loud. "Pardon?" So preoccupied with Liam, she'd forgotten about the cashier.

Elizabeth glanced at the door, hoping for one last look at him.

The cashier continued to speak, but she struggled to focus on the conversation.

"... Yeah, he takes care of those three girls like they're his own."

Those words broke through her haze and caught her attention.

"Wait! What? That's not his daughter?"

"Nah, but you'd never know by watching him when he's with his nieces. I don't reckon that'll change even when he has his own." She scanned the boiled peanuts, punched in the code for the cocoa, and gave Elizabeth her total.

Elizabeth's breath caught as she paid, picked up her snack, and thanked the lady, hoping to catch up with Liam to see if he needed her help. With the transaction concluded, she turned to walk out, but caught the cashier's parting words.

"Yeah, he's a catch, so if I were you, I wouldn't be resting on my laurels. He's worth the chase."

The brisk air did nothing to cool her disappointment when she saw Liam pull out of the parking lot. Today wasn't going to be her day.

Liam wrapped his arm around Bekah's shoulder, grabbed the bag of medicine, and guided her out the door of the pharmacy. Between helping Wrynn with the kids, stressing over his client list expiring one by one, and juggling the remaining jobs with shifts at the fire station, he was exhausted to the bone. Time was definitely not on his side. Knowing his luck, he would be the next one to get sick. If he stopped to think about it, his throat was a little prickly.

"My throat hurts, Uncle Liam, and my tummy feels funny." Bekah peered up at him, her cheeks flushed and her eyes glazed with fever.

Strep throat was running its course through the family. First Wrynn, then Maggie, and then Bekah. Liam couldn't help but wonder when it would hit Annie. He and his sister had tried to isolate the rest of the family, but so far, their plan hadn't worked. And the evidence was plain in the sick little girl next to him.

"Well, we need to get your first dose of antibiotics in you, and you need something in your stomach so it doesn't make you puke." When she burrowed into his side, he tightened his hold. "I'm thinking a milkshake would numb your throat and fill your tummy. Feel like making a quick stop in Mountain Fresh?"

Her subdued nod against his side told him how bad she felt. The normal Bekah would have been over the moon at eating ice cream for lunch. As high as her fever was, he imagined much more than her throat hurt.

"Want me to carry you?"

That earned him another small nod, so he lifted her in his arms, helped her get as comfortable as she could be, and carried her across the street to the store.

As they waited to check out, Liam juggled Bekah and her milkshake to get to his wallet. A familiar, obnoxious voice caught his attention, and when he turned to look, anger sank its claws into him.

It was Mrs. Tidwell, Wrynn's mother-in-law, and the absolute bane of his existence.

Not only did the evil woman live to torture Wrynn at every chance, but for some odd reason, she also decided to turn her particular brand of bitter evil on him and his landscaping company. Over the last two weeks, more than one of his clients had confided in him about her harassment as they released him from their employ. It seemed she was bound-and-determined to run him out of business. Her actions puzzled him, and he wasn't quite sure how to handle the situation. One thing he knew, though, was there was only one way he would tuck tail and run from her by closing his company.

Over his dead body.

A flash of blonde hair caught his eye, and he realized Mrs. Tidwell was giving *her* a severe tongue-lashing. He stepped out of line and headed straight to the ruckus.

"What's going on over here?" he asked as he joined the little group and positioned himself between the old woman and the target of her tongue.

"Aww, bless her, another sick baby?" His Marshmallow Girl rubbed Bekah's back and smoothed her hair from her face. "Ohh, she's burning up!" Her eyes widened in concern.

Liam rested his cheek on the top of Bekah's head. "Yeah, we just left the pharmacy. Sweetpea here needed a milkshake to take her medicine."

"That's two in two weeks. Not good. You feeling okay?"

"Yeah, but I–"

"Young man, you're being very irresponsible." Mrs. Tidwell bulldozed into the conversation.

"Mamaw?" Bekah raised her head from his shoulder and blinked at her grandmother. "What are you doing here?"

"You need to take that sick child home and quit spreading her germs around." The grumpy, old bat stomped her foot and pointed her finger in Liam's face.

"That sick child? You don't seem too awful concerned that *that sick child* is your granddaughter. Nor have you shown any concern when your–"

Bekah's hand cupped his cheek, bringing his attention back to her. "Uncle Liam, I don't feel so good."

Then she proceeded to throw up chocolate milkshake on his shoulder, his chest, and her mamaw's shoes.

His Marshmallow Girl bit her lip, but didn't quite manage to stop her giggle at the shocked expression on Mrs. Tidwell's face. The old woman sputtered but seemed unable to form words.

Liam closed his eyes and shook his head. "You have *got* to be kidding me." If he weren't so tired, he would be embarrassed.

When he opened his eyes, hers danced with laughter. He failed to see the humor in the situation, but of course, he was the one once again covered in vomit.

"Take two," she choked out between laughs.

"Just wait until you see my next act." He smiled and then sobered. "But seriously, one day soon, I'll catch you alone for a real introduction, but for now," he stroked his cheek on Bekah's head, "I need to get this one home."

"Yeah, you take care of her. That's what's important right now." Her hand drifted across Bekah's head and Liam's arm. "Besides, you know where to find me."

Yes, he did, and if she'd stay put, he would have cleared this mess up already.

"Grams, do you know Liam Broun?"

Elizabeth stood shoulder-to-shoulder beside her grandmother, washing the supper dishes after wonderful, home-cooked chicken and dumplings, green beans with fatback, and corn. If she kept eating like this, she would need to find a gym soon, but meals with her grandparents took some of the edge off missing her mom and dad.

"Law, child, been here over twenty-five years. Watched that boy grow up." Tootsie took the last plate and dried it. "From everything I know and hear about him, he's a mighty fine young man. You got a reason for askin'?"

"Umm, well, see…" The water gurgled down the drain, and Elizabeth wiped down the sink.

"Come on, girl, spit it out." Tootsie cackled and nudged her hip. "Somebody finally caught your eye again?"

In her freshman year of college, Elizabeth had met Jarrett and fell hard for him. They were both from small towns and close families. Hiking, camping, and being outdoors were shared passions. He loved golf as much as she did, and they played with her dad every time he went home with her. After-graduation plans were hinted at, futures discussed, and Elizabeth thought her happily ever after was within sight.

Midway through her sophomore year, her brother, Seth, got sick. She left school and, for the next couple of years, stayed home to concentrate on her family. Unfortunately, Jarrett felt neglected and abandoned, and never failed to share those feelings with her. In the beginning, his bitterness was subtle, but by the end, it was harsh. No matter what she said or did, the extremes she went to were not enough to please him. One day, between the pressure he placed on her and dealing with her brother's terminal illness, Elizabeth snapped. The frayed strings holding their relationship together unraveled, and she refused to compromise herself any longer. For her, the choice was simple. Her family. For him, his choice was one of her so-called best friends.

Since her brother's death, she'd focused on healing, helping her mother deal with her depression, and finishing her degree. What she didn't do, was think of dating. After all, Jarrett's callous treatment left her feeling as if she could never measure up. Facing rejection was not something she desired, so she simply avoided it. She never let herself get into a situation where more could develop.

Until a cold, snowy day when she'd slid on a patch of ice and slammed into Liam's back. Something about him crawled under her defenses and pulled at her. So, yes, she guessed she could say her interest was piqued.

"Well, I've run into him a few times, once quite literally, and he just seems so nice." Her cheeks heated with a blush, and she peeked through her eyelashes. "Can you tell me a little about him?"

"That would explain why he's dropped in more often lately. If I'd known that, I'd a stopped what I was doing to talk to him," Tootsie mumbled as she wrapped her arm around Elizabeth's waist and pulled her to the couch in the living room. "Well, like I said, I've watched him grow up. And to be honest, honey, he *is* nice. Comes from a good family. Dad's a carpenter and works landscaping with Liam sometimes, and his mom's a teacher. And that boy sure loves his sister and her girls to pieces. He'd do anything for them. His work ethic is above reproach. I guarantee he works hard. Maybe too hard, if you ask me. Between landscaping spring through fall, snow and ice removal in the winter, and working at the fire department, I don't know how he has time for much else."

Grams settled against the cushions, linked her fingers through Elizabeth's, and gave her a gentle smile. "But if there's one thing I've learned over time, it's that he makes time for what's important to him. See, his sister, Wrynn, she's a widow. Couple years ago, his brother-in-law, Tripp, went on some secret mission for the Army, and died. Even though Tripp and Liam were thick as thieves, Liam put his mourning aside and took over everything, and I mean everything, 'cause his sister lost it. One reason he's always so busy is 'cause she's never recovered from losing her man."

When Grams squeezed her fingers, Elizabeth glanced up at her. "He's nothing like Jarrett. He knows loss, honey, and he wasn't the least bit selfish in the way he stepped up for his sister. Don't know if she'd a made it without his help. Sure know those girls of hers would be in a world of hurt without him, though."

Elizabeth smiled as she thought of her most recent encounters with him. Grams wasn't telling her something she hadn't already figured out on her own. "Last two times I saw him, he was carrying a sick niece. He *may* have gotten puked on both times, too." She and Tootsie chuckled. "Best part was, the last time, his niece threw up on Mrs. Tidwell, too. I almost lost it right there in Mountain Fresh."

Tootsie pressed her hand over her heart, threw her head back, and hooted in laughter. "I would have paid to see that, honey child. Woulda made my day." She straightened and grabbed Elizabeth's chin in a firm grip. "Now, you stay away from that one. She's mean as a striped snake and twice as venomous. Trying to hurt that boy's business. The likes of her I'll never understand."

Those words did not sound promising. Elizabeth thought something bad was going on with Mrs. Tidwell, and now that she had an idea what it was, she didn't feel so good about it. "That's why she keeps coming in the inn, threatening Gramps, and arguing with him? I wondered what was up with that. When he saw her aggravating me, he stormed over to us like he was going to throw down with her. I will say, though, it did make me feel better. I do *not* like that woman."

"And," Grams' grip tightened on her chin, "you do *not* need to be in her presence. There's something wrong with her. Something not quite right. Some kind of evil. Stay away from her, honey. Far, far away."

At Tootsie's statement, Elizabeth shivered. The maniacal look in Mrs. Tidwell's eyes was enough to keep Elizabeth away. Still, she hoped things worked in Liam's favor, and he came out of whatever the woman planned unscathed.

"No worries there, Grams. Don't want to be near her. She kind of scares me, to be honest. And just to set the matter straight, *she* approached *me* about me talking some sense into the two of you." Elizabeth wrapped her hand around her grandmother's and pulled her chin loose. "Sure wish we could keep her out of the inn, though. That'd be awful nice."

The clock chimed eight times, and Elizabeth stood up and helped Tootsie off the couch. She knew her grandparents went to bed early, and she didn't want to be responsible for them not getting enough sleep.

"So, if Liam and I can ever manage more than a minute together without vomit involved, that'd be all right with you?"

"Let's see. Warm, kind, honest, respectful, compassionate, hard worker, and loves his family? Honey child, that would be more than all right with me." She wrapped Elizabeth in a loving hug and pressed a kiss to her cheek. "Now, it's time for us old people to head to bed, but you keep me informed, and don't be making me poke after you for information. Ya hear me? Love you, sweet girl."

"Love you, too, Grams. I need to call Momma anyway. She'll

want a Liam update. Thanks for supper and for taking time to talk," she said as she left.

As she reached the exit, the door opened, and she held it while a woman and two children walked straight to the registration counter. Her mental list of the evening arrivals didn't include a group of three. The night attendant wasn't at the counter, so Elizabeth scurried behind the desk to scan the computer for a name.

Nothing. Hmm, that's strange.

Walk-ins were rare because the inn was on the outskirts of town, nowhere near a main road. The location was desirable for folks who needed a break from their crazy world. Still, business was business, so Elizabeth filled out the paperwork, grabbed keys to a two-bedroom unit, and welcomed Melisa Case and her kids to Highlands.

Although her mind was preoccupied with her conversation with Grams, she showed them to their cabin and helped with their luggage. An overwhelming sense of sadness cloaked the family, almost choking Elizabeth with its strength. Exhaustion was visible in their tired eyes, slumped shoulders, and strained faces. The worst part was the despair etched plainly in the mother's expression. It touched Elizabeth in a familiar way she wasn't willing to explore right then.

Refusing to let the despondent mood drag her down any further, she said her goodbyes and raced to her cabin. After a long, hot shower to wash away the winter's chill, Elizabeth climbed in bed, called her parents for a quick chat, and then fell asleep to her grandmother's words.

Warm, kind, honest, respectful, compassionate, hard worker, and loves his family.

Yeah, that would work for her. Now, things would be perfect if she could get closer to him than across a busy store, congested street, or him with a sick child, *and* somehow manage not to embarrass herself by falling at his feet or mumbling whatever flew through her mind.

At long last, strep throat ran its course through the Tidwell/Broun family, sparing no one, not even Liam and Wrynn's parents. During the time the family was sick, three more clients canceled their services. Something had to give, and soon, or he wouldn't have the income to put fuel in his snowplow or purchase mulch for the spring.

His first stop upon reentering the land of the living was Buck's Coffee, where he was supposed to meet with Janet Weatherby. Not only a client, she'd also been his mother's best friend since high school and his adopted aunt. His gut told him the appointment wasn't going to be pleasant for either one of them.

The fragrance of fresh roasted coffee beans hit him when he walked in the shop. That smell never grew old. As he stomped the slush from his boots, he scanned the tables and spotted Janet in a booth at the window overlooking the street. He caught her eye, tilted his hand as though he was sipping from a cup, and nodded at her. With a grin directed at him, she lifted her own mug and shooed him to the counter.

Nerves danced in his stomach while he waited for the barista to fill his order. His thoughts went back and forth about what would happen, but Liam refused to believe Janet would fire him without a sound reason and explanation. Something told him to keep calm and listen carefully, because she was a well-respected businesswoman, a member of the town council, and a lifetime Highlander. Her finger stayed on the pulse of the community.

As soon as Elle called his order, he took a deep breath, whispered a short prayer, and joined Janet at the table.

"Liam, son, how've you been? It feels like it's been ages. Between my work and meetings, and your work and sick family, I've not had a chance to catch up with you lately. Tell me how Wrynn and the girls are. I really need to find time to run by and see them." She reached across the table, jerked his toboggan off his head, and ruffled his hair like she did when he was a young boy. "Everything okay? You seem a little, well, nervous, maybe out of sorts," she nodded at his knit cap, "and that's not like you." Her rapid fire questions were nothing new to him.

"Everything's going to be okay now that strep is finally gone. It was a little rough there for a bit, but once the girls were over it, things got a little easier." He glanced up at the ceiling and pinched the bridge of his nose before looking at her. "Wrynn's just Wrynn. No change, far as I can see. All I can do is be there when she and the monkeys need me, and pray she'll pull through. Not much else I can do, Aunt Janet."

"Oh, honey, one day it'll get better. I just know it." Her warm hand closed over his and squeezed to express her comfort. "It takes time for a broken heart to heal, 'cause first, you gotta find all the pieces. Just be patient with her, and it'll come."

"Yeah, in the back of my head, I know you're right, but you know what they say. The waiting is the hardest part." Frustration leaked into his words. "Day in and day out, nothing seems to change." Lost in his thoughts and unaware of his actions, the sleeve on his cup fell victim to his memories. Flecks of cardboard littered the table under his restless fingers.

"I miss her, the old her. The girl who laughed and lived and loved like there was no tomorrow. It used to irritate me when she'd flit from one thing to another." A small smile flickered across his face as memories of the younger version of his sister ran through his head. "Always running around without a care in the world. She was always up to something. You know. I'd give anything to see a flash of that girl again."

He pictured the current Wrynn, the one who'd given up, and pain lanced through his heart. "Instead, her eyes are dead. Her laughter's dried up. I swear she'd grow roots in the mattress if we didn't force her to get out of bed. And it kills me. Every single day, a little piece of me dies with her, and I don't know what to do about it. I want to find my own slice of happiness, but how can I be so selfish when she's in so much pain?"

Hunched over the table, he tried to sort through the mess in his brain. When he compared his sister's troubles to his empty life, guilt reared its ugly head. One day, his tomorrow would come. He didn't doubt it for one moment. What troubled him was whether Wrynn would be able to handle him finding what she'd lost. By all indications, she wouldn't, and he worried his happiness would push her further into her pit of mourning. What right did he have to want more when Tripp's death left her so broken and empty?

Why did life have to be so hard?

A touch on his lip startled him. What was that metallic taste in his mouth?

Janet held a napkin, dotted with blood, and he realized he'd gnawed the side of his lip a little too hard.

"I think I lost ya." Janet chuckled, but Liam saw the concern in her eyes. "I'd like to say you need to lose the guilt and worry about starting your own family, and I'd love to know you'd listen and do it. But …"

He opened his mouth to speak. She reacted by tilting her head and pointing a finger at him.

"Wait, let me finish. But we both know that's not going to happen. That's not who you are. You've spent a lifetime putting your sister first, and that's not going to change overnight. So," she grabbed his hands and squeezed, "this is what I'll say instead. Love your sister and those precious babies. Help them. Protect them and just be there for them. But, Liam, honey, don't close yourself off from everything else. Keep your eyes and heart open, because one day, some little gal's going to come along and sweep you off those giant feet. And when she does, I'm soooo going to love watching you fall. And don't think, for one moment, that you don't deserve happiness, 'cause you'd be wrong. I just hope you're smart enough to grab it and run. *That* has yet to be seen."

Liam grinned at the laughter in her eyes. Leave it to Janet to compliment him in one breath and insult him the next. One thing he knew for sure, being around her made the burden in his heart a little lighter. The comfort he felt with her enabled him to talk about things he otherwise kept buried. After all, a wise person once said, "Open confession is good for the soul." Never before had he spoken of the anxiety he felt about Wrynn not being able to handle his happiness. Saying the words to someone who loved him was cleansing, almost therapeutic.

Against the dingy, dirty snow, a flash of bright white moving by the window caught his attention. Every thought but her drained from his head. As soon as he saw the red scarf, his heart thudded. Her simple, unadorned beauty brightened the cloudy, gray day. His gaze followed her down the opposite sidewalk to AnaWear, a local clothing boutique. A broad smile split his face. He could be across the street and in the store in less than ten seconds. Maybe he'd finally learn her name. He scooted to the end of the bench, intending to rush out to find her.

"Hmm, that's interesting."

The *tap, tap, tap* of Janet's fingernail clicking against the table drew his attention back to her. Red burned through his cheeks and settled in the tips of his ears. Embarrassment choked him, and he coughed to clear his throat. Good grief, in his haste to leave, he'd forgotten she was there.

"Oh, Liam, I wish you could see your face. Blink before your eyes pop out of your head." Delighted laughter burst from her lips when he opened and closed his mouth, struggling to form an apology. "No, don't say anything. I can see that you don't want to be here anymore, so let's get the ugly out of the way."

Her words slammed into his brain, reminding him of the real reason he was there. Maybe she knew the answers to the problems plaguing his clients. Mrs. Tidwell was involved, no doubt, but what exactly she was doing was beyond his realm of comprehension.

"Mrs. Tidwell." He drew a deep breath in and forced it out his nose. "If you're firing me, too, I'd rather you'd just go ahead and rip off the Band-Aid. Do it fast. Hurts less that way."

"Pfft, seriously? You think I'm going to let that old cow tell *me* what to do? Honey, you're smarter than that." She rested her forearms on the table and leaned toward him. "I don't own near as much as she does, but what I do own is mine, free and clear. And let me tell you something. It gripes her tail that she doesn't have anything to hold over me. I don't have a snowball's chance in you-know-where of ever being as rich as she is, but God as my witness, if I could buy her out and run her off, I'd do it in a heartbeat.

"Now, as the preacher says, you need to listen quick, and you need to listen carefully. I'm going to spit this out and let you get onto happier things."

Liam took a deep breath and blew it out, knowing Janet was getting ready to drill something important into his head.

"She's out to ruin you," Janet began, shaking her head in disgust. "I'd say I don't know why, but we both know that'd be a lie. In her eyes, Tripp and Wrynn stole Nana and Papa's property and bank accounts from her, no matter what their wills said. She hates you. She hates Wrynn. She hates your parents. And that hatred has turned her into one bitter, old shrew. Y'all have something she's always wanted—a warm, loving, close-knit family. And at the rate she's going, she ain't never going to get it, so she wants to take it away from you.

"She thinks she owns this town, and she ain't half-wrong. Her goal is to force y'all to go somewhere else. If you work for them, they're instructed to fire you. If you don't work for them, they're ordered not to hire you. So far, almost every one of them has fallen in line with her demands."

He opened his mouth to ask her for an example, but she threw her hand up and shushed him.

"She is methodically harassing, one by one, every business that rents from her, frightening them with the cancelation of their leases. Why, she told Philbert over at Corner Wine and Cheese that she'd level the building to the ground. He's been in that same spot for more than thirty years, and even more, he's too old to start over again from scratch.

"Liam, honey, their livelihood, the way they feed their families and pay their bills, is being threatened. Their hands are tied because she has the money to string things out in court longer than they can afford not to eat."

This was news to Liam, but not a big surprise. The thought of someone losing their only source of income over a pile of mulch and spring flowers really stuck in his craw. Over the years, he'd witnessed Mrs. Tidwell harassing Tripp, Wrynn, and the girls, but this was a new low, even for the old hag.

"So, here's my advice, take it or leave it." She scooted out of the booth, stepped over to his side, and squeezed his shoulder. "You can't fight her, honey, 'cause you alone can't win. But what you can do is keep your eyes open and your ears sharp. Every single business owner knows exactly what she's doing, so find those rare few around town who don't rent from her and woo them. And for Heaven's sake, swallow your stubborn pride and ask for help. You know I'm always looking to invest in local businesses, and honey, you're a sure thing. Now, go get your girl."

She slid an arm around his shoulder, kissed the top of his head, and poof, she was gone, the bell over the door announcing her departure.

"Drop a bomb on me and then walk out, why don't ya?" a stunned Liam said to the empty space beside him.

Janet left him with some things to think about. Wow, he knew things were bad, but he had no idea the sabotage was downright evil. How did someone like her find the peace to sleep? His imagination couldn't even travel as low as her actions.

Highlands was his home, and dang if he'd let some hateful

shrew rip it out from under him. He needed to pull his head out of the clouds and find a way to work through the mess she was creating.

Pen in hand, he made a short list of things to do right away. Property search to see which clients leased from Mrs. Tidwell. Appointment with his accountant to see where he stood when those clients fired him. A call to Janet to discuss a loan or investment, just in case he needed it. He was sure he'd think of several more things over the next couple of days, but at least he had somewhere to start.

Yeah, he thought, *I can do this. She might just keep on kicking me, but dang if I'm going to let her run me out of my own town. I'm going to fight back. Now, on to more pleasant things.*

Throwing a tip on the table, he slipped his toboggan on his head and walked out of Buck's. As the door closed behind him, a red Jeep passed him. Inside it was his Marshmallow Girl.

"Dadgummit. Will I ever catch a break?"

Radio Broadcast

"Goooood morning, Highlanders! You're listening to the local news on WHLD, AM radio 1250. Today is Monday, February eleventh, and these are your community updates.

"Girl Scout Troop 30606 will be selling cookies in the Mountain Fresh parking lot this coming Saturday morning. This will be your last chance to grab those Thin Mints, Shortbreads, or Caramel Delights before cookie season ends, so get 'em while you can. Remember, no pushing or skipping line. Don't want a repeat of last year's riot, and the troop leader assures me there's enough to go around. Also note, Weight Watchers counselors will be on hand to help those members suffering from this annual guilt-filled purchase.

"A friendly reminder that you only have three days until Cupid comes to visit, so don't forget to get sweets for your sweet. And there's still time to get your tickets now for the annual Country Club's Love is in the Air extravaganza. The theme of this year's costume ball is Old Hollywood Glamour. While the gentlemen will get the opportunity to look very dapper in their suits and tuxes, the real excitement will be those slim-cut dresses, drop-waist skirts, and opera gloves the ladies will be modeling. And, as always, good neighbors, proceeds will benefit the Highlands High School Golf team.

"Speaking of good neighbors, Miss Ola needs some help from the men in our community. As you all know, the ice storm last week took its toll on the area, and this sweet lady has several fallen trees she needs removed from her yard. If you're willing to lend a hand, head on over. She made sure to tell me her blue ribbon coffee cake will be warm and waiting for you. That makes a little sweat and hard labor worth the reward.

"Mother Nature's reaction to those vicious rumors of global warming was to dump seven more inches of snow last night. Road conditions are fair at best, so if you need to go out today, please drive carefully and keep your eyes on the road while you watch the other cars around you.

"Temperatures today will hover in the low twenties with periods of below zero wind chills. Wrap up and stay warm. Seems we're in for the long haul this winter.

"And on that note, all church services in the area are canceled for this evening. Join us at 7:30 tonight, from the comfort of your own home, when the Reverend Barker from First United will lead us all in a short Bible study to round out our week.

"Now on to the national news ..."

Chapter 4

C old wind whipped through the white-covered lawn of the Endless View Farm and Inn. Liam pulled his wool cap over his ears in hopes of finding a smidgen of warmth. Frozen fingers, long numbed by the arctic air, gripped the shovel handle, dug it under the layer of snow on the sidewalk, and transferred the heavy bundle to the wheelbarrow. A sharp spasm hit his lower back muscles, and he gritted his teeth against the stabbing pain.

Normally, he wouldn't complain. After all, removing snow and ice for the local businesses and residents kept Liam's business afloat during the off-season. But this year's winter seemed to be never-ending. Almost constant storms dumped foot after foot and, with the way things were going, Highlands might never thaw. Just last week, Mother Nature dropped another seven inches, her antics forcing Liam to start his day well before dawn.

The simplicity of the task allowed time for his mind to wander. Dreams of a sunny, sandy beach competed with the vision of a roaring fire waiting for him at his sister's house. As the imagined warmth teased his frozen limbs, he turned to clear another section of the pathway. Long accustomed to the backbreaking work, he bent, scooped, and dumped his way across the concrete footpath.

Maybe Marshmallow Girl will finally be here this time. She's harder to catch than a greased pig. Speaking of, I need to stop by the Smokehouse and grab barbeque so Wrynn won't have to fix—

A shrill cry jerked him back to the present. The bright sun glared off the blanket of snow, and, shielding his eyes with one hand, he searched for the source of the shriek. Blinded by the harsh light bouncing off the white surface, he couldn't see the young girl until her body slammed into him, and her arms wrapped around his strong waist.

"You gotta save me!" she screamed as her head turned from side-to-side to look behind her. "He's going to get me." She shuddered and buried her face against his stomach.

He imagined someone coming after his nieces, and his shoulders tightened as he searched for the person trying to get the little girl. Before Liam could respond, a snowball flew through the air, smashed against her back, and disintegrated in a spray of ice. Her scream made his ears ring, and the jerk of her body forced him back a step. A slow grin spread over his face.

Snowball fight.

Relief flooded through him, followed by a hearty laugh. The situation was one he could handle with no problem. He tugged her arms loose, crouched down in front of her, and scooped up a handful of snow. After he packed it into a firm, round ball, he handed it to her and made a few more as fast as he could.

"Let's go. You lead and I'll follow."

She darted around the corner of the inn toward the cabins, and Liam jogged to keep up with her. As he left the cover of the tree line, a snowball whizzed past his head and slammed into the trunk.

"Dang, I missed him."

Liam spun to where the voice came from, caught sight of a little boy running away, and hurled a snowball against the moving target. When it shattered on the kid's shoulder, Liam raced to catch him.

Out of nowhere, one slammed into the back of his head. He skidded to a stop, turned, and was surprised to see the little girl giggling and looking guilty.

"Don't mess with my brother." She planted her fists on her hips and cocked her chin.

Liam understood and appreciated the way of things between the siblings. Though he might aggravate his sister, no one else was allowed to, and he would never hesitate to protect her.

When he lunged in the girl's direction, more weapons of ice destruction rained down from the boy's side.

"You little buggers, you're ganging up on me." Caught between showers of snowballs, he did the only thing he could. Liam dropped to his knees, and rushed to build a pile of ammunition. "You'll pay for that," he said in a silly, cartoony voice he sometimes used with his nieces.

Liam lost track of time as he focused his energy on shielding himself as best he could while returning fire from the two rascals. Laughter rang through the crisp air, and before he knew it, Liam warmed enough from his efforts that sweat ran down his spine.

"Enough. Enough." He took two steps to the side and fell back into the snow. "You win."

"Let's make snow angels." The little girl dropped down beside him and swept her arms and legs through the snow. "Momma always did this with us before she got sick."

A piercing whistle shattered the quiet. The kids immediately turned to the sound. Liam twisted his neck and shielded his eyes. Through the blinding glare, he thought he saw a woman, wrapped from head to toe in a blanket, on the porch.

"That's Mom. She needs us." The little boy stepped toward the cabin. "Come on, sis."

"Will you come back and play with us?" The little girl's round eyes filled with hope. "We don't get to play outside too much anymore," she whispered.

"Gotta go, Sissie. Mom needs us, and I'm hungry." Her brother grabbed her hand, pulled her up from the snow, and stepped in front of her as if to protect her.

Liam turned his smile down a notch, not wanting the young man to think he was mocking the way he shielded his sister. "I do the landscaping and snow removal here at the inn, so I'm sure you'll be seeing me around. Feel free to come distract me anytime I'm shoveling." He raised up on his elbow and pointed toward the cabin. "Now y'all better get a move on before you get in trouble."

Liam watched to make sure they made it safely to the cabin. Before the door closed behind them, the girl leaned out and yelled, "Bye! See you soon."

He hopped up, brushed the snow off his clothes, and went back to shoveling so he could throw down some salt before he went to see if he could find his Marshmallow Girl.

Several hours later, he was frozen stiff, from his nose to his toes. When he walked into the inn, heat seeped into his bones, making his skin prickle in darts of pain. The lobby was full of people carrying and pulling suitcases. Roger and Tootsie stood behind the registration desk, one checking folks in, and the other grabbing keys and answering questions. A thorough inspection failed to reveal the person he was looking for, and as he backtracked to the door, Tootsie glanced up and yelled at him.

"Son, you shoulda said something before now. Pretty sure she went down to the Ugly Dog to grab some supper. You make sure she gets home safe, okay?" Then she winked at him before turning back to the customer at the counter.

Finally, the break he'd been looking for. He made the drive into town in record time, all the while hoping she would still be there. When he walked in the pub, music played loud enough to keep conversations at each table private. In the back corner, he saw her blonde hair and headed in her direction.

"Who's gonna tell Aunt Lyda, Duncan's moving too far away?" She bounced back and forth, dancing in her seat as she sang some ridiculous, mixed up lyrics. The plate in front of her was all but empty. "Oh, oh, oh, who's gonna tell Aunt Lyda, that it's–"

"What in this world are you singing?"

Was she dreaming?

While enjoying her late supper, she'd been thinking about him and wondering if they would ever finally connect. Those too few occasions she saw him left her mildly obsessed and wanting more. After all, it wasn't every day she literally fell for someone. Yes, she'd been embarrassed, but she'd be lying to herself if she ignored the spark of interest she'd felt. Liam was pretty darn handsome, with his tousled, reddish-brown hair and those fascinating, turquoise eyes. Even though he towered over her, not once did she feel threatened. When he'd saved her from falling, (okay, she knew he didn't really *save* her, but a girl could dream), the muscles in his arms were firm and plentiful beneath her hands. So much so, she didn't want to let go. And when he smiled at her, her heart sighed.

And there he was, as if her mind conjured his presence.

"You do realize that's 'Jet Airliner' by Steve Miller Band, right?" Chuckling, he stepped up to the table as the server took her money and bussed the table.

She burst into laughter and lifted her coat off the chair beside her. "Of course, I do. My brother made sure to tell me every time I serenaded him with this song. It used to drive him crazy when I got song lyrics wrong, so of course I went out of my way to be creative. I'm pretty sure it's a sister's civic duty to aggravate her brother as much and as often as possible."

"Sounds like something my sister would do. Course, since she's deathly afraid of spiders, I'd probably throw one on her as payback." He held her coat for her, wrapped her scarf around her neck, and captured her hand in his. "This might sound stupid, but I realized when you dashed out of Buck's that I didn't ask your name. After chasing you all over creation, I've finally found you, and we need to remedy this situation. Fortunately, this time your grandma saw me before I left and told me where to find you, so here I am."

"Oh, she said she's seen you several times lately. She just didn't know you were looking for me." She stretched her neck to look him in the eyes and lost herself in their warmth. Deep blue and bright yellow flecks floated in the turquoise, and the outer ring appeared to be navy. From the first moment they'd met, she was fascinated, and right then was no different. There was just something different about this man.

"So, you asked Mrs. Spivey about me? I think I'm flattered."

"Hmm, what did you say?" Her gaze traveled over his face, and she liked what she saw. His tan skin, even in the dead of winter, showed he was outdoors a lot. Small, white creases framed his smiling eyes, and lighter toned laugh lines bordered his mouth. She just knew he was a man who smiled and did it often. Even the crooked bump on the bridge of his nose added to his overall masculine appeal. Simply put, he was stunning.

Beautiful.

He pinched his lips together and almost covered his chuckle, and she winced.

"Oops, I did it again."

"I have a feeling this is going to be fun." His smile revealed straight, white teeth set against firm lips. "But seriously, I don't think I'd describe myself as beautiful. You, on the other hand, fit that description to a T. Now, are you going to tell me your name, or should I just make one up for you?"

"Oh, no you don't. *I* have a feeling I'll be providing ample opportunity for you to laugh at me without you having to make up names!" She laughed at herself because she figured she would prove this statement true several times over. "I'm Elizabeth, Elizabeth Pittman." She tried to raise her hand to shake his and realized he still held it. "Is that better?"

"Perfect. It's good to finally see you without half the town or a puking kid between us." His hand was warm on her lower back as he led her to the exit. "And I'd like to apologize for it taking so long for me to make this happen, but besides this crazy weather and work, my sister, my nieces, and I have all been passing strep back and forth.

Didn't figure I should share that with you."

The cold wind slammed into her, and try as she might, she couldn't keep the strong shiver from working its way through her body. When his arm slipped around her shoulders, she took advantage of his warmth and burrowed deep into his side.

Hmm, he smells good.

Startled, she peeked up at him through her lashes, but when he didn't react to her thought, she relaxed against him. Maybe she was getting better at holding them in.

"Thanks. This cold can be a little much for me sometimes." She clicked the remote on her keys, and the headlights on her Jeep flashed. "You wanna go grab some cocoa or coffee?" Another hour or two with Liam would be a perfect ending to a long, dreary day. It sure wouldn't hurt to see if all the things she remembered from their first encounter were true or just something her mind created on its own. Even if her memories were faulty, his sharp wit was entertaining and guaranteed to bring her more laughter than the spreadsheets she spent her days with.

Please, say yes.

His arm lifted from her shoulders, and a grimace settled on his face as he looked at his watch. "I wish I *could* say yes, but my sister's expecting me for supper. She's not quite back to full speed after being sick, so I'm sure she'll need my help with the girls." His gaze roamed her face and settled on her lips before meeting her eyes. "Her situation's a little different than most. She needs me right now, and I wouldn't feel good about letting her down."

Her grandmother's words echoed through her mind. *Warm, kind, honest, respectful, compassionate, hard worker, and loves his family.* No, it wasn't in his nature to disappoint others.

"Aww, Grams told me a little about it. I can't imagine what's she's going through, but I do know she's lucky to have you." She stepped off the curb and turned back to him, uncertain what to do. Did she climb in her Jeep and drive away, or steal a few more minutes with the young man who captivated her? "Well, I guess I shouldn't keep you." When he said nothing, a small sigh of disappointment worked its way out of her mouth. "So, I'll say goodnight. Come see me sometime."

Black ice proved once again to be her enemy. As soon as her foot touched the road, she slipped. Her legs went in different directions, and her arms flailed in the air as her body flew toward his. At the moment she should have hit the ground, strong, warm arms wrapped around her waist and lifted her as though she were light as a feather.

A rush of heat engulfed her, and she didn't know if it was from embarrassment or the fact she liked being held so close by Liam. Regardless, she buried her face in the crook of his neck and struggled to catch her breath.

"What is it with me and ice?" Outside of golf, she wasn't athletic, but every time she was around Liam, she felt like a clumsy oaf. "I know it's hard to believe, but I promise I'm not usually this clumsy."

His chuckle drew her eyes to his. "I believe you. With the winter we've been having, this is an everyday occurrence." He drew her closer by tightening his hold and took careful steps to her Jeep. "Gotta admit though, you're pretty fun to catch."

After opening her door, he placed her on the seat and waited while she buckled her seatbelt and cranked the car.

"But you have to think I'm the clumsiest person, what with me falling around all over the place." She loved the hint of laughter in his eyes.

"Like I said, you're fun to catch. I guess I'll just have to make sure you keep falling for me." He pressed a kiss to her forehead. "Goodnight, Elizabeth," he said in a soft, gentle voice. "I'll see you soon. Be safe going home."

At those words, he jogged over to his truck, hopped in, and waved as he drove away. She stared into the rearview mirror until his taillights were no longer visible. As she put the Jeep in gear, she reflected over their brief encounter. One thing she knew for sure? Even though they'd just parted ways, she was already excited to see him again and hoped it would be soon.

Chapter 5

E lizabeth zipped her coat and pulled the hood snug around her face in hopes of deflecting the frigid air. Her cheeks were still a little numb from spending hours outside earlier that morning playing with the kids from Cabin Twelve. As if an icy finger trailed down her spine, goosebumps popped out on her skin. She shivered in the cold as she tugged her gloves on, tightened her scarf, and then grabbed grocery bags she'd put on the rocking chair. Winter in Highlands was beautiful, but dang, it was brutal on a warm weather girl. Life for her would be perfect on a tropical island. Instead, she felt like she was in Antarctica.

Careful to avoid the patches of ice, she stepped off the porch of her snug, little cabin. Ever since her previous Ice Capades performances, she kept her gaze glued to the path, hoping to prevent a repeat event. Since Liam wasn't there to catch her again, she knew she'd hit the ground hard.

Out of the corner of her eye, she caught movement.

Ah, there's my white knight.

"Pardon? I didn't quite catch that." Liam crossed the path to meet her.

"Darn, did I do it again?" Elizabeth covered her rapidly reddening face with her free hand and groaned in frustration. "You're going to think this is crazy, but sometimes my thoughts just pop right out of my mouth."

"I've kinda noticed, but it doesn't bother me." Liam laughed, and when she peeked up at him between her fingers, he pulled her hand from her face, but didn't let it go. "You're much too pretty to cover up." His gaze traveled over her features, and a warm feeling rushed through her cheeks. "There, much better."

"So, umm, what are you doing here?" *Did he come out here to see me?*

His lips pursing in amusement told her she'd done it again.

"Ugh, why do I keep embarrassing myself?"

"Yes, ma'am, I came out here to see you. I told you I'd be by soon." His grip tightened on her fingers, and he pulled her a step closer. "And it only embarrasses you because you don't know me, yet. We'll just have to work on that part." The wink he threw her made her stomach flutter.

He released her hand, took the bags of groceries, and placing his palm on the small of her back, guided her down the path in the direction she'd been going. "So, now that we have that out of the way, Elizabeth, what are your plans for this evening? Are you running away?" The cans clanked when he shook the bags.

"Not hardly." She nudged his solid chest with her shoulder. "A family staying in one of the long term cabins has two kids, Brittany and Grayson. I spent the morning hanging out with them at the fire pit making S'mores. Seems their mother's sick, and they don't have much in the way of food. Since no one in town delivers groceries," she cocked her head toward the bags and pointed at Cabin Twelve, "Grams helped me make a basic list, and I ran by Bryson's to grab a few things. I'm just on my way to drop them by. Then, I'm heading into town to grab some supper. I figured if they need anything else, I can stop back by the store before I come home."

"Ugh." Liam grimaced. "That's gotta suck, going on vacation and getting sick. The other day, I had a snowball war with the little boy and girl who are staying there. Now that I think about it, they mentioned something about their mom being sick, but I guess it just went in one ear and out the other." He paused and scratched the stubble on his jaw. "I gotta say, it's awful nice that you and your grams are willing to help out." His arm wrapped around her shoulder, pulling her closer to his side and steering her around a patch of ice. "Not everyone would do something like that."

"Well, in my perfect world, everyone would follow The Golden Rule. Of course, then there'd be no war or hungry children or homeless people. Oh, and the temperatures would remain a balmy, eighty-five degrees, year round."

Elizabeth glanced at the cabin and grew troubled. It was the woman she'd checked in several weeks ago. Though Elizabeth had seen the kids wandering around the property numerous times, their mother remained quite the mystery. She'd reserved the cabin for several months, yet she and the kids had been gone as much as they'd been in Highlands.

Elizabeth wondered if she should share her suspicions with Liam. In doing so, her own pain would surface. Facing the actual reality was much more difficult than merely thinking about it. At times, it was too raw to hide. What if she cried? How embarrassing would that be?

Just what I need. To look like a blubbering idiot.

"Umm, Elizabeth?" She glanced up as a look of concern crossed his face and questions filled his eyes. "Why would you look like a blubbering idiot?"

"Crap, quit listening when you shouldn't," she teased and flashed him a small smile, but she could tell he knew she was avoiding the subject. A troubled sigh escaped. "Let's just say I've seen the mother and have an inkling of what's wrong with her. And, if I'm right, it's not good. If it's what I think it is, then my family's been there, and visiting those memories is hard for me."

Stopping at the porch railing, she closed her eyes and shook her head side-to-side, and as she did, she made a decision.

He's someone I can trust. I want to tell him.

As soon as the thought passed her mind, her eyes popped open. When he didn't react, she realized she may have actually succeeded in suppressing a thought. In the little time she'd spent with Liam, she was becoming more and more comfortable with him, despite managing to embarrass herself at every turn, but only because he made an effort to make her feel at ease. For some odd reason, with him, she felt protected and secure. After all, he did save her and sweep her off her feet. Okay, she slammed into him once, and he kept her from falling the other, but still, his strength was evident, hence the protected and secure. He was tall and handsome, gentle and caring, and everything she'd seen and heard led her to believe she could trust him. It wasn't often she met someone and developed such an immediate connection. So, she went with it and prayed she wouldn't regret it.

"Tell you what. If you'll give me a few minutes to run these in, *and* if you've got time, we can grab supper to go and then come back here and eat, maybe build a fire in the pit. And if you still want to know my theory behind what's happening here, and why I think so, I'll tell you. But I'm warning you, as my grams would say, it ain't pretty."

Liam's face softened, and his gaze captured hers. "Sweetheart, how 'bout we do the food and fire pit, but you tell me if you feel like it. Otherwise, we'll play twenty questions and get to know each other better." He cupped her cheek and pressed a kiss on her forehead. "If you want to spill, then spill. But if you just want to talk about random things, then that's what we'll do. But either way, if I get to spend time with you, I'm coming out a winner."

Is he really this sweet?

"Whelp, little lady, I guess you'll just have to figure that one out on your own."

When he chuckled, Elizabeth rolled her eyes and shook her head. It didn't help to get annoyed at herself. Maybe she should put a rubber band around her wrist and pop it each time she thought out loud. Then again, she'd probably end up with a nice line of welts and bruises if she did.

"Unless they need something while I'm here, this shouldn't take long. You want to wait for me at the inn?"

Please, say you'll wait.

"Nah, the walkways and steps are icing up, so I'd rather be here to make sure you don't slip." He lifted her onto the porch and then stepped back onto the path. "Why don't I run out to my truck and grab some salt and sand while you're in there? I'll meet you back here, so don't leave without me."

He jogged away before she could respond, so she knocked on the cabin door. When Grayson opened the door, she stepped inside and glanced around the room, taking in the surroundings in one, rapid sweep.

The frail woman with dark circles and pain-filled features rested on the couch, her arctic blue eyes watching Elizabeth's every move.

The putrid smell that haunted her even two years later filled the air. Used tissues scattered on the cushions. A stained blanket tucked close for warmth. What appeared to be blood spotting the front of her pale yellow sweatshirt. Trashcan close at hand, easy to reach, and ready for quick use. Medicine bottles, with which she was more than a little acquainted, littered the otherwise empty counters. Brittany and Grayson, their eyes filled with fear, faces lined with exhaustion, and bodies slumped with uncertainty.

Her stomach cramped as the reality of what she saw churned through her. It was worse than she'd thought. Acid attempted to break free and crawl up her throat. Elizabeth didn't have to ask questions. The evidence proved her suspicions correct, and looking at the two kids, she knew, without doubt, she would do everything she could to help them. Especially the kids.

Unfortunately, the one thing they truly needed, she couldn't provide.

Their mother.

Healthy.

Strong.

And from the look and smell of things, there was a good chance that wasn't going to happen, at least not anytime soon.

Pain gripped her heart, but she fought through it. Allowing

herself to grow anxious would help no one, but then again, she feared nothing could help the situation. Her lungs seized, reminding her to breathe.

She whispered a prayer for strength. For the first time ever, she realized her loss gave her the experience and knowledge to possibly make someone else's path easier.

He never gives you more than you're equipped to handle.

Shoulders squared, mind blanked to grief, Elizabeth drew courage from deep within and set out to do what would be a temporary, but necessary, remedy.

"Hi. I'm Elizabeth Pittman. My grams sent me with a few groceries, but it looks like you need a little more help than that." She kept her voice soft and soothing, her nerves hidden, and her attention directed to the woman on the couch. "Give me a sec to put this stuff away. Then we'll get you cleaned up and in bed."

Liam glanced at his watch, wondering what was taking Elizabeth so long. Pebbles of salt and layers of sand covered the walkways and steps. Even though he rushed, pride in his work kept him from cutting corners, so it took a little longer than just a few minutes. Now, he was a little concerned because he figured Elizabeth would be waiting for him when he'd finished.

The cabin door opened, and the little girl stuck her head out the opening. "Hey. Elizabeth wants you to come in here and wait for her in case she needs your help." She yawned and rubbed her eyes as she stepped back. "Hurry, it's cold."

Well, at least he knew Elizabeth was still there, but he wondered what kind of help she might need. Then he stepped in the cabin, and his brain went on alert. Something wasn't right, but he wasn't sure just what was wrong.

The first thing he noticed was a sickly sweet, chemical scent, unlike anything he'd ever smelled before. Definitely not like any bug his nieces had ever had, and Lord knew they'd had a ton. Schools and daycare equaled shared germs and cooties, and many a time he helped Wrynn with vicious viruses such as Roto or Noro. Nope, this was not the same smell.

The second thing to draw his attention was the young boy staring into the refrigerator. A glance inside showed it to be all but empty, and he bet its contents were what Elizabeth brought with her earlier. The situation didn't look good, especially for the kids.

Liam knew he wouldn't be able to sleep unless he did something to help. Cell reception might suck in Highlands, but he used his phone for more than calling people. He opened the Notepad app, thinking the kids, much like his nieces, needed some of their favorite things to eat and snack on while their mom was sick.

Through the thin walls, he heard the shower come on, and before he could question the kids, Elizabeth joined him in the living area, her arms full of soiled sheets.

"I'm sorry, Liam, but I think I'm going to be here for a little while." Her cheeks were splotchy, and her eyes were red and tired. "You probably don't want to wait for me."

He stepped closer to her, smoothed a stray curl behind her ear, and pulled her head to rest on his chest. Her muscles were jittery and her breathing labored. Pain of the emotional variety radiated off her in such strong pulses that it slammed into him and made his heart ache. When she relaxed against him, he kneaded his fingers into her tense shoulders.

"Elizabeth, I'm not in any hurry. I'm here for as long as you need me."

She rubbed her cheek against his shirt and sighed. "Listen, you need to eat, and I really don't know how long I'm going to be here. It's not fair to ask you to wait."

Her voice was soft and filled with regret. Liam hoped that meant she wasn't trying to get rid of him, but trying to be polite and thinking of him. Then her stomach growled, and he came up with the perfect solution. Running his fingers through her hair, he shared his idea.

"Why don't you ask their mom if I can take them into town? We'll stock up on groceries and grab something easy for supper tonight. And if you're finished with what you're doing when we get back, great. If not, I'll wait until you are. I'm not in any hurry, I promise, so don't worry about time. And surely you know by now, I don't want you slipping on any ice."

She lifted her head and gave him a tired smile. "I think I figured it out. You really are this sweet, aren't you?"

He tried to read the emotions swimming in her eyes. Relief. Exhaustion. Pain. Such a random mix of things, and all he could do was tighten his arms and hold her closer. If it would help her, he would take the kids. As soon as she was finished here, he'd see to it that she rested. But until he knew what caused the pain, he was lost as to how to comfort her. And he *would* learn what was hurting her because he had a feeling she was worth the time and effort it would take to find out how to erase it.

But, for now, first things first.

"Shh, don't spill my secrets. Now, go ask, and I'll get the kids dressed and ready so we can get out of your way."

She pulled his head down and kissed his cheek. "Yeah, you really are. I'll be right back," she whispered, then walked back into the bedroom.

His heart thudded, and blood swooshed through his head, leaving him with a slight dizzy feeling. He couldn't remember the last time just being near a woman made him so happy and content. Lost in thought, he almost missed Elizabeth introducing him to Brittany and Grayson, and letting him know he could take the kids.

The next little while flew by as the two kids, afflicted with the dreaded cabin fever, thoroughly enjoyed escaping with Liam. While shopping at Mountain Fresh, he learned their last name was Case, and they were nine-year-old twins, close in age to Annie. Their mom was Melisa but went by Missy. Since their grandma died, they didn't have other family to help. When their mom found out she was sick, they'd moved to Durham a year before coming to Highlands. Neither knew what exactly was wrong with her, but both were scared it was something bad.

Once they relayed the basic answers to his questions, he asked what they liked to do for fun. Their answers tumbled one right over the other: playing outside, watching TV, and of course, video games. Neither were particularly fond of homeschooling, but with their mom's frequent appointments, it was the only way to stay caught up.

The longer they shopped, the more comfortable the children became with him, and before long, they were arguing over which cereal to get. Liam solved the problem by grabbing both kinds and throwing the boxes in the buggy.

By the time they grabbed pizza and chicken strips at the deli, Brittany and Grayson were leaning on each other and fighting sleep. Liam buckled them into the truck and then carried them one at a time into the cottage. After he fed them, he sent them to get ready for bed. When they came out in their pajamas, Elizabeth was still in the room with their mother, so Liam shooed them off to bed, climbed between them, and recited one of his nieces' favorite stories: Click, Clack, Moo: Cows That Type. After years of practice, he knew it by heart. His sound effects were perfect, and before he reached the end of the story, giggles carried through the room.

"The End." He climbed off the bed, pulled their covers up, and tucked them in for the night. "Sorry to end the fun, but it's way past my bedtime, so that means it's past yours, too. I'll be in the kitchen for a little bit if you need anything."

The kids murmured goodnight and rolled over to go to sleep. He turned to the door and stopped short. Propped against the frame, Elizabeth waited for him. Her eyes were droopy, and her shoulders were slumped. Yes, she was tired, but a smile lit up her face.

Soft.

Gentle.

Beautiful.

Liam's heart thudded at the sight of her.

He grabbed her shaky hand as he walked by and led her to the kitchen.

"Not trying to be mean, but you look worn slap-out," he whispered as he took in the lines around her eyes and mouth. "Let's get you home so you can get some rest."

"But what about supper? What about the fire pit?"

"I hate to say this, but you need sleep more than you need the fire pit. With all the crud going around, I don't want you to get rundown and sick. If you're hungry, let's take some of the pizza." He opened his arms in invitation, and she stepped into them and pressed her head to his chest. Locking his hands at the small of her back, he supported her trembling body. "Tomorrow's Friday, and my work load's a little light right now, so I'll be by sometime around four and we can talk more." When she rubbed her face against his flannel shirt, he took a deep breath. "I don't want to say goodnight, but I think it's what's best for right now."

She remained silent but burrowed deeper.

He wanted more time. Time to learn more about her. Time to maybe share something of himself. Time alone to explore those unfamiliar feelings creeping into his heart.

Maybe he was losing his mind, but arguing with himself when she was dead on her feet would have to wait. Right then, he needed to make sure she got home to rest.

He pressed his lips to the top of her head, pulled away to grab her pizza, and then led her down the path to her cabin. Once he warmed her supper and made sure she ate, he settled in her rocker while she got ready for bed. Bright splashes of pinks and purples decorated the otherwise plain room, much like the way she made his drab world more colorful. The guitar case in the corner was covered with stickers of the places she'd played.

When he left her at the door, he carried her soft, sweet kiss with him all the way home and into his dreams.

Chapter 6

L ost in deep thought, Liam walked down Main Street. He kept his head lowered as his eyes swept the sidewalk for icy patches. Possible conversations with Elizabeth and the hopeful outcomes played through his mind. Unfamiliar with the rush of nerves coursing through him, he practiced what he would say to her. Every word he came up with sounded lame.

When the aroma of fresh roasted beans drifted out the door of Buck's Coffee, his nose led him inside the shop. Based on the number of people in line, he wasn't the only one who sought relief from the bitter cold wind. After stomping the slushy snow from his feet, he jerked off his toboggan, stuffed it in his back pocket, and rubbed the static electricity from his hair. The bell over the door rang, and he stepped off the rubber mat to make way for the next person.

"Dude, I am so over this winter." A deep, happy voice boomed across the quiet coffee shop. "Is it spring yet?"

Liam turned to greet his closest friend, the owner of the loud mouth. Zack had moved to Highlands when they were in middle school, and in high school, both he and Liam had joined the fire department as junior volunteers. Over the years, their friendship had grown, and after Tripp's death, Zack's support had been invaluable.

"Tell me about it. I swear it's the coldest one in a while." Liam hung his jacket on the nearest coat rack, grabbed Zack's from his hand, and raised an eyebrow in question. "You following me?"

"Yep. Saw ya leaving the station, and I have a little time before I sign on. Figured you were heading for the truck, but I can't complain you ended up here." Zack looked at his watch and shot Liam an exaggerated wink. "You heading out to the inn to see *her*?"

"Don't make me regret telling you." Liam punched Zack in the shoulder and laughed when he got a weak groan in return. "Yeah, I'm stopping by Endless View before heading to supper at Wrynn's."

"I know how much you enjoy playing with your nieces, so if you want me to stop by and talk to her for you, I can." Zack ducked to the side when Liam's hand came toward his head. "Dude, you know I'm just messing with you. I'm all for you finding someone. You can't be a monk forever. Besides, my wife might not like me visiting your little gal."

Liam laughed at his friend and dropped his hand. "Yeah, you might be right about that. I don't think Ashton would cotton to that. I don't know about you, but I don't want her mad at *me*."

The line moved, and Liam stepped up to the counter to order for the two of them. When he got their ticket, the men waited at a table.

"We both know Ashton thinks you can do no wrong, but I found her first." Zack shrugged and rolled his eyes. "Not that you ever date much."

Liam settled back in the chair and stared out the front window. "That's about to change." His thumb rasped against a day's growth of stubble as he finished his thought. "When I see Elizabeth in a few, I'm going to bite the bullet and ask her out. None of this 'grab something and eat around the fire pit' mess. I'm talking real date."

Zack slammed his hands on the table so hard, the salt and pepper grinders rattled. When he noticed all eyes were on him, he crossed his arms, sat back in his seat, and spoke in a quieter voice. "Excuse me? Could you repeat that, please?" The higher his excitement, the louder his voice grew. "Because I thought I heard you say you were going to ask her out. And if that's true, I'm gonna need a direct quote for Ashton."

"Gimme a break." He chuckled as he said it. "Yeah, I'm going to do it."

No, he wasn't much for dating. Sure, he had been out many times over the years, but always with local girls who'd known him his whole life. Though most mothers considered him to be a real catch, the girls he grew up with understood he wasn't interested in the whole serial dating scene.

He longed to find someone to share his life with, and dreamed of having children someday. What if Wrynn wasn't mentally strong enough to lose him to someone else? Not that she would truly lose him, but the fog of her depression had kept her from seeing clearly for a while. That thought was enough to make him nauseous.

"Can you imagine what could happen if I tell Wrynn I'm dating? Is she even close to the point where she could handle it? Do I hide her or take the risk? Dang it, maybe I should just forget about it, but I really want to see what this is between us."

What if Elizabeth was his *The One* and he missed his chance? More than anything else in the world, he wanted a love like the one Wrynn and Tripp had shared, but he didn't want to hurt his sister in the process.

"Dude, shut up. You're makin' my head hurt. You're convincing yourself to ask her out in one breath and convincing yourself not to in the next." Zack shook his head, blew out a harsh breath, and threw a pack of sugar at him. "Not trying to grind your gears, but are you really using Wrynn as your excuse to chicken out? Can't you come up with something better than that? Are you sure it's not ol' what's her face?"

After a moment of confusion, Liam realized who the someone else Zack was referring to was. Lara. Somehow, anytime his future was the subject of discussion, *she* always came into the conversation.

"Really, Z? I tell you I'm going to ask Elizabeth out, and you circle 'round to this? Can't you just be satisfied I'm actually gonna take the first step? That I want to see where this could go? It's a date, not a commitment. You hearing wedding bells or something?" Liam snorted a laugh and resisted the urge to smack his friend.

"You are one confusing idiot. Do you even listen to the words you say?" Zack stretched his arm across the table and balled up his hand. "Dude, cart." He twisted it in front of Liam's face, then formed his other hand into a fist, placed it at his chest, and shook it. "Meet horse. You're getting way ahead of yourself. For once, think of Liam, and let the other crap go for a little bit. No Wrynn. No *her*. Go on a date, and see if this little gal has what it takes to put up with your lameness before you plan your future." His lips pinched in a grimace, and he ran his fingers through his hair, his mounting irritation evident.

"I'm just gonna lay this out, and because you're my friend, I won't even charge you for it. I don't want to see you get messed up again." He pressed against the edge of the table and got in Liam's face. "I get that she-whose-name-we-don't-speak did a number on you with her Houdini act, but geesh, you can't let that screw up your life. I get it, okay? I was there when you met her. Heck, we double dated 'til you guys went off to college." He flexed his shoulders, rolled his neck, and slumped back in the chair. "I was there when you came home, too. You were a destroyed, shattered shell of my best friend. I even helped you with your wild goose chase." Zack's quiet voice was filled with defeat.

Liam heard the concern and remembered the way Zack and Ashton had propped him up during those dark days, doing everything they could to help him. What bothered him right then, though, was watching Zack's ever-present spark dim right before his eyes, and knowing he was the cause. Maybe it was time to talk about something else.

"It would be so much easier to find her today. With things like Google and Facebook, it's all but impossible to hide from the outside world. It sure would have made tracking her a simple project." Liam forced a chuckle, trying to cheer up his friend.

"That's not the point I'm trying to make." Zack bit back a curse and tugged at his hair. A flush of red darkened his cheeks.

Liam knew him well enough to know he was reigning in his anger. He bent over the table, and his voice dropped to a stern whisper. "You don't need to track her. Good grief, so you had sex with her. Believe it or not, that's not the end of the world. Whatever happened between the two of you is not what's responsible for her dropping off the face of this earth. You didn't break her. You didn't destroy her." His breath rushed out in a big, frustrated grunt as his body sagged against his chair.

"I've said it before, and I'll say it again. She could have been kidnapped. She coulda run away, but, dude, she sure enough had secrets she never shared with you. I believed it then, and I believe it now. You didn't have the whole story. And you might not ever know the reasons, but you can't beat yourself up, day in and day out. Let it go. Let *her* go and move on. This is a big step for you, and it could be just the right chance for you to take, but until you take that chance, you'll never know." When Liam looked up and huffed out a breath, Zack squeezed his shoulder. "You asked God for forgiveness, but you still let it eat you up inside."

"I know you don't believe me, but for the most part, I *have* let it go." Liam frowned and stared at the wall. "What I haven't done is ask forgiveness from the one person I need it from. Lara."

The barista called out their order, and Zack pushed back from the table and stood. "I'll get it. But I want you to think about this. She isn't the one who needs to grant you forgiveness. You are. You need to forgive yourself. You can't change the past, but you can take control of the future. Just give yourself permission to open that stainless steel cage you have around your heart." Zack's shoulders slumped as he walked over to the counter.

Liam closed his eyes and mulled over his friend's words. Zack knew him better than anyone except his family. Was he right? Had Liam wasted years of his life waiting for the wrong person to grant him absolution?

The bottom line was, yes, he guarded his heart. The ache of missing Lara had lessened more every year, until he had put it behind him for good. Or so he thought. She visited his dreams on occasion, but otherwise, it was rare for him to think of her or the time they'd spent together. Only a few times had he allowed himself to remember those days after Lara disappeared, the guilt and pain he'd experienced, and the real sense of bewildered confusion clouding his mind. The idea that he'd hurt her haunted him. He'd assumed his relationship with Lara was solid and had dreamed of a future with her. She'd fit him to a T on both a mental and spiritual level, which was something he wasn't sure he'd find again.

As a young man growing up in a conservative family, he'd done everything he could to resist temptation in every form. His parents, though loving and supportive, were firm in their beliefs and strict with their expectations for their children. Work hard, study harder, stay away from drugs, and abstinence until marriage were tenets his household upheld.

And the one time he ignored the way his parents raised him? Well, it hadn't ended the way he had hoped – a ring on Lara's finger and the start of his own family. The results had been devastating to him.

In fact, to this day, he feared his lack of restraint and loss of self-control had left her with the impression that he hadn't respected her enough to cherish her forever. Years ago, he'd vowed to never to make the same mistakes again. When he found the woman perfect for him, he would treat her like precious treasure.

In the short time he'd known her, Elizabeth had brought him happiness. Maybe all the grief and turmoil was in his head because she sure made his heart do strange flips. In fact, he felt more alive than ever. He needed to move on, and this was the perfect opportunity to try.

When he opened his eyes, a steaming, to-go cup waited for him, and his best friend watched him with a careful eye.

"Here's the deal, Liam. I only want what's best for you." Zack squeezed his shoulder. "If it's best for me to support you while you run gun shy and sulk for ten more years, then so be it. But I'd much rather see you happy. You're a great guy. If you don't believe me, just ask Ashton." His eyes crinkled when he smiled. "But seriously, whatever it takes, we're here for you, dude. Just think about what I said."

"I'm thinking, promise." Liam grabbed his coffee, stood, and thumped Zack on the back hard enough to make him wobble. "I'm taking the first step today. Let's just hope she says yes."

Driving while deep in thought probably wasn't the smartest idea, but Zack's words echoed through his mind on repeat.

You need to forgive yourself and give yourself permission to open that stainless steel cage you have around your heart.

Liam turned into the inn parking lot and drove toward the front office. Come sundown, he hoped the salt and brine he'd laid on these paths earlier in the day kept them free from ice tonight. If more snow fell overnight, he knew where to plan his first stop for work in the morning.

As he neared the business office, smoke from the chiminea on the porch curled into the rafters, filling the air with a welcoming cedar scent and warming the surrounding area. His smile grew larger when he caught sight of Elizabeth in a rocking chair on the front porch, steam rising from the mug in her hand. Of course, she would be outside by the fire. He remembered the willowy body and curvy hips that tapered into slender legs.

Boy, she sure is pretty. Here goes nothing.

He reached over to the passenger seat, grabbed a small bunch of flowers, and hopped out of the truck.

"Why, Miss Pittman, you sure are a sight for sore eyes."

Liam's long legs ate up the distance between his truck and the inn. When he stood before her, he gave a low bow and presented the bouquet to her. Her musical laughter filled the air, triggering Liam's heart to beat faster.

"Alas, the gallant gentleman." Elizabeth stood and bent deep in a curtsey. "One day, I need to tell your momma how much I appreciate her raising such a refined, Southern gentleman." The smile on her face reached the depths of her cornflower blue eyes, and excited nerves fluttered in his gut. When she moved a step closer to him, the early evening sun danced off her blonde braid, creating a dazzling halo around her stunning, heart-shaped face.

Liam cleared his throat, startled by the sudden onset of nervous energy that swept through him, without doubt something he'd never experienced before now.

Talk about out of practice.

"So, um, Elizabeth." She stared into his eyes, which gave him the courage he needed. "I was wondering if I could interest you in dinner and maybe a movie tomorrow night." A slow burn traveled to the tips of his ears, and he worried his entire face might be beet red before long.

"Oh, Liam! That would be so nice." Elizabeth graced him with her full attention. "You know, I've not been off the mountain much since I moved here, and the few times I have, I spent most of that time getting the directions all mixed up and finding myself lost." She rolled her eyes in self-deprecation. "It'll be nice to go somewhere with someone who knows how to get where we're going."

Liam didn't even try to hold back his laughter. "Hasn't anyone told you yet? You can't get here from anywhere else. Highlands is in its own little world."

"Well, I suppose that might be true. I consider Highlands much more secluded than Cullowhee."

Her remark took Liam by surprise. He thought she'd told him she was from down East. Why would she be familiar with another isolated, small mountain town? As a Western Carolina graduate, he was more than acquainted with the campus and surrounding area. "I figure the only ones who know where the heck Cullowhee is, are those of us who went to school there. Talk about the other side of nowhere."

"Why, I'll have you know that I'm a Western Carolina

Catamount." She held her right hand out and flashed a dainty class ring.

This presented Liam the perfect opportunity. He reached out, took a gentle hold of her outstretched hand, and bent closer as if to inspect the ring. "Yeah, I skipped out on the whole class ring thing. Doesn't work so well when your hands are always in dirt and mulch." Creamy peach skin, smooth and soft as a feather, warmed his palm, and without thinking, he ran his thumb over her long, slim fingers, puzzled by the calloused tips.

"Guitar." Her whispered words drew Liam's eyes up to hers. She gave a nod toward her fingers. "I play the guitar. That's why my fingertips are rough as leather. No matter how much lotion I use, they never get any softer."

There it was. Pain in her eyes. The same pain he'd seen when they'd helped the sick lady.

He gave her hand a quick squeeze before turning it over and slipping his fingers between hers. "I can appreciate that. There's nothing wrong with having a talent that gives you a callous or two." He lifted her hand and pressed a tender kiss on the back. "You need to play for me sometime. I bet you're good at it."

Color rushed to her face, turning them a striking pink as she cast her eyes to the floor of the porch. Though tempted to see if her face was as warm as it appeared, Liam resisted the urge to touch her cheeks. Next to his wide shoulders and long legs, she was tiny and delicate, fragile, as if she were made of spun glass. The urge to shelter her, protect her, overwhelmed him.

"Back home, my brother and I played for hours. In college, until he got sick, we played anywhere that would hire us. Funny, but back then, I never once gave a flip who might be listening." Her lips pressed together in a thin line, and her brows furrowed as if the recollection brought back unpleasant memories. With a small shake of her head, she finished her reflection. "But since he died, I just play for myself most of the time. Too many memories. Who knows, though? Maybe someday, I'll see if I can work up the nerve to play for you. It's been a while since I've had more than an audience of *One*."

The hurt swimming in her eyes and etched on her face made his heart stutter. He knew firsthand how it felt. Did she also have the empty hole no one could fill? Did she have the urge to pick up the phone every day and share something, only to remember he wasn't there anymore? How did she spend the birthdays with no cause to celebrate? He drove a beat-up, old truck every day to keep Tripp's memory alive. Did she play her brother's guitar and think of him?

"Well, I can certainly understand that. To this day, there are places I can't hike without remembering all the times my brother-in-law was with me. His loss is something I don't think I'll ever get over. The memories are great. The pain, not so much. So, while I'd love to hear you play, I won't pressure you to do it if it hurts you or makes you feel uncomfortable." His watch beeped the hour, and Liam noticed that the time for supper with Wrynn and the girls was drawing closer. "I hate to run, but there's a trio of ragamuffin princesses at my sister's house waiting for me to come play. Wrynn's off work tonight, so I'll have time to talk with her, too. It's a win-win for me. Is six o'clock too early to pick you up?"

"Six is perfect. I'll meet you here if that's okay." With her gentle Southern grace, she withdrew her hand from his and ghosted it between her cabin and the inn. "It's an easy two-minute walk, and some handsome young fellow keeps everything nice and safe. Besides, I'm not sure if your big truck can make it through the narrow drive to my door."

"Tell you what, I'll meet you at your door and walk with you, just in case. Wouldn't want you to," he cleared his throat and grinned, "slip and fall. And this time, we're not letting anyone or anything stop us, no matter what." He grabbed her hand once more, placed a small kiss in her palm, and turned to the steps. Something about her drew him in, made him want to stay, but he'd promised to help Wrynn. With one last glance over his shoulder, he said, "I'm looking forward to it. I'll see you then."

Liam hurried to his truck, bewildered by the rush of unfamiliar emotions evoked by one little gal. He'd had to fight the urge to grab her up in his arms when she blushed. Why did her shyness bring out such a strong instinct to protect her? Nerves could be the reason his imagination ran wild. Maybe he needed to mull over the question, and sooner instead of later. Who was he kidding? His thoughts revolving around her were no less than he expected until he returned to this spot tomorrow evening. Still, he'd keep Elizabeth a secret until he was sure things were going to work out.

As he drove through town, he turned the radio on and attempted to drown out everything else. "I Drive Your Truck" by Lee Brice blasted through the speakers, drawing every thought in Liam's brain straight to memories of Tripp. He was driving his brother-in-law's truck, and a lash of pain sliced through his heart. Tripp had been so much more than just the man who had married his sister. He'd been Liam's closest friend and brother. As teenagers, their lives had entwined around Wrynn, and nothing less than the Army or college could have separated them. And separate them, it did. Even though Tripp died two years ago, not a day went by that Liam didn't remember just how good a friend, husband, and father he had been.

Those same memories set the standard for the type of relationship Liam wanted. Where he'd once thought the opportunity lost to him, his upcoming date with Elizabeth gave him a rare trickle of hope. He resolved to embrace the hope and make the absolute best of it.

Dinner with Wrynn and the girls was the normal chaos. His nieces' laughter warmed his heart. Wrynn was more rundown than normal, but reading her mind was an impossible task. The munchkins giggled through <u>Click, Clack, Moo: Cows That Type</u>, and he put them to bed before going home. By the time his head hit the pillow, his troubles were gone, and his mind was set on his date the next evening.

He tasted of
strong man,
bright sunshine,
everlasting love,
and
hope eternal.

Chapter 7

After a full day of work and dealing with Mrs. Tidwell's nonsense, Liam was ready to punch a few holes in the wall. In the last two months, his clientele had shrunk to almost half its normal size. The only bright side he could see was that few of his remaining customers did business with the old hag. This meant he was close to the point where no one else would fire him without just cause. As soon as he figured out his bottom line, he'd know if he needed to seek work off the mountain, or bite the bullet and ask Janet for help.

A hot shower washed the cold from his bones and the anger from his mind, but did little to calm his nerves. Thankfully, his excitement was enough to keep palms dry and his hands from shaking. What to wear was something he normally gave little thought to, but in an effort to look nice on his first date with Elizabeth, he chose khakis in lieu of denim, and a black sweater instead of his normal flannel. His lame attempt to control his wavy hair was a failure, but when he realized he was close to running late, he gave up.

As he walked out to his truck, he noticed Wrynn's car was parked outside and wondered how he'd missed it when he'd gotten home.

That's strange. I thought she had to work tonight.

When she didn't answer the door, Liam let himself in the house.

"Anybody home?"

A noise down the hall had him taking quiet, careful steps in that direction. As he reached the back of the house, he heard a sneeze followed by a cough coming from Wrynn's room.

"Wrynn, you okay?"

"Tripp, love, is that you? I don't feel so good."

A deep, wracking cough had Liam rushing through the door. He stopped at the sight before him. A mound of blankets covered the bed, and from the top peered a very washed-out Wrynn. Her skin was pale, almost grayish, with bright red spots on her cheeks and forehead. Wisps of hair stuck to the sweat on her face. Pillows propped behind her back kept her upright. Wads of used tissue surrounded her, and several bottles of water and medicine were on the nightstand.

"Tripp?" Her forehead creased, and she squinted at him.

"No, it's me, Liam." He was more than aware she heard Tripp's voice, but was she seeing him all the time, too? This was not good. Since she wouldn't listen to him, maybe his parents could convince her to see the therapist again. He had a feeling she wasn't going to snap out of this alone, or anytime soon.

"Oh." She shook her head, blinked several times, and her face fell as she realized who he was.

A spear of pain slashed his heart at her crestfallen appearance. He stepped toward the bed.

"Stop right there." She raised her hand. "Don't come any closer. You don't need to get sick, too."

"What in this world? You look like you need a doctor again." He walked closer to the bed, and she raised the other hand.

"Liam, stop. Dad took me to the doctor this morning. Again. Ugh … this time it's the flu." A coughing fit hit her, and the rattle in her chest scared him. "I've got medicine, and Mom's making me some soup while she and Dad take care of the girls. I just hope I didn't spread it to them."

"First strep and bronchitis, and now this. No offense, Sis, but you look awful. You really need to take better care of yourself, or you're just gonna keep getting sick."

When she made a face at him, he grinned as he closed the distance to the bed and laid a hand on her forehead. She was burning up. He grabbed a drink and ibuprofen and watched over her as she took them, tipping the bottle when her hand shook too hard. Goosebumps popped up on her skin, and she started shivering.

"I've got plans tonight, but I can cancel if you need me to stay with you." He was worried about leaving her when she was so sick and weak.

"Bubby, you're the best, but even Super Liam can't fix this." Her laugh morphed into a deep hack, leaving her short of breath. "Besides, Dad'll be bringing the soup over before too long. Go, now, before you catch it. We don't need this to run through the family like strep did."

"I can wait in the liv–"

"Liam, go."

"Fine." He tucked the blankets around her. "If you're sure you don't need anything, I'm going to leave." He swept his hands over his dressier clothes. "I'm going out this evening, but you call me, and I'll come running."

As she stretched, she moaned with pain. Liam knew what her fever induced aches felt like, and he also knew rest and liquids were the best things for her. He was really looking forward to his date with Elizabeth, but if he was needed, he would reschedule without a second thought.

He kissed her forehead, and before he got to the door, she was already asleep.

"So, if we have enough time after dinner, you still up for a movie?"

Liam rested his hand in the small of Elizabeth's back as they walked into Vito's Italian Eatery and waited to be seated.

Elizabeth turned to him and smiled. "Dinner and a movie? Sounds great." She wrapped her hand around the crook of his elbow. "I've been looking forward to this all day. It feels good to know I can sit back and relax and spend time with you."

A slight blush washed over her face, and Liam grinned. He thought it was adorable, and the rosy hue only made her more beautiful. Heck, she could be wearing a sackcloth and ashes and still put most women to shame.

"Trust me when I say the pleasure's all mine. After chasing you around all over creation, you can expect me to be a little greedy for time with you."

The hostess led them to a horseshoe booth in the corner, laid menus on opposite sides, and took their drink order as they sat across from each other.

Liam's nerves were a little jerky, but he figured they would calm down as the evening moved forward. This date had consumed his thoughts, and nothing would dim his excitement at finally getting to spend quality time with Elizabeth. Still, he wished they were sitting a little closer together. With that thought in mind, he scooted a few inches to his left.

"So, you come here often?" As soon as the words left Elizabeth's mouth, her eyes widened, and she laughed. "And no, that wasn't some cheap pickup line. It was a serious question."

Trying to see the place through her eyes, Liam glanced around. Red and white checkered, plastic tablecloths were worn but clean. Empty Chianti bottles wrapped in raffia lined the windowsills. Cream tapered candles sat in the middle of each table, the wicks dusty from never being lit. Ruffled curtains, faded from years of sun exposure, covered the top half of the windows. The décor was simple, with the definite stamp of small town.

"Yeah, I've been coming here since I was little. It doesn't look like much, but I promise, the food is out of this world." He slid over toward her a little more, wondering if she'd noticed yet. "In

Highlands, it's Mountain Fresh, Buck's Coffee, or a five-star restaurant, so anytime I want more than pizza, a deli sandwich, or a gourmet meal, I head down here."

They flipped through the menu, and after they'd placed their order, they settled back to talk.

"So, Elizabeth, tell me something about you that I don't know."

"Let's see. There's not really much about me that's all that interesting." She pursed her lips, as if in deep thought, and stared at a spot over his shoulder. "Hmm, well, I've played golf my whole life. It sounds crazy, but I love chasing that little white ball around the course. Having a golf pro for a dad makes it easy for me to get on." Her smile lit up her face. "When I was little, Daddy would take me and my brother with him when he went to work. I've met Arnold Palmer, Lee Trevino, and Jack Nicklaus. Actually attempted to play golf with Palmer, but no way will I ever be anywhere close to his level." She sighed. "No matter how hard I try."

"Is golf what brought you to Western Carolina?" He inched closer to her. A few more times and he would be right where he wanted to be.

She wiggled in her seat, excitement written all over her face. "Oh, yeah. I played in high school and earned a four-year scholarship. You know, Western has the best Hospitality and Tourism program. My concentration was Golf Course and Resort Management. I took accounting classes in case I can't break through the 'good old boy' glass ceiling."

"I handle landscaping for a couple of smaller golf courses, but I've only played a handful of times. I'd be an easy win for you." He sat back while the server put their food on the table. Elizabeth eyed his shrimp scampi, so he offered her the first bite.

"Mmm, I love shrimp." She closed her eyes as she chewed. "Delicious."

"Y-yes, it is." Liam cleared the gravel from his throat, mesmerized by the sight before him.

"Liam, you haven't even tasted it yet." Her light laughter drew him back to the conversation, her bright eyes shining with merriment.

"Right." He blinked several times and shook his head to clear the haze. "Golf. That's what we were talking about. Thaw should start soon, please, God. Maybe we can hit Wade Hampton after it warms up." His focus was so completely on Elizabeth that he didn't even taste the lemony pasta on his fork. The pull she had on him was magnetic, and he was unable to resist.

"Yeah, that would be nice. But really, I'm down with anything outdoors. I've tried to find a few waterfalls and some of the hiking trails in DuPont, but to be honest, I've gotten turned around and lost every time." She laughed at herself and paused to sample her chicken parmigiana. "What can I say? I'm just not that good with directions."

A drop of sauce on the corner of her mouth convinced Liam to close the remaining gap between them. "You have a little bit right," his thumb collected the sauce, "here."

Her gasp, when he brought his thumb to his mouth, left him feeling a little pleased with himself. Maybe he could do this flirting thing, after all.

His fork scraped against his empty plate before Elizabeth was half finished with her huge portion. He accepted her offer to share and relaxed against the back of the booth as she fed him a bite. While definitely a rare experience, he couldn't help but think how nice it felt for someone to pay that much attention to him. The sparkle in her eyes and the smile on her lips told him she enjoyed the task.

Liam managed to steer the conversation to Elizabeth and her experiences in and around Highlands. She ticked off the few places she had explored while they shared dessert. Liam shook his head when she laughed at her uncanny ability to get lost. Knowing she had managed only a handful of the thousands of things to see and do, his mind went to what new adventures he could have with her.

"That means you've missed all the great places. Have you made it to the top of Jones Knob yet?" He was eager to show her the places he loved the most.

"Are you kidding me?" She giggled and rolled her eyes. "Yeah, I know it's an old logging road to the top, but trust me, I'd be more likely to find myself taking an imaginary turn and end up in Timbuktu, or worse, sliding sideways down the mountain."

"Well, that settles it. Once the weather turns, we're heading straight to the top. It's amazing. The view stretches across the point where North Carolina, South Carolina, and Georgia meet. When the trees start budding in the spring, it's beautiful, but when the leaves start changing, the red, orange, and yellow vista is simply incredible. It's my favorite place in the world."

"That sure sounds great to me. If you lead the way, I'll follow. I'm good at that. Just don't give me a map, or who knows where we'll end up." She waved away the last of the tiramisu, wrapped her arms around her waist, and groaned. "No more, thanks. I'm about to bust."

"How 'bout this?" he said as he pushed the empty dish away. "I'll drive us there and lead us to the top. I could do it in my sleep." He leaned back to let the server clean off the table and slipped his credit card in the bill folder. When Elizabeth reached for her purse, he tilted his head to the side. "And just what do you think you're doing?"

"Covering my half?" She looked up at him and shrugged.

"Uhm, I don't think so."

"But—,"

"No buts. My invitation, my date," he winked at her, "my treat. No question."

She sighed but flashed an understanding grin. "I really do need to thank your momma for raising you right." Her hand covered his. "Thank you."

Her smile traveled to her eyes and straight to his heart. He looked at her, sitting there pretty as a picture. Her skin glowed in the candlelight, and the navy sweater dress made her blue eyes an even deeper cerulean. The funny thing was, he knew what was inside her was more beautiful than what initially caught his eye. After being around her a handful of times, he knew he wanted more. Her joyful attitude and gentle spirit soothed an ache he'd had so long, he almost missed its throb.

He helped her to her feet, and with a gentle hand on her back, guided her out of the restaurant. When she slipped on black ice, he took it as a sign. Without breaking his stride, he swooped her up in his arms and carried her safely to the truck.

"And there you go falling for me again." He juggled her in his arms and acted like he was going to drop her. "I must be doing something right."

"You've swept me right off my feet." Her laughter echoed through the night.

He didn't want to let her go, but if they were going to make it to the movies in time, he needed to put her in the truck. As he closed the door and rounded the front, his thoughts centered on her.

She feels right in my arms.

They discussed movie options on the drive to the theater, but as they pulled into the parking lot, his cell phone rang. MOM flashed on the display, and he slid his finger across the screen.

"Mom, everything okay?" He listened for a second, and then looked over at Elizabeth. "If you called the house, then you know I'm not home. I'm in Franklin, but the roads are pretty clear, so I can be there in about forty-five minutes. Want me to come to the house or meet you at the hospital?" He turned the truck around and headed back the way they'd come. "Mom, you need to calm down. I just pulled back on the road, so I'll see you at the house in a little bit."

Elizabeth turned sideways in the seat, leaned toward him, and grabbed his hand. "That didn't sound so good."

"Yeah. Sorry, but no movie tonight. Mom says two of my nieces are burning up with a fever. She's pretty sure it's the flu, so she wants to get them some antiviral medicine while it'll still work. My sister was at the doctor this morning. She's gotten worse since I checked in on her earlier, so Dad's staying with her right now." He squeezed her hand and brought it to his lips. "I'm really sorry I have to cut our date short, but they need me to watch Maggie while they're gone."

"Sick again? Oh, bless their little hearts. This year's flu is a nasty business. Momma and Daddy had it a month or so ago. They coughed their heads off for weeks." She feathered her fingers across his jaw. "Besides, if Maggie's not sick, she surely doesn't need to go to the hospital, or she'll most likely catch something while she's there. Now, tell me how I can help?"

Liam looked over at her as he stopped at a red light. "You're just too sweet to be real. Scoot over here beside me." He unbuckled her seatbelt and tugged her hand, urging her across the bench seat. "I'll just take you on home, if you don't mind. At least that way, hopefully, you won't catch anything."

When she slid to the middle and fastened her seatbelt, he lifted her chin and placed a gentle kiss on her lips. He couldn't help but notice how perfectly she fit next to him. A horn blaring behind them let him know the light had changed to green. He put his arm around her shoulder and squeezed her as he pulled through the intersection.

"I should have known something like this was going to happen. When I checked in on Wrynn earlier, I almost canceled our date, but I really wanted to see you."

"Grams told me a little about her. Says she's had a rough time, and she's really lucky she has you there for her and the girls."

"It's a day-to-day process, that's for sure. Some days are easier than others. Then something will come along, something I see, something one of my nieces says, and it seems like it just happened yesterday." He pinched the bridge of his nose, and she leaned into his side. Her warmth spread through him, giving him the solace he needed to talk about what always weighed heavy on his mind. "Wrynn's flat out in denial. She still hears his voice, and after seeing her earlier, I can't help but wonder if she doesn't see him, too. Tripp's the other half of her heart, and she has yet to find a way to let go of even just a smidgen of what they had. She struggles to get out of bed every single morning, and if it weren't for their daughters, I'm convinced she would curl up into a ball and just fade away." He drew in a ragged breath. "Sorry, but watching those girls grow up without a father and feeling Wrynn's constant heartache rips me apart. I've always wanted a love like what they had, but seeing what she's gone

through the last two years makes me kind of glad I ... Well, yeah ..."
A deep breath loosened the tightness in his chest.

"I guess I understand a little of what she's going through. My
brother Seth was my best friend and my biggest tormentor." She
rested her head on his shoulder. Her voice took on a wistful tone as
she traveled through her memories. "Oh, he was such a handsome
devil, and the bugger knew it, too. Looked just like our dad. I had to
chase all the girls away from him." She gave a light laugh. "That
stinker, he loved to hide, and when I'd walk by, he'd jump out and
scare the pee out of me. I swear that was his favorite thing in the
world to do." Nostalgia echoed in her words. "I really miss him."

He fingered a tendril of hair resting on her shoulder. "Oh,
sweetheart, what happened?" His hand wrapped around her side,
gathering her snug against him.

"Cancer." He couldn't see her face, but her voice bled with
pain. "He always shaved his head when we were kids, and he never
wore a hat. I used to tease him that all that Southern summer sun was
going to fry his brain." Her body trembled when she sighed, and his
arm tightened around her. "Sorry, remembering the good times
makes me laugh, but talking about the bad is still so hard for me."

"I really do understand, so if it hurts too much to talk about it,
then please, wait until you're ready." He rubbed gentle, soothing
circles on her arm. The thought of losing Wrynn ached deep inside
his soul, so he couldn't imagine how he would feel were it to become
a reality. He did know it wasn't something he'd ever get over.

She drew in a deep breath and huffed a quiet laugh. "Let me
finish while I can, and then we won't have to do the bad part again."
When she tried to scoot away, he held her head on his chest until she
settled against him again. "Talking about Seth always opens this deep
chasm in my heart, so I don't do it very often, but the good thing is,
it's getting easier each time." A harsh sound slipped from between
her lips. "About five years ago, I came down with a stupid cold. You
know what I mean. Stuffy head, runny nose, sore throat. Nothing
major, but it was enough to make me feel like crap. Seth had booked

80

us a gig at a coffee shop in Asheville. That's how we earned our spending money so we wouldn't drain our parents dry."

When she shifted in the seat, Liam moved his arm, and she turned sideways to face him, resting her knee on his thigh.

"Anyhow, I didn't want to go. It was getting close to exams and Christmas break, but he convinced me I had to. See, he had his eye on this little Harley Softail." She snorted a laugh, and her eyes popped wide with embarrassment. "I swear it was a piece of junk, but he thought he could fix it up nice. But first, he had to save enough money to buy it. We argued over that thing more than anything else. Bottom line, motorcycles aren't safe. He would have killed himself on these winding mountain roads."

Liam chuckled, and when he caught her glare, he zipped his fingers across his lips.

"We got to Asheville and I was miserable the whole time. He started feeling sick right about the time we were leaving, and I was beginning to feel a little better. We argued over who was going to drive back to Western." She pressed her forehead to his shoulder and blew out a deep breath. "I hate driving at night, and he always babied me and gave in, but not this time. I accused him of being selfish, when all along, that's how I was acting. Heck, I didn't want to go to Asheville in the first place, and here HE was complaining about having to drive home."

She squeezed his hand, and then pulled hers to her lap where she twisted her fingers together. Even though she didn't move her body, he felt her drifting away from him.

"Geesh, could I make myself sound any worse? I'm not sure I should tell you all this just yet. Whatever will you think of me?" Her chin dropped to her chest, and her eyes squeezed shut. "I'm normally not a selfish person, so when I think about how I treated him, it kills me. But I had no idea what he had wasn't just a cold."

He leaned to the side when she started whispering under her breath and caught her saying something about being a blubbering idiot.

Liam slowed to take a sharp curve and covered her small hands with his larger one. "Sweetheart, it hurts me to hear the pain in your voice, but you're no blubbering idiot. I promise that I'm not going to judge you over something you obviously had no control over. If it's too hard for you to talk about, you can tell me later." When she shook her head, he shrugged. "Or not. I'm good either way. Whatever works best for you. Just know I'm here for you if you need me."

"No, might as well rip the Band-Aid off quickly." She leaned her forehead against his shoulder. "I was on the mend but still tired, and here he was, genuinely getting sick. How was I to know that what was a stupid little cold for me was the beginning of the end for him. It kicked his butt. Two weeks later, he was still running a fever and barely had the energy to get out of bed. I'd finished my exams, and I don't think he took one. After talking it over with Mom, I loaded our junk in the truck and took him home. She had the power to make him go to the doctor." When she let out a watery giggle, he glanced down and saw a grin teasing at her lips. "I swear that big, strapping boy was scared of our little old momma. She could make him do anything."

Turning her head, she stared out into the cold dark night. "She took him to the doctor in Pinehurst, and his blood work came back with an elevated white count. He'd had a tick bite get infected over the summer, so Lyme disease made sense at first. But after three rounds of antibiotics and Prednisone, there wasn't much improvement. He'd be almost human one day, and the next he'd spike a high fever, have night sweats, and ache from head to toe.

"They tested him for gluten allergies, rheumatoid arthritis, fibromyalgia. You name it, they tested for it. One doctor even suggested Chronic Fatigue. Poor thing was poked and prodded and scanned so often that I kidded him about becoming a radioactive pincushion. It felt like forever, but about six months later, he hadn't improved much. So after ruling out a ton of stuff it wasn't, one of his specialists ordered a PET scan of his body and brain.

"See, he'd grown his hair out when he started college, 'cause the chicks dig it. Like he needed help." She sniffed and touched the back of her head. "The answer to all of his sickness was out of sight, growing underneath his studly locks. All those years with no hair and no hat." Her voice wavered with a sad laugh. "Told him he was going to fry his brain. And he did. By the time they found the growth on the back of his skull, it was stage III metastatic melanoma. Aggressive, too. After chemo and radiation, they found it in his lymph nodes." Her hand drifted to the side of her neck and moved to her armpit. "After the second round of treatment, it had spread to his groin and upper spinal column. It seemed like it was growing faster than they could kill it. Really, he didn't have a chance."

Knowing he couldn't bear to be near her and not hold her, he pulled the truck into a scenic lookout and put it in park. When she peered up at him, the misery and pain reflected in her eyes made his heart ache. Without giving it a second thought, he flicked off her seatbelt, lifted her in his arms, scooted to the middle of the seat, and placed her in his lap. One hand pressed her head to his shoulder, and the other secured her trembling body against his.

"Okay, sweetheart. Shh, you need to breathe." With gentle hands, he stroked her hair, trying to comfort and soothe her. As her gasps calmed, his hold on her tightened. "Let it out."

"Oh, Liam, have you ever watched someone you love, someone you admire, just give up on life? Oh my gosh, and then just wither up into nothing and die? Cause that's what he did in the end. Sure, he tried everything. It's possible the chemo and radiation slowed the progress, but there's no way to really know. After the second round, he was upgraded from stage III to stage IV. We looked into alternative medicines, but there came a point when he was just done, and no one could change his mind. Quality over quantity became his mantra. If he said it once, he said it a million times. And honestly, I couldn't blame him. He was miserable." She slumped against his chest and closed her eyes. "Nowadays, Momma struggles to get out of bed, and I just don't know if she'll ever get a handle on her depression. The thought that she somehow let him down weighs on her something heavy." Deep breaths seemed to calm her, and he was more than content to hold her in his arms.

"Most of the time, I'm able to put the bad stuff behind me and focus on the great times we had. And he really was a great brother, even if he had the habit of acting like a caveman." When she lifted her head, her smile was back, and the pain in her eyes lessened. "So, I guess I know a little about how your sister feels. It also sounds like she and Momma have a lot in common. And the way you take care of her and your nieces reminds me a lot of Seth."

Liam gathered his thoughts, cleared his throat, and glanced at the time on the dash, surprised to see almost thirty minutes had passed since his mom called. "Speaking of my nieces, I'm torn. I'm selfish because I want more time with you. I really don't want to leave you when you're so upset, but I also don't want to get you sick. And I really need to go help with the girls."

Her gasp echoed through the cab of the truck. "Oh my gosh, Liam, I'm so sorry. I started talking and forgot all about the sick babies. Forgive me, please?" Concern flooded her eyes.

"Sweetheart, there's nothing to forgive." He kissed her palm. "I hate knowing you've had so much pain in your life, but I'm glad you trusted me enough to share. Why don't you come with me to my mom's house?" His heart stopped when he realized what he'd said, but it was too late to take back the words. "Umm, it'll probably be real late, but I can take you home when they get back from the hospital."

She flipped the visor down, and the light from the mirror highlighted her red nose, tear-stained cheeks, and swollen eyes. "Are you out of your mind? There is absolutely no way I am going to meet your momma looking like I've cried for hours." She raised a brow and scrunched up her nose. "Lord, what kind of impression do you want me to make?"

Relieved at her swift rejection of his idea, Liam threw his head back and laughed. "Trust me when I say, if I brought you to my parents' house, they'd be too shocked to even pay attention to what you look like. I've brought one girl home in my whole life, and that was years and years ago." He pulled a handkerchief from his back pocket to wipe her cheeks and gazed into her eyes. "Besides, I think you're beautiful inside and out, and they will, too."

She bit her lip and thought for a moment. "Can I get a pass this time? After tonight's story time, I'm really kind of tired." Her smile radiated across her face, though a blush tinted her cheeks. "Besides, I'm too self-conscious to go like this. It'll happen, though, I promise. Just not tonight."

"Girls," Liam muttered under his breath and shook his head as he chuckled. After placing a tender kiss on her lips, he pulled back on the road and took her home.

The whole drive to his parents' house, he kicked himself. Elizabeth couldn't meet his parents without also meeting Wrynn. Even though things were moving faster than he thought possible, Liam felt, deep in his soul, that Elizabeth could very well be the piece his puzzle was missing. The piece to complete him.

Having had that and then having lost it, Wrynn might not survive seeing him love someone like Tripp loved her.

And the thought terrified Liam.

He tasted of
strong man,
bright sunshine,
everlasting love,
and

hope eternal.

Radio Broadcast

"Goooood morning, Highlanders! You're listening to the local news on WHLD, AM radio 1250. Today is Friday, March fifteenth, and these are your community updates.

"Folks, it pains me to say, but Mrs. Ivy Mae Rushton went to be with Jesus in the early hours of the morning. Ralph, the children, and grandchildren were with her until her very last breath, and they say her trip to the other side was quite peaceful. She taught many of us English and Literature at Highlands High. Her family is asking that, in lieu of flowers, folks make a donation to our local Hospice. Keep your radio tuned to this station, and I'll have more details for you in the morning.

"For a bit of great news, Zack and Ashton MacNeal welcomed a bouncing baby boy last night. For all you ladies out there who would hunt me down if I fail to give details, Carson Reese weighed in at seven pounds, and the little fella was nineteen inches long. Mom and baby are doing great and hope to come home tomorrow. Get those casseroles in the ovens, ladies. We have a new Highlander to welcome.

"Last weekend, Isabella Thomas and John Paul Gilliam snuck off to Gatlinburg. I'm happy to tell you that, from now on, she'll proudly answer to Mrs. Isabella Gilliam. The town's invited to the wedding reception, three o'clock tomorrow in the Presbyterian

Church fellowship hall. Join me as we congratulate the happy couple and wish them the best for a bright, happy future together.

"As today's the fifteenth of March, it seems fitting to remind you folks what the soothsayer said to Caesar. 'Beware the Ides of March.' The National Weather Service keeps throwing hints about a possible blizzard heading our way. Make sure to get your bread and milk before the storm hits, and keep warm, neighbors.

"Now on to the national news ..."

Chapter 8

A massive yawn hit Liam as he walked out of the firehouse at midnight. His evening had been chaotic, filled with two more chimney fires and a three-car collision. A shower, a couple hours of sleep, and at least a gallon of coffee were required before he thought of digging and throwing mulch for several hours for one of his few remaining clients. Long nights made for even longer days, and without a little rest, he would be worthless come time to spend the evening with Elizabeth.

He rubbed his gritty eyes and pulled his toboggan down over his hair. His back and neck muscles were tight with fatigue, his feet were full of lead, and his bed was calling his name. Keys in hand, he shuffled down the sidewalk toward his truck. A thick layer of frost covered the windows, so he warmed the cab while he took care of scraping it off. Exhaustion dragged at his bones. He was so tired, he realized he was sitting in his driveway and didn't remember driving home.

Before his head hit the pillow, he was sound asleep, and visions of a pretty blonde danced through his dreams.

A harsh beep broke through the silence, waking him from a deep sleep. Instinct had him reaching for his radio, even as his sleep clouded mind fought for clarity. Rising on one elbow, he flicked the channel button to receive the fire call. As the static cleared, a disembodied, electronic voice called out the code and location of the fire. When the words Endless View Farm and Inn came over, Liam jumped out of the bed and threw clothes and shoes on before snatching his wallet, keys, and phone off his dresser.

From the sound of the first beep until the moment his hand touched the door of his truck, less than five minutes had passed. The rapid beat of his heart bore evidence of the rush of adrenaline racing through his body. While this reaction was somewhat typical at each alarm, the fact that this was where Elizabeth lived made his response a little more severe. Even though the dispatcher stated the fire was contained and no one was injured, seeing it with his own two eyes was the only thing that would offer him any comfort. The tremble of his hands served as proof of how rattled he was.

As Liam approached the scene, the wet, thick smoke showed the fire not only contained but almost out. The smoldering supply shack was beyond repair, but thank God, that seemed to be the extent of any damages done.

Huddled near the path to the cottages, several employees shivered in the early morning cold. A familiar head of white-blonde hair drew Liam toward the group. While happy to see Elizabeth appeared unharmed, the shrill wheeze screaming from her chest when she took a breath alarmed him.

"Elizabeth?" Liam pushed through the crowd and stopped in front of her. A close look at her clothing revealed scorched areas of material, and sooty smudges marked her face and arms. "What in this world have you done?"

"Helped Gramps grab a few things." She rubbed her arms up and down to generate warmth, but the friction didn't stop her from shivering.

When she looked up at him, he noticed the exhaustion lining her eyes. Liam could tell she'd left her cabin in a hurry because her feet were bare and her short leggings left her ankles exposed to the cold. Her hair was half up, half down in a messy ponytail, and thick glasses covered her beautiful blue eyes.

When she shivered again, he removed his coat. As she held her arms out to put it on, Liam laughed at her t-shirt.

"Justin Bieber? *Really?* I never would've thought you'd have Bieber fever." While he zipped the jacket on her, he couldn't help but tease her, even as he gave her a thorough looking over for burns. "Is he my competition?"

She opened her mouth to reply, but a violent cough stole her breath and her words. When she managed to get it under control, the wheeze was more pronounced, and Liam was even more concerned. Just as he turned to get one of the paramedics, Elizabeth squeaked out one word. "Inhaler."

"Your cabin?" Liam asked the obvious question, and when she nodded, he turned and ran. "I'll be right back."

Elizabeth tried to yell at him, but she couldn't draw enough air in to get any volume, so instead, she followed him down the short path. When she walked through the door, the sight of Liam tossing her pillows and bedding made her giggle. He was so frantic in his search, he didn't notice her brush his arm when she walked by him.

Everything about her cottage was small, and everything about Liam was large. He looked like a giant in a playhouse. When he turned and took two steps to her kitchenette, Elizabeth slipped his coat off, calmly walked into the bathroom, and got her inhaler from the medicine cabinet. After taking two hits, she replaced it, went back to the living area, and sat in her rocking chair while the medicine took effect.

In the meantime, Liam searched every cabinet and drawer until he noticed Elizabeth nodding off in her chair. He knelt by her, gently brushed the hair from her face, and with a light touch, rubbed the tension from her shoulders. When her lashes fluttered open, the tender look in his eyes made her smile.

"Hey," she whispered as she reached up and covered his hand with her own. "I'm okay now. Promise. And just for future reference, I keep my inhaler in the medicine cabinet. You know, in the bathroom?" She pulled his hand from her neck and placed a soft kiss on the back of it. When the furrow of his brow didn't budge, she heaved a deep sigh. "I promise, Liam. I'm okay. I've been through this before. I've had asthma all my life, and trust me, this is nothing compared to some of the other times."

"Lean forward." Liam's hand landed on her shoulder, and with a little pressure, he helped her bend at the waist. When her face rested on her knees, he leaned over her and pressed his ear against her back. "Take a deep breath. Good. Let it out." He moved his ear to the other side. "In again. And out." After helping her sit back up, he checked her pulse and heart rate. "Your pulse is steady, and your wheeze sounds better, but you have rales in the lower portion of both lungs. I'd feel better if you'd let me get one of the guys to check your oxygen level." As he spoke, he laid his hands on her cheeks and took a deep look into each of her eyes. Satisfied with what he saw, he kissed her forehead and then wrapped his arms around her.

She let him rock her back and forth for a minute or two, but a yawn hit, and she couldn't hold it back. "I promise I'm not trying to rush you off, but I really need to clean up and get some sleep. I have to be at the inn in a couple of hours." His arms tightened around her when she yawned again, and her eyes watered. "This fire pretty much guarantees that tomorrow is going to be one long day, but I sure am glad no one was hurt."

Liam loosened his hold and leaned back to look her in the eyes. "You get cleaned up. I'm going to grab one of the –"

She held up her hand and stopped him midsentence. "Nope. It's okay. I promise." When she took a deep breath, he heard a slight wheeze, and with his hands near her waist, he could feel the crackles. "I seem to be promising you something every other word. But, trust me, this isn't the first time this has happened, though I hope it's the last. I truly am fine, just really, really sleepy. And if I don't get to sleep before the medicine gives me the shakes, I'm out of luck."

Liam huffed out his frustration, drawing a giggle from the heavy-eyed Elizabeth. Worry wasn't his normal reaction, but for some odd reason, his concern for Elizabeth felt natural, not overbearing, and he wore it with ease.

"Okay, you win." He kissed her left cheek. "I'll leave you be, but I'll be by early in the morning to check on you." His lips feathered her right cheek. "And if your breathing becomes more labored," he closed his eyes as his arms contracted around her, "please, please, please, call 911."

When he opened his eyes, Elizabeth shook her head, grinned, and rolled hers. "Why, yes, sir. I'll surely do just that." She giggled, and as exhaustion dug its claws into her, the chuckles changed to uncontrollable laughter. "Gotta … sleep." Her words started to slur.

Liam snatched her up and placed her on the bed. When he swung her feet over to the middle, pushed her back down, and grabbed the faded patchwork quilt, she opened her mouth to argue, but Liam narrowed his eyes and shook his head.

"Sleep, beautiful. We'll worry about getting you cleaned up tomorrow."

Then Liam did what he'd wanted to do since he walked up to the scene. He pressed his lips to hers. When he pulled back, it was his turn to roll his eyes because Elizabeth was fast asleep. He spread the blanket over her, took one last longing-filled look, and then locked the door behind him as he left.

Liam's mind refused to shut down for the night. He tossed and turned in his cold, empty bed. Though not a true close call, the fire was enough to scare some sense into him. No more games. If he were honest with himself, his wait for someone like her had been far too long. She made him feel ten-foot-tall and bulletproof. While hesitant to hope, he couldn't deny the way she made his heart lighter with just a simple glance or the way his pulse sped up at her nearness. The mere touch of her hand made him want to pull her close.

When exhaustion forced his mind to rest, visions of bright blue eyes and silky blonde curls carried him to dreamland.

True to his word, Liam stopped by bright and early the next morning and headed straight to the reception area. Since she wasn't behind the counter, he headed down the hall to search Roger's office. He stopped right inside the door and grinned when he saw Elizabeth sitting behind a desk, head leaned back against her chair, sound asleep. From where he stood, her coloring looked good, and her breathing sounded normal. Because he knew how little sleep she actually got the night before, he quietly backed into the hallway, pulled the door shut behind him, and went outside to help with the cleanup effort.

By lunchtime, his clothes were filthy, his face streaked with soot, and his hands and feet frozen, but he was satisfied with the progress he'd made on his corner of the burn site. Coffee would be good right about then. When it began to sprinkle with flurries mixed in, he wished for a moment of spring's warmth and hoped his gloves thawed fast enough to get them off his numb hands.

Until a beautiful snow bunny appeared with hot chocolate.

Her long, white parka stopped just below her knees. The brown fur lining the hood framed her face and matched the fur trim on the top of her boots. Elizabeth looked like an ice queen on a stroll across her kingdom. Snowflakes landed on her eyelashes and cheeks, and he laughed when her tongue darted out to catch some.

"Well, hello, my handsome hero." She held out a cup of cocoa. "I figured you had to be cold. Do you have a couple of minutes to sit?"

Instead of taking the mug, he pressed his hands to her sides at the bottom of her rib cage. "Sure, but humor me. Take a deep breath."

She rolled her eyes but did as he asked. "Satisfied? I did a breathing treatment this morning. Not that you could feel anything through this monster coat."

He grinned and kissed the tip of her nose. "Yes, I'm satisfied. Ya kind of scared me last night, but if you've had asthma for a while, then I guess you're used to it." He took the cup in one hand and her hand in the other, entwining their fingers as he tugged her toward the porch. "Did you enjoy your nap?"

"Nap?" She wrinkled her brow in confusion. "Did I take a … Oh, this morning." Embarrassment tinged her cheeks pink, but she smiled up at him. "What can I say? It was a long, exciting night."

"Yeah, can't argue that. My heart almost stopped when I heard where the fire was. Being as this is a small town and everyone knows everyone, it's rare we get a call for someone I don't know." He led her over to the porch swing, held it with his knee until she sat, and before taking his place beside her, set their cocoa on the deck railing. "But I have to say, I'm pretty sure I'll be happy to never, ever get the same feeling I got last night." He kept his eyes glued to where his thumb traced circles on the back of her hand. "It scared me, Elizabeth. I mean, really scared me." He glanced at her, his brows furrowed, and his mouth twisted. "A thousand thoughts flew through my head, and each one tried to convince me you were hurt, or worse. I didn't breathe until I pulled up and saw you out there with everyone else."

"I am so sorry you worried, but you know I'm okay. Right?" Her lips curled into a soft smile, and she cupped his jaw, her thumbs dancing along his stubble. "You saved me, Liam. Well, you tried to, anyhow." She winked, and he saw laughter dancing in her eyes.

"Oh, you have no idea how happy I am you're okay." His hands covered hers, traveled the length of her arms and across her shoulders, to wrap gently around her neck. He stared into the depths of her eyes. "We've spent so much time together these last few weeks, but I'm not sure I'd even realized just how important you've become to me until I got that call." He pressed his forehead to hers and looked at her through his thick, black lashes.

Her eyes widened in surprise, and as she opened her mouth to speak, Liam tilted her face up and brushed his lips over hers, catching her gasp before pulling her closer. Her eyes fluttered closed, and she melted into his warmth. When he backed away, she sighed, and a small smile bloomed.

He couldn't resist feathering light kisses across her eyes and forehead. "These freckles on your cheeks fascinate me." His lips followed the trail his fingers blazed across her face. "You're so beautiful. Breathtaking, really."

In the back of his mind, Liam heard the footsteps, but when the sound of a throat clearing hit him, it registered that he and Elizabeth were no longer alone. As she looked over his shoulder, the heat of her blush burned through his gloves.

Gloves? Dang it. What was I thinking?

Black soot marred her perfect, heart-shaped face. Now the heat of a flush reddened the tips of his ears.

There goes my good impression. I want to do this right, but I'm so out of practice that I'll probably ruin things without help from anyone else.

He turned his body to shield her from prying eyes and frowned when he saw Zack propped against the porch post.

"What's up, Z? Is there a problem?"

A grin curved Zack's lips. "Nope. Not a thing, dude. Just glad to know you're alive since you disappeared and all." He leaned around Liam and winked at Elizabeth. "Hi, Elizabeth. I'm Zack." His eyes narrowed for a split second before widening, and he barked out a laugh and smacked Liam on the shoulder. "Guess you can keep your man-card for just a little longer. You up for lunch?"

Elizabeth giggled and pushed on Liam's chest. "Go. Eat lunch with your friend. I have plenty to do here to keep me busy the rest of the day." She glanced at her hand on his chest, and when she noticed the dark streaks, she gasped. Closing her eyes, she squeaked. "Does my face look worse than my hands?"

"Yep, you two are a matched pair." Zack's grin grew wider. "But don't worry. Your pretty still shines through, but there's no hope here for his ugly mug." When she looked at Liam's filthy gloves, Zack chuckled. "Guess I'll let you two finish up. Dude, I'll be at the truck." With one last wink at Elizabeth, Zack took the steps two at a time and rounded the corner of the inn.

"Elizabeth, I'm so—"

She put a finger to his lips and giggled. "Shush it. The look on your face is priceless. It's just a little dirt and grime. Ain't nothing I haven't worn before, and it'll wash right off." She played with the fringe of hair at the bottom of his toboggan. "I will admit though," she looked into his eyes and wiggled her brows, "I think this is the best way I've ever acquired it." Her bright smile lit up her whole face.

"Huh, guess it was kind of a nice way to get you dirtied up a little. Course, I'll have to kick it up a notch." He leaned back and smirked. "After all, I'm competing against Justin Bieber."

Elizabeth groaned and slapped his arm. "Not another word about that, young man. As a matter of fact, I may burn that shirt." She stood from the swing and towered over him, hands planted on her hips. When he moved to stand, she pushed him back down, and when his hands reached for her, she grabbed them. "I'm pretty sure I've got a job ahead of me getting this coat clean. Don't add more, please."

If he hadn't seen the twinkle in her eyes, he would have thought she was upset. Instead of grabbing her waist, he latched onto her wrists and pulled her down to his level. "I'm going to let you get back to work, but we're still on for dinner, right?" When she nodded and smiled, he placed a quick kiss on her lips and let her go. "I'll be back around six to pick you up. Dress warm. The temperature's supposed to nosedive tonight, and I don't want you getting sick."

"Promise. See you at six."

Liam sat there for a minute longer, giving his heart time to slow its racing. So many thoughts battled around in his head, but the loudest one felt right.

Something about that girl makes me happy.

He tasted of
strong man,
bright sunshine,
everlasting love,
and

hope eternal.

Chapter 9

E lizabeth rushed into the lobby, her wet boots slipping and sliding across the floor. "Grams?" She slammed into the counter, and feeling the bite of the impact, rubbed a circle on her sore hip. "Ouch! Grams?"

She heard a throat clear, and whirled around to see Grams in the hall, one brow raised in question.

"You all right, child?" She crossed the foyer and peered out the front window. "Well, I don't see another fire. What's got you all excited?"

"Oh, Grams, I need to run into town." She twisted her hands together. "Liam's taking me out to dinner, and I want to go to Jolene's and AnaWear to see if I can find something to wear."

"Well, I reckon that's all right, but can I make a suggestion. Maybe two?" She picked up the phone and held it out to Elizabeth. "I talked to Gramma Gail this morning. She talked to Aunt Shelley, and it seems Shelley may have talked to your momma about the fire." She barked out a laugh. "That dang thing has rung off the hook, and I swear every other call has been your mom or dad. Why don't you call them and put their mind at ease?"

Elizabeth gasped in horror. "I should have thought to call first thing this morning, but between exhaustion, insurance agents, and fire inspectors, it plumb slipped my mind." She glanced over at her desk, and an idea formed. "Do you mind if I used the computer and Skype with them? If you're using it, I can connect my phone to Wi-Fi. That way they can see with their own eyes that I'm okay."

"Law, child, you don't have to ask permission. But here's where my second suggestion might come in handy." Tootsie rubbed her hand over her mouth, and pinched her lips together with her fingers. Her eyes traveled Elizabeth from toe to head, and when she coughed, it sounded suspiciously like a strangled laugh. "Umm, you might want to look in a mirror first." This time, she did laugh. "I, uh, wouldn't want you to scare them."

Elizabeth closed her eyes and slowly turned to face the decorative mirror beside the fireplace. When she worked up the courage to sneak a peek, her mouth dropped open, and her eyes rounded in surprise. Her appearance was much worse than she thought.

"Liam!" she growled. "That rascal. It's worse than I thought."

Soot covered as far as the eye could see. Smudged handprints caked her waist where he'd checked her breathing, wrists from his pulse check, and shoulders. Black trails where his hands traveled to hers, smeared her arms. Very little white of her white coat was evident. Her face. Dear Lord, her face. Gray mingled with black blurred her forehead and smeared one eyelid. Filthy streaks mottled her cheeks, and even the lobe of one ear was grubby. But the *pièce de résistance?* A perfect shadow of black ash outlined her red, swollen lips.

"I'm going to kill him."

Tootsie gave up the fight to keep a straight face. She doubled over, howling. "Well, I'll say one thing about that young man ..." She paused to take a deep breath. "He's nothing," gasp, "if not," gasp, "thorough." Liquid laughter streamed down her reddened cheeks. "Oh, law, you'd better ... you'd better get cleaned up before ..." She couldn't finish her sentence for cackling, so she pointed to the computer and walked away, a trail of snickers sounding behind her.

Dropping her chin to her chest, Elizabeth counted to ten.

Please, God, please, don't let it be as bad as I thought.

Reluctant to look again, she breathed in to the count of five, puffed her cheeks to blow out a harsh wheeze, and jerked her eyes up to the mirror.

"Oh, no, it's just as bad this time." She moaned in despair.

She tilted her head and rubbed at the patches on her cheek, arguing back and forth with herself.

You need to get a grip!

Yeah, right, I look horrible.

It's not the end of the world.

But his friend saw me like this.

So, what? They're firemen. You think they've never seen a little dirt and grime?

Oh, yeah. I forgot about that.

Besides, it's not like he was trying to get you dirty. He didn't even notice until Zack said something. Girl, he was caught up in you.

Her thoughts drifted to the expressions she'd seen on his face.

Liam's anxiety as he concentrated on her lungs when she breathed.

The fear in his eyes when he thought she might be hurt.

The relief that she was okay.

The surprise when he realized she was important to him.

And finally, the happiness and joy when he kissed her.

Remembering how the soot and ash came to be all over her coat and face warmed her heart and stilled any notion of mortification at her disheveled appearance. Her fingers lingered on her lips.

"Child, if you're going to stand there all day dreaming, at least let me have that coat so I can wash it."

Startled, Elizabeth pressed a hand against her racing heart and spun around to face Tootsie. "Grams, you scared me!"

"Well, I left you in that exact same spot nigh on ten minutes ago." Tootsie tugged at the coat sleeve and slipped the garment off her shoulders. "Have you called your parents?" Elizabeth shook her head. "You know you don't have to do some fancy computer thing.

They just need to hear your voice." Taking Elizabeth by the elbow, she led her to the door. "Now you go get cleaned up to go shopping, and make sure you call your momma. I'll see you in the morning."

Before Elizabeth had time to speak a word, the door was closed, and she was on the porch. Without her heavy coat, the wind cut right through her. She darted across the lawn, rushed inside, and relished the warmth. After a quick scrub of her face and hands, she gathered a jacket, her phone, and purse, and left for town.

Because it was one of her least favorite things to do, Elizabeth rushed through her shopping and made a beeline to Buck's for some liquid warmth and energy. Her plan was to grab some cocoa and connect to their Wi-Fi to Skype with her parents.

Cup in hand, she headed to the back room of the shop. The beanbag seats and papasan chairs were filled with coffee beans. She wanted to be comfortable in case the conversation turned out to be a long one.

"Elizabeth Marie, it's about time you called." Keyna's face filled the phone screen. "What in Heaven's name took you so long?"

Elizabeth grinned. "Hello to you, too, Momma. You do realize that I've run around like a chicken with my head cut off, right? Insurance agents, arson investigators, and now I've got a date with Liam to get ready for." She leaned back in the chair and jumped when her dad's face appeared in front of her mother. "Well, hello, handsome. She giving you a hard time?"

Mike winked at her. "She's hogging all the time with my favorite girl. Figured if I was gonna get to talk to you, I'd have to jump right in." His face screwed up in a wince. "Ouch, that hurt."

"Oh, don't be such a wimp. I just pinched you a little." Keyna planted a hand in his face and pushed. "Now tell her goodbye and go to the driving range."

Her dad's eyes lit up. "Well, can't say no to that, can I? I guess I better go polish my clubs first. I love you, baby girl, and I'm glad you're all right." He blew a kiss at the computer. "Be safe tonight and have fun, and I'll catch you later." Then he hooked an arm around her momma's neck and planted a wet kiss on her lips before leaving Elizabeth's sight.

"That man." Keyna giggled like a schoolgirl. "Still makes my heart pitter-patter like he did the first time I saw him." Tilting her head to the side, she peered at the computer monitor. "Baby girl, you look worn out. Are you sure you need to go out tonight?"

"Momma, I could be half dead, and I still wouldn't miss this date with Liam." She put her elbow on the beanbag, propped her chin on her hand, and stared off at nothing. "Did I tell you Liam's a fireman? He answered the call last night, and he took care of me when he got there." She took a deep breath and coughed. "I had rales last night after breathing in all that smoke, and he stayed with me until my inhaler kicked in. Well, I guess I should say until I passed out on him. Then when he came by today, he made me breathe for him." She sipped her cocoa, and grinned at her thoughts of him.

"Oh, oh, oh, he was in my little cabin last night after he walked me home, and it was just like I imagined it would be. I swear his elbows knocked both sides, and his head scrubbed the ceiling. It certainly wasn't built with someone his size in mind."

"Sounds like he's taking good care of my girl. I'll need to remember to thank him." Keyna squinted and tilted her head to the side. "Where's your good coat, young lady? I know it's still cold up there, and we sure don't want you to get sick. Sounds like that smoke did a number on your breathing as it is. Do you think it's smart to be running around in that thin jacket? You're liable to freeze to death." She stopped to take a breath, and her eyes glistened.

"Now, Momma, you stop that thought right there. My coat's dirty. Grams' washing it for me." Elizabeth tried to smile, but wavered at the worry on her mother's face. The battle to keep her mother reassured left her weary and worn. "I'm not sick, Momma. I'm not going to get sick. And you don't need to make yourself sick worrying about me. I'm not Seth." Her voice was soft but firm.

Keyna huffed in a few shallow gasps. "Baby girl, I can't. I can't not worry. I can't not be scared." Tears trailed down her cheeks and dripped off her chin. "I can't lose another child. I wouldn't live through it." Moisture glistened on the tip of her nose, and she wiped it on her sleeve. "Mom called Gramma Gail. Gramma Gail called Aunt Shelley, and Shelley came over this morning. The first thing she said was, 'Elizabeth's fine.' Then she explained about the fire, and my heart dropped right out of my chest. I called and called and called, and Lord knows Mom and Dad have to be sick of me, but I just needed to hear your voice myself."

Not for the first time, Elizabeth wished Highlands had better cell reception. If her parents could have called her cellphone, her mother's fears would have been put to rest immediately. Her chest cramped from knowing she'd caused her sweet mother a second of anxiety and pain. "I never want you to worry about me, but I just got caught up in all the stuff I had to do, and forgot to do the one thing I needed to do."

When Keyna couldn't speak for sobbing, Elizabeth's heart broke into pieces. "Oh, Momma." She touched the phone screen, wishing she could fold her mother in her arms and comfort her. "Please, Momma, please, calm down. You can see me now, hear me now. I'm okay, I promise."

Elizabeth heard golf clubs rattle, and seconds later, saw her father wrap his arms around her mom.

Mike looked at Elizabeth, compassion filling his eyes. "We're going to go, baby girl. Just know that we love you, and I'll take care of her. We'll be praying for you, sweetheart. You and Liam have a good time tonight." He kissed the tips of his fingers, pressed them to the screen, and then Elizabeth's phone went black.

Her mom had done so much better the last several months, but the panic and depression monster reared its ugly head today. Elizabeth settled back into the chair, and as quiet as a mouse, wept bitterly. Her biggest fear was the loss of her brother could eventually lead to the loss of her mother. When soggy, crumpled napkins littered the table and the dispenser was empty, she took a deep breath and tried to compose herself.

"Excuse me. I don't mean to be rude, but ..."

A pile of Kleenex appeared on the table, and Elizabeth glanced up to see a petite, blonde haired woman with smooth creamy skin and bright green eyes, swaying side-to-side. Strapped to her front was a squirming infant.

"I didn't want to interfere or interrupt, 'cause sometimes a good cry really can make things better." She nodded to the seat beside Elizabeth. "May I?"

"By all means." Elizabeth scooted the seat away from the table. "Please, do sit." She snatched a tissue off the table and mopped her wet face. "Excuse the mess," she said and sniffed. "You know, you may be right. I think I do feel better."

"Thanks for sharing your spot. Little Carson here was starting to feel like he weighs a thousand pounds, and this place is full."

Surprised, Elizabeth glanced around, and sure enough, the crowd was much larger now. "It was empty when I came in." Heat crawled up her neck, and red spots tinged her cheeks. "How embarrassing. I've been sitting here, blubbering and snotting, and who knows who all saw me."

The girl barked a laugh, startling the baby, who proceeded to squeak. "A few people mighta looked, but they were smart enough to leave you be." The infant squirmed and cried out. "AND, that's my signal that someone's hungry." She pulled a patchwork blanket from her backpack, covered herself and the baby, and after a few quick seconds of arranging things, Elizabeth heard gentle sucks and soft grunts. "There. Now we'll have a few minutes to talk. I'm Ashton, by the way." She held out her hand.

Elizabeth glanced at the table full of wet, snotty napkins, looked at Ashton's hand, and then grinned. "You might want to pass on that handshake. I'm Elizabeth."

Ashton's eyes crinkled, and a bright smile covered her face. "Yeah, that's probably a good idea." The beans inside the papasan cushion rattled as she settled back and bounced her foot. "So, you wanna talk about it, or tell me to butt out? I'm good either way."

Elizabeth chuckled at the soft-spoken but blunt lady. "Let's just put it all down to exhaustion. Last night, there was a fire where I work and live, and today has been one whirlwind after another."

"Oh, you work at Endless View? Zack went on that call last night. Pretty sure it was the only fire in these parts." She rocked side-to-side and rubbed small circles on the baby's head.

"Yes, that's where I work. I live in one of the cabins." Elizabeth tilted her head and peered closer at Ashton. "I met a Zack this afternoon. He's one of Liam's friends."

"Yep, that would be my Zack. He's about this tall," she threw a hand over her head and wiggled her fingers, "and shoulders this wide?" One arm stretched out at her sides. "Short, brown hair, brown eyes, and the sweetest smile you've ever seen?" When Elizabeth nodded, a dreamy look came over Ashton's face. "Yeah, that's my Zack, and I'm his Ashton, and this is our Carson." She sighed, a honeyed smile on her face, and for the first time since she came to the table, Ashton sat still.

"Um, yeah, I met him when I was talking to Liam, but I'm afraid I was a little, uh, dirty." Elizabeth remembered what she looked like when she met Zack, and grimaced.

Ashton shot straight up in her chair, and her mouth dropped open. "Wait, wait, wait! Whoa, whoa, whoa! I know who you are! You're Liam's Marshmallow Girl!" Excitement bubbled around her. "I'm so excited to finally meet you."

"Liam's *what?*" Elizabeth wasn't sure what it meant, nor quite how to take that title. "Um, what exactly do you mean?"

Ashton fiddled around under the blanket and pulled out a sleeping Carson. Propping his head on her shoulder, she patted up his back in a steady rhythm. "You know, his 'I've searched everywhere but can't find the girl in the white, puffy coat, have you seen her' girl. He didn't know your name, so that's what he called you." Carson stiffened and grunted, but when a huge burp exploded from his tiny body, he dozed back off to sleep. "For a while, Liam's had his eye on the prettiest, sweetest, little gal – his words, not mine – and now he wants to spend every little bit of extra time with her. Girl, that boy is G-O-N-E gone over you."

A kernel of hope bloomed warm in Elizabeth's heart, and lost in the joy of the moment, she gazed over Ashton's shoulder. "His Marshmallow Girl. Huh, who'da thunk?"

"Yeah, I probably shouldn't say anything, but really, he's crazy about you." Carson drew his knees up to his stomach, stiffened his back, and whined. "I'll just say, in the time I've known him, he hasn't dated much, and he sure as heck hasn't mentioned anyone to me in years. Until you." Ashton narrowed her eyes and pierced Elizabeth in her gaze. "I guess I'll be seeing more of you, 'cause unless I'm mistaken, you two are actually dating." At Elizabeth's hesitant nod, Ashton's stern look lessened. "Well, well. I love that boy like a brother, and if you burn him like that other one did, I will hunt you down." Carson cried out in pain, and Ashton stood. "Little fellow's getting ready to take care of some business, so I guess I need to run." She wrapped an arm around Elizabeth's shoulder and hugged her tight. "About your being sad, just remember, if you ever need to talk, here's my home number." She pressed a piece of paper into Elizabeth's hand. "Don't carry all the burdens on your own," she whispered.

And then she was gone.

Elizabeth couldn't decide if her imagination was on overdrive, or if she'd just met the Tasmanian devil. Ashton's mood fluctuated from concerned to excited to a little threatening right back to compassionate, leaving Elizabeth dizzy and a little stunned at her abrupt departure.

What just happened? And what did she mean by *burn him like the other one did?* Everyone had a past, and she knew that Liam was no exception. The newness of their relationship kept her from asking questions, but if things progressed, she would press him for more.

Elizabeth sipped on her lukewarm cocoa and replayed the conversation but could make little sense of it. All she felt was confused. Putting it behind her was the best thing she could do.

Besides, a quick glance at the clock on her phone told her it was time to get ready for her date. And as she gathered her things, the only thing on her mind was Liam.

He tasted of
strong man,
bright sunshine,
everlasting love,
and
h o p e   e t e r n a l .

Chapter 10

Running late for her date left her frazzled. Even though she purchased a new outfit that afternoon, by the time she'd gotten home, she'd doubted her decision. In the end, she'd wasted thirty minutes going back and forth between choices, and ended up going with the new skirt and sweater. Unfortunately, the thirty-minute delay meant she was ten minutes behind schedule. Parking two blocks over and watching for ice as she walked made her even more overdue.

Soft music played in the background as Elizabeth walked inside. Set back in an alcove off Main Street, she'd often thought about dropping into Ruka's Table for lunch, but for some reason, she never did. Maybe her subconscious was waiting to eat there with Liam. A quick glance around failed to reveal his dark auburn waves, so she stopped at the hostess station.

"I'm meeting Liam Broun. Sorry I'm late, but I believe we have a seven o'clock reservation." Her hands trembled as she wiped them on her skirt. She wouldn't say she was nervous, so much as her nerves were on edge. The interrupted night and crazy day were beginning to catch up to her.

The hostess grabbed two menus and instructed Elizabeth to follow her. A thorough sweep of the restaurant showed soft lighting and patrons in quiet conversation. Exposed tin roofing, duct work, and whitewashed bricks lent a contemporary, converted-warehouse feel. Bright colored paintings and modern sculptures decorated the walls and shelves.

The relaxing atmosphere was perfect, almost as though Liam anticipated her needs before she knew them. Enticing aromas made her stomach growl, reminding her how little she'd eaten that day.

While waiting for her sweet tea, she glanced over the offered selections, and bounced back and forth between a few dishes. The waiter stopped by to check on her to see if she was ready to order, but she sent him away. Liam was thirty minutes late.

Tired but content, her thoughts traveled back to the front porch swing. When he'd said, *I'm not sure I'd even realized just how important you've become to me until I got that call*, her heart almost flew out of her chest. Now, if she could figure out what he meant by important. Was he falling for her? Because she was certainly falling for him. Try as she might, no way could she ignore how special and treasured he made her feel. Jarrett had never put forth even a tenth of the effort. Of course, that could explain why getting over him hadn't been that difficult.

The front door opened, and a deep, male voice spoke to the hostess. That little flutter of hope flexed its wings again, until she glanced over and realized it wasn't him.

When the waiter stopped by a second time to take her order, butterflies danced in her stomach, and her appetite disappeared. Should she sit here, waiting, hoping, and praying Liam showed, or should she just write the evening off as a loss? After all, this wouldn't be the first time he'd not shown up for a date. Would he always be like this? That little flutter of hope was now a tiny ember of anger. The worst part was the disappointment.

Eight o'clock rolled around, and Elizabeth decided an hour was long enough to wait. It was obvious he wasn't coming, so she placed money on the table for her tea and a tip, and stood to put on her coat. Yes, she'd seen the waiter speak to the hostess, both of them looking her way. As she made the walk of shame to the door, she imagined every eye on her. As far as she knew, the hushed conversations were about her. The closer to the door she got, the redder her face grew. She wrangled with a myriad of emotions. Hurt. Humiliated. Rejected. Crushed.

The cold air on her face did little to cool the burn of embarrassment. Shoulders hunched against the wind, her eyes swept the wooden lanai.

"Elizabeth."

Her head jerked up, and she scanned for who called her name. At the end of the block, a tall figure jogged toward her. A flutter of hope tickled her heart, and she picked up her pace.

Liam?

"I'm so glad I caught you."

In his hand was a bouquet of Gerbera daisies. He took his cap off and ran his fingers through his hair.

"Zack?" Her heart fell, and her shoulders slumped. She was numb. "I thought you were Liam."

"Nah, I'm better than that loser." His loud laugh echoed through the quiet night, and he shoved the flowers in her hand. "He was at the fire house earlier. We got a first responder call, and since he's had the EMT training, he went. He asked me to get these to you, along with his apology, if he didn't make it back in time. Sorry I'm so late. He's gonna kill me for not being here earlier." His head tilted to the side, and his eyes narrowed. "You all right?"

Why was he so blurry?

"Aw, don't cry."

Cry? Who was crying? She rubbed a cold spot on her cheek, and when she pulled her fingers back, she saw the moisture on the tips.

Oh, I'm crying.

"I'm sorry, Zack. I didn't realize. I think I ... Well, it's just ... I'm probably ..." A mild throb began at her temples and between her eyes. "This day has been nuts, and I think I could use a good night's sleep."

"If it helps, he was really looking forward to seeing you

tonight." Zack wrapped his hand around her elbow. "At least let me walk you to your Jeep. I parked right beside you."

Not trusting her voice to betray her disappointment, she nodded and let him lead the way.

On the drive home, her thoughts flew all over the place. Was something wrong with her? No, she knew there wasn't, but after Jarrett, she struggled with rejection. Was she not important? Knowing Liam, his reason for missing their date would be valid. His responsibilities to his family and his jobs weren't something trivial. Was she not worth the time to make a simple call? Of course, if cell phones worked worth a flip in these mountains, she had no doubt he would've called her ahead of time if he'd had the chance.

She ping-ponged back and forth between frustration, regret, and anger, and tried hard not to let the anger fester into something much larger. The only thing that would make her pity party better was a hot shower, a pint of ice cream, and a little time with her guitar. Otherwise, she might not sleep a wink. Between the fire, her momma's meltdown, and being stood up, she needed to get outside of her own head.

So, when she got back to her cabin, that's what she did. The hot water soothed her muscles and the nagging headache, and the ice cream filled her empty stomach. After serenading herself for a while, she brushed her teeth and snuggled under her blankets. Thinking it was the best thing to do, she tried to keep her thoughts off Liam and their non-date.

Counting sheep. Reciting the alphabet. Singing the Presidents. Naming the state capitals. One foot on top of the blanket. Flipping her pillow to the cold side. Recipes. Country songs. Bible verses. Low humming noises in the back of her throat.

Nothing.

Absolutely nothing.

Worked.

No matter how tired she was, sleep eluded her. She tossed. She turned. She mumbled and groaned. By the time eleven o'clock glowed red on her alarm clock, she was so drained, her bones ached.

Thinking warm milk or another warm shower might help, she threw off the blankets, slid to the edge of the bed, and turned on the lamp. The second the room filled with light, a knock sounded on her cabin door.

Expecting Grayson or Brittany, she slipped off the chain and opened the door.

"Everything o—"

It was Liam. His cheeks were bright red, and his teeth were chattering. The fingers he rubbed over her cheek were like ice.

"Can I come in for a minute?" His voice choked out over his shivers. The light jacket he wore was little protection against the late night cold wind.

Stepping back, she nodded and waved him inside.

When he went to take his coat off, he paused. "Do you mind?" She shook her head, and he slipped it off his arms and walked over to hang it on the back of the rocker. "Are you going to say anything?"

She waited until he faced her to shrug. Then she saw the blood on his shirt. Her eyes popped open in shock.

"Are you all right?" Two steps brought her to him, and she ran her hands over his chest and shoulders, looking for where he was hurt.

"It's not mine, sweetheart." He pressed his hands to hers and held them against his heart. "It's Bekah's."

"Wait. What? Bekah's? Zack said you answered a first responder call." How did that circle back to Wrynn and his nieces?

"I did. The call was for our address. Seems she somehow got the grand idea she could fly." He covered his mouth with a fist and coughed, '*Annie.*' "Anyhow, tonight she learned a valuable lesson. If you jump off the deck, you're lucky you only break your arm."

"That's her blood?" Her hands fisted his shirt. "From a broken arm?" She scrunched her nose, and he kissed the tip. "Ewww. But is she okay?"

He took a deep breath and closed his eyes for a second. Stress etched the lines of his face. His hair was all willy-nilly as though he'd run his fingers through it over and over again.

"She's going to be fine. They set both the bones," he grabbed just above her wrist to indicate where the break was, "and stitched where they poked through the skin. Right now, she's in an air cast until the stitches come out. When I left, she was rambling something about a hot pink cast."

"Aww, honey, I feel so bad for her." She truly did. Having never broken a bone, she could only imagine how horrible the pain was. "So everyone's back home now?"

"Yeah. And I owe you an apology for not making it to the restaurant." He glanced into her kitchen, and a wry smile formed on his lips. "I see Zack made it with the flowers."

"Yes, he did." She stared down at the floor, suddenly fascinated with the grain of the wood. Did she tell him, or did he have enough on his mind? Maybe she could find the words so her explanation didn't sound like she was whining. "Thankfully, I was running a little behind, so I was only waiting for," she took a page from his playbook and mumbled into her fist, "forty-five minutes."

"That idiot was supposed to be there at seven." He slammed his palm into his forehead.

"Liam, honey, you can't really blame him if something came up. It's not really his responsibility, ya know?" She peered up at him. "That's kinda your job."

"You're right. It's my job and I failed you." He wrapped his arms around her shoulders, then looked down at his bloody shirt. "I really want to hold you when I grovel, but I'm not sure you want your face pressed against Bekah's dried blood."

"Again, ewwww. You'd be right about that." Knowing the true issue made her feel better, and helped ease the ache in her heart. Still … "I understand that none of this is your fault or mine, but if I'm honest, I'm a little hurt because I was looking forward to spending this evening with you. I swear I'm not angry, at least not anymore, but I'm kinda scared this is the ways things will always be. This isn't the first time you've dropped me like a hot potato. Is this what I need to learn to expect from you? If so, I'm not sure I'm equipped for it."

And she needed to take a big breath and calm her mind. She

wanted things between them to work out, but she hated feeling like she was ... What was the word she was looking for?

Disposable.

"What's disposable?"

"That's how you made me feel. Like I'm good enough until something else comes along." She walked around him and sat on the edge of the bed. Yes, the thought in her head popped out, but he needed to know how she felt. "I was laying here, tossing and turning, trying like the dickens to sleep, but I couldn't. This," she ghosted her hand between them, "is something I like. Something I like very, very much. But tonight, not so much."

In two steps, he was kneeling on the floor in front of her and grabbing her hands. He pressed a tender kiss to the backs of them.

"I can't promise you this won't happen again, sweetheart. If I'm working at the station, and a call comes in, someone has to go. Tonight, that someone was me. It just happened to be my niece, but it could have easily been anyone else. Not gonna lie to you. A heart attack or stroke or car accident IS more important than dinner because it means I could be saving a life." Shifting his body, he moved beside her on the bed. "I'm not saying *you're* not important. Not at all. But I need you to understand that every person in Highlands counts on us when they need us. Do you get what I'm saying? My job is important to me. You're more important to me. But you can't hold it against me if I get called out. And, if you think about it, you should probably expect it to happen again."

Irritation. Anger. Hurt. Acceptance. Conflicting emotions flew through her brain at a rapid rate. In the end, though, she realized he was right. His job at the fire station was more than throwing mulch, adding numbers, or answering phones. Lives were at stake. By refusing to realize the sincerity and honesty of his words, she was being plain, old selfish. Pure childishness.

She slumped against him, drained from everything in the last twenty-four hours. The pounding in her head took advantage and throbbed harder.

"I understand where you're coming from, and I just ask that

you be patient with me. I'm not saying I'm used to everyone's world revolving around me," her smile was weak, "but I'm not really used to being left waiting either." She wrapped her arm around his waist, and ignoring the blood, pressed her cheek to his heart. "Liam, I really don't want to feel like I'm an afterthought."

His lips mussed the hair on the top of her head, and her eyes drifted shut. Finally, now that her heart and head were settled, sleep waited to claim her.

"I like you a lot, Liam. A lot, a lot. And even though you're not my first boyfriend, so to speak, my experiences would fit in a thimble. So all I ask is you tread carefully. Very carefully. Because you're important to me, too, and I'm not sure you realize just how bad you could hurt my heart."

Chapter 11

Elizabeth learned over the following weeks that, although he was strong and tough and without doubt, all man, Liam wasn't afraid to show his kind, gentle, compassionate side. In more ways than one, he proved he was worth forgiving. The more time she spent with him, the greedier she became for more.

Snug in her warm, cozy cabin, Elizabeth talked to her mother while she got ready for bed. Strong winds whipped through the night, sleet beat against the roof, and a film of ice frosted the insides of the windows. She was thankful to be home.

"Yes, Momma, I promise I'll charge my cell phone more often." She walked to the bathroom, careful not to overstretch the cord of the phone. "Not that it'll be much use. Reception is hit or miss around here until they get those new towers turned on. You know that, silly."

"I know, but what if I need to get in touch with you?"

"What on earth would you need to get in touch with me for? Mom, we talk *every* day, sometimes twice." The hinges on the cabinet squeaked like nails down a chalkboard, sending shivers down her spine.

"Well, you just never know. Now, did you take your medicine, young lady? And *what* was that noise?"

"The noise you heard was me opening the medicine cabinet. That's where I keep my, you know, asthma medicine." Elizabeth snickered at her mother. "It's okay, Mom. I do this every night." She washed the pills down with water and used her inhaler.

This conversation occurred every time Elizabeth called home late in the evening. Her mother's obsession with her remaining child's wellbeing was a product of love mingled with anxiety and fear. Knowing that, Elizabeth tried not to let it irritate or upset her. Seth's sickness had pushed the whole family close to the point of breaking as they watched the robust, energetic young man waste away to skin and bones. Near the end, when he begged them to let him go, Elizabeth worried they might never recover. Over time, thin scabs formed, but the wounds would never truly heal.

"Elizabeth Marie, don't you get smart with me. You know I worry." Keyna's laugh brought a smile to her daughter's face. "So, are you going to keep me in suspense as punishment for worrying about you?"

Thankful her mom couldn't see her, Elizabeth rolled her eyes. "Hmm, that's not a bad idea." A huge yawn popped the joints in her jaws, causing her eyes to water. "I'm kind of tired, but no, if I don't tell you, you won't sleep tonight, and no one should lose sleep over my date with Liam, unless it's me." She slipped on a pair of leggings, an old t-shirt of Seth's, and a pair of thick, fuzzy socks.

"I was a little worried he'd cancel again, but he showed up right on time. We had supper in Asheville at this little nouvelle cuisine restaurant. It was, um, nice, and the food was good, but seriously, Momma, they sure don't give you much." Her shoulder lifted to hold the phone to her ear so she could pull her hair into a messy bun. "One of Liam's friends had suggested it, and we thought it would be different, so we tried it. We'd planned to see a movie after, but as soon as we walked out the door," she pictured him in her mind and giggled, "Liam's stomach growled. You shoulda seen his face. He turned fifty shades of red. Oh, he's so cute when he's embarrassed. So, needless to say, I suggested we find him something filling to eat.

He wants to make it up to me, so we're going out again tomorrow night."

"Have you had him over for dinner yet?" Keyna asked. "Ain't no man alive who couldn't be won over by Momma's chicken and dumplings."

"Are you kidding me? I can just see it now. Him in the rocking chair and me sitting on the bed. How romantic. Not!" She turned on the water to wash her face. "Besides, I don't call this my little cabin for nothing. Why, Liam would feel like a giant in a gnome's house if he was in here for very long."

Face covered in foaming cleanser, she tilted her upper body back and squinted to see the bright pink and yellow Gerbera daisies on her nightstand. "He brought me flowers again," she said in a quiet whisper. The vibrant colors reminded her of what he said when he gave them to her. "He said daisies mean cheerful, and every time he thinks of me, he smiles." She stepped out of the bathroom, wanting to touch the velvet petals, but the phone cord wrapped around her neck. "When he says sweet things like that, it makes my knees weak." As she rinsed the soap off with her washcloth, she noticed the brightness in her eyes and the rosy glow on her cheeks. "I don't know how to explain it, Momma, other than to say he makes my heart smile."

Keyna's loud chuckle tickled Elizabeth's ear. "Well, he *does* sound romantic." She cleared her throat and made a tsking sound. "Unlike some men." Masculine laughter and murmured words greeted her wry statement. "Yes, Michael, I'm talking about you, and no, you may not talk to your baby girl. You'll have to wait until I'm finished."

A rustling noise sounded in the background. Mom giggled, and Dad spoke into the phone. "Love you, sweetie. I'll call you sometime this week when the old ball-and-chain ain't around." A loud, distinctive oomph followed his words, which probably meant her mom had elbowed him in the stomach.

As she stretched out beneath her blankets, a vivid picture of her parents flashed through Elizabeth's mind. Their open affection, small touches, quick kisses, long embraces. No, life had not always been easy for her dad and mom, but their love proved strong enough to travel through the fire of trials and come out whole on the other side.

"You two behave." She grinned, but her voice grew wistful and serious. "I want that, Momma. What you and Daddy have. And I don't want to compromise and end up with less. I know there can be so much more, because I've seen it with you two. How did you know? I mean, do you think …"

A happy hum traveled over the line. "Oh, honey. I do believe my baby girl is falling in deep, and if he's the one, then I've been praying for him for years. *But* that doesn't mean I want you to get the cart before the horse, so to speak."

Something dawned on her, and she couldn't resist ribbing her mom. "Why, you rascal. You weren't asking if I'd cooked him supper. You were asking if … Momma!"

"Young lady, quit your grumbling. You may be almost twenty-four, and you may not live at home anymore, but part of my job as a parent is to ask these things. I just want you to take your time. Make sure he's the man for you, 'cause he seems too good to be true. That's all. Love rarely happens overnight."

In the background, Elizabeth heard a scuffle, then a thunk when the phone hit the floor.

"Mike, stop. I told you–"

"Now you listen to me, young lady." Her dad obviously won the fight for the phone. "You bring this young man to meet me, and soon, or I'm polishing up my nine iron and coming up the mountain to find him."

"Oh, Daddy, you crack me up. I guess I should be glad you didn't say your shotgun." Elizabeth giggled, imagining her dad protecting her honor with a golf club. "Tell you what. I'll talk to Liam, and, if he's free, I'll bring him with me if I can come home Memorial Day weekend, or you guys can come here to meet him. Sound good?"

"Sounds perfect. Love you, baby girl. I guess I'd better give your momma back the phone before she whacks me over the head with her cast iron skillet."

"Love you, Daddy. Goodnight. I'll talk to you later this week."

She heard the cordless pass hands, but before she could say a word, she heard her dad kiss her mom, and then he spoke into the mouthpiece one more time.

"And don't let her tell you that love can't happen overnight. 'Cause I knew, from the first moment I saw her, that she was the one for me. And all these years later, I've never had a second of doubt."

Yeah, that kind of love.

Keyna's happy sighed traveled through to Elizabeth. "That man. Don't know what I'm going to do with him, but I sure know I can't do without him."

Elizabeth laughed through a yawn and burrowed her head into her pillow. "You'll do what you've always done, Momma. Cuddle up to him when he's sweet, whoop up on him when he's not, and love him through it all." Another yawn hit her, and her eyes watered. "I think I need to go to sleep. You probably do, too."

"Okay, sweetheart." Keyna let out a heavy sigh. "Now you have me yawning. Love you, baby girl. You sleep tight, and I'll talk to you tomorrow."

"Love you, Momma." She stretched her legs out, propped a pillow against her stomach, and curled around it. "Give Daddy kisses for me, and I'll call you when I get home."

Her eyes drifted shut as her hand tangled with the cord, putting the phone on the nightstand and turning off the lamp. In the minutes before sleep took her away, she thought back over the last couple of months with Liam. He was absolutely nothing like Jarrett, and outside of that relationship, she was fairly inexperienced. But not enough to ignore what she felt was the stirring of love.

Call her old fashioned, but she loved the way he opened doors for her, helped her in the truck, and made sure, when they were on a sidewalk, she was away from the street. He gave his affection freely, and was quick to hold her hand and hug her. His kisses stole a little more of her heart every time, and left her humming for more, but he didn't hesitate to stop and push her away whenever they approached his unspoken limit. She tried not to feel rejected or confused, because Lord knew, his good certainly outweighed anything else.

And his good was what kept her wanting more of his time, attention, and someday soon, his love. Her last thought before sleep overtook her was how perfect his arms felt around her.

A knock on her door jarred her awake, and she fought the deep haze of slumber. Sleepy eyes struggled to focus on the clock. Large, green numbers showed it to be 11:15, so she knew she'd only dozed for a few minutes. A second, louder bang prompted her to throw the covers off, hop out of bed, flip on the light, and slip into her robe. Peering through the peephole yielded nothing, so she opened the door until the security chain tightened, but she didn't see anything until she looked lower.

Shivering in the freezing night air, Grayson, in only a t-shirt, sweatpants, and socks, stood on her porch.

"Oh, when did y'all get back?"

"W-week a-g-go."

Elizabeth placed a gentle hand on his shoulder, guided him inside so she could close the door, and led him to her rocking chair.

"S-s-sorry. S-s-sissy s-s-saw your l-l-light and t-t-told me to c-c-come here." Chattering, blue-tinged lips formed his words as trembles jerked his body.

When she spread a blanket over him, he hunched down in it and pulled it tight around his arms. Dark-circle rimmed eyes filled with worry and concern were too heavy for someone this young to carry.

Elizabeth knelt at his feet and rubbed up and down his legs, hoping the friction would warm him quicker. "What's wrong, honey?"

"D-d-do you have any soda c-c-crackers or p-popsicles?" Exhaustion etched his slow spoken words. "Momma's sick again." His shaking slowed as warmth seeped into his little body.

"Well, honey, you sit right here, and I'll see what I have, and then we'll go check on your mom."

A quick inspection revealed a box of crackers, two six-packs of ginger ale, and six cans of chicken noodle soup. Since she didn't know what to expect, she pulled everything out on the counter and searched for a bag.

Grayson's little head slowly bobbed, and his lids drooped heavy with sleep as he peered at her over the edge of the blanket. His eyes widened when she placed three bags at his feet.

"I don't think I can carry all that," he whispered.

Her hand grazed his hair. "No worries, honey. I'll carry it," she said as she pulled on her coat, tugged on her boots, and grabbed a sweatshirt. "Here. Lift your arms and let's put this on." After a glance at his socked feet, she rooted in a box under her bed. "Now, don't laugh at me. Just slip these on, and then forget you're wearing them."

"Um, those are really pink." His lips curled, and his brows scrunched.

The Crocs she set at his feet were a screaming, florescent pink with dark magenta zebra stripes.

"Yeah, I know. They were a gift from my brother." She shrugged her shoulders and grinned. "What can I say? He had awful taste, but they're great in the garden. Now, get 'em on, honey, so we can go check on your mom."

At her reminder, his face fell, and his eyes glistened with moisture. "It's worse than it was the last time."

Elizabeth worried about what he was referring to, and the urge to hurry hadn't left her since she'd first opened the door. "Grayson, everything's going to be okay."

"Promise?" His lips trembled as he tried not to cry.

"Promise." Guilt swamped her as the lie rolled off her tongue. She looped the bags over her arm, threaded her fingers through his, and opened the door. "Lead the way."

A thin layer of sand and ice coated the stone path, so Elizabeth tightened her grip on his hand, and carefully walked them over into the grass.

When they stepped onto the porch, the door flew open.

Brittany poked her head out and spoke in a quiet voice. "She's asleep, Gray, so y'all make sure you don't wake her up."

The sour-sweet, chemical smell of vomit hit Elizabeth's nostrils, and her heart lurched. The smell was one she would never forget. Her eyes drifted shut as her silent plea flew toward Heaven.

Please, God, tell me what to do, and then give me the strength to do it.

A jerk on her hand brought her gaze to Grayson.

"Thanks for the soup, but if you want to go back home and sleep, me and Britt can handle it."

"Yeah," Brittany butted in, "we've done this before. Mama's finished her last treatment, so she'll be better in no time."

"Umm, I don't think so." Herding the kids into the cabin, she closed the door behind them. "You've dealt with this for a while, so let me handle it tonight."

Grayson yawned, so she shooed the kids off to bed and promised to wake them if she needed their help.

Elizabeth headed to the kitchen to search for something to make ginger ale popsicles. They would serve two purposes. First, the ginger ale would soothe the stomach, and second, the ice pop would feel good on the blisters that more than likely coated Missy's mouth and tongue.

Bottles lined up like soldiers across the kitchen counter. Marinol®. Zofran®. Decadron®.

The familiar labels had taunted Elizabeth when she and Liam were there the first time, but she'd refused to accept what they meant. Seemed God wanted her back in the sort of situation she'd avoided since Seth's death. All she could do was pray for the strength and endurance to help these kids through their upcoming pain. The last thing she wanted to do was watch someone else die.

Lord, it's up to you, 'cause we both know I'm not strong enough to do this again on my own.

Chemotherapy and radiation were vile, evil, necessary things, despite the side effects which ravished the body. Having experienced this with Seth, Elizabeth knew some of the tricks to help.

She worked with what she found in the cabinets, and as she

124

poured the ginger ale into makeshift molds, she blocked from her mind what she would see, and turned her thoughts to those that made her happy.

Thoughts filled with Liam.

They spent as much time together as possible. Quick outings to grab coffee or pizza. Walks to the small waterfalls on the edge of the inn's property. Journeys off the mountain to raid garden shops and greenhouses. S'mores and hot cocoa around the fire pit. Stolen kisses on the porch swing. Any time their schedules meshed, they took advantage of the chance to spend those hours together, learning each other and growing closer.

Every time he left, she missed him the instant he was gone, and then she smiled because she knew it wouldn't be long until she saw him again. Her mornings began and her nights ended with thoughts of him, and her days were crammed with as much of him as she could get.

Something that nagged at the back of her mind was she had yet to meet his family. Liam hadn't even mentioned it since the night she cried on his shoulder about Seth, and a family emergency cut their date short. Come to think of it, several times when they'd been together, something had come up, and he'd rushed off to deal with something for his sister or nieces. A couple of times, he'd failed to show when he'd said. It wasn't that he was unreliable. It just seemed he had *too many* people relying on him, and Elizabeth didn't feel she had earned the right to complain. Yet.

She struggled not to let it hurt her feelings. When they were together, she was the center of his attention and the focus of his energy, and she tried to concentrate on that. It's not like she didn't understand his sister's loss and her inability to handle it. Having lived with the pain and the emptiness, she knew the harsh reality that came with losing someone you loved, and how difficult it was to recover. She was new in his life. Her role took on a more solid shape each time they were together, and her place in Liam's world became more certain every day.

She tried so hard, but at times, she failed, and doubt didn't hesitate to creep into her mind.

And then, when Liam was with her, any spark of resentment, anger, or jealously died out beneath his shower of affection. He looked at her as if she hung the moon, held her as if she were precious, and treated her and spoke to her as if she was a priceless treasure. Because of that, she valued every moment with him she could get. His positives far outweighed the negatives.

A cold hand touched her arm, startling Elizabeth out of her thoughts and causing her to shriek.

"Oh, I'm so sorry. I didn't mean to scare you."

Elizabeth placed her hand over Missy's and stared, shocked by the drastic changes in her appearance since she'd last seen her. Her eyes were lifeless and more sunken, and her eyelashes completely gone. Boney cheekbones and chin gave her a skeletal look. Small blisters lined her swollen lips, and Elizabeth knew they covered the inside of her mouth and tongue. Purple, broken capillaries from vomiting made her face appear bruised. What shocked her the most, but shouldn't have, was the dull flesh where long, black hair once grew.

Plain and simple, Missy looked awful. Elizabeth pressed her fingers to her lips, hoping to mask her surprised gasp.

"Oh, honey," she whispered, "is there anything I can do to make it better?"

"I know I'm not a pretty picture right now, but give me a couple of weeks to build up some energy." Missy rubbed her hands over her bald scalp. "Throw in some heavy makeup and the new wig I've ordered, and I'll be right as rain." Missy smiled, and then grimaced when a blister popped. "Sorry. I keep telling myself that this too shall pass, but it sure is taking its own sweet time about it."

"Let's get you something cold to suck on, and then, if you feel up to it later, we'll work up to chicken noodle soup and ginger ale." She tossed ice in a cup and carried it to the couch, sitting sideways to face Missy. "Brittany says this was your last treatment."

A pained look crossed over Missy's face, and Elizabeth's heart clenched tight.

"Yes, it's my last one." She rubbed an ice cube over her lower lip and touched the tip of her tongue to the moisture. "For now, at least. My doctor wants me to go back to Atlanta to get a second opinion on my next course of treatment." She sank back into the back of the couch and closed her eyes. "They can see me tomorrow, but even if I find a driver, I don't know if I'm up for the trip quite yet."

Atlanta was a good four-hour drive, but Elizabeth agreed with her. In her weakened condition, even an hour trip to Asheville might be too much for Missy.

"Where exactly do they want you to go?"

"Southeastern Regional Medical Center. It's part of the Cancer Treatment Centers of America. They took over my treatment months ago."

Oh my gosh, it's that bad.

"Yes, I'm afraid it is." Missy's eyes cracked open, and her mouth twisted in a small grin when Elizabeth gasped. "You didn't mean to say that, did you?"

"No. No, I didn't. Please, accept my apology for being so uncaring."

"You just said what I've been thinking." Missy waved off her words. "So, anyway, since I've progressed from stage II to stage III after four rounds of treatment, my doctor thinks it's the best plan right now. My last scans didn't look so good, and one of the staff there is a leading expert on my form of non-Hodgkin lymphoma. He'll run more tests to see if I'm to stage IV yet."

Elizabeth's chin dropped to her chest, and she fought to draw air into her lungs. "Oh, I've been there, and you're right. They're top notch at what they do." She heard the pain in her own voice but was powerless to cover it. Her memories of the center were not good ones because of Seth. Losing a loved one sucked, but watching the life slowly drain away killed you from the inside out. "How long will you be there?"

"As long as I need to be." Missy grabbed her hand and squeezed it. "Do you want to talk about it?"

"No, I can't, not right now." Elizabeth shook her head back and forth several times and continued speaking as though nothing was wrong. "What will you do about Brittany and Grayson?"

"Since I don't have any family and they're homeschooled, they always go with me. When this round ends, I'll bring them back here again so I can rest." Missy squirmed on the couch, and her eyes fluttered. "I hope you don't think I'm rude, but my meds are kicking in, and I'm going to fall asleep on you."

Elizabeth stood and helped Missy off the couch. "Absolutely not. You need to rest. Let me help you to bed."

After doing just that, she checked on the kids one last time before heading home. All this talk about cancer and treatments was bringing her memories back to Seth, and not in a good way. If she wasn't careful, she'd slip back into a deep depression, and she'd fought too long and too hard to crawl out the last time. Determined to think of things that made her smile, she quickened her pace and raced to her cabin.

The bright pink and yellow Gerbera daisies on her nightstand greeted her when she opened the door. Their beauty brought a smile to her face, and her thoughts of Liam carried her away to sweet dreams.

Radio Broadcast

"Goooood morning, Highlanders! You're listening to the local news on WHLD, AM radio 1250. Today is Saturday, April thirteenth, and these are your community updates.

"Friends, it pains me to say, but Mr. Robert Lee has gone home to be with the Lord after a long, hard battle. Essie says he was awake for a final goodbye with the kids and grandkids. Funeral arrangements are in the works, and instead of sending flowers, you're asked to donate to The American Lung Association.

"Remember The Ladies Auxiliary is gearing up for its annual Stop, Swap, and Shop. They're asking you to bring your gently used household items, children's clothing and toys, and books to the Methodist Church any Saturday until the end of April. All proceeds will benefit the Highlands Childcare Co-op, so get to cleaning up and cleaning out.

"Got an email from the Postmaster, asking me to remind you good citizens that the Post Office will stay open until nine o'clock pm on Tax Day, Monday, April the fifteenth, so you'll have time to get your filing mailed. Remember, render unto Caesar what's Caesar's and get that mess done.

"For all you technology users. Highlands is moving into the twenty-first century. As we told you last year, the town council approved two sites for two joint Verizon, U.S. Cellular 4G towers, and construction is nearing completion. According to the Verizon spokesperson, the towers should be up and running within the next two weeks. So, folks, not much longer until you can post on Facebook from your smartphone, while shopping on Main Street. Make sure to be detailed and do it often, 'cause inquiring minds want to know what you're eating for supper. Heck, take a picture, too.

"Keep in mind that April showers, even if they come in the form of ice, bring May flowers, and May flowers means spring has come. Not much longer now, I hope.

"Now on to the national news …"

Chapter 12

Nestled back in the cushions of the rocker, Elizabeth hummed a quiet tune. That afternoon, she and Liam had driven up on the Blue Ridge Parkway for an impromptu picnic and wildflower hunt. The more time she spent with him, the more she wanted, and Liam seemed willing to accommodate her as much as possible. Her eyes drifted shut, and she rested her head against the back of the chair. So lost was she in her thoughts, she tuned the world out.

Missy and the kids had left for Georgia a few days later than planned, and Elizabeth couldn't help but worry about them. Brittany and Grayson had started hovering over their mom, almost to the point of suffocating her. All three were feeling the stress of Missy's sickness, and none of them were sleeping much. The only thing Elizabeth could do was hope and pray the next round of treatment was successful. Otherwise, she couldn't see much sunshine through the dark clouds of Missy's situation. Cancer was evil, yet at the same time, it didn't discriminate. No one was safe, and the battle to defeat it was long and hard. The worst part, no matter how hard the fight, not everyone won.

And, then there was Wrynn. Liam said she was working herself to the point of exhaustion, and more than once, he'd had to leave work or their date to go take care of his nieces. At least he hadn't stood her up lately. When she'd explained how his blowing her off without warning had hurt her, his apology more than made it up to her. Since the April days were warming up, Liam had taken her to Stone Mountain in Georgia to see the carvings on the face of the mountain. Any feelings she had of feeling second place to Wrynn and her girls were pushed to the back of her heart.

Just that afternoon, they'd made plans to travel down to Wilkesboro later in the month. The Charlie Daniels Band, the Nitty Gritty Dirt Band, and many others were scheduled to perform at MerleFest. This was an annual event for Liam, and she was excited to go with him. He'd said something about the possibility of staying overnight, and in the next second, claimed that wasn't the best idea unless Wrynn and the girls could come. Elizabeth wondered if there was something about her causing his reaction. Or was it rejection? That was the one thought she couldn't stop from forming, and no matter how hard she tried to ignore it, it seemed to fester just below the surface.

Liam was a toucher and a kisser. His hands or lips were on her somewhere almost every second they were together, but he never crossed the thin line from affectionate to something else. It was easy for her to see he respected her, but if she were honest, she worried he wasn't 'attracted' attracted to her. Her feelings for him grew stronger and deeper every time they were together, but if he wasn't feeling the chemistry for her that she felt for him, in the end, her heart would be shattered. Because, without thinking to slow her heart, Elizabeth was falling a little more in love with Liam every day.

Something landed on her legs with a soft plop, and she jolted to awareness. Her eyes popped open to see Grams standing in front of her and a soft blanket on her lap. "Oh my, you scared me." The flutters in her heart settled, and she resumed her rocking. "I was lost in my own little world."

"Law, child, I looked out the window and thought you'd frozen to death. You do realize the temps are hovering around freezing, right? Don't expect that to change 'til least mid-May." Tootsie picked up a long stick and stirred the embers in the chiminea. The shower of sparks lit up the porch. "Your fire's about dead." A few errant strands of hair floated around Elizabeth's face, and Tootsie tucked them under her granddaughter's cap. "Why don't you come back inside and have a bowl of soup with me and Roger? It goes down good on cold nights like these."

Elizabeth realized she had missed the sun setting. Now that she thought about it, it was cold. A shiver ran through her body. "Actually, soup sounds nice right about now. I'd thought to run into town and grab a pizza or sandwich from Mountain Fresh, but if you're sure you have enough, I'd love to join you."

Tootsie grabbed her hand, pulled her from the chair, and tugged her inside. When they stepped into her grandparents' quarters, Tootsie swung the door closed behind them and led her to the table where Roger waited. Gram treating her like a little girl made Elizabeth giggle.

"Roger, look who I have here." She pulled out the chair and pushed Elizabeth's shoulder. "Now sit on down and let me fix you a bowl of soup and get you something to drink." Elizabeth opened her mouth, but before she could say a word, Tootsie stopped her. "Uh, uh, uh, no arguments. I know that look. I've seen it on your momma's face on more than one occasion."

Roger glanced up, a smile crossing his weathered, worn face. "Don't argue with that woman. I can guarantee you ain't going to win." He winked, turned toward the kitchen, and raised his voice. "Stubborn as a mule, she is, and dang if she'll back down."

Tootsie walked up behind him, soup in one hand, water in the other, and carefully elbowed him on the back of the head. "I've a good mind to give you a lap full of hot soup, you old codger."

After she sat the bowl and glass in front of Elizabeth, Roger jumped up from the table to pull her chair out for her. Once he seated her, he ran his fingers over her hair and tugged on the ends. Tootsie rolled her eyes and swatted his hand away. As they ate, the couple traded joking taunts back and forth, and at times, Elizabeth felt as though she was the guest of honor at a tennis match. One thing was sure, she felt welcome, if not a tad homesick.

The playfulness between her grandparents brought back vivid memories of her parents, and a sentimental feeling swept over her. "You two remind me so much of my parents, or maybe they remind me of you." She smiled to cover her sudden longing for home. "Not that I don't enjoy being here, but I sure can't wait to go home and visit for a little while."

"Speaking of." Roger cleared his throat. "How's your momma doing? She'll talk to me about everything under the sun, but not what's goin' on inside her head." His voice softened and concern laced his words.

"I spoke to Momma this afternoon, and she seems to be okay." When she looked at the table, she was shocked to find she'd torn the napkin to shreds. "Daddy says she isn't sleeping as much anymore, and he somehow managed to convince her to play nine holes with him a couple of times. It's been almost three years now, but..." She shifted her gaze between Roger and Tootsie.

"No momma should ever have to bury her babies. Lord, child, knowing how hard his death was on me, I can't even begin to imagine the pain of something like that for your momma." Tootsie cradled Elizabeth's hand between her own work-hardened palms. "But I guarantee she's thankful she has you, and what a blessing you are to her. A sweet, sweet blessing."

Elizabeth sniffed and laced her fingers with Gram's gnarled ones. "I don't know what to do to help her, ya know? Sometimes when she goes on and on about me getting sick or hurt, I just wanna shake her." Eyes narrowed and head tilted in thought, Elizabeth paused. "If she'd had her way, I wouldn't even be here right now. As if you two wouldn't take care of me if I needed it." A small smile curved her lips, and she peered at Tootsie. "Hmmm, wonder who Momma gets that hardheadedness from?"

Tootsie gasped in mock shock, and Roger hooted with laughter.

"Imagine the two of them together when Keyna was growing

up. It's a wonder I've lived as long as I have." Eyes filled with adoration, he leaned over and placed a gentle kiss on Tootsie's forehead. "At times, powerful things come in small packages, and what's more powerful than love? And those two sure will love you to death."

A hint of blush colored Tootsie's wrinkled cheeks, but her ears turned a bright red. "Now, Roger, you shush that nonsense." She cleared her throat, twined her arms around his shoulders, and buried her face against his chest. "You're embarrassing me. Lord have mercy, with the way my face is burning, you'd think I was having a hot flash." She sniffed and rubbed her nose on his shirt. When he grunted his displeasure, she pulled back with a laugh and turned to Elizabeth. "Enough of this mess. Now, tell me about your visits with a certain young man."

Elizabeth's eyes sparkled with delight. "Things are good. Real good, actually." Anticipation beamed on her face. "Oh my gosh, I'm so excited. I know it's only been a couple of months or so since we met, but I feel like I've waited for for-e-ver for him." Her body trembled with energy.

"Whoa, child. Slow down. Just looking at you when you're this hyper makes me tired." Tootsie raised a hand. "When are you going out again?"

"Friday night. We're having dinner with some friends of his for the first time. I can't figure out if I'm nervous or excited. I mean, I want to make a good impression, but what if they don't like me? Maybe I should do something with my hair?" Curls twirled as she turned her head back and forth, trying to see the ends. "I haven't had a trim in ages. Ugh, all this stringy blonde." She paused for breath and pushed back from the table. Butterflies fought with each other in her stomach. Definitely nerves. "Maybe I should make an appointment while I'm in town. Hmm, I need to look through my clothes. Jeans? Skirt? Slacks?" Lost in her mind, she ran through the items in her closest and didn't stop when she reached the door. "Oh, I've got the perfect sweater. Warm and cute. Now to complete ..."

Her words trailed off as she walked into the lobby and missed her grandparents' response.

Roger shook his head, his eyes wide in confusion. "What the devil was that?"

"That, my dear," Tootsie laughed, "was either Liam Broun's worst nightmare or his greatest dream come true." She looked at the closed door, shook her head, and whispered, "Go get him, girl."

Chapter 13

L iam stepped up on Elizabeth's porch, took a deep, calming breath, and knocked on the door. The last couple of months had his head spinning and his heart feeling things he thought he'd never experience again. Spending time with Elizabeth brought him to life, and for the first time in forever, he had hope when he thought about tomorrow. She was perfect in every way.

Though quiet, Elizabeth never met a stranger. Even the most anxious, fretful person calmed when she turned her attention on him or her. She had no qualms sharing her soothing spirit with the exhausted, sick Missy and lending a helping hand with Brittany and Grayson. She felt honored to pacify a crying infant and never hesitated to dole out a consuming hug to someone bereft. And should she run into someone downright ornery or grumpy, she attempted to spread humor and lift spirits with a silly joke or two. To her, life was something in which to find joy, and her mission was to spread happiness to everyone blessed by coming in contact with her.

The mention of her brother brought pain to her voice, and her eyes grew shuttered if he spoke of her playing guitar for him. Like Liam, her past intruded on her present, but that only drew out his protective nature. His mother and sister were quite used to his somewhat caveman attitude, but he knew better than coming on too strong with Elizabeth. He didn't want to scare her or run her off by applying too much pressure.

One thing he was certain of, he was falling.

Hard and fast.

The touch on his shoulder startled him.

"Honey, you all right? I've been standing here for a few minutes."

Liam lifted his eyes and saw the concerned look on her face. "No, I don't think I am," his eyes followed the tips of his fingers as they traced along her cheek, "but I will be in just a second." One hand slid up the back of her head, the other between her shoulders, and with a little pressure to pull her forward, their lips met in a warm, sweet kiss. He caught her sigh as he leaned back to speak. "You about ready to go?"

A nervous look flitted across her face, and he grinned.

"Sweetheart, you know there's no need to worry about tonight, right? Ashton's great, and Carson isn't old enough to do much more than drool on you. Zack's an idiot, but I think you'll like him when you get to know him." He grabbed her hand and squeezed it. "And if he gets on your nerves, just smack him on the head. That always works for me."

She drew in a deep breath, squared her shoulders, and made a visible effort to relax. "I know I'm overreacting, but the day I met Zack, and then Ashton and Carson, I wasn't quite at my best either time." She reached behind her for her purse. "I guess I'm nervous because I know not only how much they mean to you, but also how much you mean to them."

Liam's face twisted in confusion. "Did I miss something? I didn't know you'd met Ashton." He dropped her hand and pressed his to the small of her back to lead her to his truck.

She smiled at him as he opened the driver's side door, helped her inside, and scooted in beside her.

"No, you didn't miss anything. I probably forgot to tell you. I met her at Buck's the day after the fire." After they fastened their belts, and he pulled onto the road, she continued. "You know, so much had happened that day. Firemen, insurance people, nerves about our date that night. Oh, and let's not forget my handsome hero who finger painted me with soot and ash." She nudged him with her shoulder, and they laughed.

Liam drew her close against his side and wrapped his arm around her to hold her in place. She shared with him her worries concerning her mother's unsteady depression, and described the pressure she felt over her mom's fear of losing her remaining child. As she talked, she buried her head in his neck. Then she told him about Ashton coming to her rescue with tissue. When she giggled, he glanced down to see her eyes dancing with amusement.

"Marshmallow Girl? Really, *that's* what you called me?"

Liam threw his head back and laughed. "Well, yeah. It seems pretty lame now, but since I didn't know your name, I had to call you something. And seriously, your heavy winter coat reminds me of a marshmallow, though The Michelin Man did run through my mind." He pulled into a driveway and parked the truck.

Her mouth dropped open in an adorable O, and she punched his arm. "The Michelin Man? You have got to be kidding me." Her eyes sparked with mischief. "You'll pay for that one, buster."

Weak sunlight filtered through the windows, making her blonde curls glitter and the laughter in her eyes twinkle. Liam's heart stopped as the raw beauty of her washed over him, holding him captive. He couldn't speak, couldn't breathe, he was so spellbound.

"What's wrong?" Concern laced her quiet, soft voice. "Liam?"

"I searched for so long that I finally gave up hope of ever finding the right someone. Then, one day, a tiny little slip of a girl slammed into big, old me and knocked me off my feet in more ways than one." He heard her stuttered breath and watched as her eyes glistened. "I knew you for all of fifteen minutes, and I didn't even know your name, but I was determined to find out. For weeks, I walked around town looking for you, wondering if what I felt was crazy, and thinking it was *me* that was probably nuts." He forced his words through a throat tight with emotion.

"Everywhere I turned, I caught a glimpse of you. Standing in the checkout line. Carrying grocery bags for Old Lady Johnson. Watching an infant so her mother could tend to her crying toddler. Always doing something for someone. Those glimpses were sweet and taught me a lot about the kind of person you are, but it was never enough to satisfy me, never enough to know for sure I was right about you." He cupped her cheeks in his hands and thumbed away the tear sliding from her eye. "And then, when I finally catch up to you, you do it all over again with Missy, Brittany, and Grayson, because that's just who you are. You're giving. You're caring. You're loving, and I swear you don't have a mean bone in your body. I finally found you. And you, Elizabeth, my sweet Marshmallow Girl, you gave me back my hope, and I thank you for that."

"Liam," she choked out on a sigh as she melted against him.

Whatever she was going to say was lost when his lips took hers in a long, slow, heated kiss. All that mattered for Liam was there in his arms, and the rest of the world slipped away as he poured all he had, all he felt, into the moment.

Just the two of them.

Together.

Lost in each other.

BAM BAM BAM

Elizabeth jerked back and looked over Liam's shoulder as a bad case of nervous giggles hit her.

"Dude, you going to sit out here all night making out?" Zack threw her a wink, opened the door, and smacked the back of Liam's head. "My woman's in there slaving over a hot stove for *her Liam,* and here you are fogging up the windows."

Liam's eyes popped wide open. His jaw dropped, and mangled murmurs rumbled up his chest. A red flush started on his neck and slowly crawled over his face until the tips of his ears were bright red.

At the surprised, embarrassed expression on his face, she lost it. Her head fell back, and her laughter filled the cab of the truck, washing away the last remnants of her nerves. A feeling of calm and the sense that she was exactly where she should be filled her, and she loved it. Embraced it. Reveled in it. As tears of laughter streamed down her cheeks, strong arms wrapped around her, and she buried her face in Liam's chest.

"You okay, sweetheart?" His quiet, gentle words feathered against the top of her head.

She hiccupped and then snickered. "I'm fine, honey." Her breath huffed as she tried to get control of herself. "Sorry, I was just so nervous, but not after seeing how adorable you are when you're embarrassed."

Liam grinned. "We're a matching pair then, 'cause you're pretty darn cute when you turn all kinds of red."

"You two going to stay out here all night?" Zack's voice echoed through the truck. "I'm gettin' hungry."

Liam's chuckle vibrated against her. "Guess we'd better get in there before the neighbors come to see what all his fuss is about." His hand slid around her waist, and he helped her off the seat. "Sure glad we're finished with snow, but I'm going to miss carrying you over icy patches."

"Aww, that's so sweet, but you do know that I can walk, even if it's icy. Right?" Her eyes met his.

Yeah, I know it, but maybe I just like carrying you around."

Before she could blink, he swept her up in his arms. "

"Dude, makin' me nauseous here." Zack snorted. "Do NOT let Ashton see you like this, or I swear I'll never hear the end of it." He led us in the house, muttering under his breath. "Liam did this. Liam did that. Liam better be glad I like 'im." He threw Elizabeth another wink.

As Ashton walked into the room, Liam put her on her feet.

"Liam." She stood on her tiptoes, and Liam bent down for her to kiss his cheek. "Marshmallow Girl." Ashton wrapped her arms around her, squeezed tight, and whispered in her ear. "You never called. You doing good?"

"I'm doing great, thanks." Elizabeth returned the hug. Her eyes flew wide open when her stomach growled, and a blush heated her cheeks. "And something smells delicious. Need any help?"

"Nope, but if you come hang with me, I'll throw you some scraps." Ashton grinned at her and looped their arms together. "Zack, baby, can you set the table for me so we can get this girl some food?"

"You don't own me, woman!" Zack yelled, a scowl on his face and fists propped on his hips, but humor danced in his eyes.

Ashton rolled her eyes, tugged Elizabeth's arm, and pulled her to the kitchen. "I swear he drinks idiot juice sometimes. Here, sit." She waved her toward the table and pointed at the baby swing. "It's almost time for my little pumpkin to wake up, and before he does, I need to put a few last finishing touches on supper."

She'd no sooner spoken the words than Carson cried out and squirmed in the seat. His little body arched this way and that, and he made squeaky, little mouse noises.

Elizabeth itched to pick him up, but didn't know if doing so would upset Ashton. Any time a friend had a baby, she was first in line for snuggles and cuddles. Auntie Elizabeth worked hard to spoil the children and give their parents a brief respite by babysitting when needed, and she couldn't wait until she had kids of her own.

Oh, how precious.

"Yeah, I think he's kind of cute." Ashton placed a bottle on the table and caressed Carson's head. "I pumped earlier, 'cause I knew this would happen. If you don't mind feeding him, I'll finish up in here so we can eat."

"Oh, I would love to feed him, but I have to warn you, I'll be stealing all his kisses, too." Elizabeth beamed a smile at Ashton while she rubbed her hands to warm them. "There's nothing like that little spot of sugar under a baby's ear."

Ashton tossed a burp cloth over Elizabeth's shoulder, and after

washing her hands, she gently lifted him from the swing and cradled him in her arms.

"Well, hello, Carson. Aren't you a handsome, young man?" Dark blue eyes blinked at her as she settled back in the chair. Her heart melted. She rubbed a finger on his cheek, and he rooted against her hand. "Someone's hungry. Let's take care of that right now."

As he latched onto the nipple of the bottle and sucked, Elizabeth lost herself in the little armful. Tiny fingers wrapped around her thumb, and she quietly sang "Love Never Fails" as she swayed side-to-side, fascinated at the myriad of expressions running across Carson's little face. He peered up at her, safe and content in her arms, and she fell in love with the sweet baby boy.

A warm hand rubbed the back of her neck, breaking her from the deep trance. She glanced up to meet Liam's affectionate gaze and sighed.

"Isn't he beautiful?" she whispered.

"Yes, he is." His soft words washed over her. "Almost as beautiful as you."

"Dude." Zack's loud voice startled her from the quiet moment with Liam. "Your girl can sing. That song rocks."

Carson's shrill cry filled the room, and Ashton shot Zack a nasty look and rushed over to take the baby.

"Okay, guys, let's get this party started." She cuddled the baby on her shoulder, and his cries quieted.

Elizabeth was surprised to see the table set and loaded with steaming dishes. She didn't realize she'd been so engrossed with Carson. Everything looked delicious, and her mouth watered with hunger. Liam, ever the gentleman, held her chair for her as she sat, and before taking the seat next to her, he kissed the top of her head.

"Dude, let's eat. You can kiss her later." Zack flashed a bright smile as he sat and reached for a bowl.

As plates were filled with food, conversation flowed with ease. Elizabeth felt right at home. Ashton acted as if they'd been friends forever and made no secret that she thought the world of Liam.

And Zack? Well, Zack was just Zack. He cut up and wisecracked.

Before long, everyone finished eating, and while their food settled, Ashton and the guys took trip after trip down memory lane. Elizabeth loved getting a small glimpse into Liam's normally closed-off life and learning more about his extended family.

Everything went smooth and easy until Ashton brought up a touchy subject, and Liam went on the defense.

"So, aren't Liam's nieces just the cutest things ever?" Ashton turned to Elizabeth. "And he's so good with them. No one could ever doubt how much that boy loves his girls."

"Umm, well, I've only seen two of them, thankfully from afar, because at the time, they were kind of puking all over him." Her gaze fixed on Liam, and she bit back a grin. "Not sure they were at their cutest, huh, honey?"

"Excuse me?" Ashton sputtered. "What did you just say?" Her soft words vibrated with disappointment. "You mean to tell me you've not taken this sweet girl to meet your family? Are. You. Kidding. Me?"

"Liam's in trouble. Liam's in trouble." Zack's shoulders shook with repressed laughter. "I've been waiting for this day to come."

"Zack, not now. Shut it, or I swear…" Ashton swatted the back of his head before focusing on Liam. "You know I love you, and I always will, but I'm completely lost. You're not a player. You're not a casual kinda guy. Is it because of La—"

"Ashton, stop. Not another word," Liam cut her off. His voice rumbled with displeasure. "You don't understand."

"Then make me understand why she's here, but has yet to grace your momma's table." Ashton turned to Elizabeth and patted her hand. "Not that you're not welcome here anytime, but it feels to me like Liam's got things a little backward."

Elizabeth forced a smile, but the longer Ashton talked, the more uncomfortable and embarrassed she grew. Even though she'd asked herself the same thing numerous times, it felt strange to hear someone else voice the concern. The tips of her ears and her cheeks

144

burned, and she knew they were beet red. If she could melt into the floor, she would.

"Ashton, this is not a conversation you and I need to have over the supper table. I won't say it's none of your business because we both know you think I *am* your business." His face wiped of any expression, Liam leaned against the table, peered directly at Ashton, and raised his eyebrows. "The problem is you're embarrassing Elizabeth, and I won't have that. She doesn't know you, and I can only imagine what she thinks about your little outburst."

His words were firm, but Elizabeth could tell he wasn't angry by his relaxed expression and loose posture.

"But ... But ..." Ashton stammered, but Liam raised his hand to stop her.

"She doesn't know I'm the big brother you never had, and you have my best interest at heart. She doesn't know that you and Zack have been with me through thick and thin. She doesn't know that you want the world for me, and it hurts you when I struggle." His hand snaked across the table and squeezed hers. "I know, and I love you for it, but she doesn't, and I won't have her uncomfortable around you." He pushed back from the table, stepped behind Elizabeth, and rubbed her stiff shoulders. "Now, if you'll excuse us, I think she and I will continue this conversation somewhere else."

Elizabeth glanced at him over her shoulder. The serious look on his face threw her for a moment, but when he gave her a half-grin, she relaxed a little.

"Even if her delivery was off, Ashton's right. We shoulda talked about this weeks ago." He tucked a stray curl behind her ear. "Let's go find a quiet place."

When he pulled her chair back and offered his hand, she grabbed it and stood. As he tucked her in the crook of his arm, she knew she wouldn't have to wait much longer. After being blindsided by Ashton's reaction, she couldn't decide if she was concerned or worried about the upcoming conversation, or just plain relieved it was finally happening.

"Liam, you got some 'splainin' to do," Zack bellowed in a horrible, Ricky Ricardo Cuban accent and burst out in laughter.

"Z, I swear, one of these days you're going to be serious about something, and I'm gonna drop over dead." Ashton shook her head at her husband, stood, and approached Liam and Elizabeth. "I didn't mean to embarrass either of you. Elizabeth, I hope you'll accept my apology for putting Liam on the spot. I wasn't really thinking, 'cause he's used to my brand of crazy."

When Elizabeth nodded her acceptance, Ashton took a deep breath and turned to Liam. "Why don't you two head out back to the gazebo? Or if you want, the swing on the front porch. And then, if y'all feel up to it when you finish talking, maybe y'all could join us for dessert?" She shifted back and forth and chewed on her thumbnail. "Please?"

Liam peered down at Elizabeth and gestured for her to answer.

"If you're sure it's not too much trouble, that sounds like a good plan." She chewed on the corner of her lip. The tips of her fingers tingled, and her palms dampened, but she was ready for some answers. "The swing okay?" she asked.

His answer was to pull her closer and lead her outside. When she'd settled in the seat, Liam joined her and gave the swing an easy push.

"You okay, sweetheart? Sometimes Zack and Ashton can be a little much to take at one time."

"I'm fine. I know they love you, so I understand." Elizabeth sucked in a deep breath. It was confession time. "Liam, I have to admit I've wondered if you're ashamed of me or something?"

Liam ran his fingers through his hair. "Ashamed of you? Not even a little. It's just ..." He rested his forehead against the chain. "I don't know what to do, how to fix it."

When he turned back to her, Elizabeth gasped at the pain and frustration written in the depths of his eyes. She pressed against his side. Now that she knew it wasn't her, she needed to know what the problem was so she could help him come up with a solution.

"Talk to me," she whispered. "Tell me what I can do to make it better."

His head dropped back and stared up at the ceiling. There it was. The same selfless spirit he'd witnessed over and over again. *He* hurt her by not introducing her to his family, and *she* wanted to make things better for him.

Yeah, the steel cage around his heart? Gone, obliterated into nothingness. A zero with the rims kicked off. The hope he'd been missing? Growing. Flourishing. Rooting deep within the recesses of his being. He was not worthy of her, but no way was he letting go of her without a fight. Now, he had to figure out how to explain his concerns regarding his sister.

"It's Wrynn." There, he said it, but from the expression on her face, he knew she needed more. "She's, gah, what's the right word? Depressed? No, that's nowhere near even strong enough." His mind scrambled to come up with the right way to say what he meant, and he remembered what she told him about her mom.

"Your mom and Seth's death." She flinched, and he wrapped his arms around her. "It's like that for Wrynn, but even worse. She functions, but just barely. At times, it's like we lost her when we lost Tripp."

Elizabeth's eyes searched his face. "Okay, I get that. You told me this a while ago." Her words were slow and measured. "What I don't understand is what that has to do with you and me, and why you never mention wanting me to meet your family." He felt her take a deep breath as she pushed her face into his neck. "I've tried to be patient. Tried not to let it hurt me. But Liam, what you have to realize is this. You can't treat me like a treasure one minute, and then try to bury me in the sand the next. Your words make me feel like I'm important to you, but your actions confuse me. I can't help but think something's wrong with me, and you're afraid your family won't like me."

Frustration threatened to strangle him. How did he make her understand his wariness had nothing to do with her and everything to do with the precarious ledge Wrynn existed on every day?

"It's not you, I promise. I know my family will love you, but …" His hands cradled her jaw, and he gently lifted until her eyes met his. "I'll lay this out as best I can, but I need you to understand what we're up against. Wrynn is beyond fragile, beyond hanging on by a thread.

"See, when Tripp died, half of her literally died, too, and without him, I don't know that she'll ever be complete again. You hear people throw around the term soul mate, but with those two, it wasn't just an expression. It was a fact.

"I wish you could have seen them together. They spoke without words. Finished each other's thoughts and sentences. I swear they could read each other's minds. When one was sick, the other physically felt it. When one was hurt, the other experienced pain. You should have seen him when she had morning sickness. She'd get nauseous, and he'd throw up. They were two halves of one whole. Their love was strong and pure and blessed beyond normal. And most of all, rare. I've never seen anything like it. Not even between my parents.

"As for you and me, it's like this. You make me beyond happy. You fill holes I didn't even know were there. You fit into my life like a puzzle piece that's been missing for forever. I never even dreamed I'd find someone so perfect for me. You make me think about things I've avoided for years and want things I'd forgotten I ever wanted. I see beautiful blonde hair and bright blue eyes, but you're so much more than just a pretty face and a killer body. When I look at you, I see what tomorrow could be like.

"You're warm and kind and loving, and so dang selfless that you take my breath away. I'd be a fool to be ashamed of someone as amazing as you. You're a beautiful person, inside and out, and just knowing you is a blessing." He paused to take a breath.

"But … but … but," she stuttered, her brow creased, and her eyes scrunched. "I'm so confused."

"I can see that, sweetheart, but you didn't let me finish." He smiled and dropped a kiss on her forehead. "Plain and simple, Wrynn isn't just my sister. She's my twin. We have this sixth sense, not quite like Hollywood plays it with the mind reading and crap, but strong enough that I'm scared for her. The last time I felt for someone even a fraction of what I feel for you, she had Tripp.

"Now though, honest to God, I don't know if she could handle it. When I'm with her and the girls, I focus on them, but if I bring you into the picture, it's a totally different story. There's no way I'd be able to bury all the things you make me feel. And there's no way she wouldn't sense how it is between us, feel what I'm feeling, and remember what she's missing. And with that big, gaping hole in her heart, I just don't know how she'll react to us. I don't know if she can handle feeling what I'm feeling. Wrynn and my parents are a package deal, sweetheart. If I take you to meet them, my mom'll be calling Wrynn before we even get through the front door. Now, do you see where I'm coming from?"

"Oh. My. Gosh." She slipped her arms around his waist and squeezed him. "Liam, I had no idea, but I'll admit it makes total sense, in a weird sorta way. I've seen my momma's struggles over the last several years, and I lost myself to months of depression when Seth died. I know for a fact that the fight to get out of it is not only the biggest battle of your life, but also a fight you have to make every single day. The dark cloud smothers you until you can't breathe. It bombs your mind with so much doubt and pain, it's impossible to see the truth for the lies. It's so much easier to just give up and let go. Months after Seth died, it took everything I had to pull myself out of the pit.

"So in some way, I know exactly what she's feeling. The bad news is, short of her seeing someone for help, there's probably not much more you can do for her that you're not already doing just by being there for her and helping with the girls. Oh, I wish there was some way I could help you, though."

Relief slammed into him. "And there you go with being selfless again." He wrapped her in his arms and pressed her against him. "Thank you for letting me get that off my chest. I've worried over this since that night the girls got the flu, maybe even before, but I didn't know how to tell you. I'm just sorry that, by waiting to talk to you about it, I hurt you. I don't ever want to do that again. Forgive me?"

"Now that I know what the problem is, there's nothing really to forgive, honey. You're protecting your sister." She tilted her head and squinted at him. "But for future reference, it'd be kinda nice to know these things ahead of time so I don't think the worst."

Was it really that simple? Did a few words really wash away her hurt? How was that possible?

Her relaxed sigh reached him as she snuggled deeper into him, and he rested his cheek on the top of her head. He could hold her like this for days and never grow tired of it.

"Dude, get a room." Zack stuck his head out the front door.

"Zack, leave them alone, you idiot," Ashton grumbled as she dragged him back inside.

Liam ignored his friends and enjoyed the feel of Elizabeth in his arms. Dessert could wait.

Things in his life might not be perfect, but she was perfect for him.

Chapter 14

Liam leaned down to grab his ball cap out of his locker, and as he stood, someone smacked him in the back of his head. He heard a snicker and turned to find Zack grinning like a possum. Opposite schedules and the coming of spring had kept them from getting together for several weeks.

"Dude, Ashton loves your girl. She wants y'all to come back to the house for dinner sometime soon. Can you make that happen?" Zack took his jacket off and put it in his locker.

Liam rubbed the back of his head. "Not if you're going to be there." Using the metal door as a shield, he shifted to his left and punched Zack in the arm. "Yeah, you know we probably can. Elizabeth had a great time, too. Can't stop talking about Carson."

"Yeah, dude. She's gonna make a great mom. You done good."

"I've always wanted a family, but never figured I'd get one. I'd probably suck as a dad." His voice dropped to a low murmur, and he absentmindedly scratched the scruff on his jaw. Thoughts whirled in his head, but one specific thing stuck out at him. His eyes widened in surprise. "Dang, I've been so crazy with everything else going on, I never realized the opportunity for kids might be right in front of me. I mean, I know I ... But she's never ... I guess maybe ... Wow, kids, ya think?"

Zack burst out laughing. "Liam, if you could see your face. Talk about deer in the headlights. Priceless. Hold that pose, and let me take a pic so Ash can see." He pulled his phone out of his pocket and pretended to snap a shot. "Dude, are you scared of kids?"

"Idiot." Liam laughed along with him, having caught his shocked reflection in the mirrored wall of the gym. "You know I'm not. I've always wanted kids. Sometimes it feels like me and Elizabeth are still getting to know each other, and others, I feel like we've been together forever. Some days I think we need to slow down, but most of the time, I just plain old want more. She's turned me inside out and upside down. Truth is, I'm pretty sure I'm addicted. Like, can't live without her, addicted. But, we haven't talked about anything this serious. I don't want to scare her off. What's so funny about that?"

"Dude, I've seen you with your nieces, and there's no way you'll suck as a dad. Heck, Ashton had to tear Carson away from you the other week."

"Well, yeah. But there's a right way to go about these things." Liam ran his fingers through his hair and settled his cap on his head. "Did you see the way Elizabeth looked when she held Carson?" He narrowed his eyes and glanced over Zack's shoulder. "She's a natural, but that doesn't mean she wants her own. I guess she and I are gonna have to have a little talk about the future. The way-down-the-line future." No matter how much he thought he wanted children, coming face-to-face with the possible reality was enough to scare the crap out of him.

Zack's eyes bugged out in surprise. "Dude, what are you saying here?" He grabbed a towel from his locker and slammed the door shut. The clang of the metal echoed through the room, and the sound followed the men as they walked to the equipment room.

"Were you not eavesdropping on our conversation at your house? I'm pretty sure I was self-explanatory."

"Yeah, right. Like Ashton was going to let me hang around for that. My girl snatched my hand and drug me out of there in a flash, so talk to me."

Liam scrubbed his face with both hands. He needed to talk

someone, and outside of his family, Zack knew him better than anyone else did. He might tease him, because that was his nature, but he wouldn't hesitate to support him.

"I'm pretty sure she's it for me. No, not pretty sure. I'm sure. Yeah, I'm saying that she's the one. The thing is, we haven't talked about the future or anything like that." He shrugged his shoulders. "I'm meeting her folks Memorial Day weekend, and that's a first for me. I just have to make it through that. Then if everything works out and I think Wrynn can handle it, she'll meet my folks after the parade."

"Wow. Seriously? That's a big step. Dang, huge. Ya know what I mean?" Zack walked over to the weight machines and set his pounds before turning back to Liam. "Regardless, you're a smooth operator, but if you need help, advice, or how-tos, be sure to let me know. We both know that I'm an expert on anything to do with the ladies." Liam laughed at the absurd statement, and Zack wiggled his eyebrows. "Whatever, dude. You got time to spot me?"

Liam looked at his watch and shook his head. "Nah. Temps are supposed to hit the fifties today. I promised Elizabeth I'd show her some of the sites in the area. I need to grab a few things before I pick her up." He laughed when Zack rolled his eyes. "I'll see you later at the station."

It seemed to take forever, but spring thaw was finally there, and most of the snow was melting. Bright yellow clusters of daffodils bloomed all over the place, and their sweet fragrance filled the air.

When she had told Liam she loved being outside, she hadn't been lying. Building outdoor flower boxes was one of her first projects after the temperature started warming up. She and Liam had spent hours cutting wood and piecing it together, and they looked great on her little front stoop. She'd managed to convince him to take her to DuPont to hike to the waterfalls. Thin patches of ice on the rocks were no challenge for her.

She was more than beautiful, but her kindness and compassion made the complete package stunning. After telling him about her brother, she'd opened up more about their closeness. In a lot of ways, her stories of Seth reminded him of his relationship with Wrynn.

He stopped by Mountain Fresh to pick up sandwiches and water for the hike and made his way to Endless View. When he pulled up, she was in her favorite rocker on the front porch, her head leaned back against the top slat, and her eyes closed. She was the very picture of relaxed.

Unable to resist the temptation, he walked up the steps with as little noise as possible, and when he reached her side, he leaned over and kissed her. Her lips curved up, and her hand slipped around the back of his neck and into his hair.

"Mmm, you taste like sunshine." He nipped at her bottom lip. "And cocoa. What an irresistible combination." His hands gripped her waist, and when she offered no resistance, he lifted her onto her feet and into his arms. Her eyes fluttered open and met his, and the smile on her face grew.

"I do love your hellos." She gazed at him as if imprinting his image in her mind.

Reclaiming her lips, his kiss was slow, thoughtful, almost reverent. Moving back enough so that only a breath of air could pass between them, his lips feathered against hers as he spoke in a quiet whisper. "What are you doing to me, Elizabeth? You consume my every thought." His hands slipped up to capture her face. "I've never felt this way before."

Her fingers squeezed against his scalp. "I'm pretty sure ..." Her words halted as she cleared her throat, and he leaned over to hear her soft words. "No, I know *exactly* what you mean. When we're together, I'm the happiest I've ever been." She buried her face against the corded muscles above his heart, and Liam felt the heat rush to her cheeks. "And when we're apart, I count the minutes until I see you again."

The uneven, warm puffs of her breath fanned his chest. As though her words released something locked inside him, his grip on her tightened. Never before had he felt such longing, such need. The overload of sensations staggered him. "I ... Elizabeth, I ..." His words left him as he gave over to the wave of emotions slamming into him. "It may be too soon. I mean, I know we've only been seeing each other for a few months." He lifted her chin, gathered his courage, and stared deep into her eyes. "My words are as jumbled as my thoughts. What I'm trying to say, trying to tell you, is I'm falling in love with you."

As the words left his mouth, joy swept over her face and filled her eyes. "Oh, Liam." She leaned into him and brushed her lips against his as she spoke. "That makes me so happy because I'm falling in love with you, too."

A shiver of awareness tinged with anxiety flooded him. His heart thundered in his chest as if trying to escape. His stomach churned with excitement as he caught a glimpse of where she might take him, the future they could share. His nerves threatened to surface, but before panic consumed him, her scent floated by him on the brisk, spring breeze, and as the familiar fragrance of sunshine and daisies washed over him, his anxious feelings calmed. He knew without further question, and any doubts that may have overwhelmed him fled in the wake of his discovery.

She is the one.

The clarity of the thought shocked him, and he waited for fear or unease to seep back into his mind. When they didn't follow, peace and a sense of relief washed over him. For the first time in a while, he was content and even willing to let himself embrace it.

Needing a moment to enjoy his new awareness, he drew her into the shelter of his arms and rested his cheek on the top of her head. His eyes closed against the wind, and his breathing steadied as he fought to gain control. There would be no slip-ups this time, no error in judgment, no rush. He would focus on today. By doing so, the foundation for tomorrow would be sturdy enough to carry them through until the end of their time together. This was important because, unless he was mistaken, and he felt confident he was spot on, their future together was spelled f-o-r-e-v-e-r. Meeting his parents just moved into high priority level, and he needed to figure out how to make it happen.

When she shivered in his arms and pressed her face deeper into his chest, he realized the time had slipped by while he'd been lost in his thoughts. The sun had already begun its descent, and the air had grown downright nippy. If they were going to make it to the top of Jones Knob and back before nightfall, they needed to leave now.

"Are you still up for a hike today? We'd be pushing to get to the top of the Knob and back, but I'm game if you want to try." He rubbed her arms, hoping the friction would warm her. "Of course, as the sun drops, the temps will, too."

After exposing Elizabeth to both strep and the flu, Liam worried about her getting sick. Though a couple of months had passed and the flu bug had died down some, his protective nature frowned at the idea of her getting too cold or tired. The last thing he wanted was for her to have an asthma attack. Of course, if he suggested they stay here for a bonfire and evening picnic, he could keep her warm and feed her. An added benefit would be holding her close in his arms.

She lifted her face and peered at him. "What's that look in your eyes?" Her gaze traveled to his lips, and with a quick grin on hers, she pressed a light kiss to his mouth. "Do you have a better idea?"

"Hmm... maybe. I was just thinking that if we don't go hiking, we could always build a fire and have a picnic. I have sandwiches and water, but we could run to Mountain Fresh and grab the makings for S'mores." He knew of her love for all things chocolate and wondered if his offer would entice her to change their plans. "Maybe we could swing by the house and grab a blanket or two. What do you think?"

"Ha, you had me at S'mores!" She bounced on her feet, excitement dancing in her eyes. "Oh, we need a thermos of hot chocolate, too! That would be perfect around the fire."

He leaned over, wrapped an arm around the back of her knees, and before she knew what was happening, he scooped her up against his chest. Her musical laughter flowed through the air, and her cheerfulness warmed Liam's heart. Her happiness was one of his priorities, and he hoped to enjoy it for a long time.

When they reached the truck, he opened the driver's side door and placed her on the seat. "Your chariot awaits, ma'am." She scooted to the middle and buckled her seatbelt, and he hopped in behind her. "Store or my house first?"

"Whatever works for you will work for me. To be honest, I don't know where you live, so I don't know how far we'll have to go." She chewed her lip and looked up at him as he cranked the truck. "Um, now that I think about it, we've never much talked about you." She pushed into his side. "Not quite sure that's fair, seeing as how you know my life story."

Her voice was quiet, and if Liam hadn't seen the beginnings of a smile on her lips, he would have thought she was angry. As it was, a small bit of hurt dimmed the smile in her eyes.

"Oh, honey, don't take that personal. Please." He threw his arm over her shoulder and looked out the rear window to back out of the parking space. When he turned to face the front, he buckled up, then slid his arm down her side and pulled her closer to him. "I'm hungry to know everything there is to learn about you, is all. I guess I'm not one to talk much about myself because, well, my life is kind of boring." As he slowed on a curve, he kissed the top of her head and breathed in her fresh sunshine and sunflower scent. "Ask me anything you want."

"Do you really think your life is boring?" The confused, questioning tone of her voice caught his attention. He glanced down to see her nose wrinkled, her eyes squinted, and her head tilted to the side. "I'm positive you're wrong. You've got jobs you love, family you can see at a moment's notice, and friends who adore you. What more could you ask for?"

You, forever.

He wondered what she would say if he spoke it out loud. Instead, he thought about what she said for a moment before speaking. "Hmm, guess when you put it that way, I sound a little ungrateful. I'm not. Really, I'm thankful for all of that, and so much more." He pulled the ball cap off his head and rubbed his forehead as a heated flush swept across his cheeks. "Wow, I sounded like such a schmuck, didn't I?"

"Liam, stop." Her cool fingers traced the line of his jaw. "I didn't mean to make you feel bad. I was just pointing out a few things that I think would keep your life from being dull. Honest. That's all." When he slowed the truck again, she grabbed his chin and turned his face to her. "Please, I just listed what I'm jealous that I don't have right now." Her frown changed to a smile. "Well, except for the job at the inn. I really do love my job. You know. The job that brought me to Highlands to meet you." She made a wistful sound as she shrugged her shoulders. "Yeah, I really do love my job." She leaned into his side and nuzzled her cheek into his shoulder. "Soooo, do you live far from here?"

"Way to change the subject, little lady, but thanks for being so sweet about my bad attitude." He nodded his head toward the passenger window. "And actually, we're here. I don't see Wrynn's car, so I guess she's at work. She and my nieces live upstairs, and my place is down below." He pulled down the driveway to the back of the house.

"When we were younger, this was the cellar." He stepped out of the truck and turned to help Elizabeth down. "Tripp and I used to play on the dirt floor. Some of our best Hot Wheels races took place down here. This was his grandparents' summer house, but when Tripp and Wrynn got married, and he left for Basic training, Papa and Nana wanted them to have a permanent place to call home."

He opened the door and stepped back to let Elizabeth enter first. He tried to see it through her eyes and wondered what she thought of the wide, open space. The creamy textured walls were empty except for a few family pictures illuminated by two small sconces, thanks to his mom. Dusty white blinds covered the windows over the kitchen sink, and tan verticals concealed the French doors that led to his little concrete patio. The small, potbellied wood stove filled the air with the comforting, homey scent of burnt wood. A beige, teal, and navy sectional engulfed the living area and faced a massive TV. She walked over and skimmed a finger over his collection of DVDs.

When she turned to him and raised an eyebrow, her grin made him chuckle.

"This is quite a collection you have here. I've not had a chance to watch most of these, but this one," she held up *Finding Nemo*, "is one of my absolute, all-time favorites. Seth's nickname for me was Dory."

Liam's chuckle turned to laughter. "Dory? Really? Ohhhhh, I wonder why. Oh, that's right. You repeat things to help you remember stuff." At her gasp, he winked. "Yes, sweetheart, I've noticed that adorable habit of yours."

"Liam, you're not supposed to mention my bad habits." She snickered at herself, and he joined her until she winced. "Umm, do I do it *that* often?"

"Not as often as you say your thoughts out loud, but I wouldn't be surprised to hear you saying something about Forty-two Wallaby Way."

Her mouth dropped open, and just as he worried he might have upset her, she snorted out a laugh. When she realized what she'd done, she blushed but giggled harder. "Oh my gosh ... I cannot ... believe ... I just ... snorted." By the time she finished her sentence, liquid laughter leaked from the corners of her eyes, and her breath came in sharp, hiccupping gasps.

She glowed. This happiness was exactly what Liam was thinking of earlier. She thrived on pure joy, and he wanted to make every day like this for her. His arms wrapped around her, and he pulled her to him.

"You're so beautiful, but even more so when laughter sparkles in your eyes."

"I've never really thought I was beautiful, but I do know you make me feel that way." A flicker of a smile rose at the corner of her mouth. "And oh, so much more."

The soft lighting in the living area cast their joined shadow on the wall. The silhouette caught Liam's eyes and brought to his mind once more how perfect they fit together. Her soft curves balanced his hard muscles, and instead of towering over her, his outline appeared sheltering, protective even, around hers. He wanted to be the safe place she ran to when things troubled her, her haven against any storms that raged in her life.

Whether or not she knew it, he was hers, and he would do everything in his power to make her his.

As if struck by lightning, the thoughts racing through his mind sent desire coursing through his body. Electricity sparked along his nerve endings. His breath caught in his chest. His hands tingled. A sense of urgency threatened to overwhelm him with long forgotten feelings. The need to be closer to her, to have her, to hold her, swept everything else from his mind.

He buried his fingers in her hair and showered kisses along her jawline, savoring her taste. When she pressed closer and shivered against him, he crushed her body to his. His hands captured her cheeks, and his lips descended on hers. Staking his claim, he devoured its velvety warmth, losing himself in the slow drugging kiss.

The frantic beat of her heart thumped an unsteady rhythm against his chest. As she melted into him, he felt alive for the first time in a very long time. A small hand gripped his neck. Firm, insistent fingers pressed into the back of his head. Her body arched into his, and she quivered against him, eliciting his own shiver. Her chest heaved, its jerking motion matching his.

When his hands began to wander down her back, her heavy sigh brought him back from the almost overpowering haze. Before he completely lost himself in her, he broke the kiss. A deep breath did little to calm him when her lips detoured to his chin and forged a path to his ear.

"Elizabeth," he groaned her name. "You–" His brain rattled in his head from the strength of the shake he gave it. "We have to stop."

Taking a firm grip on her elbow, he inched back and held her until she was steady enough to stand on her own. She stared at the wall as she struggled to catch her breath. A pensive expression came over her flushed face, and she appeared to have an internal debate.

After a moment of deep thought, she edged closer to Liam and peered into his eyes.

"I think … Well, I'm not sure …" A blush stole over her cheeks. She cleared her throat and started again, this time, her voice stronger. "You're always pulling away from me, always rejecting me. If you don't want me, then I think it would be best if you take me home."

"Don't want you?" He barked a short laugh. Was she serious? The desire he felt for her was beyond anything he'd ever experienced. "How in this world could you even think that? I push you away because I want you too much. If this," he ghosted his hand between them, "was just some casual fling, I wouldn't worry what you think about my wanting to wait. The thing is, I don't want to make mistakes with you. You're too precious for me to treat you as anything less than worth the wait. If you don't understand that by now, then I'll have to work on my show-and-tell skills so you'll know without any room for doubt."

"You're not just saying that to make me feel better?" When he shook his head, she saw the truth in his eyes. Tension flowed from her frame, and hope filled her. "You sure?"

"Oh, yeah, I'm sure. You can trust me on that." One side of Liam's lips tipped up in a grin. "How about I take you out to dinner before I take you home?" Keeping a safe distance between them, Liam reached over and smoothed the stray hair his fingers had ruffled during the kiss, his hand lingering on her face. "Fire and picnic's out 'cause I'm not sure that we should be alone right now. You're just a little too tempting to me."

She nodded her agreement. "If what you said is true, then I have to agree." She pressed her palm against his hand on her cheek. "I've never felt this way before, but Liam, you have to know that you have such a strong effect on me."

"Oh, sweetheart, I not only know it, but I'm right there with you." He withdrew his hand from her face and motioned her to the door. "Let's not make this any harder than it already is. We can watch

Finding Nemo another time, and who knows, maybe I'll invite my nieces."

She laughed as she waited for him to open the door. "I'm absolutely positive they would qualify, not only as competent chaperones, but also as a great diversion from anything else."

"Oh, you have no idea." He wrapped his arm around her waist and guided her back to the truck. As he opened the door and helped her into her seat, his eyes roamed her face, and unable to resist, he kissed her forehead. "And I hope we can make that happen sooner rather than later."

Chapter 15

Each time they were together, they shared new things and explored new feelings. Liam swore mushrooms were slimy and icky and didn't belong on a pizza. Chocolate really did make the world go round and could turn Elizabeth's frown to a smile. Liam taught her regular Mason jars fit on the blender base and made fresh salsa easy to whip up for tacos. (He confessed he learned that trick from his mom, and she was quick to pass it on to hers.)

The more time they spent in each other's company, the more they wanted, so they did what they could to make it happen.

True to his word, Liam worked on his show-and-tell skills, and Elizabeth grew more confident in their relationship. Leftover feelings of rejection grew further and further from her mind. She wasn't quite sure how to resolve the fact she had yet to meet his family, but she didn't think Liam would be able to avoid the issue forever. As it was, he would be meeting her folks very soon.

A few days before Memorial Day weekend, the morning dawned sunny and warm, so when he went to see her, they walked to the private park at the inn. According to her, bright sunshine was to be experienced and enjoyed.

Somehow, in a way only Liam could, he convinced her to play a game of pickup basketball. His every shot swooshed through the net with no effort on his part, his movements smooth as silk. He made it seem easy. Elizabeth couldn't tear her eyes from him.

Until he passed the ball her way.

Instead of watching its path, she watched Liam raise his eyebrows and open his mouth to speak.

"Elizabeth, watch out!" He jogged her way, but the ball beat him to her, bouncing up to smack her in the head.

"Ouch." She rubbed the tender spot above her ear and grabbed at the offending object. Within minutes, she discovered the ball was her natural enemy. No matter how hard she tried to catch it, it slipped through her fingers every time. Her dribbles went willy-nilly all over the place, and she spent a lot of time chasing the ball around the court. The basket may well have been on the moon, because even with all her upper body strength behind her throws, at no time did any one throw come near it.

She gave it everything she had, but in the end, sprawled on the asphalt after taking a ball to the head for the second time.

"No more, Liam." Her breath caught in her chest when he loomed over her and shaded her from the bright sunlight. "No more. I suck at sports."

There she was, all sweaty and short-winded, and he looked like he'd been playing cards or Monopoly.

"Well, Michael Jordan, you ain't." A smirk curved his mouth as he held his hand out to help her off the ground. "How's the head, Ace?" His shoulders shook, and he clamped his lips together.

"Don't you laugh at me, you rascal. It's all your fault, ya know?" She planted her hands on her hips and scrunched up her face.

"Hmm, really?" He cleared his throat, and she grinned as he tried to look serious. "How is it, exactly, my fault?" He cut a chuckle off with a cough.

She stepped closer to him and rubbed the back of her fingers along his cheek. "I couldn't see the ball for looking at your handsome face." When he raised his eyes to the sky and sighed, she snickered. "Why, you liked to bowled me over with your good looks." Her voice dripped sugar sweet in a sarcastic, overly Southern tone.

"Well then, I guess we'll just have to find something else to do."

Prepared to hear him tease her for her lack of athletic ability, she was surprised when he swept her off her feet, plopped her down on the tire swing, and spun her around until she was too dizzy to sit upright.

"You crazy boy, stop it right now." Giggles bubbled out of her as she slouched against the chains. "Oh my gosh, STOP. I'm going to puke."

He grabbed the chains and slowed her rotations, and when the tire stilled, he snatched her up, threw her over his shoulder, and ran for the slide. She felt safe and secure, but seeing the ground rush by upside down made her stomach clench and her dizzy head spin even more. Kicking and screaming, she buried her face in his back and wrapped her fingers through his belt loops. When she nibbled his side, he spun in a circle and laughed as she shrieked.

Taking the rope stairs two at a time, they reached the top, and he hopped into the chute. Down they went. At the last second, he twisted so she sprawled across his body. He hit the ground with a soft "Oomph," and a laughing Elizabeth squirmed on top of him. So filled with happiness, she couldn't hold it inside after seeing the smile in his eyes.

"You've lost your mind." She gave into the urge and pressed her lips to his. As soon as his arms tightened around her, she snuggled closer and deepened the kiss. He left her breathless and flustered, but serene at the same time. Being in his arms felt like home to her, like she belonged in them, and she would happily spend all day in this exact spot with him.

He rolled them to their sides and drew back to peer into her eyes. "Yeah, I've lost my mind," he whispered, his voice husky. Strands of loose hair drifted around her face and tickled her nose, and his gentle hand brushed them behind her ear. "I've lost my mind over you." His work-roughened fingers traced the bones in her jaws and cheeks. "You take my breath away, Elizabeth. Before I met you, I always felt like something major was missing in my life." He paused to clear his throat, "Now I know it wasn't a *thing*. It was you. When I'm with *you*, my world is right. It's whole. You're what I've been looking for, for so, so long."

She drew in a deep breath, but before she could speak, he buried his face in her neck and whispered, "You're so beautiful, really, but it's not even close to that." The arms around her waist tightened. "I know I keep saying it, but the gift you are inside is even more precious than the lovely package wrapping it. What you are, in here," his palm pressed against her heart, "is what draws me to you like a moth to a flame. You're perfect for me."

"Oh, Liam, you're one to talk." She scratched her fingers through the scruff on his jaw and feathered her thumbs over his chin. "You're so strong and handsome, but you're so much more than that. You're kind and compassionate, brave and loyal. You work harder than anyone I know, and yet you still find time to spend with me and help your sister with her girls. Your love for them fills my heart with joy and tells me that, one day, you're going to be such an amazing father." She leaned into him until her lips brushed his. "I just hope and pray I'm around for that," she whispered.

His arms clenched tight around her, forcing the air from her lungs.

Oh, no, did I say the wrong thing?

He flipped her onto her back and his body followed, his elbows holding most of his weight off her. "No, sweetheart, you didn't say the wrong thing." His smile was gentle, but his eyes flashed with something she couldn't quite read. "Not the wrong thing at all. I just keep questioning how I can feel something so big and so strong in so little time."

"You're right that it's only been a few months. In some ways, it feels like I've known you forever, but try as I might, my brain can't get my heart to slow down." Elizabeth squirmed when Liam stared at her but didn't speak. "Oh, gosh, I *did* say something wrong. Are you upset, honey?"

Liam's soft laughter calmed her nerves, and his words reassured her.

"No, sweetheart. I'm just thinking that I don't know how I got to be so lucky or what I did to deserve you."

His eyes captured hers, and she saw a flash of something that made her heart skip a beat. Was she reading him correctly? She wanted to ask, needed to know if he felt the same as she did.

"Liam?" she whispered.

"Shhh." His lips met her in a deep, soulful kiss, and her hands gripped his head, pulling him closer.

She felt it all in his kiss and never wanted it to end. His affection. His protective nature. His happy spirit. His gift to her … himself. Her hands flexed when he tried to pull back from her.

"You didn't let me finish, sweetheart." His lips feathered over her cheek to rest at her ear. "You consume me. When I'm awake, my thoughts constantly travel to you. When I can see you. When I can hold you. When I can kiss you. At night, in my sleep, you invade my dreams. Dreams of tomorrow when I can have you for forever. When I can make you mine for every day, in every way. I love you, Elizabeth, and I love you more every day." When her breath caught, he pulled back to look at her and smile. "So, no, when you say you hope you're around, you're not saying the wrong thing. You're saying the absolute right thing."

Tears threatened. She fought them but lost the battle. Her breath hiccupped, and her heart hammered in her chest. Wave after wave of joy washed through her.

He.

Loves.

Me.

Yay!

He grinned as he shook his head, and she knew she'd once again shared her thoughts. But right then, she didn't care. Because he loved her.

Pressing hard on his shoulder, she managed to roll him to his back. Happy tears dripped from her cheeks to his. "Honey, I love the way you make me laugh." Her lips grazed his forehead. "I love the way you comfort me when I think of Seth and cry." She placed gentle kisses on his eyes. "I love the way you make me feel safe and protected." Her nose brushed the tip of his. "I love the way you worry if I'm cold or hungry or tired or having trouble with my asthma." She nibbled along his strong jawline. "I love the way you love me," she paused to take a breath and wipe her face, "because the way you love me is perfect." With his face captured in her hands, she pressed her lips to his in a mind-numbing kiss. "I love you, Liam, with every fiber of my being," she whispered, her voice light and joyful.

Mother Nature celebrated the dawn of new love. The sun shone brighter as the white clouds danced across the clear, blue sky. The wind whispered through the budding leaves of the trees, carrying the scent of spring flowers. Birds serenaded them while crickets chirped their own song. But Elizabeth missed all of it because her heart and mind focused on Liam. On being at home in his arms. On the bubble that encapsulated them.

Love protected. Love trusted. Love hoped. Love endured. But most of all, true love never failed, even when tested. And neither Elizabeth nor Liam knew how much their love would be tested in the weeks to come.

Radio Broadcast

"Goooood morning, Highlanders! You're listening to the local news on WHLD, AM radio 1250. Today is Thursday, May twenty-third, and these are your community updates.

"With only a couple weeks until summer break, our schools are looking for End of Grade Testing proctors. If you're interested in monitoring the students during these state-mandated tests, please give Mrs. Jean a call during school hours at 555-4982. If you've got a couple of hours to spare, she sure could use your help.

"It's time to get ready for our annual Backpack Kids food drive. Collection boxes are located around town at all the banks, grocery stores, convenience stores, and Ace Hardware. If you'd rather donate money instead of ready to eat foods or just need more information, contact Carole Hogsed at 555-KIDZ. That's 555-5439.

"It's time to begin our annual countdown to Memorial Day weekend with a couple of reminders concerning the holiday festivities. Sunday evening, bring your picnic basket and meet up with friends and family at Highlands Park for Memorial Day fireworks show.

"Join us downtown at Town Hall, eleven thirty Monday morning for a time of quiet reflection and gratitude for those brave men and women who gave their lives to defend our freedom.

"At noon, Highlands' Veterans of Foreign War will lead us in

"The Star Spangled Banner" as our Flag rises from half-staff. Folks, this is a beautiful sight you don't want to miss.

"Then hang around for our annual Memorial Day parade and enjoy the quirky, funny, and sometimes strange floats created by your neighbors.

"I'll leave you with this quote by G. K. Chesterton. 'The Flag does not fly because of the winds that blow it. The Flag flies because of each Soldier's last breath blowing past. For those who have fought and died for it, freedom has a taste that the protected will never know. The true Soldier fights not because he hates what is in front of him, but because he loves what is behind him.'

"Now on to the national news …"

Chapter 16

Liam couldn't believe Memorial Day weekend was already upon them. If he said he wasn't nervous about meeting Elizabeth's parents, he would be lying. This was a huge step forward in their relationship, but he knew he was ready for it. He still felt guilty, though, for not introducing her to his family, but come the weekend after the holiday, that little task would be marked off his to-do list.

A quick glance at the clock let Liam know he needed to go see Wrynn and the girls right then, or he might be late leaving for the inn. After throwing his bag and a light jacket in the backseat of the truck, Liam headed around to the front of the house.

As he stood on his sister's porch, giggles, love, and warmth escaped through the door and seeped into the deepest recesses of his heart. When he heard Wrynn's telephone ring three times, Liam turned the knob and found it unlocked. As he opened the door, he heard laughter down the hall and watched in amusement as Wrynn tiptoed backward toward the kitchen. Since it was obvious that she was trying her best to be quiet, he decided to announce his presence as he walked into the house so he wouldn't startle Wrynn and make her scream.

"Knock, knock."

Liam wanted to go see what the munchkins were up to, but

when he walked further into the house, a familiar voice from his past drew him toward the kitchen.

"Hi, Wrynn. This is Lara. It was so good to see you again today. I hope we can get together again real soon. We've got a lot of catching up to do. Anyway, we're not going to be able to make it to supper tonight. I'm really sorry, but some things have come up. Talk to you soon. BEEP. MESSAGE HAS ENDED."

Liam felt as if someone punched him in the stomach. After a decade, *her* voice was not one he wanted to hear. Though unanswered questions still plagued him at times, he was content with his life and excited about moving forward. More importantly, though, he'd finally taken Zack's advice and forgiven himself in order to take a chance with Elizabeth. The last thing he wanted to do was even think of her.

He hadn't seen or heard a word from Lara since their freshman year in college, and he classified her as a most definite part of his past. He knew, without doubt, Elizabeth would be a part of his future. His plans over the weekend included a long talk with her father while they played golf, so, when she met his family the following week, everything would be in order for his next step.

And now this.

He didn't know what to do with this knowledge that she was back. Surely, Lara wouldn't return to Highlands and expect everything to be as it was a decade ago. Surely, she knew he wasn't the same person anymore. Surely, she didn't think he was there waiting for her to come back.

But what if he was wrong?

Guilt grabbed him by the throat, strangling the air from his body. Confusion threatened to drown him. No, he wasn't confused about his feelings for Elizabeth. He loved her, plain and simple. He adored everything about her, right down to her strange, little quirks. But because he'd failed to share so many times, she knew nothing of his past.

Wrynn spoke to him, but his thoughts consumed him and drowned out her words. When the girls scurried into the kitchen, and his sister rushed them right back out, the only thing that crossed his mind was leaving, getting away from the haunting voice, so he fled. He rushed right out the front door and straight to the truck without even looking back, but when he grabbed the truck door, Elizabeth's face floated in his mind.

As he left Wrynn's house, Liam thought about heading down to DuPont State Forest to hike out his confusion and frustration, or making the trek to the top of Jones Knob to throw his conflict and uncertainty in the rushing wind. The flicker of guilt over Lara's disappearance reared its ugly head and sprinkled doubt on all his plans. He wanted to run, to hide, to find a way to organize all the thoughts going through his head.

He slammed his fist against the steering wheel. To be honest, he was angry. Angry at Wrynn for hiding Lara's return from him. When did they see each other? Angry at Lara for never getting in touch with him over the years. Why did she wait so long? And furious with himself for even thinking about taking the coward's way out and hurting Elizabeth. Love did not act that way. So no, he refused to flee like a scaredy-cat.

Instead, his heart led him to Elizabeth.

When he arrived at the inn, his mouth was dry, and his hands were locked tight to the steering wheel. Why did he say he'd spend the night at Endless View? The evening was a huge event in his and Elizabeth's relationship, and he prayed for positive results. He fought back a nervous case of the 'what ifs'.

What if her parents didn't like him?

What if he couldn't mask his confusion?

What if he said or did something to hurt Elizabeth?

What if? What if? What if?

The door to the inn opened, and his time for reflection ended. A couple of deep breaths helped somewhat calm him, and he slid out of the truck, determined to put everything behind him but the beautiful woman waiting for him on the porch.

Even though he was anxious about meeting her parents, she wrapped her arm around him as soon as he walked in, and her loving warmth put him at ease. After introductions were made, they settled into easy conversation, and Liam was quite proud of how he hid his inner turmoil.

Elizabeth blushed when her parents shared tales of her growing up years, and when Seth was mentioned, Liam saw and felt Keyna shut down for a little bit. His stories of his nieces' silly antics were greeted with laughter, and the mood sobered when he spoke of Tripp's sacrifice for their country.

By the time they finished eating supper, they treated him as if they had known him for years. He caught Elizabeth giving her mother a strange look when Keyna asked him how he liked the chicken and dumplings, but he had to admit they were the best he'd ever eaten.

Everyone pitched in for cleanup, and in no time, the leftovers were put away and the dishes washed. Laughter filled the small kitchen, and Liam felt right at home. The lingering glances and little touches between Elizabeth's parents and grandparents reminded him of his own parents, and he realized that this was where Elizabeth learned her affectionate ways. The actions modeled by them were ingrained in her. Like him, she grew up with an open display of love, and therefore, didn't hesitate to express her feelings in the same manner.

Once everything was finished, Elizabeth cuddled next to him on the couch, and talk turned to the activities planned for the holiday weekend. As he relaxed beside her, a stomach full of food, physically tiring days of landscaping, and long nights at the fire station caught up with him, and he nodded off several times before drifting into a series of clipped daydreams. Bright, vivid images played across his mind.

The icy blue of Lara's eyes.
The sun glinting off Elizabeth's long, blonde hair.
The emerald green dress Lara wore to their senior prom.
Tripp's foot connecting to a yellow kickball.
Elizabeth's soot-streaked face.
A bright red t-shirt on the desk in a messy dorm room.
A mangled tent at Merlefest.

Elizabeth's puffy, white coat.
An empty bed.

Flash after flash hit him, the past mixing with the present, one forgotten as the next began.

A burst of laughter jolted him back to his surroundings, and when he opened his eyes, everyone was looking at him. For a split second, muddled thoughts glued him to the spot, and his heart raced as he struggled to shake off the vicious hold his dream had on him.

The last sequence, him waking up to an empty bed, lingered in his clouded mind. When he blinked, he could still see the indention in the pillow and his red shirt she'd worn to bed. Feel himself wondering why she wasn't beside him. Smell a faint hint of her perfume.

He was hollow, an empty shell.

"Liam, are you okay?"

Elizabeth's warm hand caressed his cheek, and guilt struck a cruel blow to his heart.

What was happening to him? After all the time that had passed, Liam was right back in his dorm room. Right back to wrestling with confusion and anger. Right back to feeling abandoned and alone. Right back to a time in his life he thought was finished.

But one stupid phone call brought it all crashing back down around him.

Half of Liam was sitting on the couch beside the gentle, loving woman who represented his future. The other half was trapped in the memory of waking up alone ten years ago. His yesterday was colliding with his tomorrow. The time to share with Elizabeth had arrived, and he hoped he felt better after the telling of it.

Maybe forgiving himself had been an illusion, but regardless, he needed to share this with Elizabeth. He waited too long, as it was, and intended to fix the problem. Now.

"No, I'm not, but I will be." He grabbed her hand, staggered up from the couch, and pulled her to her feet. "I'm not trying to be rude, but I'm not going to be any good tomorrow if I don't get some sleep. If y'all will excuse us, I'd like Elizabeth to walk with me so I can see her to her cabin." He made an extra effort to be polite, but he wanted to drag Elizabeth from the room and get the coming conversation behind him.

In his rush to leave, he failed to see the look of concern on Elizabeth's face. If he'd sensed her alarm, he might have been prepared for her reaction.

What in this world just happened? One minute they were on the couch, relaxed and enjoying time with her family. The next, they were out the door, and Liam acted as if the hounds of hell were on his heels. Though, if she spent much time thinking about it, he was off kilter when he walked in the front door, and somehow he managed to hide it as the evening progressed.

She'd thought it was cute when he dozed off. A full stomach and two jobs would do that to a man. Having shared with them how hard he worked, her family was more than understanding. When he stiffened and jerked in his sleep, she figured the couch wasn't the most comfortable place to nap. But the lost uncertainty in his eyes when he woke worried her. He didn't look at her. He looked *through* her, as if she wasn't even there. And she watched the shutters close over his eyes as he shut her out.

His reaction when she touched him shocked her. He'd jerked away and panic was evident in every line of his face. While she would admit she'd learned a lot about him over the past several months, *that* Liam was new to her, and she didn't particularly like the way it made her feel.

After his parting words, no one had a chance to speak before he was dragging her out the door, and she doubted he noticed the bewildered looks her family gave his back or their worried murmurs rising at their abrupt departure. Her mind ping-ponged back and forth over what could possibly be the matter, and of course landed on the worst thing she could think. The conclusion she reached made her heart cramp and left her short of breath.

Oh, my gosh, he's realized he doesn't love me.

Liam stopped so fast, he jerked her arm, and pain shot through her shoulder.

"No, never. Don't ever let me hear that again." His words were short and clipped. "I *do* love you."

"Well, what am I supposed to think?" Panic bubbled in her chest and seeped out into her voice. "You didn't see the look on your face. Liam, I felt you freak when I touched you. That's never happened." She struggled to suck air into her lungs, startled by the shrill wheeze her efforts produced.

"Shh, sweetheart. Calm down, please or you'll have a full blown attack."

"Calm down? *Calm down?* Are you kidding me?" she asked between noisy gulps of air.

When his arms wrapped around her, she planted her face in his chest and concentrated on breathing, on easing the constriction in her airways. The less oxygen she drew in, the dizzier she grew until her strength left her, and she slumped against him.

The next thing she knew, she was over his shoulder, and he was racing toward her cabin. The door banged against the wall. He dropped her on the bed and disappeared into the bathroom. Before she had time to blink, her inhaler was at her mouth, and he administered two puffs.

"Breathe in, Elizabeth." He glanced around the room as he pressed her down onto her back. "Where's your nebulizer?"

She closed her eyes, determined to focus on drawing in a full breath instead of the worry on Liam's face. As the medicine kicked in, the tight bands around her chest loosened. His weight settled on the bed, causing her to roll against his thigh.

"Sweetheart, I'm so sorry I caused this. I handled the whole situation wrong." His voice was strained. "Can you forgive me?" Calloused hands drifted softly over her face and hair.

"For what, Liam? I still don't know what the heck is wrong."

She peered up at him through her lashes. "Can you please tell me what's going on? I really don't like this feeling in the pit of my stomach."

"I'll make you a deal. I'll talk while you do a breathing treatment. Now, where's your nebulizer?"

"Liiiaaam," she rumbled in frustration. "The inhaler worked. I'm fine, or I will be when you tell me what's wrong." She almost smacked him when he pressed the side of his head to her breastbone. "Wh- wh- what are you doing?" This forward of a move from him shocked her.

"Shh, don't talk. Just breathe."

Then she realized what he was doing. He was reassuring himself she could breathe again. He proved this when his hands pushed firmly against the lowest part of her lungs and paused for her to take a few breaths.

She fought it with true, valiant effort, but she was helpless to stop the giggle from bursting out of her mouth.

I can't believe I thought he was feeling me up!

Liam's head jerked up, and his eyes flew to hers. She watched as the pain washed through him. His reaction confused her even more.

"No. Not that. I just needed to know you could breathe." He moved too close to the edge of the bed, fell on the floor, and raised his hands in the air. "I swear, it was strictly clinical."

"That's it." She sat up and reached for his hand. "Get your tuchus up here, and tell me what the devil is wrong with you."

He scooted away from her and buried his face in trembling hands. To say his reaction stunned her would be an understatement. But even more, she felt a twinge of fear. The Liam on the floor was not the one she had grown to love. She didn't recognize that person. She moved to the edge of the bed, planning to join him.

"I met this girl right before my senior year of high school. Her name was Lara. We dated for close to two years. Everyone, including me, thought we were perfect together."

When his quiet words reached her ear, she froze, and her heart turned over.

"Then near the end of our freshman year of college, she disappeared. The police found nothing, and Lord knows I searched to the ends of the earth and found not one clue."

Okay, so his story was tragic. She understood that. But it was also a very long time ago. Surely, he didn't beat himself up about it ten years later. And she couldn't help but wonder how exactly this Lara figured into him and her.

"Here's the thing. All these years, I've thought I did something that caused her to run, and now, after this afternoon, I'm pretty convinced it was my fault." He drew a deep breath and forced it through his nose. "I was raised a certain way. Not everyone agrees with it, but for me, that's the way things are. It's what my parents taught me and my sister, and I never doubted, not for one minute, that what they taught us was what they thought was best for us."

Confused. Puzzled. Downright bumfuzzled. The more Liam talked, the more baffled Elizabeth grew.

What the heck is he talking about?!

Liam got up on his knees and shuffled over to the bed. "That's what I'm trying to explain, sweetheart, but I think I'm making a mess of it. I woke up, and she was gone. Just disappeared into thin air."

Pressure built behind her eyes, and she pinched the bridge of her nose. "Liam, quit talking in circles and just spit it out. You're giving me a headache."

"Lara and I ... Well, w-w-we ...," he stammered and stuttered as a blush crawled up his neck.

"Liam, so help me. Spit. It. Out!"

"We slept together!" he shouted, his words echoing in the small room.

"So?"

"Don't you get it? We had sex. That's not the way I was raised. It went against everything I was taught. We'd talked about it at length, and that's not what we agreed on."

"Are you forgetting that I, too, was raised in a small Southern town in the middle of the Bible Belt? If you think my parents taught me something different, you'd be wrong. Now my question stands. *So?*"

"But right after, poof, she was gone. Something I did hurt her and she ran." His chin dropped to his chest in defeat and he rested his forehead against the mattress. "I don't know what it was, but I know it's my fault, and I'm scared to death I'm going to do something to hurt you, too."

"Liam, that's crazy. You can't think that way. You don't have it in you to hurt me." She ran her fingers through his hair, hoping to soothe him. "You have no way of knowing what she was thinking or what she was feeling, but I'll tell you right now, if she ran from you, she's crazy. If she *was* kidnapped, it's not your fault, and you've wasted all these years worrying for nothing. What if she's dead?"

"She isn't."

"You don't know that, Liam."

"I *do* know that, sweetheart." He lifted his head to look at her. Pain morphed his features until he looked years older than he was. "I stopped by Wrynn's today before I came here. I heard her voice on the answering machine. She's here, in Highlands."

"Ho-ly cow, are you serious?" Her eyes widened. Her mouth dropped open. And she could only imagine the shocked look on her face. Now she knew what was bothering him and wished she had an idea of how to help him.

"Yeah, I'm serious. See my problem? I have to see her." Hope shone in his eyes. "Now I can get answers to the questions I've had all these years. Find out what I did wrong. I've worried that I rushed her or hurt her or showed her disrespect or something. This may be my only shot at forgiveness."

Finding his answers would require him to approach Lara in person. His worries were buried too deep to be satisfied with a short phone conversation. By his own admission, he thought they were perfect for each other. If she supported him, she ran the risk of losing him to her, but if she didn't, wasn't the risk of loss as great? Would she be able to sleep at night if she begged him to stay away from this Lara? No, she wouldn't. An act that selfish would destroy

180

her, and in doing so, put an end to any chance of sharing a future with him. Her brain hurt from the thoughts crashing through it.

What do I do? What do I do? What do I do?

"That's the beauty of it, sweetheart. All I want you to do is be there with me and hold my hand, if you're comfortable with that. No more secrets between us." He brushed a lock of hair off her cheek and tucked it behind her ear. "I need to know. Can you see that? Cause if I can find out what happened, then I can make sure I never make the same mistake with you."

"You want me there when you talk to her? Like, in the same room?" She puffed out her cheeks and blew out a long gush of air as she mulled it over in her head. "Okay, I think I can do that. What I'd like to know though, is why didn't you tell me about this before now? And is this Lara the one Ashton was talking about when she said you'd been burned?"

"Ashton said that?" He chuckled when she nodded. "Figures. She's worse than a mama bear. And yes, after Lara disappeared, I was pretty worthless for a while. I kind of cut myself off from my friends and family and buried everything deep inside because I didn't know how to handle it." Moving beside her on the bed, he wrapped an arm around her shoulder and drew her closer to his side. "I didn't date. I rarely socialized. I just didn't want to. I thought *that* part of me had died. I finished college and came back home to take over Dad's landscaping business. Then when Tripp died and I saw what it did to Wrynn, heck, what it still does to her every day, I started to think that maybe I was the lucky one, ya know. You can't lose what you don't have."

She couldn't imagine a Liam withdrawn from the world. He lived life at full speed, laughing and making others laugh with him. Gracious, the way he took care of his nieces without complaint was more than anyone could ask of him. No, a world without her Liam would be a very sad place, indeed.

Wonder what changed.

The instant the thought passed through her mind, his arm tightened, and he chuckled.

"Do you really not know the answer to that question?"

"Ugh, one of these days, my big mouth is going to get me in trouble." She groaned when she felt the heat rise to her cheeks. "But no, I don't. To me, you've always been, well, for lack of a better word, normal. Happy, even. And that doesn't match up with what you've told me. Not that I'm saying you aren't telling me the truth, but honestly, I've never seen that side of you."

"Well, let me explain it in a way that even my nieces would understand. Once upon a time, in a land far, far away, there lived a beautiful princess named Elizabeth."

"Oh, I love fairytales," she said through a laugh, and he grinned. "Well, don't stop. Tell me more about this beautiful princess."

"One day, Elizabeth decided to travel from her home in the Flatlands of the East to the picturesque mountains of the far West, not knowing the land was filled with dangerous snow and treacherous ice. On her quest for the best hot cocoa in the land, she found herself sliding on the slippery surface. Unbeknownst to her, a handsome prince was standing in the perfect place to rescue the beautiful princess. When she slammed into his back, she somehow managed to shatter the cage around the prince's heart. At the time, the prince was unaware of the princess's brave feat, but before he knew it, he was hopelessly bound by her magical spell. You see, this beautiful princess was much more than a pretty face. She was gracious and humble and giving to all those who were blessed to meet her. The prince could do nothing but fall in love with the beautiful princess, and she loved him, too. The end."

"The end? That's it?" She poked him in the chest. "There's no 'and they lived happily ever after'?"

"Well, my love, maybe I should say to be continued." The love in his voice swept over her, leaving a trail of goosebumps in its wake. "That part of our fairytale has yet to be written, but if things go the way I hope, we'll finish the story together."

"Oh, Liam, I hope so, too."

She tipped her face up to him, and he placed a tender kiss on her lips before backing away.

"I need to go, sweetheart. Golf with your dad tomorrow and that whole 'lead me not into temptation' stuff." His arms enveloped her, and he pulled her tight against him. "I love you, sweetheart," he whispered against the top of her head. "Thanks for listening."

"Oh, honey, you're welcome." She snuggled closer in his embrace. "I love you, and I'll see you sometime tomorrow evening." A grin blossomed on her face, and she hid it against his chest. "Good luck with my dad tomorrow. The best advice I can give you is to run if he comes after you with his nine iron." She pictured it in her head and giggled.

Come tomorrow, she might have to sneak out to Wade Hampton and spy on her two favorite men.

He tasted of
strong man,
bright sunshine,
everlasting love,
and
hope eternal.

Chapter 17

L iam had forgotten how much he *didn't* like chasing a little white ball around a sea of green turf. The course was busy due to the holiday weekend, and the delay between tee-offs was long. After five and a half hours of hurry up and wait, they were on the final hole. This day was never going to end if he couldn't get his ball to go in the right direction. It was a good thing he enjoyed being around Mike, but he was growing more anxious the closer they came to the end of the course. He knew The Talk was coming, had waited for it all day, and he wanted to get that particular conversation out of the way before they joined Elizabeth and Keyna for supper.

"Remind me again why I agreed to play golf with a pro," Liam grumbled as yet another ball plopped in the small pond. The urge to throw his club was there, but he fought it. Barely. Few things ruffled his feathers, but the last hole's water hazard was getting the best of him. He wished Mike would just go ahead and broach the subject of Elizabeth so his heart would quit trying to jump out of his chest. "How many drops do I get?"

"As many as it takes, son. As many as it takes." Mike threw his head back and roared with laughter. "Just making me look better and better." He blew on the end of his fingers and scuffed them on his shirt.

"Like you need my help," Liam muttered. His score passed one hundred several holes ago, much to Mike's delight. "I'll remember this the next time."

"Drop the ball, son, and let's see if you can shake off that awful hook of yours." Pulling a towel from the side of his bag, Mike concentrated on wiping off the face of his club. "So, you think there's going to be a next time? Let's talk about this a little."

And there it was. Liam didn't know if he should be nervous, scared, or relieved, but he was ready to get it out of the way.

"You know, Mike, I've been waiting all day for this, and now, the perfect speech I've practiced all morning just flew right out of my head." His grip slipped on the shaft, and he stopped to wipe his sweaty palms on his khakis. "I've never been one to beat around the bush, so I'll say it straight out." He shifted his body a few inches to the left and swung his club. Both heads turned to follow the ball. "You and Keyna raised an amazing daughter. She's kind and compassionate and the most selfless person I've ever met." When the ball landed near the green, Liam pumped his fist in the air. "Yes! Finally."

"Good job, son." Mike threw him an exaggerated wink. "Sure took you long enough."

Liam took no offense at his joking words. "Yeah, but I can take you at basketball. Name the time and place."

"Not going to argue that one, son. Go ahead and finish what you were saying about my baby girl. So far, I agree with you one hundred percent."

They stuck their clubs back in the bags and hopped in the cart.

"This is going to sound strange, but just hear me out." He wiped the moisture off his brow and hoped he didn't sound foolish. "The first time we met, I knew, right there on the spot, that your little girl was something special. It was like she invaded my thoughts and dreams. I couldn't get away from her, and it almost drove me crazy. I thought about fighting it, but I just wasn't strong enough." He gazed out over the greens, lost in his memories. "I chased her around town for forever, and then finally, one day, I caught up with her. Funny thing about that? She was even better than I remembered. She told you about the sick mom and her kids, right?" He looked over to see Mike's nod. "You would have been so proud of her. She's stepped right in, dealt with the situation like a pro, and in no time, has everything organized and under control. Simply stunning, and she acts like it isn't a big deal, because to her, it isn't. She saw something that needed to be done, and she did it. And she's always doing things like that."

"Yeah, that's my baby girl. She's been like that since she was a little thing, and I hope she never changes." Mike's face glowed with pride.

"See, there's this part of First Corinthians, and she lives it every day of her life. Love is patient and kind. Love is not boastful or proud." He stopped to swallow around the ball of anxiety lodged in his throat. "Mr. Pittman, I'm in love with your daughter, and if there's one thing she's taught me, it's that true love never fails." His nostrils flared as he drew in and blew out a deep breath. He slouched down in the cart and stared down at his bouncing knees. "We still have a few things to work on, but I'm letting you know right now, I'm here for the long haul, so I hope to Heaven y'all like me." Acid churned and tossed in his stomach.

"Son."

"Umm, so, I know it seems awful quick, seeing as how we haven't known each other for very long, but you know what they say, the heart knows what it wants." A loose thread on the seam of his khakis fell victim to his nervous destruction.

"Son."

"I wasn't looking for anyone, but now that I've found her, I'm not letting her go."

"Son, stop."

Surprised at Mike's sharp words, Liam straightened and turned to look at him.

"I'm sure you know, but Keyna and I are very close to our baby girl. Rarely a day passes that we don't talk several times, and lately, a lot of our talk has been about you." His voice softened the longer he spoke. "I honestly can't think of one thing she's said that would make us *not* like you. You're a gentleman and *soooo romantic*." Mike spoke the last part in a prissy voice as he fluttered his eyelashes and pressed his hands to his cheeks. "But seriously, she's told us how you pitched in to help out with that sick lady's kids. How you take care of your nieces like they're your own. How your sister's depression might even be worse than Keyna's, and you take care of her, too. Not because you have to, but because you want to. And that's just the tip of the iceberg. The way my baby girl talks, I'm pretty sure you set the moon and the stars in the sky." He crossed his arms over his chest and glared at Liam. "Course, I might need to change my way of thinking, seeing as how it sounds like you want to take her away from me."

Liam bit back a chuckle and settled on a grin, thankful Elizabeth's kind words to her parents had made The Talk easier for him.

"A while back, when our Seth was sick, Elizabeth's beau, Jarrett, thought her attention should be on him, not on her family. It was subtle at first, but it got ugly pretty fast. His kind of thinking is so far outside of her nature that she had no idea how to deal with it. That boy hurt my little girl, treating her like that during the worst time in her life, and it still makes me see red. I know you're supposed to forgive people who do you wrong, but I gotta tell you, I'm still working on that part, and it ain't been easy."

This was new to him, but the thought of someone treating Elizabeth that way made him furious. "Are you kidding me? Who in their right mind would–?"

Mike cut him off midsentence. "And I may have just overstepped my boundaries, son, seeing as how it seems like she's not shared this with you yet. I'll ask that you not push her on it, though, because those days were dark for all of us, and it's not a time we like to visit too much. But there's a reason I told you that story, and that reason is this. From the things she's told us, you don't have it in you to treat her that way. Seems to me, you know just how special and precious my girl is, and I'm trusting you to keep treating her just like you do now." Mike stepped out of the cart and reached for his putter.

"That, sir, is an easy promise to make and keep. She is precious to me, and I have no trouble whatsoever treating her that way." Liam was relieved. The Talk wasn't near as bad as he'd built up in his head, and having no prior experience with such things, he'd almost made himself sick with dread. Now that it was over, he was looking forward to hitting the stupid ball in the hole so he could spend more time with Elizabeth.

"I'm going to hold you to that, son. Now, let's finish this dance so we can get back to our girls." Mike walked over to his ball, but before he swung his putter, he looked over his shoulder. "And if you ever hurt my baby girl, I'm–"

"Coming after me with your nine iron." At the shocked look on Mike's face, Liam laughed. "Yeah, she told me to run if you came after me today. Now, come on, let's get this done so we can leave."

With minutes to spare, he pulled up at his parents' house for their normal Sunday supper before the annual fireworks show. Leaving Elizabeth behind was hard, but with her family in town, he knew she wanted to spend their last night and day with them. Then, after the Memorial Day parade and they saw her parents off, he was taking her to meet his family. He couldn't wait for them to meet the girl who stole his heart.

The call to his mom earlier in the morning had eased some of her worries, and as expected, Wrynn had already told her about Lara's call and Liam's reaction. Regardless, he still expected Wrynn to give him the third degree for the way he ran out of her house on Friday.

Sure enough, as soon as he walked in the door, she flew at him to offer comfort. He compared hearing Lara's voice to the way he used to rip duct tape off her arm and tried to play it off as best he could. Yes, the phone call upset him, but not for the reasons she thought.

Thankfully, his parents wanted to share about their mother's retirement, so after joking around with his parents, conversation centered on their news. When the meal was finished, he was relieved he'd avoided being grilled about his weekend, but while his nieces were getting dessert with his dad, his mom cornered him. When he glanced over at Wrynn, she smirked at him and slouched down in her chair. Guess he wasn't getting any support from her.

"Now, if we're going to make it to the fireworks tonight, we need to have this discussion quickly." Mom went into full teacher mode, which meant listen fast but carefully, because there might be a test at the end. "Liam, I understand you were surprised to hear Lara's voice on Wrynn's answering machine, but you didn't give Wrynn a chance to explain what happened. You just rushed out of the house, and let us all worry about you for the last couple of days." She leaned over, covered his hand with her own, and squeezed. "Wrynn ran into her in the parking lot of Mountain Fresh. It was out of the blue. They sat and talked for a bit, and Wrynn invited her to supper to talk some more. Nothing more, and nothing less. Before Wrynn had the time to talk to you about it, Lara called to cancel. That's as far as it got."

Mom stood and moved behind Liam, wrapping her arms around his shoulders and squeezing, offering the comfort only a mother could. "I know she hurt you, baby, but you need to understand that she's back in town to stay. You also need to know something else." She knelt in front of him and grabbed his hands. "I saw her near the school on Friday. There were children in her car. You need to prepare yourself for the fact that she has a family and may have a husband. You know that you WILL be running into her, and as small as this town is, it will be soon."

Liam rested his forehead on his mom's, and as he opened his mouth to tell her he was okay, his dad walked through the kitchen door with one monkey on his back, one in his arms, and one riding his foot, all chattering up a storm. That signaled the end of the conversation.

"These girls are ready for some fireworks." All four of them looked raring to go. "Let's get this show on the road."

Mom gently rubbed Liam on the head. "We will finish this conversation later."

Yes, they would, but not in the manner she thought. By the next night, everyone would know Liam didn't spend his time pining over Lara.

Liam stopped by the gym for a quick workout when he left the fire station. It was almost time for the Memorial Day parade. Every year, he rode on top of the fire truck and threw treats to the crowd.

When he'd told Elizabeth goodbye Sunday evening, they made plans to meet after the parade for an early supper with her parents before going to his parents' house. Liam left for the firehouse, happy, hopeful, and content, but little did he know, life planned to get in the way.

Riding high on top of the fire truck gave Liam the opportunity to keep an eye out for Wrynn and the girls. He watched the crowds on both sides of the street until he spotted Maggie perched precariously, feet tapping an excited rhythm, on her mother's shoulders. The tops of Annie and Bekah's heads were beside Wrynn.

Three things happened quick as lightning, like dominos tumbling across a table.

First, Maggie saw him, and her kicking legs went wild, catching her mom off guard. Second, a stunned Wrynn stumbled toward the edge of the curb. Third, (and what worried Liam the most), was the strange man who, a few steps away, watched every move Wrynn and the children made. At her first unstable lurch, the unfamiliar man raced to her side, grabbed her elbow, and prevented her from taking a nasty spill.

Without a thought, he scurried down the fire ladder and into the crowd. As Liam plucked a bucking Maggie from her mother's shoulders, Wrynn turned to look at her rescuer.

At Wrynn's distressed cry, Liam moved to separate the children and her from the stranger who drew such deep anguished wails from his sister. When he grabbed Wrynn's chin in an attempt to help her settle, she shook him loose, buried her face against his chest, and begged him to get her out of there.

After settling a frantic, panicked Wrynn and confused girls at the firehouse, Liam fought deep to control his anger and turned to face this man who was responsible for causing his sister more pain.

"Who are you?" When a keening wail came from Wrynn's cowering body, Liam curled his fingers into a tight fist and then shook some of the tension out of his hands. "What did you do to my sister?"

The man jabbed his fingers through his closely cropped hair. "I'm Master Sergeant Randall Lee Underwood. Tripp and I served together from Basic on through Fort Benning." He extended his hand, and Liam hesitated for a second before he shook it. "Has Wrynn been like this since Tripp's crash?"

Anything concerning Tripp set her panic and despair off in a flash, and here was a big flesh and blood reminder. No wonder she was all but catatonic.

"For the most part, yes, but the last week or so, she's done a little better, faced a few demons, and made some real strides toward healing. There've been times in the past two and a half years when I thought she'd just give up, but heck no, she's just kept right on fighting. I guess seeing you brought it all back."

Randy paced away, and when he turned back, pain etched the lines of his face. "I was there when Marcus told her Tripp was gone. It was one of the worst days of my life." He pinched the bridge of his nose, visibly fighting for composure.

"Well, that certainly explains her reaction when she saw you." Liam ran his hands through his hair. Now that he knew the part Randy played in that fateful day, Wrynn's reaction made complete sense and didn't worry him as much. "There's nothing you could have done that would've made it easier for her. A piece of her soul died that day, and she'll never get it back."

"I love that man like a brother. Love that little gal in there, too. It liked to have killed me when she collapsed and went into labor. Thank God she and the baby were okay, but still." Randy stopped and looked over at Wrynn and the girls. When he looked back at Liam, his eyes glistened. "Listen, I'm going to head on out. I never intended anything like this to happen. My plan was to keep an eye on her, not make things worse for her. I hope you know that." Randy dug out his wallet, removed a business card, and handed it to him.

Liam tucked the card in his shirt pocket and choked out a short bark of angry laughter. "Well, I sure as heck hope not. But yeah, that might be the best thing for her. She'll come around soon, I'm sure." It was Liam's turn to look over at Wrynn. "No, I know she will. I'm looking out for her. I'll take care of it."

"If she needs anything, would you please call me?" Randy ran his fingers through his hair and glanced back at Wrynn and the girls. "When she's better, would you please let her know my wife and I miss her, that we want to see her? Spend time with her and the girls?"

"Oh, absolutely, I'll tell her. I don't know when I'll do it, but I'll make sure she knows. And as for calling you, don't count on that happening any time soon." As nonchalant as possible, Liam nudged Randy toward the exit. While their conversation was informative, comforting his sister and nieces was his priority, not playing nice with the person who, no matter how unintentional, wreaked havoc in their day. When Randy finally walked out the door, Liam rushed back to Wrynn and the girls.

As Wrynn became more aware of her surroundings, he helped her get his nieces into the car. He held her in his arms until she stopped shaking, and then waited to see them safely on their way. Only then did he look at the time and realize he was almost two hours late picking Elizabeth up to meet his parents. Since he'd planned to surprise his mom and dad, they would never know he and Elizabeth were running late.

Prepared to grovel to get back into her good graces, Liam

called to apologize and let her know he was on his way. Her cell went straight to voicemail, so he called the inn. When Tootsie answered the phone, she politely informed Liam that Elizabeth, after seeing her parents off and waiting around for him to show, had gone to Asheville with a few employees from the inn and wouldn't be back until late that night.

When Liam hung up, his gut told him he'd messed up big time, and his mind went in different directions, trying to think of a way to make things up to her. Regardless, he couldn't do anything about it right then, but if the fire station was quiet tonight during his late shift, he would have time to come up with something great.

A two-car collision out in the country kept him busy until time to leave, and when Liam finally crawled into bed, the sun peeked over the horizon.

He tossed and turned, filled with worry and anxiety. About Wrynn. About the girls. About Elizabeth. Exhaustion ate at his bones, but his mind didn't shut off long enough to find rest. Giving in to sleep's evasiveness, Liam dragged himself out of bed to shower, hoping the hot water would revive him. Time was running away from him. Anxious to see Elizabeth and make things right, he rushed out the door without coffee or ibuprofen to ease his headache.

With the thought of making her smile, he stopped to grab a cup of her favorite cocoa and a bunch of bright Gerbera daisies, and ended up annoyed for having to wait in line for a price check. The slight pounding in his temples changed to a strong throb when, two blocks from the store, he saw a woman trying to change a flat tire. Though he wanted to ignore her, he couldn't. He would want someone to stop and help the women in his life. By the time he threw the flat in her trunk, his feet were filled with lead, his shoulders ached, and his patience was gone.

To make matters worse, as he slid in the truck, his knee hit the cup holder, and the lukewarm cocoa spilled down his leg to pool in his shoe. No way was he going home. His need to see Elizabeth was stronger than his wanting clean socks. He banged his head on the steering wheel several times, which made his head hurt worse, and counted to ten to get a handle on his frustration. Then he sped through town, but the drive to the inn felt like it took forever. He watched inch by inch go by in slow motion.

When he finally parked in front of the porch, she was curled up in her favorite rocking chair. For the first time in the long, dreary day, he smiled. His headache eased its thump. The tension drained out of him. She was his cure.

As he slid out of the truck, he heard her speak.

"I thought I might see you sometime today."

Her voice was soft, too soft, and filled with a depth of anguish that terrified him. Something was wrong, very wrong. Forgetting the flowers, he slammed the door, bounded up the stairs, and dropped to his knees in front of her.

"Elizabeth, sweetheart, what happened?"

Red rimmed, puffy eyes looked over his shoulder, and a trail of tears carved a path on her cheeks. He moved into her line of vision, but she turned her head away from him.

"Sweetheart, please, tell me what's wrong." He cupped her cheeks, but she drew back from his caress. Panic stole his breath. She'd never refused his touch.

"Do you have any idea the things that went through my mind when you didn't show up, didn't call?" The whispered words drifted to nothing when she gritted her teeth. "I thought that maybe you'd had an accident, so I went looking for you. I searched up and down every road that leads here, but didn't see your truck. So I drove into town. When I got near the fire station," her head jerked side-to-side, and she clenched her eyes shut before piercing him with her glare, "w-w-want to know wh-wh-what I d-d-did see?" Her words stuttered, and her breath hitched. "I saw– I saw– I saw you hugging her. Was that Lara? Were you with her when you were supposed to be with me?" She bit out the angry words.

Pain-filled eyes met his, and his heart lurched at the tears dripping off her chin. What the devil was she talking about? As his mind replayed her words, he realized she'd seen him comforting Wrynn and thought she was Lara. Having never met his sister,

Elizabeth didn't know any better. But she trusted him, didn't she? It stung that she would even think that of him. What had he done to make her believe he would betray her like that?

"Sweetheart, that wasn't Lara." He captured her chin in his hands and forced her eyes to meet his. "That was my sister, Wrynn. Something happened at the parade, and she fell apart and needed me. That's why I was late. I couldn't just leave her and the girls. I had to stay, but when I called to explain, your grams said you'd gone to Asheville." He spoke in a calm tone, hoping to soothe her hurt.

"Liam, please, just save the excuses," she screeched. Jerking his fingers from her face, she planted firm hands on his shoulders and pushed him away from her. "Lara or Wrynn, does it really matter which one? Lara's suddenly popped back into your life, and Wrynn's always going to be there." Her shrill voice stabbed knives into his temples. "When, Liam, when? When do I get to be first place in your life? What do I have to do to get there? Disappear for a while? Fall apart? Or do I just wait and wonder if I'll ever get there?" Her body folded in the chair as she buried her anger reddened face in her knees.

A stunned Liam slumped down on the porch. How long had she felt this way, and why had she never mentioned it to him before? The bitterness he sensed was about more than what happened the day before. More than Lara's return. More than a few missed dates. What was going on here that he couldn't see?

"You say you love me, but I gotta tell you, pushing me aside again and again, and always making me second best doesn't feel like love." The force of her sobs shook the rocking chair.

What did she want him to do? Abandon his sister? Yes, he'd not shown up a couple of times, but he always called her to let her know what was happening. Yes, he'd been late more than once. But dang it, Wrynn needed him, and even more, the girls needed him. He fought back a tiny spark of anger. Annie, Bekah, and Maggie were REASONS, not excuses, and he never once hid the fact that his nieces were a priority for him. Was he wrong to put them first? Would Wrynn be better off if he left her to fend for herself and forced her to handle everything? No! She would crumble. The girls would suffer. And he wasn't willing to let the thought become a reality.

"So, let me see if I understand what you're saying." He took a deep breath and struggled to speak in a composed voice. "When the man who told my sister her husband was dead showed up at the parade yesterday, and she completely, totally lost it, I was supposed to just leave her there and hope for the best? Is that what you're saying?"

When her head flew up and her startled eyes met his, he ignored her. His headache was back, and it felt like it brought jackhammers with it. His muscles ached with fatigue and stress. Between Lara's call, meeting her parents, Wrynn's flipping out, and Elizabeth's assumptions, Liam was at his limit. The spark became an ember and thrashed through his veins, leaving him powerless to stop it.

"Her girls, MY girls, were right there beside her when it happened. Was I supposed to pat them on the head and walk away?" The ember grew to a raging inferno, and he unleashed it without thought or hesitation. "Oh, girls, I'm sorry your momma's blacked out on the couch, but I've got a date. Y'all take care of things, and I'll check in with you later when I have time. Are. You. Kidding. Me?"

He stood up, gripped the arms of the rocker, and leaned over in her face. "I give you everything I am, every last second of time I have in me, everything I've kept hidden for years, and this is what you do? You jump to conclusions without letting me explain? You hold stuff in for God knows how long, and then throw it in my face? I don't think so, and you know what? I don't need this right now, not after the crap morning I've had. Maybe I could have found a different way to handle the situation, stopped to call you, something, but you weren't there. You have no idea what happened because you didn't give me a chance to tell you. You say you love me, but *that* doesn't feel like love." He stomped to the steps and threw his parting words over his shoulder. "She's my sister, so let me ask you this. What makes this any different from what your dad told me that Jarrett guy did to you?"

He heard her gasping cries but was too livid to stop and look at her. He had to get away right then. As he slammed the door of the truck, she ran after him, screaming his name, but it was too late. He couldn't see anything past the red film covering his eyes. The sweet smell of flowers turned his stomach, so he rolled the window down and tossed them to the gravel as he drove away from the inn. From Elizabeth.

The anger coursing through his veins kept him company on his drive home. The windows rattled from the force of him crashing through the front door. He wanted to kick the couch or punch the wall to work the fury and resentment out of his system. Rage warred with exhaustion. He needed sleep, but first he needed to shower the cocoa off his leg. Maybe that would cool his temper some.

Numb to the bite of the gravel, Elizabeth dropped to her knees as Liam sped off, and clutched the battered, bruised daisies to her chest. Halfway through his rant, she'd realized how petty and stupid she'd sounded, but he didn't give her time to say anything. Not that she blamed him, but he needed to know she'd been wrong not to listen to him in the first place. Everything was her fault for feeling sorry for herself. After her hissy fit, he might never believe she trusted him. She did, truly, and he'd never given her reason not to. She had to find some way to make him forgive her.

What did I do? Oh, God, help me. What did I do?

When she'd looked for him the evening before and found him in some woman's arms, a part of her crumbled. A sorrow she'd not known since Seth passed away filled every crevice of her being. Overcome by an ignorant, irrational jealousy, she leapt at the chance to run away to Asheville with a couple of girls from the inn, but no matter how far she ran, she couldn't escape what she'd seen. Anger replaced sadness. Bitterness washed away every last shred of hope. All night, it stewed and stirred and grew so enormous that by morning, her gut churned like hot lava in a volcano, waiting to erupt. By the time Liam showed up, she was ready to explode.

And explode she did.

Without warning. Without explanation. Without restraint.

She'd spewed all her venomous insecurities, all her shortcomings, all her anguish at the one person who made her whole and happy and content.

Oh, dear Lord, what did I do?

His words repeated in her brain. *What makes this any different from what your dad told me that Jarrett guy did to you?* He was right, and she was wrong about so many things. But could she repair the damage she'd done? His hurt and anger had been so thick, she'd choked on them. Was this a wrong she could right? Would he forgive her? There was only one way to find out.

Blood rushed to her head, and pins and needles attacked her feet when she stood. Shaky legs barely held her upright. Afternoon was rushing toward evening. Panicked she might run out of time, she ran to her cabin to grab her purse and keys, jumped in her Jeep, and threw gravel as she raced out of the parking area.

Finding Liam to apologize was her only option. She only hoped she wasn't too late.

He tasted of
strong man,
bright sunshine,
everlasting love,
and

h o p e   e t e r n a l .

Chapter 18

Water dripping from his wet hair, Liam plopped down on the bed and tossed and turned to find a comfortable position. The hot shower did nothing to relieve the tension in his shoulders or the pounding in his head. When comfort eluded him, he stared at the ceiling and watched the fan rotate. Exhausted didn't quite cover the way Liam felt. A combination of drained, defeated, and depleted came closer. The hurt in his heart throbbed. The pounding in his temples left him nauseous, and a night of no sleep was catching up to him fast.

A day that started bad had made a slow descent straight into a pile of hot, stinking manure. He couldn't remember a time he'd ever been that angry. And he knew, to a certain extent, he'd overreacted. But dang it, she gave him no time to explain before she attacked.

The problem was, every time he closed his eyes, he saw the pain written on her face, the tears in her eyes, and then the anger taking over her little body. She went from broken to furious in a blink, and her actions triggered his reaction.

If he could start the day over, he'd try to find a way to make her listen. He'd control his temper and give her a chance to calm down. Since he couldn't, he was sprawled across the covers, watching the dust motes dancing in the afternoon sun, searching for a way to

FINDING HOPE FOR TOMORROW

make things right. It appeared a short nap was out of the question, too. No way was he going to be able to shut his mind off and sleep.

When no easy solution appeared out of the air, he slipped out of bed, threw on some clothes, and did the one thing left to do. He grabbed his keys and rushed out to his truck.

Finding Elizabeth to apologize was his only option. He only hoped he wasn't too late.

Good grief, the drive through town never took this long. His impatience made every minute feel like an hour. When her little Jeep flew past him, he hit the brakes, turned the wheel hard left, and did a one-eighty in the middle of the road.

Her brake lights flashed as she pulled onto the shoulder, threw open her door, and raced toward his truck.

Skidding to a stop, he jumped out and ran to her as fast as his feet could carry him.

"Liam!" His name on her lips was the most beautiful music he'd ever heard.

"Elizabeth!" He bent his knees and braced himself as she jumped in his open arms.

"I'm so—,"

"I'm so—,"

Their words tumbled on top of each other.

"Sorry. Forgive me," they whispered together.

"I'm sorry. I'm sorry. I'm sorry. I'm sorry." Elizabeth showered kisses over Liam's face.

"Forgive me. Forgive me. Forgive me." Liam wiped her cheeks and claimed her mouth with his.

Time stopped for the two of them, and the world around them faded to the background.

Lips poured forgiveness. Hands soothed aches and pain. Murmured words provided peace of mind. Arms shared strength.

Hearts beat in perfect sync, together in love.

Forgiveness was bliss.

The blare of the horn from a passing truck startled them apart, and a teen in the back yelled, "Get a room."

Elizabeth's mouth dropped open, her cheeks reddened, and she sputtered out a mortified huff. "Oh, my gosh, how embarrassing!"

"That's the perfect shade of pink on you," Liam teased, and the rosy hue darkened even more. When she narrowed her eyes, he laughed and pulled her tight against his chest. "We need to talk, and I know the perfect place. You free for the next couple of hours?"

She sighed and burrowed deeper into him. "For you, I'm free forever. Where are we going?"

"That easy?" He bent down and found himself drowning in the love shining in her eyes.

"I jumped to conclusions, accused you without listening, overreacted in a flash, turned into a screaming shrew, and threw your love in your face. I love you with all my heart and don't want to lose you, so yes, that easy." By the time she finished her rush of words, she was breathless.

Relief washed over him and weakened his knees. Shame followed quickly on its heels. "Sweetheart," he murmured in a pained voice. His eyes closed and his arms tightened around her. "Let's not do this right here on the side of the road. I need more time to grovel." He stepped back and ran his hands down her arms to clasp her hand. "You want to ride with me or follow?"

She glanced at their surroundings. "How about you take me somewhere to leave the Jeep, and then I'll ride with you."

"Easy enough. Follow me to the school."

A soft breeze blew the scent of honeysuckle and wild roses through the laurels and rhododendron. Hawks circled the air, searching for their next meal. White crops of rock jutted here and there, and green trees covered the mountains as far as the eye could see. The valley below looked a hundred miles away.

The view was breathtaking.

"Liam, what is this place?" She threw her arms out to the side and twirled in a circle. "I've never seen anything so beautiful."

"I have." He grinned at the confused expression on her face. "I'm looking at her."

The sun shimmered off her hair. Several short strands floated around to frame her pink cheeks. The blue of her eyes matched the clear, cloudless sky. Her happiness was so bubbly, so vibrant, so alive that he felt it. The vision of her, there in his favorite place on Earth, quite simply took his breath away.

"You're so silly." The wind carried her giggle to him.

He spread a blanket on the ground and dropped the backpack on it. On the way out of town, they'd stopped for sandwiches, snacks, and water since they had no immediate plans to leave anytime soon. They had a lot to talk about, and neither wanted to rush.

"This, my dear, is God's country, also known as Jones Knob. I've wanted to bring you up here for the last couple months, but something always came up." He joined her on the ledge, wrapped his arm around her waist, and pulled her back to his front. "I think I'd feel better if you didn't get quite so close to the edge, though."

"My tall, handsome prince will protect me." She peered up at him and batted her lashes. "Now, tell me what I'm looking at."

His chin rested on her shoulder as he pointed out certain features. "Here on the right is Whiterock Mountain. Below us is the Tessentee Valley. Somewhere here on the left is where Georgia, South Carolina, and North Carolina meet. I've hiked that part of the Bartram Trail, but dang if I could tell you where it is from up here." A turn of his head put his mouth at her ear. "Welcome to the top of the world, sweetheart," he whispered.

Turning her with him, he walked them over to the blanket and helped her sit. "I, uh, didn't have much of an appetite today, so I was hoping we could eat while we talk. That okay?" Guilt flashed over her face. "Nope, none of that. Now that we've calmed down, we know that we both were wrong." Dumping the sack like a typical guy, he separated everything, handed her a sandwich and water, and grabbed two for himself. "I'm not mad anymore, promise. But I am confused about what brought on your reaction."

She picked at the label on the bottle and avoided his gaze. When the silence stretched out too long, he lifted her chin and pressed his forehead to hers.

"Sweetheart, I'm not talking about you seeing me hug Wrynn. If I saw you in some strange guy's arms, I'd probably punch his lights out and ask questions later." That earned him a little smile. "I'm talking about this second place crap. Where did that come from?"

Her chest rose and fell as she blew out a deep breath. "Umm, well, I can't lie to you. We've talked about it before, a little. Sometimes, it just seems like, if you need to drop something, I'm the one who gets the boot. I know it sounds lame, but I can't help it. Liam, you didn't just blow me off this time. You kind of blew off my parents, too, and that left me scrambling to make up excuses for you. Not to mention, I was supposed to meet your parents last night."

She was so nervous, he could feel it. Her hands fluttered and jerked so hard, she almost spilled her water. When he captured them between his own, she peered up at him through her lashes. He braced himself, knowing he might not like what she said next.

"What happens if we get married, and when it's time to have kids, I go into labor and Wrynn needs you for something?" Her whispered words wavered, so she cleared her throat. "Are you going to hand me my suitcase on your way out the door to go help her? See, here's the thing, I can picture you as a permanent part of my future. I want that so bad I can taste it, but Liam," her hand rubbed the area over his heart, "I have to know I'm first in here. I deserve that, and I won't accept anything less. I refuse to be second best."

He lay back on the blanket and tugged her down beside him, wrapping her up in his arms. "Okay. Wow, I'm glad I asked. Ya know, I've been helping Wrynn so long that it's become second nature to me. Most of the things I do aren't really even for her. I love her, don't get me wrong, but I worry what will happen to the girls if I'm not there." He felt weighted down under his burden and tried to shrug it off. "The last couple of weeks, she's seemed a little better. Not quite so weepy. Not quite so needy. A little more together. I don't know if you've noticed, but I've been around a little more, and that's part of the reason." Her quick nod against his chest and her arms tightening around him made him smile. "The other part of it is because Mrs. Tidwell finally quit putting every bit of her energy into destroying my business. Since February, she'd singlehandedly run off over half my customers."

Elizabeth shot up off the ground, surprise mingled with anger on her face. "Half your customers? You have GOT to be kidding me! I just thought she'd been harassing Gramps and a couple of his friends. I had no idea it was so much more. Why didn't you say something? I'd a said something to that mean, old woman."

The fire in her eyes and the way she scrunched her face made Liam chuckle. He sat up and tugged her back into his arms. Right where she belonged.

"Whoa there, my fierce, little protector, let's slow down for a second. I know we've never talked about finances or anything like that, but remember, I'm a single guy who lives in his sister's basement. My overhead is low, and while I couldn't live out the rest of my life on my savings, in a pinch, it'll do me. I panicked at first, and then I spent some time stewing on it, but when I pulled my head out, I talked to my accountant, made some contingency plans, and found an investor in case I get to the point I need one. So, don't you worry your pretty, little head about it for another second." He gathered their trash and shoved it in the bag.

"So, let me see if I've got this straight." Her voice was so soft he had to lean closer to hear her. "You've been stressing over your business. You've been running yourself ragged between landscaping and working at the fire department. You're playing therapist to your sister and father to your nieces. And you're with me every second you can be. Did I about get that right?" When he nodded, she jumped to her feet and threw her arms in the air, shaking them to emphasize each word. "Why. Didn't. You. Tell. Me?" Her yell rang out across the mountain range and echoed back to them. *Tell me. Tell me. Tell me.*

The fury in her face. The anger in her voice. The rigid hold on her body. Her hair flying wild around her face. She was incredible, yes, but she was also hilarious in her snit.

Blame it on worry. Blame it on lack of sleep. Blame it on their fight. Whatever it was, Liam lost it. He rolled to his stomach, buried his face in the blanket, and laughed until he couldn't breathe. His quiet, petite, fairy-like sprite was so cute when she was angry, but he didn't think it would be smart for him to say that to her. At least, not at that moment.

"Oomph." He grunted when she plopped on his back. Being the smart man he was, he quit laughing.

"What in this world is so funny? Have you lost your mind?"

Her elbows dug in his spine, so he rolled beneath her, brought her chest to his, and then flipped her to her back. When she looked up at him, he lost himself once again, but this time in her eyes. "Yes," he whispered and kissed her sweet lips. "I've lost my mind and my heart. You have them now. Keep 'em safe for me, okay?"

She pursed her lips and blew out a sigh. "Let's just hope I do a better job than I did earlier today."

"Pot," Liam pointed at her, and then jerked his thumb at himself, "meet kettle. Quit trying to hog all the blame for yourself." He threw her a wink. "I'm not exactly an innocent party in this argument. I needed an attitude adjustment before I got to the inn this morning. Between worrying about you and Wrynn, not being able to sleep after my shift, a headache to beat the band, and a shoe full of hot cocoa," he wiggled his foot and paused when she giggled, "I was already in a bad mood. It scared me when I saw you crying, but when you wouldn't look at me or let me touch you, I panicked. And then when you lit into me, I'm sorry to say I lost control of my anger. That rarely happens, and I hope to God, you never see me that way again."

He rolled them to their sides and brushed her hair out of her face. Her sweet, innocent spirit reminded him how blessed he was. A future without her would be empty and bleak. It was time he told her how he really felt and what he wanted, no, needed to survive.

Her, with him, forever.

His heart near bursting, he stood, took her hand, and pulled her to her feet. With a slight tug of his arm, he led her to the edge of the knob. He swept his arm out at the view and hoped what he said made sense.

"Below us are mountains and valleys. Some days it snows. Others, the clouds hover low, or the sun shines bright. No matter what, though, it's always beautiful.

"Thing is, the storms can be scary. Snakes and bears hide in the brush. At times, no light gets in through the leaves.

"But most of the time, it's so stunning it takes your breath away. Seeing it all by myself is great, but when I share it with you, it's indescribable."

His heart thumped against his chest, and nerves tightened his throat.

"This vista is like us. We're going to fight and argue and have crappy days. That stuff's all a part of life. But what we have together is so stunning it takes my breath away. And our good always outweighs the bad.

"We can stand here on this ledge until the end of time. There's nothing wrong with that. It's safe. It's easy. Or you can take my hand, and together we can jump off the ledge and discover what life has in store for us. We'll weather those storms, gaze at the stars, and bask in the sunshine, and once in a while, we'll get caught in a storm, but we'll do it together.

"I'm a simple man, sweetheart. I don't have fancy words or grand, romantic gestures. Heck, I didn't even know this was going to happen today, so I'm a might bit unprepared, but here goes.

"Too fast or too slow, I don't care. It's not my place to put a timespan on love. I know what I want, Elizabeth, and that's you. Today. Tomorrow. Forever." He knelt down on one knee, stretched his hand out, and held his breath. "I love you, Elizabeth. Will you take my hand?" Sweat gathered on his brow, and his knees shook as he anxiously waited for her answer.

She stared long and deep into his eyes, as though she was reading his soul. A heart-stopping smile spread across her face. She grabbed his hand in one of hers, wrapped the other around his neck, and pulled his face up to hers. With her lips feathering his, she answered. "Liam, I love you, and I will gladly take your hand."

With hands and lips joined, they took a leap of faith, and their first step to tomorrow.

Together.

He tasted of

strong man,

bright sunshine,

everlasting love,

and

hope eternal.

Chapter 19

That night, as they sat atop Jones Knob, peering out over God's handiwork, something changed between them.

Something so huge, so all encompassing, mere words could never explain or describe.

When it happened, she didn't question. She accepted with an open mind and willing heart.

Once she took Liam's hand, they didn't stumble. They didn't fall.

They soared.

The fear. The worry. The anger. The doubt. Everything evaporated, blown away to nothing, as if they'd never been there. Love, trust, honesty, and respect swept in to fill the void.

Every glance, every murmur, every touch took on new meaning. The set of his jaw, the look in his eyes, the angle of his head, she read them all with ease. The soft caresses, the whispered words, the feathered kisses proclaimed love, passion, commitment.

This something turned the dial on *them*, and the static faded, leaving them attuned to each other.

She felt safe. Protected. Loved. More so, she was excited to envision their future, together.

The intensity of the clear connection with the man she loved was immense and beyond beautiful. The communion of their souls was so pure and innocent, and yet, so shockingly intimate, she struggled to take it all in.

They spent hours staring out at the vista, pouring out their souls, and embracing the promise of tomorrow. Nature's symphony serenaded them as God stroked a brush and painted an extraordinary red and orange sunset across the evening sky. As the night sky darkened and the stars twinkled to life, the circles under Liam's eyes deepened. He fought to keep from yawning. The stress of the last few months was catching up with him, and Elizabeth knew he needed rest. And knowing she would see him the next day, she convinced him it was time to go home.

She, on the other hand, couldn't shut her mind off as she tossed and turned and jerked the covers. His forgiveness was a gift she would treasure forever, and she hoped never to need it again.

When her eyes would drift shut, vivid dreams about the evening jarred her from sleep, and when she woke, she relived every minute in her mind. It was on constant repeat, creeping back in once the reel ended. Then, anticipation of her upcoming lunch with Liam took over, leaving a frazzled mess behind. Knowing she had a pile of work to do didn't settle her one iota. With thoughts of him clouding her brain, she rushed through her morning routine, sparing not a glance to her appearance, and a jumpy, jittery Elizabeth plopped down at her desk, hoping the hours would quickly pass.

For the first time since she arrived in Highlands, her mind strayed from her work. Spreadsheets and reservation calls made her want to scream. A clogged toilet in unit nine and lost keys to twenty-seven made her skin crawl with irritation. Wrong entries were caught and corrected. Coffee soaked a stack of invoices. She caught herself tapping her pen on the desk. Her knee refused to quit bouncing, and the rattle of paper clips when it hit the drawer irritated Grams *and* her. Impatience wasn't a familiar trait for her, but the minutes passed as slow as molasses. By the time eleven o'clock rolled around, Elizabeth was ready to run from the building.

Only one more hour until she saw him again.

"Baby girl, *that* is enough!" Grams snapped, rolled Elizabeth's chair away from the desk, and spun her around to face her. "What's got you so all fire jumpy this morning?"

Elizabeth brushed tangled strands of hair out of her eyes and took a deep, cleansing breath. Her mind raced. Her heart thundered. Her hands shook. Tumbled words tried to escape, fighting over which ones got to go first.

"He. Loves. Me." Exhilarated laughter bubbled out, and she twirled circles in her chair. She felt like a giddy school girl. "He loves me, Grams, like really, really loves me." If she looked in a mirror, the joy on her face, the sparkle in her eyes, the happiness coloring her cheeks, all those would reflect in her image.

"Oh, Grams, he was all 'take my hand and step off the ledge and forever.' Oh, my gosh, he was down on one knee." Her squeal echoed throughout the lobby. "It was amazing. I'm the luckiest girl in the world."

Silence greeted her. Deafening silence. After a few seconds, it became uncomfortable silence. She lifted her head and peeked over at her grandmother.

Elbows propped on the counter, chin resting on laced fingers, and an amused grin on her face, Grams stared directly at her. "You 'bout done, or you just catching your breath for the next round?"

Elizabeth pulled her lips between her teeth and pressed her fingers against them.

"So, let me see if I got this straight. The same fella who left you crying in the gravel also put that glow in your cheeks?" Grams lifted an eyebrow when Elizabeth's mouth dropped open. "Yes, I saw. I also heard most of the conversation. It's not like the two of you were quiet about it. Roger said he figured the two of you were smart enough to work it out on your own, so he wouldn't let me go outside. Looks like he was right." Her eyes softened, and Elizabeth soaked up her grandmother's love. "I'd say you've learned a good lesson. Forgiveness is a mighty powerful thing. It doesn't erase what happened, but thank goodness, love doesn't keep a record of when you're wrong."

She cringed as she remembered her disgraceful behavior the day before. "Oh, Grams, I hurt him so bad. To forgive that flaming shrew I turned into, he has to love me an awful lot. Wouldn't you say? I just don't know what came over me to act that way. I've never been like that before." Shame colored her quiet words. She wasn't as quick to forget as Liam was, but after last night, her guilt wasn't as heavy.

"I'd say you got bit by the green monster, Jealousy. I'd also go so far as to say you'll protect against it in the future and likely won't overreact next time. IF there's a next time."

The chair squeaked as she straightened and dug deep to go back to her joy of moments ago. "Grams, I floated in here on a big, ol' bubble of happy this morning, and you busted it by reminding me of the stuff I wanted to forget." Her face crumpled in a pout as she whined. "I better get it back before lunch, or you're in big trouble."

As if she'd just finished making biscuits and was shaking off flour, Grams dusted her hands together. "Well then, let's put this topic behind us, 'cause I'm curious about something else." A mischievous grin slid across her face.

"Should I be worried about that look?" Elizabeth squirmed in her seat. Even though she loved everything about her grandma, Tootsie was known to get a wild idea and run with it. There was no telling where she was going with this.

"Well, sugar, I was just wondering who dressed you this morning?" Grams scanned her from head to toe. "Don't get me wrong. I know young folks these days like to be quirky and different, but that getup you've got on is a stretch for you."

Afraid to look down, she closed her eyes. "Is it that bad?" she whispered.

"Mmm hmm." Grams cackled. "I know Seth gave you that shirt for Christmas, but where in this world did you find orange pants with ... Is that black cats?"

Elizabeth gulped in a deep breath, and with a trance like slowness, she rotated around to face the mirror in the lobby. Sure enough, in her hurry to dress, she'd grabbed the Justin Bieber shirt and a pair of Halloween pajama leggings. To make matters worse, her shoes were different colors, and her hair was a tangled mess. Her thoughts drifted back to before she left her cabin. She couldn't remember brushing her teeth.

"Oh, my gosh, Grams. Why didn't you say something?" she shrieked in embarrassment. "People have been in and out of here all morning, and you just let me sit here like this?"

"Sweet child, I tried to several times, but you haven't heard a word I've said all morning. You've been all up in that bubble of happy, and wearing a Do Not Disturb sign, to boot." She ran her hand over Elizabeth's head and down to cup her chin. "Why don't you go ahead and leave now? Maybe take a shower. Have a cup of coffee and a Xanax, though one might counteract the other."

"Well, seeing as how I'm meeting my Liam for lunch, and I sure can't go like this, I think I'll take you up on that offer." She wrapped her arms around her grandma's waist and gave her a light squeeze. "Love you, Grams. Thanks for taking care of me."

"Always, baby girl. I love you, too. Now shoo. You get on out of here and get dolled up for your fella."

Elizabeth took her Gram's advice and left. Maybe it would help make noon get there sooner.

Liam rolled over and blinked, trying to figure out what the buzzing noise was that woke him. After a long stretch to work the kinks out of his muscles, he wandered into the kitchen to fix coffee.

When he crawled into bed the night before, more relaxed and happier than he'd been in a long time, sleep wasted no time claiming him. He dreamed of her smile and the way she felt perfect in his arms. Things were definitely looking up for him.

With only a couple of hours until lunch, his list of things to do was longer than his arm. He propped a hip against the counter, took a big sip, and made his mental notes.

First thing, he needed to talk to his parents and find a good time to bring Elizabeth to meet them. More than enough time had been wasted. She deserved for him to show her off to his family, especially since she was so honest about how much it had hurt her that he hadn't. They would love her as much as he did. How could they not?

Shopping, a chore he hated, was next on the list. Maybe he would browse the jewelry store before lunch. Some might think it too soon to give her a ring, but quite frankly, he was finished with worrying about how others might react or what they might think. Elizabeth was a blessing, his blessing, and it was high time he showed everyone how he felt. No more running. No more hiding. No more worrying about Wrynn's reaction to his happiness. Elizabeth was there to stay, and as a permanent part of his life, people needed to get used to her being around.

He was shedding the coward's mantle and stepping out into the light.

A quick stop at Mountain Fresh for picnic supplies was easy. Chocolate would melt in the truck, so those were out of the question. Since he wanted to spoil her with flowers, a quick stop at the florist was necessary. He hoped they had Gerbera daisies. The smile they put on her face made any effort worthwhile, and the bright colors reminded him of her. Besides, if he was making it official and giving her a ring, things needed to be done in a certain manner. He planned to woo her until she didn't know what hit her.

A quick glance at his desk reminded him he needed to deliver invoices as he ran around town. Every penny was now more important than ever. On top of the stack of envelopes, his cell phone vibrated and beeped, and a light flashed on the screen. At least he knew what that noise was now.

Reliable cell service was new to Highlands, and he was still surprised every time the thing rang. Like most people he knew, an answering machine sat next to his home phone. He would admit, though, how nice it was that if there was an emergency, people could get in touch with him in a hurry.

KATHRYN M^CNEILL CRANE

The screen showed two missed calls and two voicemails. Now, if he could remember how to retrieve them, things would be great. Maybe he should ask Annie to teach him. After all, young kids were born with technology programmed in their brains. A few fumbled attempts later, and he found the access he needed.

The first message was from Mr. Huáng, asking Liam to meet with him later in the week to discuss upcoming jobs at a few of the family properties. The second was the grounds manager at a small golf course in Cashiers, asking Liam to find time to work a couple of canceled projects back into his schedule.

The phone slipped out of his numb fingers and clattered on the desk. His scrambled mind worked to process what he'd heard. Two of the largest clients he'd lost were asking him to come back. Their business equaled half his losses, money wise.

Wrynn had told him she would speak to Mrs. Tidwell. What on this earth did she say to get such results?

He flew into action, showering and dressing before heading around to Wrynn's front door.

"Wrynn, are you here?"

When he got no answer, his nose led him to coffee, and everyone knew Wrynn could be found anywhere coffee was. Without it, she couldn't function. If any coffee was left in the pot, he was better off doing all the talking unless he wanted her to snarl and spit at him.

"Morning. You're up early." He dropped a kiss on her hair and went straight to the coffeepot. "Do I smell bacon? Oh, you're making strawberry syrup. Pancakes?"

She didn't say anything, but at the early hour, he didn't expect conversation from her. No one would accuse her of being a morning person. His stomach growled, reminding him of the little he'd eaten the day before.

"I just dropped by to give you an update, but now, I think I'll stay for breakfast."

Again, she remained quiet, but Liam sensed a newfound peace

in his twin. He knew better than think it would last, but while it did, he wouldn't question her and risk pushing her back to her old ways.

"I don't know what you said to her, and really, I don't want to know. Well, maybe I do, but still, I got a call from two of my clients, and it seems they've had a change of heart. Looks like I've got work to do this week."

Ah, there it was, a spark of life in Wrynn's eyes. Something he wanted to see happening more and more.

He hung around for breakfast, helped the girls dress and get breakfast, and then gave them a ride to school. He was so glad to see a flash of the old Wrynn, and prayed it lasted more than a day.

Next stop, his parents. His mom, a teacher, would be at work, but his dad's shop was in the garage. Sure enough, his truck was in the driveway.

A burst of nerves hit him, but he brushed them off. If his parents were upset, and they would be, they'd just have to work through it. Even so, he was glad his dad was alone. Okay, maybe he was a little afraid of his mom. Once he shared the news with his dad, he figured his dad wouldn't wait to tell her when she got home, leaving one less thing for Liam to worry over. Her initial reaction, be it anger or tears, would be long gone by the time he brought Elizabeth home with him.

"Son, you gonna stand out there all day, or you gonna to join me for a cup of coffee?" his dad yelled from his workbench.

"Morning, Pop." Liam pulled him in for a sidearm hug and then sat down on the worn out couch in the corner. "Not sure I have time for coffee. Had a couple of messages this morning about a couple of the jobs I lost. Something's happened, 'cause they want me back. We've got to schedule a time to meet."

"Well, I guess Wrynn's visit with Mrs. Tidwell is bearing some fruit. Haven't heard about any more harassment, either. Maybe she'll finally leave my girl alone. She's got enough to deal with without that old bat bothering her."

Avoiding the subject he came to discuss, he told Pop about the flash of the old Wrynn he saw at breakfast. He was just as stunned as

Liam was. When he ran out of things to tell him, he summoned his courage. Maybe the coward's cloak wasn't as gone as he'd thought.

His collar tightened to choke him. A fine sheen of sweat popped out on his forehead. His clammy palms wouldn't dry on his jeans. He swallowed around the words stuck in his throat.

"Son, you all right?" Pop grinned when he nodded. "This wouldn't have anything to do with that pretty, little blonde you've been squiring around town, would it?"

The floor dropped out from under him. Liam's mouth gaped, and his eyes bugged out of his head. "What ... Who ... How ..." he stammered, shocked to the core.

"Seriously, son? *How?* Still clueless as ever." Pop's laughter bounced off the walls. "I've seen you with my own two eyes. You do realize I live here, too, right? As for who? Everyone. More than a dozen people have approached me in just the last two weeks. By the way, is your golf game any better than it used to be?"

He's not mad. He's laughing. Holy cow. I wonder if Mom knows?

"Liam, son, your face is still just as expressive as it was when you were a teen. Those narrowed eyes mean you're worried about your mom. Don't be. She not only knows, but she's dying to meet her." Pop joined him on the couch and put his hand on Liam's shoulder. "We figure there's a good reason you've been hiding her?" His statement sounded like a question, and concern filled his voice. "We want you to be happy. You know that. And since we learned Lara's back in town, we've spent a right fair amount of time worrying about you."

Liam's limbs loosened, and he relaxed into the couch. "I've been trying and trying to figure out how to introduce y'all without Wrynn knowing. I don't want my happiness to be a reason for her to stay in her dark hole. But now, it's too late," Liam scrubbed his hands over his face, "since I sorta, kinda asked Elizabeth to marry me last night, I kind of need to get this introduction business out of the way so y'all can fall in love with her, too."

Pop fell against the back of the couch, eyes wide as he stared at Liam. "You sort of, kind of did what?" he yelled. The look of stunned confusion on his face almost made Liam laugh. Almost. "You asked her to marry you, and we haven't even met her? Have you lost your mind?"

"Yep. Yes, sir, I have. Lost my mind and lost my heart. If you want to see 'em again, you'll have to wait until you meet her." Liam's broad smile split his face, matching the smile in his heart. "And I didn't exactly say the words 'will you marry me,' but that's what I meant. She's a smart girl. She'll figure out what *forever* means if she hasn't already." His dad's mouth opened and closed like a fish, and Liam quit fighting his laughter. "Now, I need to know when I can bring her to supper, because I've gotta hit the road. I've got some ring shopping to do. We're meeting up for lunch, and I'm hoping to find something before then and make it official."

"Son?" He poured his unspoken question into one word.

"I'm sure, Dad, absolutely, positively, one hundred percent, beyond a shadow of a doubt sure. She's *the one* for me. She is to me like mom is to you and like Tripp was to Wrynn."

Pop stared at Liam, searched his face for answers until Liam felt like a caged monkey at the zoo. He wouldn't be surprised if someone poked him or threw peanuts at him.

"Umm, Dad, you okay?"

"Give me just a second, son." Pop dashed into the house.

For a moment, Liam felt a hint of concern, but before he had time to investigate it, his dad rushed back in the garage. In his hands was a small, faded black jeweler's box Liam didn't recognize.

"Son, I've waited for this day for years. Prayed about it for almost three decades. If what I read in your eyes is true, my prayers have been answered." He rubbed his thumb across the top of the worn box and handed it to Liam. "It's not much, but it was my mother's, and in my heart, I know she would want you to have it."

Liam swallowed the lump in his throat and flipped open the lid. Inside the velvet-lined box was an engagement ring and wedding band. He wasn't exactly jewelry savvy, so he didn't know if they were white gold, silver, or platinum, which considering their age, he doubted platinum. What he did know was this gift was beautiful for so many different reasons. The biggest was it meant his father accepted Elizabeth, sight unseen.

Teary eyes met teary eyes, and the two men embraced.

"Thanks, Dad. I don't have words to say how much this means to me." Liam's voice trembled with emotion and appreciation. "You're going to love her, promise. There's no way you can't."

Pop huffed out a deep breath and cleared his throat. "I'll talk to your mom, but unless you hear anything different, let's plan on Friday night, just the four of us. I'm assuming Elizabeth knows about Wrynn's situation, so we'll put our heads together then and see if we can figure out how to handle her."

Some things never changed. One thing Liam could always count on was his parents' unwavering support. Since he was a young child, they'd always taken the time to listen and help him jump over any hurdle he met. As he grew older, he leaned on them less and less, but time didn't diminish the love they gave, or his gratitude for them.

Liam breathed a sigh of relief. "Yes, she's more than aware of what Wrynn's going through. I know I keep repeating myself, but thanks. You'll never know how much this," he lifted the jewelry box, "means to me. I never even knew you had this, but I can tell you that I know my Elizabeth will love and appreciate it more than anything I could buy her. This is, well, it's perfect for her."

"Then, unless something happens, we're all set for Friday. I have a feeling you've got a few things to do before this lunch, so I'll let you get to it." His work-roughened hand captured Liam's chin. "I love you, Son, and I'm so proud of the man you've become. If you say we'll love her, I know we will. Now, go on, boy, and get your things done so you can shower your little gal with all the attention she deserves."

After exchanging hugs and goodbyes, Liam walked to his truck, heart lighter, mind cleared, and filled with excitement. He was seeing Elizabeth again in just a couple of hours.

Elizabeth turned into the gravel pull off and parked her Jeep. Hooker Falls was another one of the places that she and Liam always talked about visiting, but never had time to go. He'd assured her of the easy hike and clear, marked trails, so she followed the signs to the backdrop of two of her favorite movies, *The Last of the Mohicans* and *The Hunger Games*.

After leaving Grams at the inn, Elizabeth showered, drank a cup of coffee, and played her guitar. Something about her fingers plucking the strings and creating beautiful music soothed her soul, and, Lord knows, she needed something to calm her spirit. Since the night before, she'd been on a natural high, so a few minutes of peace were good to help settle her.

She bounded up the trail, jumping over rocks and branches, and gasped when her foot hit the icy water. No matter how hot the day, the water was always cold and refreshing.

A bright red blanket covered a table rock, and on it sat a picnic basket and bottles of water. Beneath the mist of the falls was another blanket. To the side of it, she saw him at last, and her heart thumped hard in response.

The bright sun brought out the red in his brown hair. His strong, broad shoulders, so wonderful to lean on, cast a huge shadow against the cleft of the rock. In his hands, he held a bundle of vivid orange and red Gerbera daisies. He looked like a fierce Viking, waiting to claim his prey. The love in his eyes wrapped tight around her like a blanket on a cold winter's night.

He made her heart smile.

"You're here. Finally. It feels like it's been years since I saw you." He helped her over the last of the slippery rocks and folded his arms around her. The mist cooled her skin as his touch heated it. A gentle kiss completed his hello. "I've missed you."

Safe. Warm. Secure. Protected. All of this washed over her, but the most prevalent thing she felt was the sense of home. In his arms, surrounded by his love, she was home where she belonged.

"You look rested." She tipped her head and peered up at him. His appearance had changed overnight. The dark circles under his eyes and the stress lines around his mouth were gone. Tight muscles were relaxed. He seemed happy and peaceful, his smile light and easy.

"I am. Best night's sleep I've had in a while, and I have you to thank for that." He gestured to the blanket and helped her sit before handing her the flowers and stretching out beside her. "I needed that solid eight because this morning has been crazy in more ways than one."

"Really? Is everything okay?" Her eyes held his, and she caught flashes of something moving in them. Excitement? Nerves?

What's going on?

He grinned at her spoken thought, and she rolled her eyes.

"We'll get to that later. I'll start at the beginning with some excellent news." He brushed loose tendrils of hair off her face and cupped her cheeks, his thumb feathering over her bottom lip. "When I woke up, I had messages from two different clients wanting to rehire me. I have no idea what's going on because I haven't met with them yet, but I'm not looking that gift horse in the mouth." His eyes drifted to her mouth and followed the movement of his thumb. "These jobs have the potential to restore at least half the income I lost, so hopefully I won't have to take on the outside investor."

"Liam, that's wonderful. No wonder you're more relaxed." She pressed a kiss to his palm. "That will definitely make things easier for you."

"Hmm, us, not me," he murmured in a distracted tone. His hands tightened on her cheeks, and his eyes narrowed, as if he was searching for something on her face. "Definitely easier for us. Now my savings can go toward a house instead of materials and fuel. Unless you'd rather build. I'm fine either way. Someplace to call our own. Ours. Yeah, I like that." His voice was strange, almost like *he* was thinking out loud.

"Liam? Earth to Liam. Where are you?" When he didn't

acknowledge her, a curious sensation curled in her stomach. He was carrying on a conversation with himself, but she liked what he was saying. No, she loved it. Needing answers, she snapped her finger beside his ear, drawing his attention as he blinked. "A house?"

"Well, sweetheart, I guess we could live at Wrynn's, but I'd rather not. Of course, we can stay there for a little while if you want to build instead of buy." His tone uncertain, his fingers ruffled through his hair, and he shrugged. "You do want a house, don't you?"

"So, is now the time to explain just what's going on?" His perplexed expression made her want to giggle. Instead, she bit the corner of her lip and raised a brow in question. "If I know more, maybe I can, say, contribute an educated opinion on all these plans of yours."

"Oh." His mouth formed an 'O', and his tongue peeked out at the edge of his lips. "Yeah, I might be getting a little ahead of myself." A flush crept across his cheeks, and the tips of his ears burned red. "I knew I'd mess this up," he mumbled under his breath.

Oh, my word, he is soooo stinking cute. Look at those pink cheeks. Bless it, he's embarrassed.

His eyes narrowed, and his head tilted to the side. "Are you making fun of me, sweetheart?"

She clamped her lips between her teeth, wrapped an arm around her waist, and fought laughter with every breath. "Nope," she squeaked, and a small snicker escaped. Her eyes popped wide when he crossed his arms over his chest, and she lost it. Streams of giggles bubbled up and over, the light, happy sound echoing back from the rocks.

"Elizabeth." Exasperation tinged his voice. "Elizabeth!"

With her hand held palm out, she gasped for breath as her laughter slowed. "Sorry, sorry, sorry. I'm okay. I wish," she wheezed as she spoke, "you could have seen the look on your face." She gulped a lungful of air and grabbed his hand. "I promise I wasn't making fun of you, but honey, you looked so dang adorable, I couldn't help myself."

He rose to his knees and loomed over her. She read his intent and scooted back an inch.

"Liam Broun, don't you da—"

"I'll give you something to laugh about."

His fingers latched onto her waist and dug in, tickling her until her lungs begged for air and she was afraid she was going to pee. Somehow, during the scuffle, she ended up on her back, and he straddled her thighs and loomed over her, so when he stopped all of a sudden, she was looking straight in his eyes. Everything he felt shone back at her, and she was certain he read the same for him in hers.

"Your laughter is music to me. Do you have any idea how much I love you?" His voice was a quiet, soothing caress. Her nod earned her a bright smile. "You know? I believe you do. I went to see my dad this morning." He fumbled for something in his pocket and closed it tight in his fist. "Imagine my shock when he wasn't the least bit surprised about you. Seems he and Mom have seen us together 'round town, and were just biding their time until I mentioned you." His eyes softened, and he caressed her cheek with his clenched fist. "I'm sorry I haven't taken you to meet them yet, but I'm fixing that big mistake, hopefully on Friday."

"Liam, honey." She covered his fist with her hand. "I understand, I promise, and you don't have to apologize for it again. I get it."

"I know you do, sweetheart, and that's just one of the millions of reasons why I love you." He sat up straight on his knees, stretched his neck side-to-side, and cleared his throat. "So, while Dad and I were talking, it occurred to me that I may not have made myself one hundred percent clear last night." After swallowing several times, he tugged at the collar of his t-shirt until it stretched loose around his neck. "Wow, I can't believe how nervous I am. Could you sit up, sweetheart?"

While Elizabeth did as he asked, her mind raced a hundred miles a minute.

Was this …? Was he …?

Then her time to think ended.

"Last night, when I asked you to take my hand," he stretched his out, and she grabbed it and held tight, "what I was really asking was this. Will you take my hand and walk beside me, wherever life may take us? Will you be my yesterday, my today, and my tomorrow? Will you be my life, my love, my joy, my hope until the day I die? Will you, Elizabeth Marie Pittman, do me the great honor of marrying me?" He opened his fist and presented a ring.

Centered between two bands of white gold was a continuous circle of Celtic eternal knots. Nestled in the center of each knot was a small diamond, and set at the top was a larger round diamond surrounded by a circle of emeralds. It was obviously an antique, and quite possibly a family heirloom, but even more so, it was perfect because Liam came with it.

Her brain screamed, "Yes," but every muscle in her body froze. Her throat convulsed with her effort to respond. Her mouth twitched as she tried to force out the single most important word in her life. When nothing else worked, she finally managed a slight nod.

When she did, every ounce of tension leaked from his rigid stance. He slipped the ring on her finger, gathered her tight in his arms, and sealed his promise with a kiss like never before. He tasted of strong man, bright sunshine, everlasting love, and hope eternal. As often happened with those two, they lost themselves in each other, and the world faded away.

Until the squeak of a small animal and the tearing of paper drew their attention to their picnic lunch. Perched on the edge of the basket, two white squirrels wreaked havoc on their food.

Their eyes met again. Liam grinned. Elizabeth shrugged. And the kiss resumed.

A little while later, their stomachs reminded the lovebirds they needed to eat. It was, after all, close to suppertime, so they dropped Elizabeth's Jeep off at the inn. While there, they placed a Skype call to Elizabeth's parents and shared the news with her family. Keyna cried what she called tears of joy. Mike threatened a visit with his nine iron. Tootsie wept as she smothered them with hugs. Roger stood back, arms crossed over his chest, and point blank told Liam he wasn't good enough.

This started a good-natured argument between Roger and Mike because Mike felt it was *his* place to say that to Liam. It ended when Roger told Mike he still wasn't good enough for Keyna, no matter how many years had passed. Mike rolled his eyes, and smack dab in front of the web camera, he laid a long kiss on his wife. Keyna melted in his arms. Roger mimed puking. Liam, Elizabeth, and Tootsie laughed at them.

When asked about the date, Elizabeth's response was they hadn't discussed it, to which Liam replied with one simple word. "Soon." Laughing at Elizabeth's scrunched nose and narrowed eyes, he told her family they'd get back to them with more details, disconnected the call, and dragged her out the door.

"Sweetheart, soon." She grunted, and Liam pulled her close to whisper in her ear. He thought her little snit was cute, but he needed her to understand exactly what he meant. "Soon, and by soon, I mean as quick as we can get it arranged. I want you to be mine forever. In. Every. Way." Her eyes widened, and he grinned. Now, she understood. "The best way to avoid temptation is to either remove it or remove yourself. I have no plans to remove myself from you until I take my last breath, so that means we've got to remove the temptation."

She blushed to the roots of her hair, but quickly nodded her agreement. "Okay," she said, her voice weak and breathless.

"I see you understand me now." He lifted her into the truck and slid in behind her, and they headed to Mountain Fresh.

Pizza on the table and drinks in hand, their conversation turned to the wedding.

"You may not know this, but Wrynn and Tripp got married out

by the pond at Endless View. It's a beautiful location, and I bet we could sweet talk the owners into giving us a good deal for the reception and ceremony."

"Oh, buddy, I wouldn't be too sure about that. Have you *met* them? 'Cause they're crazy." Elizabeth giggled and smacked him on the bicep. "And there's this certain landscaper who works there. I keep a close eye on him, 'cause one of these days, I just know he's going to take off his shirt." She wiggled her eyebrows and grinned. "Seriously, though, that's a great idea. Lucky for me, my man's smart. And just so you know, by good deal, I hope you mean free."

"No." Liam shook his head and narrowed his eyes. "I'm not taking advantage of your grandparents by asking for handouts."

"Pfft, well, too bad, sooo sad, not sorry. They're my family, and to use your word, soon, they'll be your family, too. I can guarantee you they won't charge us a dime, and if we give them a day or two, they'll come up with the idea themselves. They'll be over the moon with excitement, and I won't let you throw it back in their faces." She leaned over and pecked him on the lips, probably trying to take the sting out of her honest words. "Now, if a certain landscaper wants to offer his services in exchange, shirtless, of course, who I am to argue. But I gotta warn you ahead of time, that idea will more than likely be shot down."

Liam frowned at the table, uncomfortable with the idea of not paying his way. Everything he owned, he worked hard to get. His sweat on the baseball diamond and basketball court provided his college education. His back and hard labor paid for his necessities and allowed him to build a nest egg. The only thing he'd been given was Tripp's truck, and he didn't *need* it. He *wanted* it to keep the memory of his brother alive.

Pride goeth before a fall.

The thought trickled through his brain. Was that his problem? He considered himself a simple man and made every effort not to be arrogant or conceited. Vain, egotistical people irritated him, and he stayed far away from their superior attitudes. Now, he asked himself if he was acting the same way, and his answer was a loud, resounding yes.

"Well, that's some conversation you're having with yourself. Of course, if you were me, you'd think out loud, and I would've heard what was going on in there." Her soft hand caressed his face, rasping against the stubble on his cheek. "Please, Liam, don't fight me on this. It's not worth it," she whispered and gazed at him with concern-filled eyes.

He gave a sharp nod and conceded the fight. "You're right. It goes against the grain, but it's not my decision to make. If that's their gift to us, then for you, I'll gladly accept it."

The smile she beamed assured him he'd made the right decision, and he would work hard to see it on her face as often as possible.

"So, I guess we need to check with them to see when's the soonest we can have the wedding there." He bit his lip to keep from grinning when she groaned. "Keep in mind we're in season, so we may have to wait until after the Fourth of July."

"Liam," she gasped, "That's just a little over a month away. Surely, you don't expect me to put a wedding together in that short amount of time. It's impossible. I need at least three months, if not more."

"You want me to go away for a while?" He wrapped his arms around her shoulder and spoke softly in her ear. "Temptation, sweetheart. I love you, and make no mistake, I definitely want you, but I'm determined to do it right this time, and you tempt me to the edge of my control." She burrowed her face into the curve of his neck, and he kissed the top of her head. "I'm going to need your help, whether it's six months, six weeks, or six days. What I feel for you isn't going to go away, and the one thing we *can* control is when I get to quit fighting it. So please, for me, soon."

She drew back, chuckled, and sarcasm rolled off her tongue. "Okay. Okay. Okay. I'm irresistible. I get it. 'Cause, you know, you don't tempt *me* in the least." She rolled her eyes and smirked. "So, soon. I'll get right on that, for the both of us. That way we can get to the good stuff." Despite the impish look on her face, pink crept up her neck and cheeks.

"Lord, you're cute, but you know you're not helping me in the least." Liam groaned and banged a fist against his head. "Get to the good stuff," he mumbled under his breath.

Elizabeth threw her head back in laughter, and Liam stared, held captive by the joy on her face. He had a feeling she would always be able to find a reason to laugh, to be happy, and to share her love of life with everyone blessed to meet her. As her sparkling eyes met his, his heart fell just a little deeper, beat just a little harder, felt just a little lighter, and he knew she would keep it safe for him.

The ring of his cell phone startled him.

"I don't know if I'll ever get used to this stupid thing, but that new tower sure works." He leaned up to pull it out of his pocket and read the display. "Hmm, it's my mom. She never calls, so I better take this."

Elizabeth gazed over his shoulder, and a worried look settled on her face as she stood. "Okay, honey. I'm just going over to the deli counter and check on Missy. I wonder if she's gotten any news on her next treatments yet."

His mind already on the call, he gave her an absentminded nod, and hit the button to answer as she walked away.

"Hey, Mom. Everything okay?"

She talked so fast, he struggled to keep up with her stream of words.

"Elizabeth and I are at Mountain Fresh eating supper."

"Yes, I'm sitting down."

"Mom, slow down. I can't understand what you're saying."

"What? Wait, say that again." He felt the blood drain out of his face and a woozy haze moved in its place.

"Did you— Did I hear— Are you serious? Wrynn?"

"Yeah, we'll be there as fast as we can."

Numb fingers dropped the phone. Trembling hands covered his face. Strong shoulders shook with silent sobs. Liam broke down in the middle of the café and cried like a baby.

"Liam, honey?" Soft, warm hands rubbed circles on his scalp. "You're scaring me."

"I'm okay, sweetheart, great actually." His hands muffled his voice, and he felt her lean against him. "But we've gotta go right now." As he stood, his hand latched onto hers.

"Then let's go. I'll drive while you talk to me. Okay, honey?"

Liam picked her up and whirled her in circles, oblivious to the grins and stares coming from the other patrons. Lifting her high in the air above him, he threw his head back and yelled at the top of his lungs. "Tripp's alive!"

Applause broke out around them, but quickly quieted to hushed murmurs. The town's grapevine was officially activated, and by that same time the next day, preparations to welcome home one of Highlands own would be well under way.

Elizabeth's mouth opened, her eyes bugged out, and then she grabbed his face and buried him in kisses.

"It's a miracle." He slid her down to the floor and claimed her mouth for a real kiss. "This is the best day of my life. You said yes, and my brother's come back from the dead." His arms tightened around her until she squeaked. "Now, let's go home. I've got a lot of introducing and catching up to do."

And then he glanced over her shoulder, looking straight into the eyes of his past.

"Lara?" He shook his head to clear the sudden cobwebs, and tilted his head to examine her more closely.

Something about her appearance was not quite right, but he couldn't figure out what it was. The heavy makeup caked on her face was new, but ten years had passed since he last saw her. Maybe it was normal for her now. As a cross country runner, she'd always been trim and fit, but now, she looked scarily skinny, almost emaciated, even. Her trademark long, black hair was dull and lifeless, where she once prided herself on its sheen. Her posture was stooped over, and every few seconds, a pained grimace twitched on her lips. Yeah, something was definitely off with this picture.

"Where?" Elizabeth turned and glanced around the store. "Is she here? What's she look like?"

"Right," Liam pointed a shaky finger at the woman in front of them, "there."

"No, that's Missy Case." Elizabeth grabbed his hand and squeezed it. "You know, Brittany and Grayson's mom. We've been helping her out when she's sick from her treatments?" She spoke soft and slow like he was a child she didn't want to upset. "You've just got a lot going on in your head right now."

"No, sweetheart, that's Lara Feldstein." He circled an arm around her waist and drew her closer to his side. "At least, I think it is."

His heart stopped as his mind settled enough to latch onto one prominent thought. If this was Elizabeth's Missy, then Lara was more than just a little sick, which would explain the changes in her appearance and the small, rolling walker she leaned against. But why the heck was she in Highlands after all these years?

"No, you're both right, but I don't think now is the time to explain things. I heard what you said about Tripp, and I know your family needs you right now. There's too much to tell and discuss and plan for." Lara's voice cracked, and her gaze pierced him. "Liam, we'll catch up soon. Real soon. Preferably before the day ends. What I need to discuss with you is very important, and as you can see, I've waited too long as it is. Come to the cabin when you're done."

Without giving Liam or Elizabeth time to argue or question, she turned and shuffled away, leaving two very stunned people in her wake. Only then did he notice Brittany and Grayson waving at them as they trailed behind her.

"Did that just happen?"

"Is that really Lara?"

"How the heck did I miss this?"

"Oh, Liam, what are we gonna do?"

Their questions tumbled out one on top of the other, and unfortunately, neither of them could produce the needed answers.

"Oh, my gosh, Liam. The kids—"

His ringing cellphone cut off her words. MOM flashed across the display.

"Crap, I can't believe I forgot." Liam grabbed Elizabeth's hand and led her out to the parking lot as he answered. "We're on our way."

He tasted of
strong man,
bright sunshine,
everlasting love,
and
hope eternal.

Chapter 20

T he short ride to Liam's house would appear calm to anyone on the outside, but Elizabeth's mind whirled up a storm. She wished she was behind the wheel to occupy her brain. Instead of concentrating on driving, though, she was sifting through memories of the past several months, trying to figure out how she missed such a huge chunk of vital information. The thoughts whirled through her mind like a smoothie in a blender. How those new developments would change the way they moved forward terrified her, because if . . .

"You okay?" He draped his arm over her shoulder and pulled her closer to his side. "I'm kinda used to hearing your thoughts, but you're awful quiet over there."

Startled from her musings, she glanced up at him. Happiness sparked in his eyes. A soft smile rested on his lips. His muscles were hard and firm, but nowhere near tense, whereas, she was a bundle of active nerves. Her insides jumped and quivered, waiting for the next thing to happen.

Oh, my gosh, how can he be so relaxed with everything that's going on?

His laughter filled the truck, and she buried her face in his chest. Yes, she'd done it again. More than aware of her habit, she pinched her lips together and curled a hand over her mouth.

"Already told you, sweetheart. You said yes, and my best friend and brother is alive. Best. Day. Of. My. Life. And today's just the beginning."

If she weren't on the edge of a complete freak out, she would laugh because, unless he was a master at hiding things, Liam didn't have the first clue.

She had a feeling Liam was in for a very, very, VERY big surprise, a revelation that would rock his world even more than Tripp being alive. Unless she was reading him wrong, Liam had no idea whatsoever that he was a father to two precious children, Brittany and Grayson.

Two young children uprooted from their home to chase medical care for their mother.

Two helpless children who watched their mother grow sicker and weaker every day.

Two unsuspecting children whose very lives were close to the point of an upheaval so extraordinary, years may pass before they recovered.

Was she ready for the responsibility that came with two grieving children? Was she equipped to help them navigate the new world they didn't choose?

And what about Liam? Would the knowledge change what he wanted? Of course, she had no way of knowing what he would think of his instant family, but what she did know was he was not one to shirk his responsibilities. He would face everything head on, determined to do the right thing. A flash of insecurity ripped through her, leaving her wondering if Liam would see her as part of the solution. A breath later, she calmed her racing heart, secure in knowing he did love her, and together, they would work things out together.

The truck stopped in front of Liam and Wrynn's house, and she was once again jarred back to the present. Having no idea what to expect on the other side of the door other than Liam's family, panic cackled as it set its claws in her. Opening her mouth to suggest she stay in the truck, the joy written on Liam's face stopped her. She refused to be the one to squash it.

I think I'm gonna puke. What if they hate me?

"You can't be serious. No way could anyone hate someone as loveable as you." He climbed out, and reached in to help her. "Wow, this is it, isn't it? I know you weren't expecting to meet my family until Friday night, but I can't think of a better time than now. Introducing them to my *soon*-to-be wife is icing on the cake."

She laughed at his emphasis on soon, but grabbed his hand to keep him from pulling her out of the truck.

"Honey, stop for a second, and think. Are you sure this is the right time for everyone to meet me?" When his head tilted and his brows furrowed in confusion, she pressed a kiss to his chin. "Don't you think enough is going on without throwing me into the mix? Won't my presence, our news, take away from Wrynn's day?"

Liam threw back his head and laughed. When he calmed down enough, he swooped her up in his arms, kicked the truck door shut, and all but ran up the walkway.

"Take away? Are you kidding me?" He shook his head and chuckled, his arms tightening around her. "Sweetheart, there is no way under Heaven you could ever take away from today's joy. If anything, your being here will multiply it."

Before she could respond, the front door opened, and an older woman stepped onto the porch. Elizabeth's first thought was to be embarrassed because Liam was carrying her. Nerves quickly changed to concern as she studied the woman she was sure was Liam's mother. Her face was pale. Red rimmed her eyes. Her hands alternated between fluttering and clenching. Elizabeth searched her face for joy, and found only anxious worry. Something wasn't right.

"Sorry it took so long, mom. You won't believe who—"

"Elizabeth, honey, it's nice to meet you, and I hate to throw you into this mess without the time for a proper introduction." She grabbed Elizabeth's hand, and her eyes begged for understanding. "I promise we'll get to it later. But, right now, Liam, honey, Wrynn needs you." She turned and led them inside the house.

Elizabeth heard a low whimper, but a quick glance didn't reveal the source. Then Mrs. Broun closed the door and pointed to the corner behind it. Bare feet, a white robe, and a curtain of mahogany hair were all Elizabeth could see of Wrynn. Curled in a protective ball, she rocked back and forth, mumbling something under her breath, oblivious to their presence.

Liam set Elizabeth on her feet, kissed the top of her head, and walked over to crouch down in front of his sister. When she didn't respond to his hand on her shoulder, he wrapped her in his arms and whispered in her ear.

Her head lifted, and her face was a portrait of misery. Wide, wild eyes darted around the living room. She grabbed Liam with claw-like hands and jerked him to her.

"He was here, Liam. I know he was here." She buried her nose in the neck of her robe and sniffed several times. "I know I always hear his voice in my head, but this time's different. I swear I can still smell him. Tell me I'm not losing my mind. Tell me he was here and I didn't imagine it." When she peered up at Liam, the look of despair on her face made Elizabeth's heart shudder. "Tell me it's not all in my head. I don't think I can take it if it's all in my head."

Liam's quiet murmurs seemed to agitate Wrynn instead of soothing her. He tucked her into his body, shielding and protecting her much as he did Elizabeth, and turned to his mother.

"How exactly do you know Tripp was here?" His mere whisper bled a lifetime of pain.

"She called me to get the kids, Liam, and I *heard* him tell her to say goodbye. I waited and waited for her to call me back, and, when she didn't, I left the kids with your dad and came straight over. *This* is how I found her." Frustration written plainly on her face, she knelt down beside her children. "I heard his voice with my own two ears. He was here. I'd swear it."

"Think, Liam, think." As he talked to himself, he dropped his chin to his chest and pressed the heel of his hand to his forehead. "There has to be a way to tell if he was really here." His head jerked up, and he stared straight at Elizabeth. "Sweetheart, would you check their bedroom for any signs he was here? I can't leave her like this."

Trying to remain as invisible as possible, Elizabeth nodded. She headed down the hall, but it dawned on her she didn't know which room was theirs. The sight of Liam tending to his sister stopped the question before she asked. From the little she'd already seen in the last few minutes, the bond between brother and sister was unbreakable. Once more, she felt the sting of guilt for ever begrudging the times his sister needed him, and wondered if part of her reaction had been due to jealousy. After all, the option to lean on Seth would never again be available to her.

Thankfully, the first door she opened was the master bedroom. Sheets covered the windows, hanging crooked over the rods as though they were thrown up in a rush. The bed was rumpled, and half the covers were strewn across the floor. Silver picture frames lay on a pillow, and towels littered the floor outside what she assumed was the bathroom door.

What exactly was she looking for? A thorough perusal of the room revealed nothing in particular, but the objects on the bed piqued her curiosity. Upon closer inspection, she discovered snapshots of Liam's nieces and sister. Yes, she was definitely the woman Liam was hugging after the parade.

She searched the faces for similarities to Brittany and Grayson. At first, they were vague, but the more she inspected them, the clearer the details became. Bits of Liam and Wrynn were woven in with pieces of Lara. Though age had changed each of the adults, once Liam was presented with the idea, no way would he be able to deny those kids were his.

A knock on the door frame drew her from her speculations. "Sweetheart, did you find anything?" His face was pinched with stress, and his hands were fisting his hair. "I hated to ask you to look, but she's really losing it this time. I don't know what we'll do if she just imagined he was here, so we have to find some kind of proof."

"Well, honey, to be honest, I have no idea what I'm looking for. The bed's a mess. Towels are on the floor. And these sheet curtains aren't quite what I would expect, but for all I know, this is normal." She gathered the pictures and held them out to him. "The only thing I really find odd is these pictures on the pillow. I know it's not much, but it's all I got."

"If they're pictures of Tripp, I'm not surprised she'd sleep with them. The sheets on the windows are what strikes me as off, but with the way Wrynn's been acting lately, who knows?" A crooked grin covered his lips, and he huffed out a laugh. His shoulders lost some of the tension holding them rigid. "I can't imagine what you think about my crazy family. I feel like I've known you forever, but I haven't. I've thrown you into an uncomfortable situation, and given you an impossible task, and you do it all without complaint because you're you. How did I get so lucky?" He wrapped her in his arms and pressed a kiss to her lips. "I hate to say this, but I need to take advantage of that for just a little bit more. I'll make it up to you, I promise."

Didn't he know she'd do anything for him?

Her arms tangled around his neck, and she snuggled closer for a short moment before she stepped away. She wanted to get him across this hurdle before she presented him with her theory about the children, and in order to do that, the search must continue.

"Tell you what. I'll check the bathroom. I assume it's behind this door, since these are here." At his nod, she picked up the damp towels. "You check in there." She pointed to the other door in the room.

The bathroom, like the bedroom, was in complete disarray. The cabinet under the sink was open. Clean, folded towels were on the floor outside the small linen closet. The shower curtain hung outside the tub, and a trail of water on the floor let her know it had been used in the last several hours. Nothing caught her eye as evidence of Tripp's presence, though. As she turned to leave, she noticed a trash bag on the floor beside the toilet. Hope fluttered in her chest as she picked it up and opened it.

The foul odor was the first thing she noticed. She fought not to gag and pulled the collar of her shirt over her nose for the next breath. A quick peek inside revealed filthy camouflage.

"Liam, I think I've found something." She twisted the top of the bag closed and ran back to the bedroom. "It looks like some kind of uniform."

Liam rushed out of the other door, his face glowing with elation. Something silver dangled from his fingers. "Dog tags. Found them on the closet floor." He grabbed the bag, threw his arms over his head, and shuffled his feet in a strange victory dance. "He was here. Let's go." He dashed for the door, and she followed. "Wrynn, he was here. He was here. We've got proof."

Like the day they met, Elizabeth slammed into his back when he came to a sudden stop, but instead of stepping back, she wrapped her arms around his waist and held onto him.

"These dog tags were on the floor of the closet beside a bunch of letters and other stuff."

Wrynn came up on her knees, her hands clasped against her chest. Hope radiated in her eyes. He stepped closer, pulling Elizabeth with him.

"And Elizabeth found what appears to be camouflage in the bathroom. Gotta tell ya, sis, they stink to high Heaven, but I'm pretty sure it's his uniform."

Wrynn snatched the items out of his hands, and pressed them close to her heart. The moment she touched them, peace poured over her. "Oh, my gosh, Liam, I thought I was completely losing my mind." Though the evidence of her tears remained, the wild look in her eyes drained away, and the tension left her body so quickly, she wobbled. "He was really here." She drew a deep breath and crinkled her nose when the odor hit her. Relief washed over her face, further erasing the signs of stress. "Oh yes, I definitely remember this smell." Her eyes blinked rapidly against a fresh batch of tears. "Oh, Tripp, why did they take you away from me when I just got you back?" A deep sigh reverberated through her chest.

Elizabeth stumbled forward when Liam dropped to his knees

in front of Wrynn, but his strong arm caught her around the waist and eased her down beside him.

"Sis, do you know who he went with or where they took him?"

"No." Her anguished whisper made Elizabeth shiver beneath the weight of pain in that one simple word. "We heard a knock on the front door. He told me to stay in the room while he checked. When he came back, he told me he had to go, but he would see me again soon. I didn't have time to ask questions, Bubby. He kissed me and squeezed me so tight, I'm sure I'll have bruises. Before my head quit spinning, I chased after him, but he was … just … gone. After a few minutes, I couldn't stop thinking that maybe I just imagined everything."

Liam's eyes narrowed, his brow puckered, and he stared at the front door, but looked as though his mind was a million miles away. Elizabeth started when he surprised her by snapping his finger, jumping to his feet, and tugging his wallet out of his back pocket.

"That Underwood guy? Could he know something about this?" He rifled through his billfold and pulled out a business card. "Let's give him a call."

"Randy!" Wrynn grabbed the card so fast, her hand was a blur. She darted into the kitchen, her mother on her heels, and jerked the phone from the wall cradle. Her hands shook as she dialed the number and waited. As her questions poured out, her sense of relief was so strong, it cloaked everyone around her. She stopped to listen and melted against the wall. Mrs. Broun collapsed into a chair and pulled Wrynn onto her lap before she hit the floor.

The phone clattered against the tile and the two women embraced.

Now that the panic had passed, Elizabeth took advantage of the situation and watched Liam as he embraced his sister and mom. The previous tension and stress was gone, and in its place was a joy that stole Elizabeth's breath. A single tear slipped down his cheek, creating a dark spot when it landed on his mother's blouse.

"Talk to me, Sissie." His voice broke, and he took a deep

breath. He lifted a shaky hand and brushed the hair out of his sister's eyes.

Wrynn's mouth opened and closed, but produced no words. She pressed her fingers to her lips, drew in a shuddering breath, and laid her head on his shoulder.

"She was able to talk to Tripp for just a few seconds." Mrs. Broun said in a soft voice. "My baby girl's gonna be okay."

The moment was almost too perfect for words.

His love for them was written in the lines of his face and body, and gave her a glimpse of her future. A man who treated the women in his life as precious treasure was a man who should be valued and held onto. No, he wasn't perfect. Neither was she. But they were perfect for each other, and in the end, that was all that mattered.

She finally allowed herself to relax and appreciate the life-changing moment with his family. A miracle such as what happened that day was rare, and no matter what would happen in the future, worrying about it wouldn't change the outcome.

He caught her by surprise when he spun around, dashed over to her, and, lifting her in the air, he twirled them in a circle. Beneath her hands, his body quivered with excitement.

"Best. Day. Of. My. Life."

She lost herself in his kiss, forgetting where she was and why she was there. He consumed every last fiber of her being.

Until his mother cleared her throat. The burn of the blush traveled up her neck and settled on her cheeks and the tips of her ears. Mrs. Broun and Wrynn leaned against the archway outside the kitchen, their eyes glued to Liam and her.

"Liam, put me down," she whispered. When he lifted her higher and gave her an unabashed grin, she glared down at him. "Put me down, or I'll choose New Year's Eve as the date," she threatened through clenched teeth.

Her feet touched the floor in an instant. His eyes bugged, and his mouth dropped open. She bit back a grin at his astonished expression.

"You wouldn't dare," he whimpered, a crestfallen look on his face. "Sweetheart, that's just plain ol' cruel."

Laughter bubbled up from her chest, and she swallowed it back. "Honey, *now* isn't the time to talk about this." Her eyes cut over to his mother and Wrynn. "Let's finish up here first, okay?"

"Wrong answer." He made a sharp, buzzing noise. "Now's the perfect time to introduce my fiancée to my mom and sister."

"Excuse me? Did you just say fiancée?" Wrynn raised a brow in question, tilted her head to the side, and swept her gaze up and down. Her inspection was so thorough, Elizabeth felt like a germ under a microscope. "Does this fiancée have a name?"

"It's Elizabeth." A soft smile crossed Mrs. Broun's face as she gazed at Elizabeth. "Liam, I never thought I'd see the day, but your dad's right. You've found her." She extended her hand, and Elizabeth shook it. "I'm Faith, and I'd like to be the first to officially welcome you to our family. Bill's going to be so ticked that I got to you before him." Stepping closer to Elizabeth, she held out her arms and rolled her eyes at Liam. "And I would love to hug you if my son will allow it."

"Sorry, Mom. Of course, you can." Liam's voice was gruff with emotion. He loosened his hold, but not by much.

His mother threw her shoulders back and propped her fists on her hips. "William. Russell. Broun. Are you going to let her go?" The angry look on her face startled Elizabeth until she caught the sly wink directed her way and knew his mother was teasing him.

"He's always been stingy. He never let me play with the good toys." Wrynn giggled as she moved closer to them. "You'd think we'd be used to it by now." Her voice was hoarse, and her face swollen, but a new light shone in her tired eyes.

"Oh, I see how it is. Y'all think you're gonna gang up on me. Here, you can hug her, but I don't think I'm ready to leave you two alone with her yet." Liam dropped his arms, and his hand on her back urged Elizabeth forward a step. "Sweetheart, take everything they say with a grain of salt."

Mrs. Broun tugged her into her arms and squeezed her tight.

"That boy. Keeping him on his toes can be such a chore," his mom whispered in Elizabeth's ear. "You have quite a job ahead of you, I'm afraid."

"Yeah, but think of all the fun I'll have." Elizabeth peered over her shoulder and grinned at Liam as Wrynn joined their circle.

"So, Elizabeth, did Liam tell you about the time–"

"Kitty, I'm warning you," Liam growled. "Don't make me have to go hunt down a spider."

Wrynn grimaced and shivered. "Ugh, then don't call me Kitty, and I won't tell your fiancée all the crazy things you used to do to me."

"Are they always like this?" Elizabeth asked their mother as the two traded barbs back and forth. She was enjoying the spirited banter between the siblings and was also relieved to feel not a drop of jealousy. If it were her and Seth, they too would kid and joke. Oh, how she wished he were there to meet Liam and give his approval. She imagined the two would become fast friends.

"Elizabeth." Wrynn's hand on her arm drew her out of her wistful musings. "I'm so glad to meet you, even under these weird circumstances. I feel kinda stupid ..." She blew out a harsh breath, and a crooked smile settled on her mouth. "No, you know what, now's not the time for lengthy explanations. And trust me, explaining all my crazy the last few years will take a while. Now is the time for me to say thank you."

Wrynn glanced over at Liam. Love for her brother was written in her eyes. "He's been the glue that's held me and my girls together, but I've always wanted more for him." She turned back to Elizabeth and nodded. "And I can tell that you're his more, and I can't wait to get to know you." Her fingers slipped through her tangled curls and toyed with the ends. "But the thing is, and I hope you don't think I'm being rude, I kinda need to get cleaned up and go get my babies. I just want to hold them in my arms, knowing their dad will be with us soon. I've still got a million things to figure out."

Liam nudged his way between them and pulled them close to

his sides. "You kicking us out, sis?" His playful words brought a radiant smile to Wrynn's face.

"Yes, Bubby. I love you, but it's time for you to go do something other than babysitting your sister." Wrynn inched up on the tips of her toes and pressed her forehead to his. "Thank you. For everything. Tripp says ..." Her whisper caught on a gasp. Her voice cracked, but her eyes glowed with happiness. "Thank God for such beautiful words. Tripp says his briefing is being fast-tracked, and he'll be back in less than two weeks. Until then, he can't give me any more details." She drew in a shuddering breath, took a step back, and grinned. "I've taken so much from you. Not gonna say I won't need you again, but for now, I *think* everything's going to all right. So, get on out of here, and go live a little for you."

"Love you, sis. Always have. Always will." Liam ruffled Wrynn's hair, kissed his mom's cheek, and then grabbed Elizabeth's hand and pulled her to the door. "We'll see y'all Friday."

Once they were buckled in the truck, he turned to her and grinned. "Welcome to my crazy family. If you're thinking about running, just remember that I'm faster and I'll catch you."

Chapter 21

E lizabeth was quiet on the drive back to the inn. Her head rested on his shoulder, and since he caught her yawning a couple of times, Liam figured she was tired. The day had been long and hectic. Truth be told, he was exhausted, but doubted his mind would shut off anytime soon and let him rest. After all, it wasn't every day a man salvaged his business, gained a fiancée, and recovered a dead brother.

As he pulled the truck into the parking area near Elizabeth's cabin, his headlights skimmed over someone scrambling off her porch, reminding him they still needed to visit Lara. When he hopped out of the truck and reached in to help Elizabeth down, a small body collided with the back of his legs.

"Mr. Liam, Miss Elizabeth, come quick. Mama fell." Grayson's breath came in rushed pants. "We can't get her up."

Liam brushed past them and ran to their cabin. As his feet stomped across the porch, Brittany threw the door open and stepped back for him to enter. His clinical assessment made his stomach clench and his knees weaken. Lara was sprawled facedown across the hardwood floor. Her left arm was at an odd angle, as though she'd tried to break her fall. A gash on her forehead dripped blood on the floor. Crimson drops mixed with foamy spittle trailed from her lips and splattered the collar of her shirt, and the blanket twisted around her body. Her eyes and cheeks were sunken and her skin was gray. His only clue she was breathing was the slight rise and fall of her chest. Each inhale screeched like nails on a chalkboard. Each exhale produced further bloody, frothy bubbles. If he hadn't seen her earlier, he wasn't sure he'd have recognized who she was.

Why she returned to Highlands months ago and hid from him was a mystery he didn't care to unravel. Her reasons were her own, and he wasn't the least bit concerned with them. Even though she'd once meant the world to him, she'd thrown him and everything he would have given her away when she'd left without a word. Any feelings for her, outside of his guilt, had long since faded. His only concern was to keep her alive for her children.

Please, God, don't let her die in front of her kids.

His training kicked in, and he dropped to his knees. Moving as though in a thick fog, he dialed 911, identified himself, and rattled off her stats. He rolled Lara to her side to clear her airway. Beneath his fingers, he detected a faint pulse. Her heartrate was slow, and her pupils were nonreactive. When asked for her medical history, he searched for Elizabeth and found her huddled on the couch with the kids, their faces buried in her sides.

"Sweetheart, what's wrong with her?" His voice was abrupt and professional as he untangled the blanket from her limbs and covered her body.

"Large B-cell lymphoma." Her voice was quiet and calm. "Recently upgraded to stage IV B."

"Do you know the affected area?"

She nodded, nibbled the corner of her lip, and glanced down at each of the children. When she gazed back at him, her eyes were glazed. He knew what she was going to say wasn't going to be good. Pain and regret flashed in her eyes.

"Lungs, brain stem, spine." Her breath hitched, and he knew she was thinking of Seth. "Pretty sure most if not all of her lymph nodes are involved."

Once he relayed the information and heard when to expect the ambulance, Liam closed his eyes, dropped his chin to his chest, and let the emotion come. Even with his limited knowledge of cancer, he knew stage IV was almost always synonymous with The End. Her family, if she had any, would need to be notified as soon as he could find out something. But right then, he needed to learn as much as possible about her condition, deal with getting Lara to the hospital, and find someone to care for her children while she was there. And in order to do those things, he would start with the kids and pray they could help.

"Brittany, Grayson, I need you to understand what's going on here." Two sets of eyes met his. The fear in their depths froze the words in his mouth. The firehouse in his small town doubled as an EMT station, and on more than one occasion, Liam was the person who gave bad news to the family. No matter how many times he did, though, it never made the next one easier. Even though Lara was still alive, all signs pointed to her not being that way much longer. "Your mother is very sick. In the next few minutes, an ambulance will be here to take her to the hospital. I know you're scared, but I need you to help me so I can help her." He rose to his knees and shuffled to the couch. "Do either of you know where your mom keeps her important papers? Medical records? Insurance forms?"

As one, they nodded and burrowed deeper into Elizabeth's sides, linking their hands together on her lap.

"In case there's a fire ...," Grayson said.

"... she keeps them in the trunk," Brittany finished her brother's sentence.

"Do you guys think you could show Miss Elizabeth?" He scooted back over to Lara, pressed two fingers to her inner wrist, and checked her pulse, thinking it seemed a little stronger. "I'd really like to be able to give something to the doctors at the hospital."

Both heads bobbed. They crawled off the couch. Brittany grabbed Elizabeth's hand while Grayson got the keys out of Lara's purse, and then led them out the door.

"Lara, can you hear me?" Her fingers twitched. The involuntary muscle spasm gave him a moment of false hope. "Lara, it's me, Liam." He knew patting her cheek would do nothing, but he did it anyway.

Nothing.

"Lara, Brittany and Grayson need you to wake up. I need you to wake up." When she didn't react, he ran his fingernail from the heel of her foot to beneath her toes.

Nothing.

His hands traveled up her legs to her torso, stopping to pinch and prod along the way. He remembered her being ticklish, so he feathered his fingers across her sides. Her lack of response to his attempts worried him.

Seconds after he heard the wail of the ambulance, the paramedics burst through the door and wasted no time assessing Lara. Elizabeth and the kids followed inside behind them. Liam met them at the couch and took a folder from her. Pulling his keys from his pocket, he asked Elizabeth to get the kids in the truck, and as Lara was loaded on the stretcher and pushed out the door, he gave the file to the EMT.

"I don't know what's in there, but make sure the doctors get it." He locked up and followed them off the porch. "We'll be right behind you."

His hand on the truck door, he stopped to take a deep breath, rolled his stiff shoulders, and said a quick prayer. Instead of finding any measure of peace, a bad feeling settled in his stomach.

While Liam had been focused on Lara, Elizabeth had spent the time examining every similarity between him and the kids. Any shred of doubt she'd had was gone. How she hadn't seen it before was beyond her. Her only excuse was her focus had been on Liam and their growing relationship. Losing herself in him had quickly become her favorite pastime.

Sometime in the next little bit, she needed to let him know what waited in Missy's trunk. When she'd opened it and seen neatly-labeled boxes and envelopes, her hands itched to tear into them. Hoping the answers Liam wanted were inside them, she'd almost brought everything in the cabin. Brittany handing her the binder clearly marked 'Medical' helped her to focus her attention and energy where they needed to be: Missy and the kids.

Time was critical. Having been at this juncture once before with her brother, she knew Missy didn't have much time. The signs her body was shutting down couldn't get any clearer to her. What happened after that was yet to be seen, and as cliché as it may seem, life as she and Liam knew it was going to take a drastic turn, and soon. She could only hope, when the time came, that the love and support she offered Liam, Brittany, and Grayson was enough to help them through the worst of everything coming.

The next few hours would determine a lot of things, the least of which was her upcoming role in the Lara/Missy saga. Stress and worry filled the truck to the point the air was heavy. Liam's grip on the steering wheel was so tight his knuckles were white. His neck was so stiff his heartbeat was visible in the protruding veins. She wished she could take the burden from him, do something to help him relax, but at the moment, Brittany and Grayson needed her more. Settled in the backseat between the two, she offered what comfort she could, holding the two trembling bodies tight against her.

Searching for something simple to occupy them, she convinced Liam to go past the hospital to grab takeout from Wendy's. After all, what kid didn't like chicken nuggets and a chocolate Frosty?

She was trying to stall the inevitable – hard hospital chairs, the never-ending wait, the antiseptic smell, the noise of the ambulance bay – but most of all, she wanted to give them a taste of normal in an otherwise abnormal situation. Having lived this very experience, she knew preparing them for what was to come was impossible. All she could do was be there for them, no matter how hard it was on her.

The kids remained silent as they picked over their food.

Neither had spoken since they'd led her to the car. As worried as she was, they had to be nothing short of terrified. She'd spent lots of time with them over the last several months. While well-behaved, they were also nine-year-old children, and most of the time, they acted it. What she wouldn't give to see them cut up and tease each other.

Walking into the hospital was an exercise in restraint. Elizabeth wanted to snatch the kids up, grab Liam's hand, and run as far in the opposite direction as they could go. Brittany and Grayson curled up beside her while Liam talked to the receptionist.

"Miss Elizabeth?" Brittany's voice was so soft and quiet, Elizabeth bent over and placed her ear level with her lips. "Is it time?"

"Is it what time, sweetie?" She lifted her arm and showed Brittany her watch. "You want to know what time it is?"

"No. The doctor in Georgia said it was almost time. Is it?"

Chills traveled through Elizabeth's body as if someone had walked over her grave.

That time. Oh, dear Lord, how to answer that question.

She took a deep breath, trying to figure out how to explain the situation, but she knew from experience, words carried no meaning at times such as these. No matter how she tried to dance around the truth, the fact was, it may not be the *exact* time, but it wasn't much longer.

Thankfully, before she had time to answer, Liam came back with information. His head was tilted to the side. One eye was narrowed. Confusion was written all over his face. She and the kids ran to meet him, and he led them down a hall.

"Nurse said it's, uh, a slow night, so she's already in a, in a room." His words were fumbled and slow. "Um, she's still not conscious, but we can go ... uh, go back and, and sit with her." His mouth pursed on one side as he scratched the stubble on his jaw. "Um, Elizabeth? Did you look at what was in that file?"

"The file? No, I brought it straight to you." Now it was her turn to be confused. "Was there something in there?"

He led them to the room and asked the kids to wait on the couch.

"The doctors are in with her right now. I need to talk to Elizabeth for a minute, so we'll be right there."

Brother and sister held hands, hung their heads, and slowly walked into the room. They looked so pitiful and so very small. Elizabeth's heart ached for them. When the door closed behind them, Liam moved so they could look through the glass and keep an eye on them. As soon as the kids sat down, he turned back to her.

"Elizabeth, have you and Lara talked about any of her arrangements? I get the feeling their father's never been in the picture, and I know her mother passed away several years ago, but surely she's made some sort of plans for the kids? Did she ever say who to get in touch with? Friend? Cousin? Anything like that?" He ran his fingers through his hair when she shook her head. His foot tapped a steady beat on the tile and his muscles tensed. "Cause I gotta tell you, I was shocked to the bones to find out she had papers drawn up a week ago where she named the two of us as her Medical Power of Attorney."

"What?" Elizabeth gasped in disbelief. "Why would she do that, especially me?"

"See, that's the thing I don't understand." He stared through the window, but looked as though he was miles away from her. "I haven't seen her in years, and you barely even know her. Why would she trust us to make those kinds of decisions for her?"

Elizabeth leaned against the wall, brushed her hair out of her face, and closed her eyes, trying to understand the implications. Thought after thought tumbled through her mind. *Why me? And why didn't she say something? She's had plenty of time to just ask me. That would be the polite thing to do. But if she'd asked, what would I have said? She knows I went through this before. Why would I want to do it again? Thank God, I didn't have to make decisions for Seth. Why did she do this?*

Finding herself responsible for someone else's end of life medical care certainly wasn't something she looked forward to. Despite the time she'd spent taking care of her and helping with the twins, their relationship was superficial. If they'd been friends for years, Elizabeth would understand, but for Heaven's sake, they'd met a few months ago. The only thing she could come up with was Lara must have been desperate and alone. Lara's reasoning behind such a monumental decision was beyond Elizabeth's ability to understand, but it looked as though the time for questions and answers had passed.

A warm hand gently squeezed the tight muscles in her neck. When she opened her eyes and saw the confusion and concern written on his face, she was sure it mirrored her own.

"I don't understand. Why me?" Elizabeth voiced the question they both were thinking. "It's not like she's my BFF," she quirked her fingers in air quotes, "and we've planned this all along. She barely knows me."

"Yeah, I know what you mean, but in a way, I kinda understand. You're warm and friendly, kind, compassionate, and loving. Your nature is to help and nurture. I'm pretty sure it's impossible for you to be anything else, and there's no way she could miss something like that. It's just who you are. But me?" He wrapped his arms around her and pulled her against him. "I'm nobody to her. That's the big thing that confuses me. *She* left *me*, not the other way around."

His chest heaved as he took a deep breath. "And here she is, storming back into town, just like she left. No warning. No explanation. No nothing." His arms tightened to an almost painful point, and when she squirmed, his hold loosened. "I just don't get it. She's been here off and on for months, and somehow she's managed to hide in plain sight. It's obvious she didn't want to see me before today, but now, it's too late for me to get the answers I need. I'll never find out what happened." His voice broke, and her breath caught at the pain in his eyes. "I'll never get the chance to ask her to forgive me."

"Liam, honey, we've not had much time to talk about all the crazy things that've happened this evening, but I need you to listen very carefully to what I'm about to say." She raised up onto her tiptoes, cupped his cheeks, and looked directly into his eyes. No matter what, he needed to find it within him to close the door on his past so he could focus on the future, because the time was quickly approaching when she would have to tell him the truth about Brittany and Grayson. "If Missy, sorry, Lara was upset with you or holding some kind of grudge over something that happened a long time ago, she wouldn't have sought you out. Trust me, I know how girls think, and there's no way she would have come back to Highlands if you'd ruined her life. So, you really need to get those crazy kinda thoughts out of your head."

His mouth twisted to the left, his nose crinkled, and his eyes squinted. She bit back a grin at how hard he was thinking over her words. Her deepest hope was that he would listen to the wisdom behind her words, and maybe finally quit torturing himself over his supposed indiscretions. How he'd lived with such guilt for so long was beyond her ability to comprehend. Knowing what a loving son, brother, and uncle he was, she knew beyond doubt he'd blown things to huge proportions in his head. No way he'd been careless or ruthless with Missy. He wasn't made to be that sort of person. Such behavior was simply beyond his nature.

And he's mine. All mine.

He raised a brow, and his lips curved in a smile.

"Annnd, I said that out loud." She flashed him a grin and shrugged. "Well, it's true, so why shouldn't I say it? And I also managed to draw a smile out of you. After everything we've gone through in the last couple of hours, I'll take it."

The light in his eyes dimmed, and she regretted her words for a second. Then something else dawned on her.

"Liam, honey, let me put it to you this way, okay? If she was upset or holding some kind of grudge or hated your guts, would she have named you her Medical Power of Attorney? No woman in her right mind would do something that important if she didn't trust you with every fiber of her being. Do you hear what I'm trying to say? You're the only one who still has an issue with the past." She flicked her hand toward the door and stomped her foot. Her patience was waning, and she wondered if she'd have to beat the truth into him. "You. Did. Nothing. Wrong. Why can't you get that through your thick skull and just accept it as fact and move on?"

His right brow lifted, and the left side of his mouth twitched.

"Don't you dare laugh at me, you rascal. I'm being serious here." She propped her fists on her waist and popped her hip. "Yeah, I can tell you're soooo scared of me."

His low chuckle, though sounding tired and stressed, made her heart take flight. Maybe he *was* listening.

When he pulled her to him, she rested her cheek against his chest and sighed.

"Thank you, sweetheart. I hear what you're saying with my head, but my heart's a little slower. I promise it's sinking in." His arms tightened for a moment, and he kissed her hair. "For the last ten years, I've carried this guilt and shame around with me, kinda worn it like a suit of armor. It protected me from letting anyone else get too close to me, and me to them." Lifting her chin, he gazed down into her eyes. "And then there was you. Heck, in no time, you'd hacked my armor to pieces, and wormed your way inside the cracks. Most of those pieces have washed away, but I need you to be patient until the others are gone, and I need you to keep reminding me, every day if need be, to just let it go. Think you can do that?"

"Well, I guess I can." She rolled her eyes and groaned, biting back a giggle. "The things I do for love." A yawn hit her, making her eyes water, and she covered her mouth. "Oh, excuse me. I think I'm feeling the effects of the last couple of days. Lord, please don't let me get the hysterical giggles. I do that when I'm overtired."

"Yeah, I'm 'bout wore slap-out myself. Let's see if we can get an update, and then I guess we need to figure out what to do with the kids tonight." He looked through the glass at Brittany and Grayson. "Any ideas?"

"Oh, I'm planning on staying with them at their cabin tonight. Their stuff and their momma's stuff's there. Poor things don't need anything else to worry about right now." An idea hit her, one of those lightbulb moments. "Liam, we still need to go through her trunk. There's no telling what we'll find. Think you can stay with us so we can look before we bring the kids back in the morning?"

"Beautiful *and* brilliant. How did I get so lucky?" He stretched his neck and rotated his shoulders. "Maybe we'll find instructions for the kids and her next of kin, things like that. It'd sure be nice to have some kinda idea of what she wants."

"Then it's settled. Let's talk to the doctor and get those babies home." Her hand grazed down his arm, and she entwined their fingers and pulled him to the door. And after the kids were asleep, she would break the news.

He tasted of
strong man,
bright sunshine,
everlasting love,
and

hope eternal.

Chapter 22

L iam rolled over onto his back, confused about whose arms were wrapped around him. When he squinted at the body next to him, he couldn't help but smile at the sight he saw. Grayson was curled up next to him. On the other side of the bed, Brittany and Elizabeth were tangled together, blonde hair mingled with auburn, still sound asleep.

His heartbeat doubled as his imagination traveled to the day it would be his own child or two nestled against his soon-to-be wife. The little cabin nestled in the woods. Picnics on Jones Knob. Family hikes and campouts. Maybe one day coaching Little League or Upward Basketball. Two things he knew for certain: one, he would never be lonely again, and two, Elizabeth held more than his heart in her hands. She also held his dreams. He couldn't wait to get started on his life with her.

Weak sunlight peeked through the cracks between the blinds. Lingering exhaustion let him know he needed more sleep, and a quick glance at the bedside clock told him the others did, too. Too few hours had passed since they'd fallen into bed.

Convincing himself to get up and face the day, he slipped from the bed and headed to the kitchen to see if he could find the makings for coffee and something to eat before they searched through Lara's belongings. He yawned and scratched his chest, realizing he'd forgotten to grab his shirt from the floor.

As the sleepy fog drifted from his brain, last night's events flooded his mind. When he and Elizabeth had gone back in the room to talk to the doctor, the initial news they received left them confused.

After learning how bad things would get near the end, Lara had signed a living will and had Do Not Resuscitate orders drawn up by her attorney. Because of it, their medical POA was a useless piece of paper because all decisions were already made. Why did she do it in the first place? If Lara was trying to make some sort of statement, neither Liam nor Elizabeth understood what it was. The whole mystery surrounding her left them perplexed and baffled as to her intentions.

All bewilderment fled as the doctor explained what had happened to Lara and what to expect in the very near future. The tumors growing around her vertebrae had finally cut off all neurotransmission, leaving her paralyzed from her ribs down. Fluid in her chest cavity placed pressure on her lungs and heart, wreaking havoc with her oxygen levels and blood flow. Last, but not least, the mass around her brain stem was beginning to compress, reducing her kidney and liver function to an almost nonexistent level. Her body responded to shutting down, system by system, by slipping into a coma.

Her limbs were ice-cold due to dehydration and slowed, sluggish circulation. Every breath she took rattled and wheezed in her throat. Her cheeks were hollowed, the bones sharp and jutting out in her profile, and her eyes were sunken into their sockets. Gone was the beautiful, long black hair Liam remembered, and in its place was a flakey, mottled, fuzzy skull. The veins in her neck, arms, and hands resembled crazy blue and red lines on a haphazardly drawn road map. And her skin, her once glowing, radiant young skin, was see through like onion paper and marred with purple and yellow bruises. To Liam, she looked everything like an elaborate Halloween decoration and nothing like the woman he'd first given his heart to.

A simple inspection of her proved the doctor's prediction of Death's imminent visit to be true. No way could her body take much more punishment. His words brought a quiet panic to the room, and Liam's heart broke into pieces when Brittany and Grayson, refusing to leave their mother's side, tried to climb in the hospital bed. Tearing an IV from Lara's hand ended their struggles and earned their reluctant acceptance of their leaving her. As Liam and Elizabeth gathered the sobbing, hysterical children, her heartrate slowed and the harsh gurgle of her breathing stopped.

Alarms and alerts blasted their ears. The doors flew open, and they were pushed to the side as several nurses ran in the room and rushed around the bed. IV lines and monitor wires were inspected. New bags of fluids were attached. The head of her bed was raised higher to relieve pressure from the fluid on her heart and lungs. Though the doctor had previously reassured them she was in no pain, Fentanyl was pushed intravenously. When all legal medical intervention allowed by her DNR had been done, the doctor examined her pupils, listened to her lungs, and turned to them. The simple shake of his head told Liam all he needed to know. He gathered the children in his arms, carried them over to the bed, and did what he would have wanted done for him. He let them say their goodbyes to their mother, and held them close until Lara took her last breath.

No amount of soothing strokes or words would take their pain away. He could still feel their bodies quivering against his, could still hear their gasping sobs echoing in his ears, could still remember the exact same reaction from his sister and nieces when they got word of Tripp's death. Too much for them and too little from him, but God help him, he didn't know what else to do.

Liam pressed his hands to the counter, squeezed his eyes closed, and dropped his chin to his chest. Slow, deep breaths helped loosen the tight bands around his heart and clear some of the pained fuzz from his head.

The soothing fragrance of coffee scented the air. The toaster clicked and bread popped up. Birds in the tree outside the window chirped and pecked at the bark. In the distance, a horn blew. These ordinary things signified another ordinary day, but not for Brittany and Grayson. Their days of normal were gone for a while, and all he could do was pray for a quick healing. They would never forget their mom, but as time passed, her memories would bring them comfort, not grief. Losing a friend who was like a brother was all but unbearable, but his mind refused to even entertain the idea of losing a parent. Yes, it would happen one day, but that didn't mean he had to think about it right then.

Warm hands snaked around his waist, startling him from his morbid thoughts. He felt lips ghost a light caress on his back before a cheek rested against him. The small touch erased his frown and reminded him of all the good things to come.

"Morning, honey. You get any sleep?" Elizabeth's voice was quiet and groggy. The brush of her breath sent goosebumps across his skin as her thumbs traced circles on his ribs.

The urge to turn around, to snatch her in his arms and run as far, far away from what was to come, hit him in a flash. If they stayed there, memories of the days after Seth's death would be shoved in her face everywhere she turned, causing her pain he didn't want for her. It was one thing to talk about the aftermath of death, but quite another to experience it firsthand. Yes, as he squinted his eyes and stared off into nothing, the plan to take her away from everything solidified. He would call his parents to come look after Lara's children, and he and Elizabeth would go somewhere, anywhere else but there. The coward's way didn't make him proud of himself, but it did give him a moment of false relief.

He twisted around to grab her hands, intent on doing just that, but stopped short when he saw movement out of the corner of his eye. The kids. His shoulders dropped in defeat, and a sense of shame washed over him. Elizabeth, Brittany, and Grayson deserved better from him. Fully intending to greet the twins, he glanced up.

From right outside the bedroom, turquoise eyes stared back at him. Brittany.

One good look was all it took for time to come to a standstill.

Auburn and mahogany curls framed a pixie-like face. Taller and thinner than he remembered, and her face was more rounded like Lara's than oval, but if he didn't know better, he would swear he was staring at a young version of ...

The vision from his past walked toward them. The bands around his chest tightened again. Blood pounded a syncopated rhythm through his brain. His breath froze in his lungs, refusing to release. Bright white spots danced in his eyes. Rapid blinks failed to remove the fog in his head. Sweat beaded on his forehead. Clammy hands clawed at Elizabeth's arms.

His brain short-circuited. At least, he thought it did, because there was no way, absolutely, positively no way he was seeing what he thought he was.

As reality slammed into him, his shaky knees gave out on him. He braced against the cabinet and prepared to meet the floor.

"You're– They're–" His mouth opened and closed, the sudden dryness choking off his words. Lightheaded from lack of oxygen, he slid down to the floor and grunted when something heavy landed in his lap.

Elizabeth gasped as she slammed into Liam's knees and fell against him. What in this world just happened? One minute, she was resting against his back, wishing she could sleep for another hour or ten. The next, Liam had become a whirling dervish before collapsing and taking her to the floor with him. Maybe he'd made himself dizzy with that quick spin.

Concern flared at the grayish pallor of his skin. His chest wasn't moving, and his face was frozen. Shocked, wide eyes locked on something over her shoulder.

"Liam, honey, are you okay?"

His mouth gaped like a fish but produced no words.

"Sweetie, you're scaring me. Talk to me. Please, talk to me." She cupped his cheeks in her palms, shocked by how clammy his skin was. He wasn't talking. He wasn't blinking. His body was as stiff as a statue.

What began as mild concern was quickly morphing into pure, unadulterated panic. Did she wait to see what happened? Call 911? If he'd had a stroke or an aneurysm, he needed medical help immediately. Praying she wasn't being foolish, she yanked against his hold on her arms, but his grip tightened, keeping her in place.

"Is he okay, Miss Elizabeth?"

The quiet, scared voice startled her, but at the same time, relieved her. She slumped against Liam's chest, waiting for her heart to quit thumping against her breastbone. When she could take a full breath, she looked over her shoulder at Brittany.

Yep, except for a few small differences, Brittany closely resembled one of the little girls from the pictures in Wrynn's bedroom. Now that she knew what had caused such a shocking reaction from Liam, the relief was so overwhelming, her tensed muscles eased, and her breathing resumed. The rush of adrenaline leaving her body left her feeling like a bowl of limp noodles.

"Holy cow, Elizabeth."

She tilted her head back and met Liam's eyes. Wonder and awe, and more than a little fear beamed back at her. Nibbling her lower lip, she gave a hesitant nod at his unspoken question and braced herself in case he was mad at her for not sharing with him.

"You knew?" His soft, shocked whisper teased the tendrils of hair on her cheek. "How? When? You didn't tell me." Confusion laced his voice.

Worried the children might overhear their conversation, she pulled his head down and spoke quietly in his ear. "I just figured it out yesterday when we were at Wrynn's house. Those pictures I showed you." A quick glance behind her let her know the conversation needed to be finished somewhere besides the kitchen floor because the kids were inching closer to them. "Let's fix them something to eat and then take this outside the scope of little ears. K?"

Liam closed his eyes and banged his head against the cabinet several times. When he spoke, his words were tinged with a trace of bitter. "Sure. Looks like I've waited almost ten years, so what's a few more minutes, right?" As soon as he bit out the last word, his face fell. "I'm sorry, sweetheart. I'm not quite sure just what the heck I'm thinking right now, much less what the heck's going on around here, but I do know better than take it out on you."

Elizabeth smiled at him as she traced the stubble on his jaw. "I would imagine you feel like a dinghy stranded in the middle of the ocean, but if you'll let me, I'll try my best to anchor you in place." She wiggled out of his lap and pulled him to his feet. "But first, you might wanna put on a shirt while I scrounge around and see what we have to eat."

Liam left to grab his shirt, and when he returned, they worked together to put a very late breakfast of scrambled eggs and toast on the table. Conversation was awkward and quiet. The kids spoke when something was asked, but Elizabeth knew they were still in shock. She couldn't help but wonder when Lara's death would hit them, and hoped she and Liam were strong enough to get them through the coming days.

"While you two shower and dress, Liam and I are going to go look over some of the things in your mother's trunk," Elizabeth said as she cleared the table and grabbed the keys to Lara's car. "And when we're finished, we'll figure out what we need to do next."

Her statement was met with slow nods. Brittany and Grayson pushed back from the table, and joining hands, walked to the bedroom they shared.

She ran her fingers through her hair, pulling lightly at the roots. So many things to do, people to call, arrangements to make, and she had not one clue where to start. An idea would start to form, and before she could fully grasp it, another pushed it out of the way. Making a mental to-do list was an impossible task with her mind so jumbled and mixed.

"They're finished with school for the year, so we don't have to worry about that right now. But Liam, they're too old to be sharing a room. We really need to think about getting someplace bigger so they don't have to. They're getting to the age where they'll want their privacy. When I was Brittany's age, I didn't want Seth to even–"

Liam's hand on hers stopped her ramblings. "Sweetheart, take a breath."

So, she did. Her lungs expanded with her deep inhalation, and her eyes drifted closed. She held it for a second, and as she slowly blew it out, some of her anxiety drained out. It felt so good, she did it again.

"Thanks, that was just what I needed." She peered at him through her lashes, worried she'd overstepped her boundaries. After all, he found out only moments ago, and there she was telling him what they needed to do. What if he didn't want her input? "Sorry for just jumping right in there with both feet. I know it's not my place."

Warm arms folded around her. "Well, I got news for you, little lady. If you think I'm doing this without you, you got another think coming." His lips brushed against her hair. "If I'm not mistaken, you'll be Mrs. Broun before too long, so I reckon this ... situation is something we need to talk about because we're going to be dealing with it together." He stepped back, grabbed her hand, and pulled her to the door. "Unless," he furrowed his brow and frowned, stopping so quick she stumbled, "well, unless you've decided this isn't something you want to deal with right now. After all, you've known for a little longer than I have, so you've had time to think about it. And if you don't, you know I'll under–"

"Now who's rambling?" Elizabeth giggled at the puzzled look on his face. What she wanted, no, needed, was to ease his burden and make him smile. "You know, you're just so darn adorable when you frown." A quick, firm tug on his hands closed the distance between them, and she pulled him down the steps and led him to the car. "Don't you just love those flashes of doubts and insecurities? The crazy things that run willy-nilly through our minds. The way we second-guess ourselves and the people we love? But see, my mind's already traveled the same path yours just went down, except I was worried *you* wouldn't want *me* there, that I'd just get in your way. Know what I decided?" She grinned at him as she wiggled her brows up and down. "I figured you could do it on your own, but guess what? I'm not gonna let you. I'm not going anywhere. So there. Stick that in your pipe and smoke it."

The tight creases around his eyes loosened, and the pinched lines around his mouth disappeared. The darkness in his eyes was replaced with a happy spark. The rigid muscles in his shoulders relaxed. Right before her eyes, the tension he'd held on to since Grayson had found them last night drained away.

And the best part was when his lips met hers in a firm, quick kiss. It would seem her Liam was making his way back to her. Now to figure out how to keep him there with her.

"Not gonna lie, sweetheart," his radiant smile reached straight to his eyes, "I didn't even know how much I needed to hear those words. How you could put up with someone as stupid and knuckleheaded as me is beyond my comprehension, but you said it, and I'm holding you to it. You, my little wife-to-be, are stuck with me."

"And you think I'm going to argue with you?" Relief flooded through her. She laughed, releasing the rest of the stress of the last few days. "Not gonna happen, buster. Knuckleheaded, I totally get, but why, pray tell, do you think you're stupid?"

"Elizabeth, honey, did you see how much she looked like me? Like Wrynn and the girls? How the heck did I miss something so obvious? Geesh, I mean, over the last several months, I've spent more than a little time with them, and I didn't have a clue. Not. One. Clue. So yeah, stupid or blind … or something." Liam's sigh was filled with regret. "How on God's green earth did I miss it? It's not like the signs weren't right there in my face." His cheeks reddened and his eyes flashed. "I'm scared and confused, but most of all, I'm mad. Mad at her for keeping such a huge secret from me. Mad at her for wasting time I could have spent with them, getting to know them. Mad at her for dying, cause now I can't yell at her or ask questions.

But most of all, I'm mad at myself for not realizing sooner that those two sweet children in there are my own flesh and blood.

"They think that they're all alone now, and it's my job to break the news to them that they're not, and I have no idea how to do that. Do I just pop up and say, 'Hey, I know your mom just died, but surprise! I'm your Dad!'?" The more he spoke, the more sarcastic his words became. "Or how 'bout, 'Y'all don't have to call me Mr. Liam anymore. Just call me Dad.'? Think one of those will work? Cause I got tell ya, I'm lost here. Got no idea whatsoever how to handle this situation. What do I have to offer them? Nothing, that's what. And sweetheart, what if they hate me? What'll I do if that happens?"

As if. Elizabeth couldn't decide if she was amused or irritated at him. He had no idea just how loveable he was, the stupid man. Sure, he was nervous and anxious, but seriously?

Nope, she was going with irritated. Her eyes closed as she drew in a deep breath.

One. Two. Three. Fo–

"Um, why are you counting?"

"Don't interrupt me. Four. Five. Six. Seven." When he tapped her on the shoulder, she glared at him through narrowed eyes. "Eight. Nine. Ten. Okay, I'm pretty sure I need to keep going, but we're running short on time right now." She pressed a button on the remote and the trunk popped open. "You, my dear, are being ridiculous." Without waiting for him to help, she sorted through the boxes and started shoving them in his arms, lecturing him as she worked. "By getting you, they're also gaining grandparents, and an aunt, and cousins … not to mention me. Those kids have lived in several different places in their short lives, so you'll also be providing stability. After leaving what they know and losing the only family they think they have, you'll be giving them love and family and a place to live. That's huge, Liam. Huge. Okay. I think that's it." With the last one in her hand, she slammed the truck and turned to him.

"That may be a good thing." He peeked around the boxes stacked higher than his head and grinned at her.

"Oops. Mighta gotten a little carried away." She stood on her tiptoes to grab the top box, but he backed away from her.

"I got this. Where do you want 'em? Your cabin or theirs?"

She wasn't sure how he was going to react to her next suggestion, but she wanted to remind him of the people who loved and supported him. He needed to understand he wouldn't have to go through everything by himself.

"I'm thinking neither." When he tilted his head and furrowed his brow in confusion, she pushed back her uncertainty and forged ahead. "No, I think we should put everything but the one marked 'Legal' in your truck. Then, we need to go through it and get as much done as we can toward making funeral arrangements. After all that's finished, we should load up the kids and head to your place or your parents' house. I'm pretty sure Brittany and Grayson could use a change of scenery by then. Whatcha think?"

She guessed, since he headed straight for the truck without another word, he agreed with her.

"Thanks."

Confused, she stopped on the bottom step and looked over her shoulder. "For what?"

"For knowing what I needed. For making me laugh. For sticking by me. For giving me the strength to get through this." His smile lit his eyes. "For being you. For loving me. Need I go on?"

"Nope, I'm pretty sure that's enough for right now. Just as long as you know how lucky you are." The love on his face wrapped around her like a fuzzy blanket. "We'll get through this, honey. I promise."

Yes, the days ahead were going to be difficult, but they would make it because they had each other to lean on for support. What they had was worth every hard time to come, no matter the fight or struggle.

The easy part was finished, and there was no way the kids wouldn't love him. She just hoped whatever Lara left behind answered some of Liam's questions.

Or his heart might never find true peace.

He tasted of
strong man,
bright sunshine,
everlasting love,
and
h o p e   e t e r n a l .

Chapter 23

"I can't wait to get this monkey suit off." For the first time in days, Liam plopped down on *his* couch in *his* home and loosened the tie around his neck. Since the kids were resting on his bed, he was out of luck. Long accustomed to jeans, t-shirts, work boots, and flannel, he'd never quite felt comfortable in a suit. Head falling to the cushion behind him, he closed his eyes and rested.

Nights with little sleep left his eyes red, swollen, and gritty. He was so tired, his bones ached. His skin was twitchy with nerves and too much caffeine. If pressed, he'd swear his scalp was crawling with critters. The last few days were catching up to him. The fact that his brain wouldn't shut off didn't help the situation at all.

When he and Elizabeth had walked back into the cabin, – *Wow, was it really just three days ago?* – the kids were on the couch, waiting for them. Shock glazed their eyes, and the fear around them was so thick, Liam choked on it. At that exact moment, he realized just what was at stake, and put his own concerns, which paled compared to theirs, to rest. Whatever he learned from what Lara had left behind would have to be enough. He would make sure of it.

Because *his* children – and he marveled at how fast he accepted that as fact – were what was important. What surprised him most, though, was how fast his genuine like for them was evolving into love. He vowed to do everything in his power to make the difficult transition as fast and as easy as possible for them, and put his anger at their mom behind him.

Thanks to Lara's immaculate organization, within minutes of opening the box, Liam knew which funeral home she wanted to use, who to call about her memorial stone, and the name of her attorney. After looking at the complete picture, he realized she wanted to be laid to rest in Highlands because she'd known he would never leave his family and home.

While Elizabeth took the kids to feed the fish in the pond, Liam made the necessary calls. Because she'd known her death was imminent and had prepared for it, he had very few arrangements to make. Less than an hour later, the date and time had been set for her service, the details finalized for the delivery of her cremation niche, and an appointment set with the attorney for the reading of the will, among other things. One great thing about small town life was, though everyday things moved at a much slower place, the willingness of others to rush to help when a loved one passed.

Her planning was methodical, almost clinical and cold. No detail, other than her date of death, was left uncovered. From what he could tell, she'd completed all the arrangement in the three weeks since she returned from her last treatments.

Maybe she was trying to make things easier for the kids. That, he could understand. Unfortunately, his mind didn't stop at that thought.

Maybe she wasn't the sweet, shy girl he remembered from his past. He had no idea what her life had been like for the last decade, but seriously, how could she not let him know? How could she hide this from him as though having children wasn't important?

Maybe she'd hated him as much as he'd hated himself for years. He'd always thought he'd done something to hurt her and drive her away. Was this how she paid him back?

Of course, she would show up when he'd finally let go of the self-loathing and guilt and found someone who brought joy into his life. Maybe she knew he was finally happy and was trying to sabotage his new relationship.

Maybe. Maybe. Maybe. Those could go on for days.

Whatever else, one thing he knew without doubt: her timing could have been better by at least a few days.

He fought back a brief flash of anger, knowing that, regardless of how he felt, nothing more could be done. She'd waited too long to approach him, and now it was too late. Recalling his vow to put it behind him, he talked himself down and changed the course of his thoughts. His happiness was waiting for him at the pond.

Not wanting to miss another minute with his new family, he walked out to the water. Where he hoped for some sort of laughter, a worrying silence greeted him. His concern evaporated when he saw everyone huddled together on the dock, sound asleep. Though he'd accepted the kids were his, and even felt the beginnings of love, the sight of them tangled around and entwined with Elizabeth did strange things to his heart.

There on the weathered, battered wood was everything he'd ever wanted. His family. His own slice of Heaven. His tomorrow.

And recognizing the gift for what it was, made it easier to forget his anger at Lara and made him hopeful he might be able to forgive her someday soon.

Later in the evening, the not so fun part of parenting appeared. No matter what he or Elizabeth said or did, nothing made the children happy. They fussed and grumbled through supper. Brittany refused to eat and threw her food in the trash. When she burst into tears and ran to the bedroom, Grayson squatted outside the door, taunting and teasing her over nothing and everything. That led to her tackling him to the floor, and the fun began. In the matter of seconds before Liam and Elizabeth forced them apart, hair was pulled, ribs elbowed, and shins kicked. Both were snotty, blubbering messes.

Holding the squirming, wiggly boy tight against his chest, Liam tried to get a better grip before Grayson slipped out of his arms.

Poor Elizabeth wasn't faring much better with Brittany fighting against her.

"Stop it. Right. Now!" His frustrated yell was sharp with irritation, causing them to cry harder. If this was his first true challenge at being a parent, he was certain he'd just failed.

Until Grayson dove for Brittany, wrapped her in his arms, and dropped to the floor. Rocking her back and forth, he held her gently and whispered, "I'm sorry, Sissie," over and over until she cried herself to sleep.

Realizing they were as exhausted as he was made their outburst more understandable. It also drove home the fact he had a lot to learn, and only a little time to do it.

"Bless their hearts, these babies are plumb worn out." Elizabeth sat down beside them and pulled Brittany into her arms. Grayson leaned against her shoulder. "I think it'd be good if we all got ready for bed. Don't know about you guys, but I could use a good night's sleep."

When Grayson nodded, his eyes fluttering shut, Liam helped him to his feet, picked Brittany up, and reached down for Elizabeth. To say the last twenty-four hours drained them would be a gross understatement. Too tired to do anything more than brush their teeth, they crawled under the covers, and within moments, were sound asleep.

The following morning, the kids seemed more like robots than children. Their movements were stiff and their voices hollow. They spoke when spoken to, but rarely raised their gaze from the floor. He wondered if learning of his relationship to them would make things better or worse, but because they'd slept late, they were already pressed to make their appointments on time.

They went by the funeral home to meet with the director, Leon Schultz. When Liam introduced the kids as Lara's children, Leon looked back and forth between them and Liam. His eyes widened in shock, surprising Liam at how his old friend saw in an instant what Liam himself had missed.

"They ... You ... Lara?" His mouth opened and closed as he clearly searched for words.

The quick nod Liam sent Leon's way seemed to convey both his yes and his request to discuss it later because Leon dropped the topic. He was still trying to come up with the best way to let Brittany and Grayson know he was their father.

After explaining to them that Lara wished to be cremated, Leon helped them choose the urn which would hold her ashes. Before they left, arrangements were made to meet the next afternoon at the cemetery.

Their next stop was the florist where Brittany and Grayson chose flowers to place on their mother's niche. Liam hoped for some sort of emotion when he asked about Lara's favorite flowers, but was disappointed when he received nothing more than a mumbled reply.

His final attempt to break through their indifference was head to Mountain Fresh. A milkshake always worked on his nieces, but no such luck with them. Nothing seemed to break through to them, and shortly after returning to the cabin, everyone went to bed.

Something warm pressed against his leg. Soft fingers threaded through his hair, pulling his mind from the memories. The soothing hand felt so good, he slid down and put his head in Elizabeth's lap.

"Mmm, that feels great, sweetheart." A huge yawn made his jaw pop and his eyes water. "You're gonna put me to sleep."

"Honey, the kids are napping. Why don't you go lay down while I scrounge up something to eat? A little rest'll do you good."

"Nah, I just needed to rest my eyes for a minute." Liam glanced up to see his favorite smile. "What I wouldn't give to be able to just call and get a pizza delivered right about now. So," he paused to remember what his cabinets and fridge held, "I think I've got chicken nuggets and fries, maybe a frozen pizza or two, and probably some soup, but I'm pretty sure any produce I might have is bad by now. Let's go see what we can come up with."

He stood and helped her to her feet, and together, they explored the kitchen. When he realized how bare his cupboards were, he apologized and explained he ate with his sister and nieces most of the time.

"Tell ya what, we'll give the kids another hour or so to sleep, and then we'll head into town and grab a bite." He drew her back to the couch, prepared to snuggle for the next little while as they talked. Nothing like having built in chaperones. "So, I've been thinking. Now that we've got the memorial service out of the way, I need to let the kids know I'm their father. It's probably also a good time to let them know we're getting married." He scrunched his nose and shivered. "Oh, the wicked stepmother. You've got big shoes to fill, my dear." Laughter danced in his voice.

"Yeah, about that." She stared over his shoulder. Her mouth twisted to the side, and her brows furrowed. "We kinda need to talk about things."

His breath stopped in his chest. Every muscle in his body froze. She'd changed her mind. He knew it was too much to ask her to take on a readymade family, but after her speech a few days ago, he honestly thought she was willing to take them all on at one time. Pain such as he'd never felt jolted through his heart.

"You ... You've ch-changed your ..." He struggled to speak around the lump of fear lodged in his throat.

Panicked eyes met his. She grabbed his cheeks and shook his head side-to-side.

"Lose that idea right now, buster." Her lips met his for a second before she pressed her forehead to his and closed her eyes. "In no way have I changed my mind, and I've a good mind to kick your tuchus for even thinking such a thing."

Relief flooded through him, and he took a deep breath to calm his heart.

"So, to quote you, I've been thinking." When he narrowed his eyes, hers lit with laughter. "We may have a problem."

"Yeeeesss?" he questioned, confused at the direction the conversation was taking.

"So, when I was talking to Momma and Daddy yesterday and telling them about everything that's happened in the last couple of days …" She took a deep breath and shook her hands. If he touched them, he knew her palms would be damp. "They know things have been crazy, crazy, and um, we're both definitely in over our heads and coping the best we can." A blush stained her cheeks and Liam bit back a grin at her discomfort. "The thing is … Well, the thing is, they're not so happy about us practically living together. 'Even with the kids here to chaperone'." Her voice dropped low to mimic her father. The pink tint on her face turned red and crept down her throat. "It's not that they don't trust you, it's just, well, um, I'm their baby girl. They say I need to go back to the inn. Alone." She clenched her eyes closed and made a sound deep in her throat.

"Did you just growl?" Liam couldn't hold back the chuckle. When her eyes popped open, he slapped one hand over his mouth, and grabbed her hand with the other. Sure enough, he was right. Her palms were as slick as a greased pig.

"Fine. I don't know why I'm so nervous." She squared her shoulders and looked him straight in the eyes. "Heck, I'll just spit it out. Momma and Daddy are coming up tomorrow to, and I quote, 'check out this situation.' They want to meet the kids and spend a little time with them. Knowing my parents, they'll spoil Brittany and Grayson rotten. But Liam, I kinda need to warn you that, between Momma and Grams, you should seriously be prepared for some not so subtle pressure."

Her embarrassment and uncertainty made her even more beautiful. He opened his mouth to tell her, but stopped when she leaned away from him.

"And … Daddy maaayy have said something about beating you with his nine iron?" She tilted her head to the side and nibbled her lip. "But we both know he's full of it." When she finished, she melted against the couch cushion, as if relieved to be finished.

"Okay, I can handle that. And if you think about it, their coming here to confront me isn't so strange to imagine. Seriously, if I had a daughter –" Sitting straight up in surprise, his eyes flared as it hit him once again. A euphoric feeling rose in his chest. "Holy cow, I *have* a daughter. It feels so weird to say that." He stared out the window as he tried to organize the clown parade of exciting thoughts rattling around in his brain. "They're right, though. Even though our situation is different, neither of us was raised this way. Is this the example we want to set for our kids? Nah, probably not, so we'll have to fix it.

"So, you need to have your parents bring your birth certificate and, just to be on the safe side, your social security card. I'm sure Mom knows where mine are at, so that shouldn't be any problem. And I guess this means we need to make a trip to Franklin first thing Monday. That'll give us next week to look at places to rent. If we find something we like, Zack and Ash can help us move what little stuff we have. Then once we're a little more settled, we'll figure out a solid long term plan.

"And then I guess you women will come up with a thousand things you need to do before next weekend. Ugh, flowers and cakes and dresses. I remember all that stuff Mom and Wrynn and Nana had to do. I know it's probably not going to be what you dreamed of when you were a little girl, but I promise you'll never regret it. I promise I'll make you happy, or die trying." He stopped when Elizabeth covered his face with her hand and pushed him against the couch.

"Earth to Liam, Earth to Liam. Stop and take a deep breath, and then, if you don't mind, explain to me what in this world you just said." Her blue eyes danced with laughter. "You were talking so fast, I'm not sure I understood a word."

His gaze traveled over her. She had no idea how much he needed to make her his, needed her as a permanent part of his life. Now that he'd had her around the clock, one day without her laughter and support and sincere joy for life was too much. Once she understood, his idea might seem crazy, but not near as crazy as he was for her. With her parents coming to town to check on them, things were falling into place. This was his shot at keeping her forever, and no way was he missing it. His job right then was to convince her.

"Okay, here it is in a nutshell. If you don't have them, you'll need to call your mom and get her to bring your birth certificate and social security card to you tomorrow. First thing Monday morning, we'll head down to Franklin and get a marriage license." Her eyes widened and she blinked several times, and he grinned at her shocked expression. "Then on Saturday, we can get married. You realize this means next week is gonna be cram-packed full, right? My mom has one week of school left, but I'm sure our parents will help get everything together. With me so far?"

He waited for her to say something, but when she didn't, he continued.

"After taking the last few days off, I need to work some, but we should have plenty of time in the evenings to find a place big enough for all of us. If it's okay with you, we'll just rent for now. That'll give us time to decide if we want to build or buy. So, you with me, or have I just been talking to myself?"

Her silence was starting to worry him. He touched her hand, and she jerked as if she'd been shocked.

"Saturday?" She spoke in such a soft voice, he leaned closer to hear. "Next Saturday?" He moved back a little as she spoke louder, but she stopped him from getting too far by grabbing his ear. "As in a week from tomorrow, Saturday?" Okay, so maybe she was screeching just a little. "Have. You. Lost. Your. Mind?" She held firm to his lobe as he tried to shake his head no. "Don't you shake your head at me. I know exactly what you're doing. You weren't kidding around when you said soon. But ... but ... Uhh," she shrieked.

Okay. Now she was panicking. Maybe he wasn't as smooth as he thought. When she jumped up, he braced himself, wondering what was next.

A flood of feelings welled up inside her and swirled around like a tornado.

Panic. Shock. Excitement. Anxiety. Worry. Frustration.

She couldn't sit still any longer. Hopping off the couch, she marched the length of the room back and forth at a frenzied pace, trying to wrap her brain around everything he'd thrown at her.

He's lost his ever loving mind. I swear he has. Seven days to plan a wedding. Seven days to find a place to live. Seven days to uproot everyone and everything. Only a man would think it's that easy.

Her hair whipped around in her face and stuck to her lips when she skirted a side table, and she pulled it back in a messy bun.

Flowers. Cake. I need to call Ashton. She'll have to find her own dress. There's just no time for us to do it together. Dress! Oh my gosh, I need a dress. I don't even know where to start. Geeze, Louise. In seven days. Deep breath. Deep breath. You can do this.

She stumbled in her heels, wincing at the twinge of pain, so to be on the safe side, she kicked them off to the side.

Wouldn't do to break my leg. How the heck would I walk down the aisle? Hmm, maybe Liam could carry me. That man is crazy. Yeah, but he's crazy for me. He'd do it, too.

A heavy sigh left her as she stopped at the window and pressed her forehead to the chilly glass. Now that she'd talked it through with herself, she felt much calmer. Would this be the wedding she'd always dreamed of? No, not even close. Would she be marrying the man of her dreams? A man who would love her and cherish her until his dying day? Absolutely, and really, that was all that mattered.

Only one topic was left that they needed to discuss.

"Liam, it seems like now would be a good time to talk to the kids." Exhaustion swept through her as the short burst of adrenaline left. The cold window was a soothing balm against her heated face. Her eyes drifted closed for a second to enjoy the relief. "We can't do anything else until we tell them you're their father. It's not fair to keep it from them."

"Elizabeth." His soft word traveled through the quiet room.

"They have to know, Liam, before we throw anything else at them. Honey, they need this."

"Elizabeth, sweetheart, they know."

The hushed giggle behind her didn't sound like Liam. In a flash, her brain caught up with what her ears heard. Her spine stiffened. Her eyes popped open. As she turned around, her breath caught in her throat.

There, sitting on either side of Liam, were Brittany and Grayson. A chill traveled through her body. Mortified by her careless delivery of such important information, she wanted to run and hide. Instead, she moved toward them, stopping at the edge of the couch.

"Brittany, Grayson, I'm so sorry." Her heart skipped at the lopsided smiles they wore. "You needed to know, but not like that. I shouldn't have just blurted it out like that."

"We already knowed," Brittany whispered and shrugged her shoulders.

"Momma told us last week." Grayson grinned at Elizabeth. "She said he'd tell us 'vent-ua-ly."

Liam's eyes met hers, and the shock she felt was written all over his face.

"Yeah, she said we were lucky, cause when she was gone, we'd get another family to take care of us. Not everybody's as special as us." Brittany's mouth quivered. Squirming against the cushion, she gazed at Elizabeth, her eyes filled with cautious hope. "She said they'd love us just as much as she does. Will you?"

And there it was. The question to end all questions.

Elizabeth knelt down in front of Brittany and gathered the little girl in her arms. "Oh, honey, I would be honored to be part of your new family." She rested her cheek against the top of Brittany's head. "I'm pretty sure I'm the lucky one."

Looking at Liam holding Grayson, she realized that everything she'd ever wanted and needed was right there within her reach.

Life. Love. Healing. Hope.

He tasted of
strong man,
bright sunshine,
everlasting love,
and

h o p e   e t e r n a l.

Radio Broadcast

"Goooood morning, Highlanders! You're listening to the local news on WHLD, AM radio 1250. Today is Saturday, June eighth, and these are your community updates.

"Folks, I'm here to tell you that miracles never cease to happen. Join me in welcoming back one of our very own who we thought was gone forever. Channing "Tripp" Tidwell has returned from the dead. Rumors have run through town like wildfire this last week, but I gotta tell you, if I hadn't see him standing beneath the flagpole at Highlands School with my own eyes, I wouldn't have believed it myself. A community celebration is in the works, but the family asks that we give them a little time to reunite in private.

"The Broun family is on a roll this week, friends. They would like to invite you to join them for a celebration in honor of the nuptials between Liam Broun and Elizabeth Pittman Broun. The wedding reception will be held at four o'clock at First Presbyterian.

"Our 2012-2013 school year has come to an end, and many teens in our area are looking to keep busy by helping you out with whatever you need done. For a complete list of who's available for yardwork, childcare, and various other jobs, contact Ms. Shumaker, Highlands School Counselor, at 828-555-1515, Monday thru Friday, from eight AM to three PM.

"All you dog lovers out there, the town council would like to remind you to please scoop your poop from all public areas. Ain't nothing much worse than stepping in a pile of it and carrying that mess into your house or car. So be a good neighbor and tend to your dog's business.

"The Civitan Club's annual 'Shaggin' Til Ya Drop Beach Party' was a rip roaring success. You helped the group raise over a thousand dollars to build wheelchair ramps and widen doorways for several households in our area. Thank you, Highlanders, for being good neighbors.

"Now on to the national news…"

Epilogue

From the balcony of the home he and Elizabeth had built, he watched his family and friends move about the yard. Everyone he loved was there, in one spot, even if only in memory.

Liam would love to say everything over the years had been as smooth as silk. If he did, he would most certainly be lying, and maybe even a tad delusional. What he *could* say was life was more full and rewarding when he conquered the obstacles thrown his way. The fight for his family had drained him at times. His knees had hurt when he fell. But through it all, he'd picked himself up, brushed off the dust, and staggered back onto the path of life. Never once did he doubt its worth or promise. Though challenged many times over the years, he'd enjoyed each step of the crazy journey. Bumps and hurdles were expected because raising children was hard.

It wasn't often he thought back to the day he let go of the last remnants of his guilt, once and for all, but the occasion called for it. After all, Lara was responsible for giving him two of his biggest blessings.

After retrieving Lara's boxes from his truck, the plain manila envelope marked *Liam: Open First* had been promptly ignored for the many albums full of pictures of the kids from birth. Only after everyone was asleep did Liam consider opening it. His hands shook as he removed the letter written in her familiar scrawl. The warm hand on his shoulder gave him the courage to read.

Dear Liam,

By the time you read this, I'll be gone. I can only imagine the questions you wish you could ask me. Unfortunately, the answers I *could* give would only spark more questions, and I don't have those answers.

When I was three-ish, my father disappeared. I've always had a feeling he was murdered. For years, it was just Momma and me, running from one shadow after another. We moved so often, I learned the hard way to never let myself get attached to the people I met. Why bother when things could change at the drop of a hat?

And then, you came along and showed me what I was missing. You snuck past all my walls, and for the first time I could remember, I felt safe. I belonged somewhere because someone loved me. You became my home, my haven.

When Momma came to your dorm that morning, I fought her with everything I had, but the thought of dragging you into the life we lived and the danger we always ran from scared me. Cliché as it may sound, a part of me died that day when we walked away. I all but curled up in a ball and gave up on life. I look back on that time, and to this day, it breaks my heart.

I'd love to tell you I snapped out of it when I found out I was pregnant, but that'd be a big, fat lie. It made it worse. The biggest news of my life, and I couldn't share it with you. If anything, I floated through my pregnancy on a cloud of depression. My only reprieve was in my dreams because that was the only place I could be with you, talk to you, hold you. Oh, how I missed the little things that were *my* Liam. The way you'd always talked to me on the phone when I couldn't sleep. The way you'd show up with coffee when I needed to cram for a test. The way you'd stand for hours at my cross country meets. The way you held my hand when I was scared or sad. You looked at me like I was perfect and treated me like I was your greatest treasure. *I. Missed. You.*

My wake-up call came in the form of Brittany and Grayson. Their need for me slowly replaced my need for you. I didn't have the time or energy to miss you anymore. In my very darkest hours, they became my reason to live. They were the only piece of you I had left.

Leaving you was the hardest thing I've ever done until the day I found out the cancer was winning and I'd have to leave them. This time, knowing you'll keep our precious babies safe when I'm gone gives me the peace I need. I have no doubt whatsoever that you'll see them for the treasure they are.

For what it's worth, I like Elizabeth. She's beautiful inside and out, and I think she'll be a wonderful mother to our kids. Watching her love for you grow over these months has given me nothing but hope for your future together. Leave your past behind, and embrace tomorrow. I have a feeling it's going to be spectacular. I wish I could be here to see it.

Please tell my babies that their mother loved them so, so much, and don't let them forget me.

Thank you, Liam, for loving me so long ago, and know I never stopped loving you, not for one breath.

Always yours,

Lara

Loud sniffles behind him brought a broad smile to his face. He would never have all the answers he wanted, but what he ended up with was worth so much more. The hardships and joy along the way had brought him to the sweetest moment in time.

"You look so beautiful, sweetheart." Elizabeth, his love, his soul mate, his heart, fought tears as she clasped Lara's pearls around Brittany's neck.

"Sissie, you look like a princess." Four-year-old Ivy, their youngest, fluttered around, fluffing out the length of white satin. "I can't wait to throw the flowers."

Seven-year-old Abigail and ten-year-old Emma, practiced their walk down the aisle.

"This is taking forever," grumbled Seth, their thirteen-year-old son. He straightened when Liam glared at him. "But you do look pretty."

"That's better." Grayson thumped Seth on the shoulder as he walked over to his twin. "You're absolutely breathtaking, Britt."

"Oh, Gray, I'm so nervous I could puke." Brittany raised her shaking hands and covered her mouth.

"You'll be fine, promise." With a tug on her wrist, he pulled her into a gentle embrace. "I love you, sis," he whispered.

Liam fought his own tears, and sent a silent thanks to Lara. Without her gift to him, that day would have never come. The day when he would give his Brittany to another man, one he prayed would love, honor, and cherish her until her last breath.

His puzzle was complete, the pieces interlocked with an unbreakable bond, and the joy he felt made his heart ache. Gathered in the small room was the tomorrow he'd once hoped for.

Then Elizabeth turned her beautiful blue-sky gaze to him, and his heart was lost all over again.

The End

About the Author

Kathryn is a simple country girl who likes to spend time with her family. Born and raised in North Carolina, she loves to travel, but can't imagine ever leaving the mountains she's come to call home. She holds Jeremiah 29:11 very close to her heart and believes it with every fiber of her being. "For I know the plans I have for you," declares the Lord, "plans to prosper you and not to harm you, plans to give you hope and a future."

For more information, and ways to connect with Kathryn Crane, visit *About.me/kathryn.crane*

www.ingramcontent.com/pod-product-compliance
Lightning Source LLC
Chambersburg PA
CBHW070654180626
46817CB00006B/2370